MUCH ADO ABOUT MAGIC

PATRICIA RICE

sourcebooks
casablanca

Published by Sourcebooks Casablanca, an imprint of Sourcebooks, Inc.
P.O. Box 4410, Naperville, Illinois 60567-4410
(630) 961-3900
Fax: (630) 961-2168
www.sourcebooks.com

Originally published in 2005 by Signet Eclipse, an imprint of New
American Library.

Library of Congress Cataloging-in-Publication Data

Rice, Patricia, 1949-
  Much ado about magic / Patricia Rice.
    pages cm
  Originally published in 2005 by Signet Eclipse, an imprint of New
American Library.
  (trade paper : alk. paper) 1. Artists—Fiction. I. Title.
  PS3568.I2925M87 2013
  813'.54—dc23
                          2013028273

    Printed and bound in the United States of America.
          VP 10 9 8 7 6 5 4 3 2 1

Prologue

London, Spring 1740

"LUCINDA HAS SUCH A LOVELY ARTISTIC TALENT. WHYEVER did she choose to draw a *casket*?" Hermione Malcolm Childe, Marchioness of Hampton, leaned closer to study her niece's chalk sketch on the easel. "That isn't..."

She raised up abruptly to glance at her sister Stella standing beside her. They were in the nursery, dressed for the ball they would attend later. Surrounded by the innocent toys of childhood while garbed in the security of wealthy society, Hermione didn't fully comprehend the dire subject of the painting. "Is that the young prince?" she whispered in horror.

Stella Malcolm Pembroke, Duchess of Mainwaring, nodded her regally powdered head, concealing an expression of concern. A plume from her headdress bobbed and brushed her nose, but she was watching the children romping and didn't seem to notice the feather. "Lucinda saw him in the park yesterday."

Both women turned to watch their offspring. Hermione's eldest daughter, Leila, was ordering her younger siblings and cousins into line. Leila's sister, Christina, was climbing across dressers rather-than following orders. Stella's eldest daughters weren't nursery age any longer, but her younger children willingly joined in the romp—all except Lucinda.

Seven-year-old Lady Lucinda sat quietly in a corner, sketching with a charcoal pencil, unobserved by the rest of the nursery occupants. Every so often she looked up at a laugh or a protest, then returned to laboring over her work. Her long, slender fingers flew over the artist's pad. She'd tied her wavy silver-blond hair back with a discarded string to prevent it from falling in her face and distracting her. Her porcelain features reflected sheer pleasure as the picture appeared beneath her pencil. She'd smeared her blue silk gown with chalk earlier, and the lace at her wrists was dirty with charcoal smudges, but she seemed oblivious to her disarray.

"She is such a happy, quiet child," Stella explained with love and fear in her voice. "She never asks for anything except for someone to look at her drawings. How can I tell her not to show them to outsiders?"

As the younger of the two Malcolms, Hermione was unaccustomed to being consulted by her far more powerful and talented sister, but as a family they were familiar with these perplexing questions of dealing with their gifted daughters. Sometimes, it took the entire clan to chart the course of a single child. Or to shield her.

"She'll want an art teacher," Hermione predicted gloomily. "He'll gossip. Everything she does will become public. Can you imagine what would happen if the prince dies after she's drawn him in a casket?"

Stella nodded. "She would be publicly pilloried and ostracized. Her father would be removed from his royal post for fear he caused the prince's death. And then people would start sneaking around the back door, asking to have their fortunes told." She sighed. "I've asked the duke to find a teacher who only speaks French. Lucinda is adept with languages, and France has the most skilled artists."

Hermione brightened. "Even if the teacher tells others of what she draws, he'll be dismissed as just another foolish Frenchman. Excellent." As another thought occurred, her pretty, round face fell. "She doesn't really have your second sight, does she? It's a terrible burden to bear."

Stella sighed, and powder gathered in the wrinkles that

were deep before her time. "Only in her drawings, and she isn't aware of what she does."

Hermione caught the scarf floating from her shoulders and idly tucked it into her bodice, then looked around for the fan she'd left lying on a child's desk. "She will understand soon enough, I fear."

As if to prove her prediction, the artist in the corner gave a cry of dismay, stared at her drawing with loathing, and crumpled it into a ball. When she threw it away from her, the other children raced to retrieve the paper as if it were a new game.

Before they could open the wrinkled drawing, the duchess swept across the nursery, her full brocade gown swirling with authority. Appropriating the paper, she gestured toward the exit. "Go give your fathers a kiss before we leave for the ball."

Lucinda dragged herself unhappily from her corner to follow her sisters and cousins. The duchess let her go without a word or a hug, although her powdered and rouged features hid a world of sorrow.

When the children were gone, the two women opened the drawing.

A charming depiction of dancing, laughing little girls filled the page.

"It's lovely," Hermione exclaimed. "I've not seen better in the royal art gallery." Then, taking a closer look, she gasped.

Stella nodded as if she'd expected it. "I thought she'd quit drawing her own image some time ago. I suppose she lost herself in the moment."

Hermione gazed at the pencil drawing in bewilderment. "But whatever does it mean?"

Stella traced the outline of the ominous shadow hovering in the corner just behind the image of a little girl sketching. "I am hoping it means her future is uncertain. Otherwise…"

Hermione briskly removed the sketch from her sister's hand. "It doesn't show anyone in a casket, does it? It's just a shadow. Children have strange imaginations."

Stella rearranged her momentarily vulnerable features into

her usual dignified expression. "Of course. We will see that she marries well when the time comes, and we will all be there to cast light on any shadows. That is what families are for."

And that was why Malcolms stuck together.

One

LADY LUCINDA MALCOLM PEMBROKE PULLED THE HOOD OF her gray mantle around her face and hurried down the nearly empty halls of the art gallery ahead of the morning crowd. She didn't halt until she reached a full-length portrait of a laughing gentleman on a galloping white stallion.

Not precisely a gentleman, she supposed, trying to be honest with herself. Romantic fantasies needn't be gentlemen. Looking up, she fell under the spell of the subject's mysterious dark eyes all over again. It was as if he looked just at her and that they shared a wonderful secret. She'd painted the portrait, so she knew its secret: the dashing gentleman didn't exist anywhere except in her imagination.

But that wasn't how rumor had it.

With a sigh, she admired the gentleman's exotically dark complexion, rakish smile, and unsettling eyes. She loved the contrast between his scarred, piratical features and his elegant clothes. She'd deliberately given him a romantic white stallion and painted the innocent background of a festival to contrast with his aura of danger. Amazingly, the playful setting seemed to suit him.

The man didn't exist. If he had, she would never have embarrassed herself and the subject by entering the oil in the exhibition. She had even signed the painting with just her initials, to avoid any potential harm, except that there were enough people familiar with her style to set rumor rolling. She would never understand why people saw more in her art than she intended.

She couldn't imagine why the Earl of Lansdowne would want to ruin her triumph and this magnificent painting with his scandalous accusation. If he hadn't suffered an apoplexy immediately after seeing the portrait and making his furious allegations, she would demand an apology. She would never paint a *murderer*.

The sound of footsteps warned her that the first arrivals at the gallery were approaching the back hall more quickly than she'd expected, probably heading directly for the scandal of the moment rather than examining the better-known works in the front hall. She had no intention of making a spectacle of herself by appearing in public with the portrait. Looking around, she located a small niche across the hall where she could sit, unobserved.

Her fingers itched for the sketchbook and pencil in her pocket. She'd like to have a drawing of the exhibition for posterity. After this episode, her father wasn't likely to let her enter another oil, and she couldn't blame him. She'd never meant to achieve notoriety. She'd only wanted others to admire the portrait into which she'd poured her heart and soul.

She peered around the corner of the niche as a tall man strode determinedly in her direction, the skirt of his elegant coat rippling about his legs with the strength of his stride. The coat was tailored to fit shoulders and a chest wider than that of most gentlemen. The lapels and cut were of precisely this year's fashion, except that the coat was *black*. No gentleman wore black in London, not even for mourning. How very odd.

His neckcloth was a pristine white with just the right amount of starch for crispness without an inch of foppery. His breeches were of a tawny silk that matched the elaborate embroidery on the coat's lapels and pockets. His long vest matched his breeches and was embroidered with black in a simplicity that caused her to sigh in admiration. More gentlemen should accent their masculinity in this way instead of dressing as peacocks.

But when he was close enough for her to see his face, she gasped in horror and drew back as far into the niche as she could go.

❧

Crossing his arms over his new, correctly tailored and damned expensive clothes, Sir Trevelyan Rochester studied the ridiculous portrait hanging in the Royal Art Gallery for the entire world to see. Fury bubbled at the outrage perpetrated on a perfectly respectable piece of canvas that would have been better used in making sails. He dropped his gaze to the artist's signature, *LMP,* and his ire flared anew. The coward hid behind initials.

He'd spent twenty years working his way up from impressed sailor to owner of his own ship, and not one man in those twenty years had dared insult him in such a flagrant manner—not and lived to tell about it, anyway. He'd defeated bloodthirsty pirates, captured French privateers, gained his own letter of marque from the King of England himself, only to be humiliated by an unknown artist on the other side of the world who could not possibly know more than rumors of his exploits.

Had it not been for his desire for peace and a home of his own, rather than preparing for yet another senseless war with France over the colonies, he would never have walked the streets of London again. Had the artist counted on his not returning to England?

He would make the damned man walk the plank at sword point and dispense with the gossipmongering, scandal-provoking scoundrel as a favor to society. It was the duty of any self-respecting privateer to rid the world of enemies to king and country.

Except he wasn't a privateer any longer, and Mr. LMP had provoked only him and not king or country.

A deep scowl drew his eyebrows together as he studied the details. It was his likeness, all right, unless he had a twin somewhere he didn't know about. Given the propensities of his noble family, that was possible but not likely.

The painting depicted *him*—Sir Trevelyan Rochester, knighted by His Majesty for action beyond the call of duty— riding a prissy white horse adorned with red ribbons on a beach in the midst of what appeared to be a summer fair. Trev assumed Mr. LMP had intended to poke fun by decking out him, a feared privateer, in macaroni attire of fluffy lace jabot and useless cuffs that spilled lace past his fingers. The artist had given him boots instead of clocked stockings, but the boots were cuffed and shiny and foolish for riding.

The subject of the portrait was defiantly hatless and wigless. A deep blue riband tied his hair back, and one black strand blew loose to fall across his battle-scarred cheek. Trev had to admit the artist had captured his olive complexion and sharp features with painful accuracy. His mother's mixed Jamaican heritage could not be denied. Brushed with tar, his noble grandfather had called his coloring, just before the old man had let the navy take Trev to do with as they would.

Still, the painting was hopelessly silly. The man in it managed to look romantically dashing despite a touch of savagery behind his flashing dark eyes. Trev didn't mind that so much, but the contrast between the man and the frivolous white horse was laughable.

No wonder people were talking. Still, he did not see what had sent his cousin's widow into such fits when he'd arrived at her door. He'd spent all his adult years on the other side of the world, and she couldn't know him from Adam, but she had barely given him a minute to introduce himself before slamming the door in his face.

It was James, their old butler, who had sneaked out to explain about the portrait all London was talking about. The preposterous painting was so well-known that word of it had spread even to the rural village in the south of England where his late cousin's family resided. James hadn't had time to explain *why* the portrait was so scandalous. Or perhaps he hadn't known.

If he didn't know better, he'd think his grandfather had planned this humiliation.

He studied the portrait, but he could see no reason for alarm, except for the smirch on his masculinity. That could cause difficulty in his search for a wife, but he doubted any sensible woman in his presence would question his virility.

He was about to spin around and stalk out when a whisper from the crowd gathering behind him caught his ear. He eavesdropped unabashedly.

"They say the earl had an apoplexy right on this spot." The whisper was distinctly feminine and horrified.

Trev crossed his arms and pretended to study the portrait.

"It's a Malcolm prediction, of a certainty," another voice said in awe. "See that boat sinking in the corner? It's the viscount's. The red is quite recognizable. They say he's been missing at sea for months."

Trev ground his molars and waited. Malcolm? The M in LMP stood for Malcolm? He would know the full name of the blackguard who'd put his face upon a wall without permission.

"There could be other red yachts," a male voice said scornfully. "But the man certainly looks a pirate. No wonder the earl recognized him."

"But Rochester hasn't been in England since childhood," the first female voice protested. "How could the artist have painted him so accurately that the earl could recognize him, without having seen him?"

"They don't hold fairs on the shore in Sussex," a bored male voice drawled. "It's a hoax."

Trev couldn't agree more. The silly little boat in the painting was hardly noticeable. The grieving widow standing on the rocky shoreline was buried in veils and could be anyone. An artist's ploy, contrasting laughter with grief or some such flummery. His cousin had gone down at sea months ago, so to add his yacht to the background was the artist's deliberate scandal-mongering, not foretelling.

Now he understood why his cousin's widow had slammed the door in his face—the portrait showed him laughing as his cousin's yacht sank. He'd have to wring the artist's neck after all. Laurence had been a good, decent man, and his death was no laughing matter.

"The shire held a fair this year," a timid voice countered. "The new Duke of Sommersville sponsored one. That is when the yacht went down."

The crowd murmured more loudly as the conversation picked up in several places at once. "He looks dangerous enough to have murdered his cousin," someone said in response to a comment about his scar.

Trev snorted. No self-respecting murderer would wear that much lace, he wagered. It would get all bloody. Just try using a sword with lace wrapped around the fingers!

"Now that the viscount's gone, if the earl dies, Rochester could claim the title," said a female, followed by a horrified, "The man should hang!"

Trev figured neither spectator knew what she was talking about, since Laurence had left an infant son as heir and his grandfather had declared Trev illegitimate. Truth never fazed good gossip though.

Both comments overrode the more sensible voice that said, "But the man says he just arrived in England, and the viscount died last summer."

"I know Lady Lucinda," a timid female interjected. "She always paints one of her kittens into the landscape. See the orange tabby in the tree? It died of old age in April. That oil was painted last winter, well before the viscount's yacht went down. I saw her working on it."

A gasp of awe escaped the fascinated crowd, and Trev gritted his teeth at this nonsense.

"If the Prophetess painted it, then it must be true," said another woman. "She painted Pelham in his grave before he died."

"She painted my mother walking across Westminster Bridge before it was finished."

"Lady Roxbury fainted when she saw the Prophetess in the park—painting Roxbury with a woman that wasn't her and children that weren't theirs."

"You know his mistress is bearing his child," someone else murmured.

The whispers grew riper and louder, but Trev disregarded all the gossip except the relevant—a woman artist! Rocked by the enormity of such perfidiousness, he had only one thought in mind—to locate this attention-seeking, kitten-drawing *Prophetess* who had depicted him as his cousin's murderer and throttle her until she admitted to all London that the painting was a hoax. Furious, he swirled around to cut a path through the crowd.

Confronted with the man in the portrait come to life before their eyes, the crowd recoiled in horror.

Feeling as murderous as they believed him, Trev stalked off without looking right or left.

Lucinda slid deeper into the shadows of the alcove and held her breath until Sir Trevelyan swept past, bronzed features scowling, Spanish eyes flashing, and manly muscles rippling.

Her gaze dropped to the lethal rapier emerging from his coattails, and she trembled.

Foolishly, her traitorous fingers itched for her paintbrushes. This time, she wanted to paint him as a thundercloud in the form of a man. She could see now that her first attempt was sadly lacking in comparison with the reality.

The man actually existed! The Earl of Lansdowne had been right. She couldn't believe it. How could she have painted a man in her head only to see him walk out of a crowd like that? Could the other gossip be true then? Had that man, that *pirate*, been in England during the fair as she'd painted him? Could she have actually seen him last winter, when he'd filled her dreams?

She didn't think she wanted to be around to find out. He looked angry enough to commit murder, but oddly enough, she'd been drawn to the sadness in his dark eyes. There was something in the way he held himself... She couldn't put her finger on why he fascinated her.

That's what she deserved for listening to romantic tales of heroes and villains told by silly women with nothing better to do. The tales they'd told of commanders at sea and warriors on land and knights of old had given her dreams until she'd had to capture them on canvas.

She supposed they had talked of privateers like Sir Trevelyan, who had captured a renegade French warship that had blocked a British harbor a year or so ago. She remembered the story anyway, but she'd not been thinking of it when she'd painted the portrait. At the time, she'd thought the painting showed a fantasy hero with a romantic, fun-loving nature. She'd thoroughly enjoyed the contradictions of character she'd conveyed.

She could dash that foolery right now. She couldn't imagine anyone less romantic or more dangerous than the man who'd just left the gallery. Perhaps there was some truth behind the rumor of his being a murderer after all. After all, privateers were licensed to kill.

She shivered, and, tucking the hood of her mantle more securely over her distinctive white-blond hair, hastened to a back exit.

If rumor were true, Sir Trevelyan Rochester had murdered his cousin to claim the title and estates his grandfather had denied him.

If rumor were true, her painting provided evidence that Rochester had been in England when he had said he was not, destroying his credibility and alibi.

She knew the last rumor was based on false assumptions, but how would she ever explain the coincidence of the resemblance? She couldn't. And now a dangerous privateer knew her name.

She'd caused scandals enough in the past but none of this magnitude. It was past time she left London, before the privateer stormed the walls of her home to murder *her*.

⤜✦⤛

Lucinda pushed a quilted petticoat into her brocade valise and looked around at the clothes scattered across her bedroom, trying to decide if she could squeeze in anything else. It had taken her the better part of the afternoon to carry out all the details of her plan to run away from home.

Without warning, her younger sister Cecily burst into the room. At seeing the disorder in her sister's chamber, she halted abruptly. "I thought you told Mama you had the megrims and could not attend the ball."

Lucinda winced at being caught in the first of what might become many lies. "I'm feeling better."

"You cannot go, Sinda," Cecily whispered in horror, finally making the connection between luggage and gossip. "Mama will think of a solution."

Mentally berating herself for not having bolted the door, Lucinda tugged the valise buckle closed. "No," she said simply.

"What do you mean, *no*? Mama always thinks of something. Remember when you were twelve and you painted the pretty lady on her new silk sofa? And over the mantel you sketched in a portrait of the Stewart prince, only he had blood on his hands? Mama warned Papa, who told the king, who called the troops home in time to prevent a bloody war."

Lucinda shook her head and a tear crawled down her cheek. "She prevented a bloody war in *England*, but not in Scotland. If I hadn't painted that picture, would all those brave young men have died at Culloden?"

Too young to remember that period in history, Cecily shrugged carelessly. "If not there, somewhere else. What matters is that Mama can make this right, too. She and Papa can do anything. Papa is a *duke*."

"Papa could not prevent all London from believing my painting means Sir Trevelyan murdered his cousin." Bitterly, Lucinda flung her box of oils on the bed with her valise.

"It is a very good painting," Cecily said. "Everyone says so."

It was an *excellent* painting; in all respects, an oil as fine as any that hung in the royal galleries. She had simply chosen the wrong subject. Again.

Just seeing innocent Cecily, with her blond curls and anxious expression, sealed her decision. At sixteen, Cecily had come out only this year. She already had a dozen brilliant beaus who had been conspicuously absent these past weeks of controversy. The portrait had forcibly reminded them that a man had to be strong and brave—or desperate—to marry a Malcolm.

Lucinda must leave town to give her three younger sisters

a chance to marry. At twenty-two, her own time on the marriage mart had passed. Six years was long enough to show she had tried. Malcolms with dangerous gifts had been known to disappear from public sight from time to time. It wasn't as if she would be setting any precedents. There was freedom in anonymity.

"I won't go far," Lucinda promised. "Cousin Felicity has said I can stay with her and Ewen until I decide how to proceed. I'll travel to Scotland incognito and live under an assumed name. I can make my living by painting landscapes. I can't harm anyone by drawing trees. I think I'll be much happier away from London."

She'd repeated those lines to herself enough times that she managed to sound cheerful while she said them. They did sound good, even if she was lying about her destination to throw Cecily off her trail. She had never lived without her family and had almost no idea how to go on by herself, so she wasn't foolish enough to think she could completely run away. It was just that she'd been quiet and obedient for so long, she needed to establish her new self and her new life before her family could talk her out of it.

It wasn't as if she didn't have a marketable talent. Landscape paintings were all the rage. And surely it would be safe to paint grass and trees.

"How will you go?" Cecily asked in an awed whisper. "Scotland is a very long way and the roads are bad."

"It's better that you don't know so you won't have to lie if asked. Go and forget you saw me this evening. In a few days, your beaus will be back on the doorstep, and all will be well."

Cecily looked even more stricken. "There are thieves all over St. James these days! I heard Papa say it is not safe to walk the streets. You cannot go without a footman and a linkboy."

"I've made arrangements, I promise," Lucinda swore, and this time, she was completely honest. She wasn't a brave person.

She hugged Cecily to reassure her. Still unhappy, her sister tiptoed out the door with Sinda's gentle shove.

After her sister was safely gone, Lucinda glanced around for anything she'd forgotten, then slipped to the balcony window with valise and paint box in hand. She must be gone before Cecily started feeling guilty. Their parents had left for a dinner and ball, but that didn't mean they couldn't be found before she made her escape.

She'd planned everything to the last minute. She had a chair waiting to take her to the inn where the Sussex coach would leave within the hour. She no intention of running off to chilly Scotland.

Taking one last look at the pretty room that had been hers all her life, trying not to imagine what would happen in the morning when her younger sisters discovered she was gone, Lucinda swept away a tear. Mouth set in determination, she dropped her valise and paint box off the balcony into the shrubbery below, then pulled her concealing mantle over her face and hurried from her room toward the servants' stairs. She'd traded a fine muslin morning dress for a maid's coarse wool gown, so she wouldn't appear out of place at a common inn. She would look a mess when she arrived, but that was the whole point, wasn't it—not to look like herself?

A high wall surrounded the yard, so there was no one to see when she retrieved her bags. Dusk fell early this time of year. An owl hooted from the old oak, but owls didn't scare her. From here, it would be easy. She knew where to find the gate key.

The gate creaked a little as she stepped into the mews, but the servants were all in the hall having their supper. She could scream bloody murder and they wouldn't hear.

She almost did scream when her first step into the alley brought her up against a tall, cloaked figure that materialized out of the darkness. *Thieves!*

A strong hand caught her shoulder, and her heart nearly leaped from her chest.

Her accoster released her, and she hastily backed toward the gate and safety. In the dusky light, she recognized the powerful form and black coat of the man who had made such an impression on her in the gallery. Not a thief then— a *murderer*.

Sir Trevelyan had come to kill her.

"Steady on now, lass." His voice was like deep velvet. "What's your hurry?"

Not soothed by his tone, she shrank into the shadows of the vines spilling over the walls. Behind her, she fumbled for the gate latch while feigning ignorance for as long as she might.

"Who are you?" she demanded in a manner totally unlike her, hoping her voice didn't shake. "There should be none back here but the duke's men." That seemed the thing a spirited maid might say.

Feeble illumination from the stable lantern at the end of the mews cast shadows on the pirate's striking features. He was taller than her father and even wider of shoulder than she remembered. His black tricorne tilted rakishly, concealing his expression.

"I'm just a visitor seeking a shortcut." He swept off his hat and made a deep bow. When he stood upright again, the light fell on the sharp blade of his nose and his deeply set eyes.

She'd painted that face, knew it intimately. He was far more imposing and dangerous close up than she had dreamed. The heart-pounding, knee-weakening sensation returned. This time, she recognized it as abject fear.

"And who might you be?" he inquired. "Not many stroll these alleys at night."

Trying not to stutter, she kept her voice low. "'Tis none of your concern, sir. Be off about your business, if you please." She'd never said a saucy word in her life. What had possessed her to say such a thing now? She dropped her gaze in fear, to seek the hilt of his sword. He'd left it off, thank the goddess.

He didn't seem offended so much as amused by her reply. "It seems I've stumbled on a little hedgehog. Tell me, if you will, is the duke about this evening? I have business with him."

Oh dear, oh dreadful dear. Would he challenge her father to a duel over the painting's insult to his reputation?

Now that she had set about a career of anonymity, she supposed she must become accustomed to storytelling. "He is not, sir. The family is away for the season."

"But the stable lanterns are lit as if someone is expected," he contradicted with a knowing grin. He produced a gold piece from his pocket and let it gleam in the light. "I've a coin for you if you can tell me when the family will return."

Shocked at his audacity, she sank deeper into the shadows and prayed her cloak concealed her features. The gold between his gloved fingers twinkled, and she thought of her meager purse. She'd never been one to save her allowance when it could be spent on a new oil paint.

What would it hurt to tell when her father was expected home? It was not as if a carriage with four horses could arrive surreptitiously. All Rochester had to do was linger, and he'd eventually see her parents.

She needed to be rid of him so she could make her escape before they returned. The sedan chair she'd hired wouldn't wait much longer.

"The duke has been at Whitehall all day," she lied, "and is past due home. His family has gone to the Beresfords' ball without him." Just enough detail for plausibility, she hoped. Her father never left her mother waiting, and it would be the wee hours before they returned.

"Very good," he said, sounding pleased. "And your name, should I call again?"

What would the name of a servant avail him? Trembling, she shook her head. "The master doesn't know I'm out. I'll not tell you that."

He laughed. "And where are you off to, then? Shall I escort you? It is not safe for a fair maid to walk the streets alone at night. There is danger in the dark."

His whole face altered when he smiled. He looked like a laughing pirate, a man who took life to excess and reveled in it. Sinda admired the flash of his white teeth against his dark coloring and wished she could know him better. A man like this was rare in society.

Dangerous, she reminded herself. She was the dreamer and certainly not the smartest of her family, but she knew better than to dally with an acknowledged privateer. "I daresay I'll be far safer alone than with you, sir. Pray, let me pass."

His dark eyes narrowed and he hesitated. Then he chuckled and held out the coin, which she snatched quickly, trying not to notice the heat of his hand.

"I thank you, then." Bowing, he returned his hat to his head and strode off as if they'd just exchanged a pleasantry.

He disappeared around the far side of the carriage house. She gave him a moment or two to get ahead of her.

He was devilishly attractive. His velvet voice alone could make a woman swoon. And no doubt he would have strangled her had he known who she was.

Gulping in relief at the near miss, grateful she'd chosen to leave London, she hastened down the alley to peek into the street. She wanted to be certain Rochester did not linger at their door. She saw no sign of the man.

She hadn't realized how very *dark* the streets were without a linkboy to carry a lantern for her. Or how lonely they were without one of her sisters laughing and talking at her side.

To her relief, the sedan chair waited. Dragging her valise and paint box, she hastened to take her seat, proffering the coin Rochester had given her and speaking her direction. She felt no guilt at using his money to make her escape. It was his fault that she must do so.

❧

Standing in a doorway near the waiting sedan chair, Trev listened to the girl give her direction. He wasn't the kind of man to laugh off an insult or let grass grow under his feet. And sometimes, he had the devil's own luck.

He'd wager everything he owned—and that was currently a considerable sum—that the chit with the paint box he'd just helped run away was the *Prophetess* whose neck he'd come to wring. She'd raised his curiosity several levels upon this mischance meeting. She certainly hadn't been seeking attention this evening.

He'd spent these last hours investigating Lady Lucinda Malcolm Pembroke, learning she was a well-known trouble-maker and the haughty daughter of a powerful duke. All thought of the peace and civilization he'd come home to find fled his head. Twenty years at sea had taught him to attack first and ask questions later.

But he'd never attacked a woman. Trev's temper faltered under a wave of bitter anguish. Seeing the artist in person reminded him that the lady hadn't caused his cousin's death.

Laurence had been the only decent Rochester he'd ever known. He'd been looking forward to their reunion after all these years. A few months younger than Trev, Laurence had been as purely aristocratic English as Trev was not—golden-haired, rosy-cheeked, and jolly-humored when he'd last seen him. Granted, that had been when they were both fourteen. Time could have wrought changes, but Trev would have preferred to judge that for himself.

Scowling blackly, he went in search of his carriage.

He'd stormed his grandfather's house an hour ago to see for himself that the Earl of Lansdowne was truly comatose from the apoplexy that had stricken him at the art gallery. He wouldn't have put it past the old man to have instigated the whole nefarious plot to discredit him, but beyond proving the earl was bedridden, he'd learned nothing else. Believing Trev to be the murderer the earl had accused him of being, the earl's servants had risen up against him in fear. He'd been fortunate to escape without broken bones.

If he was to find out why he'd been framed for a murder he hadn't committed and regain any chance of courting a lady and having a family, Lady Lucinda Pembroke was his only lead. He'd have to follow her, then force her to admit his innocence.

Planning by what means one might force a lady into anything, Trev grinned, swung his walking stick, and signaled the carriage waiting for him around the corner.

Two

THE SEDAN CHAIR THEY FOLLOWED SLIPPED DOWN A SIDE street. Trev's bays couldn't take the narrow turn. He swore beneath his breath as his carriage halted for the third time in the heavy traffic delivering their befrilled and bewigged occupants to Beresford House.

"That's what you deserve for playing the Prince of Pomp in a damned carriage," Mick, his driver, called. "You shoulda brought Rex."

Mick was a good man, a hard worker, and stalwart sailor. Before he'd been impressed into His Majesty's Navy, he had been a stableboy. A week ago—the day Trev had arrived in England—he'd bought the stallion, Rex, and handed it over to Mick. Mick would have walked through gunfire in gratitude, but he hadn't an obedient tongue in his head.

Neither did Trev. Society's manners held no appeal except as a means to an end. He'd thought to practice propriety when he returned, court a pretty maid, and marry. It seemed as if fate—or his grandfather—had decreed a different path, as usual.

Watching his prey escape, Trev leaped down from the carriage's confining interior. He'd heard the direction the girl had given the sedan bearer and had no intention of losing her so easily. The inn she'd named was in the part of London he remembered from his youth.

He should have strangled her there in the alley, but the

audacity of a duke's daughter playing the part of maid had amused him. She should have recognized him when he'd removed his hat, but she hadn't so much as flinched at the sight of his scar. He admired her courage. So he'd let the leash out a little longer, hoping she would lead him to the true source of her treachery.

"I'm going on foot, Mick. Meet me at the Lion."

"There's been thieves in the alleys hereabouts these last weeks," Mick warned from his perch behind the horses.

Trev laughed and saluted him in acknowledgment before striding off.

It had been nearly twenty years since he'd seen London, but unless the Red Lion had moved, he shouldn't have difficulty finding it. It was only a street or two distant from his grandfather's home. The West End of London was not large.

He took a cross alley behind the earl's home. Hurrying through the darkness, he heard a rustle and a footstep follow him into the narrow passage—undoubtedly one of the predators said to be helping themselves to the fat pocketbooks of the wealthy lately. He sighed with impatience at a possible delay. He'd traversed far more dangerous paths than this one, in areas where outlaws had to be swift, invisible, and heavily armed to survive.

This was St. James. A thief merely needed a big stick and the brains of a dormouse to make a living. Trev strolled onward as if he hadn't a care in the world.

Apparently believing brute force was on his side, the brigand didn't even have the good sense to be quiet. The heavy footsteps quickened as the thief reached the darkest shadows in the most obvious place to close in for the kill. The man had set up his ambush as if he did this often.

With a growl of exasperation, Trev stepped abruptly sideways to place his back against the wall. Deprived of his target, his assailant stumbled with cudgel still upraised.

In one swift motion, Trev grasped the end of the stick, thrust out his foot, and brought the cudgel down sharply with both hands. Thrown off balance, the footpad tripped and sprawled face-first into the mud.

"I suggest you find another alley to inhabit," Trev said, stepping over the bulk of the would-be thief. "I frequent this one, and next time, you'll not come off so easily. I haven't the patience to deal with you tonight."

Without bothering to incapacitate the cursing thief, he carried the cudgel away. Survival was risky even in the wealthy realms of London, it seemed.

Trev had hoped that by returning to England, he could exchange his wealth for the peace he hadn't known since childhood. But even in England, trouble followed. If it hadn't been for that accursed painting, he could be at the Willows now, helping his cousin's grieving widow and child.

He arrived at the Lion just as a coach rumbled out, horn blaring, harness jingling. Sturdy horses struck hoofs against cobblestones, and lanterns swayed on the outside. A drunken sailor hung over the top rail, casting up his accounts, much to the distaste of his fellow topside passengers—all male.

Trev tried to see the interior of the carriage as it passed, but it was too dark and crowded. Dismissing the possibility that the sedan chair could have arrived already, leaving an inexperienced miss to manage her heavy luggage, buy tickets, and secure a seat so quickly, he kept an eye on the yard for her arrival and scanned the crowd outside the inn.

He methodically eliminated the usual inebriated gentlemen, country squires, and assorted fat farm wives. He studied a slender woman in a brown travel cloak, but her shoulders were slumped, and she looked beaten down by her situation. Governess, he pegged her. Not finding anyone with the proud carriage of a duke's daughter or the paint box of an artist, he leaned on his cudgel and waited.

A doxy eased up beside him, reeking of gin and cheap perfume. "Got some time, guv'nor?"

He had time but not the inclination. Rather than risk pox in every port, he'd learned to control his randiness until he'd reached known harbors.

Trev held up a silver coin between his fingers. "Look inside to see if a lady in a hooded cloak, carrying an artist's paint box, is there."

"Lor', guv'nor, she must be somethin' to set eyes on to earn that." She snatched the coin and shot inside before he could change his mind.

Some minutes later she returned with a full flask and an expression of utter contentment on her slack jaw. "Scarce a lady in sight, as should be."

"Thank you." He hadn't expected any less. The tavern would be full to bursting at this time, far too rowdy for a woman traveling alone.

Mick swung Trev's pair of bays neatly through the gate as passengers from the next arriving coach emptied into the courtyard.

"I've lost her," Trev told his driver with disgust. "Keep an eye on the crowd in the yard while I talk to the ticket seller."

Inside the inn, he scanned the chalked list of departures. The Sussex coach had been the one he'd just missed. Only coaches traveling along turnpikes departed in the evenings. The only other scheduled departure had left for Oxford earlier.

He stepped up to the ticket window. "Did a young lady travel out on the Sussex coach?" he inquired with a bored drawl that concealed his intense interest.

"None that I recollect," the old man said, scratching his gray head. "Just gentlemen going that way. One of the gents had his cook with him, but she weren't young nor a lady."

For some insane reason, Trev was struck with a bolt of concern. The girl was young, naïve, and alone in the dangerous streets of London at night. He'd seen her wave around the golden coin he'd given her. Perhaps her sedan chair carriers had pegged her as a wealthy target. He could be responsible for harm done to an innocent young woman. Someone should be notified that she hadn't arrived at her destination.

Admittedly, if she was the malicious twit whose painting had stirred the gossip about him, he should be furious with her, but even budding bitches didn't deserve what could happen to them on city streets. He ought to know. He'd been down that road and still had nightmares.

With resignation, Trev returned to his carriage, and after

ascertaining that the chair still hadn't arrived, he ordered Mick
to return them to the Duke of Mainwaring's palatial mansion.

✥

"What the bloody hell do you mean, am I missing a daughter?
Do you have any idea what time it is?"

Leaning against one of the marble columns embellishing
the duke's front door, legs crossed carelessly at the ankles,
Trev retrieved his gold watch from an inner pocket, consulted
it with deliberate care, and nodded. "Half past two in the
morning, Your Grace. A trifle early for leaving a ball, but a
man burdened with as many duties as yourself has little time
to play, I assume."

Tweaking a duke's ill humor was not the path to peace
and prosperity, but he'd spent a damned long time cooling
his heels on the front step waiting for the man's return. The
butler had refused him entrance. Someone would pay for that
insult—it might as well be His High and Mighty Grace.

Aristocrats who thought themselves the right hand of God
didn't impress Trev much, although the Duke of Mainwaring
was an imposing figure in his curled and powdered wig and
satin evening suit. Though surely past his prime, the duke
didn't appear to have an ounce of flab on him, and his eyes
flashed with dangerous intelligence. Trev wouldn't want to
come upon him in a dark alley.

But it was the formidable matron in paint, patches, acres of
velvet, and towering headdress who awed him. The duchess
breathed fire without speaking a word. Hell, if he'd been a
girl, he would have run away too.

He almost felt sympathy for the troublemaking chit when
the duchess deigned to speak in a voice icy enough to turn a
man's balls blue.

"And what concern is the whereabouts of my daughters
to you, sir?" she demanded with the air of an English queen.

"The concern of any gentleman for a lady wandering the
dangerous streets of London at night, Your Grace. As you
may have heard, there are brigands about." Trev noticed the
footman at the door shiver, then gesture to someone inside.

He wouldn't be surprised if a troop of cavalry rode down the stairs in a moment. He had yet to be invited in, even though he'd introduced himself. "But if you care not—"

A wisp of a girl in white appeared in the doorway, interrupting his tirade before he could launch it.

"Mama! Sinda's gone! She ran away to Scotland hours ago."

Scotland? Bloody hell. He'd fretted these last hours for naught. The female had *tricked* him. She'd given the chair bearer a false direction to throw off his pursuit. She hadn't gone to the inn at all. She'd gone to the docks. The lass must be mad.

Deviously, lethally mad. He'd wring her neck of a certainty.

The duchess shrieked. The ethereal creature in white wept. And the duke started shouting orders to his carriage driver. Lanterns and torches flared upstairs and down throughout the impressive ducal edifice.

Deciding he'd done his duty and that a search more thorough than he could launch was under way, Trev walked off, swinging his souvenir cudgel like a cane. Noble families had a habit of misplacing offspring, it seemed. Perhaps his own case was not so out of the ordinary as he'd thought.

He suffered a twinge of anxiety at the possibility that he'd sailed the wrong course, but he hastily suppressed it. Old wrongs must be righted.

He was thirty-two years old and couldn't expect to live forever. He'd nearly lost an eye to a backfiring cannon, hovered on the brink of death from a rapier wound to the chest, and almost sacrificed a leg to a gator. If he wanted to live out his remaining days raising young Rochesters to inherit his fortune, he had to start now, while he was still in one piece.

He had to talk to the artist of that damned portrait and make her confess in front of witnesses that she was part of his grandfather's nefarious plot and had never seen him before in her life.

Considering the accuracy of the portrait, how likely was anyone to believe either of them?

Sinda rubbed her eyes as the coach slowed to stop at the Sommersville inn in the early dawn. No highwaymen had dashed madly out of the hedgerows to halt her escape. She hoped that meant Sir Trevelyan hadn't followed her. Even so, her father would be looking for her in every coaching inn in England. It had been a flash of inspiration to send the sedan driver to buy her ticket. And the flash of a gold coin that had paid for the service.

Her mother would figure out where she was, of course. The duchess always knew where everyone was, even when they didn't want to be found. It was a gift of hers.

Stepping wearily from the coach, Sinda didn't try to surmise what her mother would do. A normal mother would tell her husband where to find their straying lamb, or she would race down to berate her daughter for being a coward and a fool or simply send servants to collect her.

Stella, Duchess of Mainwaring and acknowledged head of the Malcolm clan, was no normal mother. Thank goodness.

Sinda hadn't notified her cousin Christina of her impending arrival, and it was far too early an hour to do so now. She'd been in the area before and was familiar with the inn. She would have a bite of breakfast and wait until the sun was fully up.

By all the goddesses, she wished she knew how she had come to this sorry pass. She was a modest, unassuming sort, loyal, obedient, doing all that was expected of her. Her only desire was to paint, not cause trouble. It wasn't as if she'd *meant* to paint Sir Trevelyan, after all. And the summer fair was simply coincidental. Why did people insist on seeing things in her art that she hadn't meant at all?

It was a mystery to her. The day Lady Roxbury had fainted in the park, all she'd done was capture the likeness of a passing gentleman, then painted in a pretty lady and some children to accompany him. How was she to know the gentleman had recently taken a mistress? She thought the lady's faint more a matter of silliness than her own prescience.

Sipping hot chocolate brought to her by an early-rising servant, watching dawn awaken through the wavy glass of a mullioned window, she wished she could transform herself from the glaringly public daughter of a duke to a simple villager. No one would notice her then.

A few minutes later, she looked up in surprise as an auburn-haired woman in dark mantle and hood slid onto the bench across from her.

"This inn isn't quite as respectable as it once was," the woman warned.

Stunned, Sinda froze with cup in midair to study this forward intruder. Not a complete stranger, she decided. There was something familiar about her. They must have met briefly on her earlier visit, but her weary brain simply didn't recognize her table companion under these different circumstances.

"I'm Mora Abbott. My father is the vicar." The new arrival held out a slender hand.

Unaccustomed to such directness, Sinda hesitantly accepted the hand. Mora's grasp conveyed warmth and... interest? Curiosity? She must be exceedingly tired to think such things.

"I'm..." Sinda blinked. Who was she to be? If she wished to remain anonymous, she must adopt a new name. Why hadn't she thought of that earlier?

"You look too much like your cousin, the duchess, to be anyone but a Malcolm," Mora warned her. "Perhaps if you colored your hair or hid behind spectacles you might escape notice."

This was ridiculous. It was as if this stranger could read her mind. Or knew her predicament. Although, Sinda supposed, if Christina had chattered to the vicar's daughter—and her cousin always spoke everything on her mind—Mora probably did know about her.

"I was just wishing I could be someone else for a while," she replied. "I'm Lucinda, but I wish I could be a Mary or Anne or Peg and live in a simple cottage to be left alone with my work."

"Welcome to Sommersville, Lady Lucinda," Mora said. "I fear tales of your fame precede you. It is difficult to disguise true talent."

She hadn't thought of that either. She hadn't thought of

very much at all except escape. She had assumed Christina would help her concoct a scheme to keep her hidden. Christina was excellent at scheming, and her cousin was a duchess now, with all the attendant power if not the wealth.

"I only mean to paint landscapes," she answered. "And I am not so very well-known. Women artists are considered beneath notice. That one portrait is all I've ever displayed in a gallery."

"Nevertheless, your fame precedes you. Or, shall I say, notoriety? All society watches and emulates your family. Everything you do is talked about and repeated, even this far into the countryside."

"I'll never live down Bonnie Prince Charlie, will I?" Rubbing her eyes and sinking back against the faded cushion of the high seat, Sinda wished for nothing more than a warm bed and a good night's sleep. Maybe then she could sort this through. Right now, talking to a complete stranger as if she'd known her all her life seemed to make sense.

"If you just paint landscapes, you might," Mora said reassuringly. "The duke owns a cottage not far from here. It's not rented at the moment. Shall I take you there? I can send word up to the manor that you've arrived. That way, no one will know of your connection to the duchess."

Lucinda brightened. "Would you?" As the idea caught and held her imagination, she felt better than she had in days. "By chance, would you know anything of changing hair color?"

Three

HAVING LEARNED WHAT HE NEEDED TO KNOW IN LONDON, Trev set his sights on Sussex and the Willows the day after his encounter with the duke. The carriage horses trotted down the long drive leading to the late Viscount Rochester's home—the home that should have been Trev's.

The home that *would* have been his had his grandfather not paid London solicitors to declare his father's Jamaican marriage illegal and null. The Willows had been part of his grandmother's dowry, entailed to her younger son upon his marriage. With the marriage annulled, it had returned to the earl's coffers, to be dispensed at his will.

The elderly earl despised his mixed-blood grandson. He wouldn't return the estate.

"Reckon the welcome won't be any friendlier than it was last time," Mick noted laconically.

Sprawled beside his driver, flicking his whip and watching a golden-red leaf drift by his nose, Trev drank in the crisp autumn air as if it were the finest brandy. "Reckon I care?" He mocked Mick's thick accent.

"Reckon you do," Mick replied darkly. "You can pretend you're a care-for-nothing, but I been beside you through war and hurricanes. No captain ever saw to his crew like you. And that's a grievin' widow and her lost little lambs up there. You ain't never turned a cold heart to a woman or child yet."

"Aye, and tell that to Raw Patty. She's rotting in a Jamaican jail because I put her there." Trev scoffed at the imbecility of thinking he was soft.

"Patty weren't female. She's a hellcat, and well you know it. If you cared for nothing, you'd move into the earl's big house and tell his servants to go to hell, instead of pining after this puling little place of your cousin's. You got as much right to both as the widow, seein' as how the earl's too ill to look after them."

Trev flicked the whip and caught a bronze beech leaf. He could argue, but he wasn't much on explaining himself.

The tidy square manor house coming into view was the only home he'd ever known. He clung to the memory of every honey-colored block of limestone and each arched red-sandstone cornice. He remembered the polished mahogany banister that he and Laurence used to slide down. The humid aroma of the orangery had given him his first taste of the tropics. The rolling acres of green through which they passed filled his heart with longing. Those memories had kept him alive in those first years of near slavery.

He didn't want the earl's fortress in Somerset that had been entailed to his cousin Laurence. Trev wanted to bring a loving wife to the home where he remembered being happy—the estate Laurence had promised to sell him. The estate he couldn't claim because now that Laurence was dead, the earl was executor, and the earl would rather see him rot in hell than sell him one inch of land. Trev's hatred of his grandfather hid the ache of his cousin's loss, but seeing his childhood home now stirred longings best tamped down.

"My grandfather's estate has a steward," he responded to Mick's talk of taking over guardianship of the earldom. "My cousin's place does not. There should be workers in the fields, scything hay for the winter, moving sheep to winter pastures, and harvesting the grain before it rots. I'm not much of a farmer, but I can drag lazy men from their beds and set them to work."

Mick chuckled. "Aye, you can do that if the widow will let you."

There was the problem in a nutshell. So far, the widow

had not acknowledged him as even a Rochester, much less guardian to her children. She'd never met him, after all, and he certainly didn't look like any Rochester she knew. He understood. He didn't have to like it.

Anyway, it wasn't as if he could bring home a wife to a house that was already occupied.

Trev gazed at the sparkling glass in the ancient mullion windows of his home and knew suspicious eyes gazed through at least one of them.

Lady Rochester had a right to be suspicious of his intent under the circumstances. He didn't know how to tell her that he didn't scheme to usurp the rights and estates belonging to her late husband or her infant son. His nephew could have the earldom and all its wealth. He only wanted the Willows, which rightfully belonged to him.

"There should be a school of social skills," he grumbled, grasping the post and swinging down to the ground as the carriage halted at the front stairs. "How do politicians learn to lie and connive and persuade?"

"Snakes raise snakes," Mack said prosaically. "You're a cat raised by wolves. Ain't no wonder you don't know how to get on."

Trev grinned at the image. "A puma, my good man, not any old house cat."

Mick snorted. "Right you are. Black pussycat." He whipped the horses toward the stable, leaving Trev standing on still another doorstep, on the outside looking in.

He still had the whip in his hand. Cursing his clumsiness, he held it behind his back as he rattled the knocker. He knew damned well the household had seen his arrival. He could just imagine the anxiety heightening behind the doors. He wondered if this time they would let him in. Despite his efforts, nothing had changed with his hasty trip to London. He gave another curse under his breath to the missing artist.

To his relief, one of the tall oak doors swung open beneath his impatient knock. A stranger stood there, a slight woman in drab gray with a coronet of auburn braids hidden beneath a lace cap. A new housekeeper?

He'd meant to have cards engraved but had forgotten. It was a blamed nuisance trying to scrounge up distant memories of youthful lessons on a gentleman's duties. He tried to look innocuous, but his scarred visage didn't wrap well around civility.

He'd forgotten his hat and held a whip in his hand. He was like to scare the servants to death.

"I'm Trevelyan Rochester, here to see Lady Rochester." He saw no point in bowing and scraping before a servant, so he stood there stiffly, waiting for the door to slam in his face again.

"The viscountess is resting. Won't you please come in?"

The maid didn't curtsy, but Trev was too stunned at the invitation to care. Should he expect muskets and sword point if he crossed the threshold? With no small degree of trepidation, he took a deep breath and entered the hallowed foyer where he'd last seen his parents alive.

The scent of baking bread greeted him. He inhaled the aroma, almost closing his eyes in an ecstasy of homecoming. This was the way it should be. Brisk autumn air, baking bread, a roaring fire—and a woman to welcome him home.

That kind of sentimentality would get him killed. He scanned the imposing balustrade rising to the second floor, searching for hidden weapons or assassins.

Finding nothing to fear in the foyer, he stepped across the parquet to check the blue salon, then studied the silent woman with hands folded in her skirt.

"You are?" he demanded curtly.

"Mora Abbott." Still no curtsy.

This time he noticed, and a scowl formed across the bridge of his nose at the impertinence. A friend of the viscountess? In those rags? His instinct for trouble stirred, and he continued to stare at her with suspicion.

"The vicar's daughter, to be precise." She watched him through keen eyes the pale aqua of a summer sky before a storm gathered. "As is understandable, Lady Rochester is unwell."

"In the absence of the head of the family, I have come to look after the lady's interest. I must speak with her," he told her.

Her dark-lashed eyes didn't flicker. "Would you care for some coffee? I can seat you in the salon."

He followed Miss Abbot into the sunny front room reserved for visitors. His boots resounded like death knells against the hardwood floor.

The woman indicated a seat she'd turned toward the fire. "I'll have someone serve you directly."

Rather than take the delicate silk chair and wait idly, tapping his fingers, Trev paced the long salon. He didn't have many memories of this room. Children had been banned from playing near the expensive, flocked silk wallpaper, century-old furniture, and Ming vases, but that had only confirmed it as a good place to hide in a rowdy game of hide-and-seek. He'd probably had his rump tanned for his misbehavior, but winning the game had been most important then.

And now? He didn't know. When he'd received Laurence's letter saying the earl was in ill health, Trev had been torn between his abiding need to beat the old man at his own game and the overwhelming desire to simply come home to the peace he remembered from childhood.

Now Laurence was dead, the earl hovered on the brink of the grave, and winning had lost its glitter. He hadn't even been given an opportunity to grieve.

"Is the earl dead?" whispered a voice Trev could almost imagine came from his own head since there was no other in the room.

He stood in front of a window, hands behind his back, so he glanced out. He saw only rolling hills, trees, contented cattle—and a drop of nearly twenty feet. No pixie fluttered outside the glass.

Pixie. His gaze fell to the expensive puddle of drapery at his feet. He had a sudden recollection of his youthful hiding place. With his boot, he inched the drapery sideways, uncovering a child's buckled shoe.

"Last I heard, your great-grandfather lives," he informed the draperies gruffly.

"Then we don't have to leave." Defiance more than relief tinged the reply.

"You won't ever have to leave if you don't want to," he promised with the fervency of one who had been denied his heart's desire. Immediately, he regretted his words. Of course, he wanted them to leave, to go to the earl's home where they belonged.

"Even if Mama's baby is a girl?" the child whispered back.

Baby? Laurence had written when his wife had borne him a son and a daughter. He had not written of pregnancies. But what difference would it make if the baby was a girl or a boy? Laurence already had his heir.

"My nanny says my nasty cousin will throw us out." The child wept, and the draperies trembled with the force of her grief. "My daddy won't know where to find us when he comes home."

He'd taken too long to answer. Pained that he'd caused his niece—and undoubtedly her mother—such distress, Trev awkwardly dropped to one knee, to the approximate height of the unseen child. He tried to sound reassuring—not easy for a man who was more accustomed to shouting against the wind. "This is your home. You can live here forever and ever. And so can your mama and your brother and whatever baby comes along." He cursed himself for three times a fool. Laurence's wife had probably sent the child apurpose to soften him.

He might have the blood of men on his hands, but he couldn't harm a child. Mick was right.

A flaxen head and big blue eyes peered warily around the damask. "I don't have a brother. He died, and Daddy cried."

Trev swallowed and tears sprang to his eyes. He had no idea how to go on. Laurence had lost his son? He must have been devastated. But the little girl was waiting for his response, and he couldn't take it all in at once. "I'm sorry to hear that, lass. Shall I order cakes when Miss Abbot returns?"

She smiled blissfully, revealing tiny dimples. "Would you, please? I'm fearfully hungry."

Standing, Trev held out his big lummox of a hand to take her tiny one. She hesitated, then slipped her fingers into his and let him help her over the puddle of draperies. She had freckles across her pert nose and a smear of jam on her rather dusty neckerchief. And she looked like a miniature Laurence as Trev remembered him. His heart wrenched painfully.

"You're very dark," she chirped, searching his face. "My daddy won't let my mama use powder to hide her freckles. Do gentlemen not use powder?"

"Charity, you're not supposed to be in here," a sharp voice scolded.

The demure witch of a vicar's daughter stood in the doorway, tray in hand, watching them with those odd eyes of hers.

Unbalanced by the spate of innocent chatter and the child's easy acceptance of his fearsome visage, Trev refused to release the girl's hand but gallantly led her to the silk chair at the fire. "Miss Charity and I would like some cakes, please," he ordered as if he had every right to do so.

And he did, he realized with such startlement that he almost fell into the chair. If Laurence's heir had died... He couldn't think of it. He'd never thought of it. Laurence was the only son of the earl's eldest son, heir to the earldom, and that's the way it was meant to be.

No wonder his grandfather had had an apoplexy. If both Laurence and his son had died, then the earl's only heir was Trev, the son of the younger son, the swarthy result of a mixed marriage and named bastard by his own family. Unless the child the viscountess carried was a boy... He sat frozen, trying desperately not to think of it.

Charity touched his hand and beamed up at him. "Thank you, my lord," she said with the pride of a child who has learned a new trick.

Trev didn't correct her use of a title he'd never coveted nor thought to have.

Four

"I STILL CAN'T BELIEVE YOU DID THAT TO YOUR HAIR," Christina, Duchess of Sommersville, grumbled as she and Lucinda sauntered through the village green at the end of September.

"It's just henna. Mora said it will wash out gradually. I rather like it. It makes me feel rebellious and someone else altogether."

"I rather prefer you as quiet cousin Lucinda. And your real hair is such a lovely silver-blond. Quite distinctive."

"Precisely," Sinda said dryly, stopping before the cottage she had called her own these past weeks. "And you must behave as if we are virtual strangers, unless you wish to see murder and mayhem on your doorstep."

Tall, slender, and just beginning to show her pregnancy, the duchess tied the blue ribbon beneath her straw hat and checked the green for bystanders. Finding plenty, she sighed and gave a regal nod rather than enter the cottage. "I heard Sir Trevelyan stormed off to London to petition Parliament for guardianship of his grandfather's and cousin's estates while the earl is ill. If he can prove that his father's Jamaican marriage is legal in British courts, then he stands to inherit the whole. I doubt he'll be seen in these parts again."

Sinda shivered. "I cannot believe I was so unlucky as to choose the same village where his cousin used to live. Perhaps I should have gone to Felicity in Scotland."

"I daresay the earl has an estate there as well. This is a very small island, after all. You cannot hope to hide forever."

"I can hope to hide until the earl dies, and Sir Trevelyan has too many other matters on his mind to look for me." Glancing over Christina's shoulder, she adopted a smile. "Hello, Mrs. Flanagan. How are the children today?"

Reminded of the role she was playing, the duchess gathered her skirts and handed the pretty basket on her arm to Sinda. "I am so glad you will be sketching my kitten, Mrs. Jones. I hope you enjoy your cottage."

Turning to the matron closing in on them, she smiled gaily. "Dear Mrs. Flanagan! Just the person I needed to see. You know the altar cloth for…"

Sinda grinned as her cousin Christina threw herself into the diversion and led her suspicious neighbor away. A duchess who preferred traipsing the woods or climbing haunted towers to society's rules understood role-playing well enough. Pretending she didn't know Sinda was a trifle more complicated.

Letting herself into the lovely house she'd borrowed from Christina's husband, Sinda hugged herself with pleasure at the cozy nest she'd made there. The duke had told her to spend whatever she needed to make it comfortable for the next tenant.

Knowing the duke's coffers were bare, she didn't like to take advantage of his generosity, so she'd limited her purchases. Even so, she'd enjoyed herself thoroughly.

She had a good eye for décor that might pay the duke back someday. It didn't require a lot of coin to adorn the small windows with muslin dyed with indigo from Mora's endless supply of useful plants and herbs. A rug woven of rushes dyed in blues and reds covered the worn plank floor. An easel stood in the sunny front window—a relic rescued from Duke Harry's attic, as was most of the rest of the furniture.

Sinda liked pretty things around her and wished she could indulge more, but for a first home, she had done well. Once she sold a few landscapes, she would do better.

Christina had commissioned an oil of Harry's monstrous

mansion, thus giving Sinda reason to visit whenever she needed. The ugly mixture of Tudor timber, castle stone, and contemporary brick hadn't inspired her to paint it yet, but she enjoyed sketching the village. Both Mora and Christina had promised to spread word to neighboring manors of Sinda's talent. The squire's wife had already made an inquiry.

She missed her sisters, but it was too soon to let them know where she was. All hue and cry had died soon after she'd arrived, so she assumed her mother had discovered she was safe with family.

Sinda hoped Sir Trevelyan forced Parliament to acknowledge his right to the estate so he no longer had reason to be angry with her. She rather enjoyed her new anonymity, but she dearly wished to see her family. Had Cecily's suitors returned? Had Belinda saved any more kittens?

About to hang a kettle over the fire for tea, Sinda halted at a knock on the door. Perhaps it was Mrs. Flanagan, escaped from Christina's clutches.

Smiling in welcome, she opened the door—and froze.

A petite, heavily pregnant woman cloaked in rich velvet, with lace covering her powdered curls, stood on the doorstep. Shadows marred her eyes and sleeplessness haunted her gaunt features. An elderly maid hovered at her elbow, as if waiting for the lady to topple at any moment, as she gave every impression of doing.

"Are you the artist?" the elegant visitor asked. She carried herself proudly, but her voice broke on the question.

Stunned by the grief emanating from a wealthy lady who ought to be all peaches and cream and smiles on the eve of her child's birth, Sinda recovered quickly. "I have some skill in the arts, yes. Won't you please come in?"

As the woman nodded and stepped over the threshold, Sinda dusted off the chintz pillow on the wooden settle before the fire. "I was just about to make tea. Would you like some?"

"Tea? How lovely, thank you." The lady sank awkwardly on the bench with the aid of her maid. "I fear weariness has robbed me of my manners. I am Lady Melinda Rochester."

Rochester? Sinda nearly dropped the kettle. She only

managed to steady her hand by reaching for a towel. This was the woman who must have suffered the torments of the damned after the scandal caused by Sinda's painting of Trevelyan. If she'd induced any small portion of the lady's grief, she wished she could repair the harm.

"Welcome, my lady." Years of living in society paid off. She could respond to the social niceties without giving them a thought. "I am Lucy Jones." Her nanny had used to call her Lucy. Jones had seemed innocuous enough when she'd renamed herself.

As she performed the ritual of heating the teapot, counting out expensive spoonfuls of loose tea, and waiting for the kettle to boil, she realized tea was not something commonly served by those who counted their pennies, but it was too late to correct her error now.

Presenting her guest with a delicate china cup of steaming Keemun, Sinda sat on the hearth pillow and waited. The viscountess didn't look at all well. She wouldn't press her.

"Do you... could you..." Her guest cast a helpless glance at the sketch on the easel. "I hear you are very talented. Are you quick?"

Forcing her eyebrows not to fly off her face, Sinda sipped her tea. "It depends on the medium, my lady. Oil is time consuming. Chalk is quick. Watercolor is only good for some subjects."

The woman made a moue of frustration. "I so wanted an oil, a grand painting of my daughter sitting in the blue salon. Or on the grounds with the topiary. Or in the orangery where Laurence—" She fought back a sob, and the maid hastily provided a handkerchief.

"I cannot do portraits," Sinda said, wishing it could be otherwise, but she had no intention of further harming this woman who had already suffered so much. If there was more grief in the lady's future, she didn't want to paint it for her.

The viscountess dried her eyes with the finesse of one who had to do so often. Renewed determination colored her voice. "My husband's heir is in London, obtaining the approval of his peers to turn us out of our home."

The rotten no-good cad! How could he do that to this lovely woman and her children?

"A sketch of the house if you could," the lady continued. "Or the spaniels. I do not know when he'll return or if he'll allow us to keep anything."

Lucinda caught her breath and considered the request. Did she dare brave the grounds of the man who would like nothing better than to cut off her head? The old, quiet Lucinda would have hid in her room at the thought.

The new, anonymous Lucy, the one with the red hair, laughed boldly to herself. Just let Sir Trevelyan try to stop her!

⟨❧⟩

Early October

Galloping down the lane to the Willows, Trev cursed fluently in every language he knew, needing to vent steam before entering the stifling environment of a house of bereavement.

Mick emerged from the stable where he'd been tending the horses. Leaping down from his weary stallion, Trev brushed his servant away from the reins and walked the horse himself. He needed to cool down as much as Rex did.

"Wouldn't accept your papers, would they?" Mick asked prosaically, walking with him, grabbing a rein to control the stallion's tossing head.

"I don't think they'd accept me if I resurrected my father from the grave."

"Don't imagine ye asked politely, did ye?"

"I was bloody polite! Showed them the affidavits from witnesses to the marriage. Showed them the wedding ring and the letters my parents exchanged calling each other *husband* and *wife*. But the marriage took place almost forty years ago, in a primitive village in a foreign country. The contract wasn't written, no church was involved, and once my parents were no longer alive to testify to their willingness to the marriage, my grandfather's solicitors had it labeled a *secret* marriage and thus null. It's all flummery. Parliament representatives said they'd have their attorneys look at the case anew in due time.

I know that ploy." Trev ground his teeth and walked faster. "So I hired my own lawyers to sit on the tails of their solicitors until they examined my documents."

"Aye, that's the way of it. Play 'em at their own game." Mick nodded sagely. "Did ye sit in their coffeehouses and share yer drinks with them? Smile pretty at their daughters?"

"What daughters? They wouldn't let me within a mile of any. They all think I murdered Laurence!" Trev set off a stream of invectives.

"The widow hired an artist," Mick said with studied nonchalance.

Trev halted in midstream. "An artist?"

Mick kept the horse walking. "Pretty little thing. Claims she's a widow too. She's sketching the orangery."

"The orangery?" Trev had a sour taste in his mouth for artists these days, particularly lady artists.

"Aye. She has the dogs in there." Mick's weather-beaten face couldn't look innocent if he tried, but his voice was all that was virtuous.

"Does the artist have a name?"

"I heard tell it's Lucy, Mrs. Lucy Jones, nice simple name for a lass. Since you had an interest in lady artists, thought you might have an interest in this one."

Trev could lay every grievance he'd suffered these past weeks at the feet of a certain lady artist. Flinging down the horse's reins and leaving the animal to Mick, he stormed off in the direction of the orangery and a suspicious artist with the name of *Lucy*.

⌘

Sketching the lazy spaniels in front of the soaring glass windows of the orangery, Lucinda was grateful for her placid nature. Otherwise, she might be tempted to look for a stick to take to the despicable cad who threatened to evict the viscountess and her daughter from their home.

While Sir Trevelyan spent his hours harassing London society, the lady lived in terror and grief. What a wretched world if a widow could lose her home for not bearing a son!

Perhaps the viscountess would birth another boy, and the ill earl would recover, and that would be the end of his pirate grandson.

Sinda hated to believe that the romantic hero she'd painted had the soul of a villain, but she'd seen the coldness of Sir Trevelyan's eyes in the gallery. He had looked fully capable of swinging the wicked sword he carried. Of course he swung swords. He was a pirate. He killed people! How could she expect him to be anything but evil?

And to think that even for a moment she'd allowed herself to be attracted to him! If her judgment was that easily swayed, it was a good thing she had chosen to become an old maid.

Perhaps there was something one of her family could do to prevent Sir Trevelyan from evicting the viscountess. She would write to her father, except her father would probably like to lock up his straying daughter right now.

One of the spaniels lifted its brown-and-white head and sniffed. Sinda frowned and waited for the animal to lie back down. She'd never before painted animals from real life. She just had visions of them in her head that she copied. She could probably sketch the spaniels without their posing, but their movements disturbed her concentration.

The other dog yipped and stood up, tail wagging. Giving up, Sinda looked around for Charity. The child loved to watch, although she couldn't sit still for long. Or remain quiet. She'd chattered of the baby brother she'd lost, of how she watched every night for her daddy to come home, and how she hoped the new baby would make her mama laugh again. It was all Sinda could do to keep smiling through her tears for the child's sake. She plastered that smile on now as she waited for Charity to appear from amid the greenery.

Instead, a tall, distinctly masculine figure shoved his way through the palm fronds.

She froze. The day was cloudy, and the glass reflected only shadows across his harsh features.

A shadow of whiskers gave a dangerous cast to his angular jaw. He wore no hat or wig, and his jabot was askew. His garb was as simple and elegant as on the first day she'd seen him, except his long vest and coat were unfastened to reveal his linen beneath, as if he were in the privacy of his own chambers. She could easily imagine the muscular breadth of his chest beneath the gaping silk of his vest. She gulped and tried not to lower her gaze to where his shirt met his breeches, but his eyes were such a study in fury that she did not wish to look at his face, either.

Taking a deep breath, she adjusted the long lappets of her lace cap and reached for a broader pencil. How well had he seen her that night? It had been dark and she'd been wearing a hood. Would he murder her immediately or wait until he found her at home in the dark?

"Mrs. Jones, I presume?" His tone was not only disbelieving, but also sarcastic. She could sense his massive presence towering above her where she sat.

Shuddering inwardly, she declined her head in acknowledgment and returned to her sketch. Her hand shook.

At her non-response, he scowled. She could feel it.

He stood behind her, gazing over her shoulder at her sketch. She tried to steady her hand as she rubbed in the featheriness of the dog's tail. Both animals lay back down but they watched the newcomer with delight.

"*Lucy* Jones?" he continued, conveying layers of irony.

"And you are?" she asked without looking up.

Nonplussed, Trev stared at the nape of her neck. A reddish curl escaped her cap at the nape. Could he be wrong? The duke's daughters were said to be fair. She was sitting so he couldn't even tell if she was of a height with the girl in the alley.

And she was abominably rude. A duke's docile daughter no doubt merely dabbled in watercolor and wouldn't maintain the unsociable habits of the artists he'd met in his travels. This woman certainly possessed the impertinence of a professional artist dedicated to her craft.

He wanted to snatch off her cap and make her face him, but beneath the rough exterior he'd garnered in his years at sea was still the gentleman his mother had made him. Almost.

"I am Trevelyan Rochester, Charity's cousin." He waited

to see if she would acknowledge his presence, his name, or that she even knew of his existence.

"Pity," was her response.

"*Pity*?" He kept his voice to a low roar. What the devil did she mean by that?

"Charity would prefer a cousin more her age to play with," she said with a degree of absentmindedness while she sketched the dog's tail.

He could fling the canvas on the ground and stomp on it, or he could play along awhile longer. He'd always been fascinated by the way artists worked. She was quite talented, if he was any judge at all. She'd sketched the structure of the orangery's ornate frame and glass in a few brief strokes. The dogs were rapidly taking shape. In the background, he could see the lines that would become the plants framing the dogs. He envied her sureness.

"Our family is a small one," he said. "We have a habit of losing members faster than we replace them. Perhaps I should bring in children from the village for Charity to play with."

"I'm sure she would like that, although I would recommend asking the viscountess for permission first. She's not at all well."

"Her condition has worsened?" he asked in alarm.

She gave him a scathing glance from beneath darkened eyebrows. Not fair, then, but redheaded. Interesting. And lovely. Her long lashes prevented him from seeing as much of her eyes as he would have liked.

"The child grows heavier and Lady Rochester grows weaker. She's lost a son and a husband within the space of a year, and she's in dread of losing her home. But then, I'm sure you wouldn't understand a woman's fears."

Trev winced at her coldness. She didn't sound like the saucy imp from the alley. This was a woman grown, not a child, and she looked as if she'd like to spear him with her pencil.

"I'm not here to steal her home," he corrected. "Only to run it as someone must. I have encouraged her to move to Lansdowne where she belongs, that is all."

"So you may throw her out when you come into the title?"

She returned to sketching, although her strokes were bolder now, indicative of her fury. "How very generous of you."

"I won't be coming into the title!" Not if anyone in the British aristocracy had anything to say about it, anyway. "Lansdowne is closer to London and the best physicians. If she's bearing the next earl, she should take up her rightful place in the earl's household. The old man could use a woman's help."

"Did Lansdowne invite her?" she demanded. "Are *you* in the habit of going where you're not invited?" She held up her pencil and studied the stroke she'd just made. "Oh, I forgot. You weren't invited here."

"By Jove, you've the tongue of an adder! Should I let the harvest rot in the fields while the silly woman grieves? I'm not the devil, you know!" he roared in a tone that had once sent men scattering.

"And not a gentleman, by any means. Were I Lady Rochester right now, I'd be in tears. No wonder the woman hides in fright in her own home."

She said that so calmly that Trev blinked in surprise. His normal reaction would be to order her thrown down the hatches. She leveled him with her directness.

"And thus you are not a lady for you do not fear my shouts?"

She shrugged delicately. "You are the usurper. I was invited here."

He couldn't decide if he wanted to howl curses and wring her neck or cackle like a lunatic, take a seat, and see if he could rattle her as she rattled him. He couldn't remember the last time anyone had stood up to him. He could make a pirate crew cringe with his roars.

"The dogs aren't waving their tails," he pointed out, comparing her drawing to the lazy spaniels who once more slumped in repose.

"They were. And they will again. The study needs movement. If I wished to do a still life, I would leave out the animals."

It annoyed him that she paid no heed to his presence. He might have a harsh, unfashionable visage, but ladies usually liked to use their wiles on him. Did he make her uneasy? He hoped so, because she certainly disturbed him.

He stepped between the easel and the dogs. She continued sketching as if he were not there. A long strand of auburn hair fell down her cheek. She did not pin her hair well. She wore a white linen apron over a dull blue bodice and skirt, presumably to protect them from the charcoal dust. She had pencil smudges all over the apron and on her nose. She kept her head bent so he couldn't discern more than the flawless cream of her cheek. He couldn't tell if she was the girl from the alley. He thought not. She was simply too forthright to be the daughter of a duke, trained in society's artful evasions.

"Do you do portraits?" he demanded, forcing her to look at him, recognize him, and acknowledge his presence.

She glanced up. Her eyes were the color of the sea at its finest, and a longing for his ship, the *Pirate Lass*, stole over him. He loved sailing. He wasn't certain what he was doing here, besides making an ass of himself, except he had no business on the sea any longer. With the wealthy Spanish nearly driven from the West Indies and war with France on the horizon, it wasn't worth risking his life or that of his crew to ask for his letter of marque to be continued.

"I don't do portraits," she said flatly. "And if you continue to stand in my way, I'll paint the spaniels from memory and be gone."

She had a lady's cultured voice and the soft hands of a woman not accustomed to hard work. After he got past the shock of her eye color, he could admire her fair, unpowdered cheeks. Surely a duke's daughter would wear cosmetics or retain an unhealthy pallor from their use. She had a rosy color all her own. He either embarrassed her or made her angry.

"There's no reason for the lady to hide in her own home. I wouldn't harm a hair on the head of my cousin's widow. 'Tis not my fault she's a weeping milksop," he asserted brashly.

She glared at him. "Do you tell her so?"

"How can I tell her so? She hides when she sees me coming."

"And are you yelling when she sees you, as you yell now?"

"I'm not yelling! Only fishwives yell." But he lowered his voice a decibel or two.

A hint of a laugh tugged at her lips. Trev wanted to take umbrage, but she was too pretty and the subject too silly.

"A man needn't shout to be heard," she told him primly.

"He does in gale force winds or if he wishes the crow's nest to hear him. Men respond to shouted orders, not namby-pamby requests."

"Women respond to flowers and politeness and an occasional smile and flattery."

"I should flatter the she-devil who ordered the door slammed in my face when I first heard of my cousin's death?" He was shouting again. Even he could hear that. "Did she not think I grieved his loss too?"

She raised a lovely curved eyebrow, and Trev growled and stepped out of her way. He ought to walk down the aisle of greenery and keep going. He had no use for artists or scolds, and he had work to do.

He stalked back to a flimsy excuse for a palm tree. He turned around and paced back toward the dogs. She was still sketching. A shadow very like a man had taken form beneath her skillful fingers. She began rubbing it out the instant he breathed down her neck.

"I must talk with her. Come with me and keep me from shouting."

She cocked her head to stare at him incredulously. Trev crossed his arms and willed her to heed him. He tapped his fingers against his upper arms.

Apparently seeing that he was a force to be reckoned with, she glanced away, obediently set down her pencil, and wiped her fingers on a cloth. She neatly packed her pencils in a careful arrangement inside her box. She closed her box. She drew a sheet of foolscap over her sketch. She removed the sketch from the easel.

When she began packing up her easel, Trev had had enough. He'd been played the fool by aristocrats far more powerful than she these last days, and his patience was exhausted. He'd given her an express order—one dedicated to helping the viscountess and the estate—and she intended to walk out on him. Well, to hell with that. She was a female, so he couldn't heave her down the gangway as he would an insubordinate sailor. He chose the next best solution.

Grabbing Mrs. Lucy Jones by her lovely waist, he hauled her feet from the ground and, bracing her against his hip, carried her, kicking and struggling, skirts sailing, into the house.

Five

CAUGHT BY SURPRISE, SINDA TRIED TO KICK FREE OF SIR Trevelyan's grip, but she realized quickly that he couldn't feel her soft shoes through her layers of petticoats. He was so tall that even though he held her from the floor, her head still didn't reach past his ear. Not that she could reach his ear from this awkward position, or she would have bitten it off.

He wasn't hurting her. He was carrying her with such ease that he probably was only half aware of what he did. She'd just pushed him to some edge visible only to him, and he fought back in the only way he knew—with brute force.

Someone needed to teach him a lesson in manners.

His broad arm grasped her at the waist of her boned bodice, right below her breasts. If she struggled more... She froze.

He shifted her to a more comfortably upright position. He had muscles like iron. She grabbed his upper arm with both hands, leaned over, and sank her teeth into the silk and linen over his shoulder. That would teach him not to leave his coat unfastened if he was intent on settling arguments by manhandling her.

"Stop that." He glared at her and kept walking out of the orangery and down the back corridor toward the front of the house.

Well, biting had held his attention for all of three seconds. New tactic needed. "I am capable of walking," she said with as much dignity as she could muster.

"Then you should have done so when you had the chance. I do not tolerate insubordination."

"Insubordination! You're not my master. You cannot tell me what to do."

He plunked her down on the octagonal floor of the foyer. She hastily settled her skirts and brushed surreptitiously at those places on her person that still burned from his touch.

"I pay your fees. That puts me in charge." Clasping his hands behind his back now that he had her where he wanted her, he pulled his coattails back and looked down on her as if he were still captain of all he surveyed. The gleam in the dark eyes above the formidable scar was dangerous.

Sinda stuck to her argument, although all that broad linen-covered chest right before her eyes muddled her mind. "The lady pays my wages."

"The lady hasn't a ha'penny to her name. Neither has her family. Laurence lived off the land and our grandfather's allowance. The earl is his executor. The earl is comatose. There are no funds but mine."

Sinda opened her mouth to cut him down to size, but staring into his implacable, dashing visage, she was reduced to silence. She wasn't normally an argumentative person, but she wasn't normally assaulted by strangers either. Right now, amazed by his proximity and his revelation, she couldn't think straight enough to put words together at all. A strand of his long dark hair had come loose in their struggle.

"You're paying the servants?" she finally had the sense to ask, tilting her head to study Sir Trevelyan's exotic features. Did she imagine it, or did the scar twitch under her observation?

"Someone must, else they'd starve or seek new employment. Now do you see why I must speak with the viscountess?" His dark eyes flashed with some incomprehensible emotion.

She did understand. She honestly did. But she'd just been manhandled by a pirate who turned out to be a philanthropist, and she could not quite comprehend the duality while reeling from the heady stimulation of his presence. Her gown still held the scent of him—a smoky, spicy aroma that she might remember the rest of her days. Her waist tingled where he'd held her.

She was the daughter of a duke. *No one* had ever treated her so.

When she didn't speak, he made an impatient gesture and advanced toward the stairs. "I will try not to yell," he grumbled.

He meant to confront the viscountess looking like… looking like… a pirate. The lady would faint of a certainty.

Gathering her wits, Sinda ran to the bottom of the stairs. "Wait! You cannot go like that."

He halted and looked over the balustrade at her. "Like what?"

She gestured at his unfastened clothing, windswept hair, and beard-darkened jaw. "Like a pirate! She fears you. Is that what you want?"

"That's why I wanted your help, but you have not offered it. I cannot coerce you into acting as buffer between us, so I must bully my way in. There are things we must speak of whether she wishes it or not."

Sinda brushed a strand of hair out of her eyes and regretted that she'd had to leave her maid behind. Even a silly cap couldn't keep her hair from escaping its pins. A few minutes in the pirate's company and she looked as disheveled as he. "Then speak to her as gentleman to lady, not pirate to victim. Have you no valet?"

He scowled, and it was like watching a thundercloud pass over his dark features. She shivered before the storm.

"Why do you think I wear these fribbles?" He held up a cuff trimmed in lace.

Although there was far less of it than most men wore, it was exceedingly fine lace, and the wrist revealed when it fell back was more bronzed and muscled than any she knew. Sinda tried not to admire too obviously, but she really wished she could paint the power of his arm.

She reminded herself that she wasn't painting portraits anymore.

"Find your valet," she said sternly, to disguise that she was shaking in her shoes. "I'll tell the gardener you would like some flowers. Prepare some flattery. When you are ready, I will approach the lady first, but if you yell at her, I shall kick you." She never, ever spoke to people this way. She must be possessed.

She swore he stared at her for a full minute. She felt the brunt of his coal-dark eyes and began to understand the fascination of their intensity. She did her best not to melt. He didn't flinch at her rudeness.

"You'll not run away," he demanded, not asked.

"Do I look like a coward?" she replied, though she knew in her heart that she was. She had run away from him once before.

As if he knew that, he didn't answer but proceeded up the stairs without a backward look. She supposed that put her in her place.

Had he recognized her? Was that why he treated her as he had? Should she run again? It would be easy to go to Christina and hide in her husband's huge mansion. An entire army could not get at her there.

But there had been pain behind his eyes and concern in his voice, even when he was yelling. If he spoke the truth and he was paying the estate expenses—with no hope of return— then perhaps she ought to help him. A little.

She had no real reason to believe him a bad man as others did. She knew what others did not—her painting did *not* show Sir Trevelyan in England at the time of his cousin's death. The painting merely showed the imagination of an overfanciful spinster.

He could still be a murderer. Pirates or privateers did not tend to be too nice about who they killed. But did pirates care if their cousin's widow had a roof over her head?

Not having any experience with pirates, she couldn't say. She would simply have to rely on her ability to judge character—which seemed appallingly lacking in the case of Sir Trevelyan—and hope for the best.

❧

Shaved, powdered, and pomaded, Trev shrugged his shoulders uncomfortably against the confines of buttoned vest and tightly tailored coat and avoided looking in the cheval glass. His mincing valet was in ecstasy that he'd actually donned the colorful vest with the peacock feather embroidery. Trev had almost forbid the hair powder to keep the fop from floating off the floor in his gibbering delight, but in the end, thinking of the stern little peahen waiting for him downstairs, he'd relented.

By Neptune, but Lucy Jones was an armful! He yanked at his neckcloth to loosen it rather than let his thoughts dwell on the swell of her breasts crushed against his side and the suppleness of her waist in his hand.

She'd scolded him as if he were a lad of ten.

He'd concentrate on that. A woman who called him a scoundrel and a fool was not the kind of sweet, gentle lady he craved for his own.

Descending the stairs, he found her arranging a colorful assortment of fall flowers and leaves in a vase on the foyer table. Her cap had fallen to her shoulders and soft waves of red hair escaped from their pins. In the watery sunlight from the overhead windows, the loose tresses contrasted strikingly with the creamy expanse of bosom above her lace-trimmed bodice. She'd removed her apron and washed her hands and the smudge on her nose. She no longer looked like an artist but like a lady as proper as any he knew. Not that he knew many.

He might not crave a snapping turtle for wife, but he craved those luscious curves in his bed. He hadn't had a woman since his return. He really ought to seek one soon if he was thinking of the prickly hedgehog in that way.

He craved a friend who could help him. What should he say to keep her on his side? She was humming happily, snipping stems, bending the blossoms, creating a graceful bouquet out of a handful of weeds, and looking like Persephone personified. He was hoping she would translate his gruff words to ones Laurence's wife would comprehend. He couldn't untie his tongue for the life of him.

He must have made some noise on the stairs because she looked up, and the beauty of her smile almost tripped his feet. She actually had his heart thumping like some untried lad's. That wouldn't do.

He clattered down the rest of the stairs in the damned high-heeled shoes his valet had foisted upon him. "Now that I look like a woman, will she approve?" he growled.

Her smiled widened, and he almost believed he saw appreciation in her gaze, but that was his pride wiggling out from beneath the layers of frills. He resisted the urge to jerk at the lace jabot irritating his chin and rubbed powder off his nose instead.

"You look very much the elegant courtier, sir. I must commend your valet." She tilted her head and admired his powdered and beribboned queue. "With your dark coloring, that style suits you very well."

Sweeping back the long tail of his buff coat, Trev made an elegant bow. He had employed the obeisance enough these past weeks to no longer be quite so rusty at it. "Your servant, madam. Shall we beard the lioness in her den?"

Her smile disappeared. "I have sent her a message that you would like her to join you downstairs for tea, but she has declined."

Before he could growl and stomp toward the stairs, she thrust the vase into his hands. "She may feel safer in her own rooms. I will go up first and pave the way. Remember, flowers and flattery."

Trev watched her swinging skirts until she disappeared in the hall overhead, then he stuck his nose in the bouquet and sneezed. A leaf fluttered to the floor. He set the weeds back on the table and paced. If this were the stern of his ship, he could command the bosun to haul the coward from her hammock. Life was much simpler at sea.

Simpler, but without the niceties of a woman's laughter or the softness of her skin or the fragrance of her perfume. Hearing Charity chattering to her nursemaid somewhere above, he wanted the uncomplicated love of a child of his own. He couldn't have those things at sea.

He wished Laurence were here to steer him right. His cousin would know if he should pursue the artist for his bed or a lady for his wife. He would know what ladies were open to pursuit. He would laugh and pound him on the back and offer him a brandy or a good gallop instead of pussyfooting around, expecting him to dress like a fop and mince like a dandy.

Surely Laurence hadn't submitted to foppery to please his lady.

The thought appalled, and Trev was grateful when he heard a door open and voices travel through the hall. He hurried toward the stairs. He wanted to get this over now, before he turned tail and ran for his ship.

As he ascended the stairs, he could hear the low murmur of protest from the viscountess's chambers. The artist's reply was a little more distinct. He couldn't discern the words but the tone was reassuring, cajoling even, as one would speak to a recalcitrant child.

He ought to wonder why Lucy Jones did him this favor when all else thought he was a murderer, but he was more concerned with having his way than attributing motivation right now.

"He is your husband's cousin, my lady. Whose judgment would you believe, your husband's or his grandfather's?"

Aye, there was an excellent argument. Trev strained to hear the reply. He wanted to believe Laurence hadn't married a ninnyhammer.

The lady's first words were lost to him, but as he approached the door, he caught the last angry argument.

"...what if I carry a boy? Will he murder my child too?"

Pain shot straight through him. Reacting without thinking, he shoved open the bedchamber door. It hit the wall like cannon shot, and both women stared at him, startled and wide-eyed. "I am not a murderer!" he roared. "I don't want the bloody title. I only wanted to come *home*!"

The viscountess screamed. The artist heaved a sigh and pointed at the door. "Flowers," she said calmly. "Then flattery."

He tried staring her down. He knew his dark coloring and scarred cheek were fierce enough to terrify most men. She met his gaze without flinching. Spinning on his high red heel, Trev stalked out, muttering.

A clatter of shoes against stairs, much grumbling, and a few moments later, he reappeared, vase in hand.

Sinda had to hide a smile behind a cough. Garbed in lace, powder, and buff coat and breeches, Sir Trevelyan was a formidable sight to see. His elegant stockings certainly needed no plumpers to pad his muscled legs.

But behind the lethal cheekbones and flashing eyes, he looked so unutterably apologetic, bewildered, and angry that she wanted to hug his neck and tell him everything would be all right. She daren't tell him any such thing, and hugging his neck would most definitely give him wrong ideas. She'd just never seen so masculine a man reduced to such bewilderment by a woman's tears.

And he was quite correct about one thing: lace and heels on a man this virile were ridiculous. He should dismiss his valet.

"My lady, my sincerest apologies." He entered the chamber to bow and present the flowers. When Melinda didn't take them, he set them on a dresser in front of a mirror. "I know I have arrived at a delicate time for you, but you must know that I am equally grief stricken. Laurence was my oldest and best friend. I only mean to help as he would wish me to do."

At mention of her late husband, the grief-stricken widow grabbed a handkerchief and sobbed into it. Sir Trevelyan began to look impatient. He sent Sinda a "what do I do now" look.

"You wish to pay your respects to your cousin's grave," Sinda whispered, slipping behind him and toward the door. "Would she care to accompany you?"

He stiffened in resistance. His jaw tightened in that stubborn line she'd noticed earlier. He wanted to discuss estate matters with a grieving widow, the silly man. He'd been long from society if he thought that would occur anytime soon.

"My lady, I would like to pay my respects to Laurence's grave. Would you care to accompany me?"

Sinda smiled in delight and started for the stairs. She intended to grab her materials and run as quickly as she could before all went wrong and he took to hauling her around again. She'd completed her duty here. If she'd done him a disservice by painting the portrait in the first place, she'd accomplished what little she could to right her error.

As she started down the stairs, she heard Melinda's voice ring out in teary rage, "I did not even have his body to bury!"

Oops. Wincing, Sinda hurried down the stairs. She hadn't known that.

Not wishing to hear the pirate's surprised response, she hit the landing running, grabbed a newel post to maintain her equilibrium, and continued her race of escape.

High heels clattered down the stairs after her.

At the bottom, she darted behind the staircase and pressed herself against the wall. Sir Trevelyan stormed past without looking.

To her surprise, he flung open the front door and ran out roaring for his horse to be brought around.

What in heaven's name had the viscountess said to him to send him haring off like a man afire?

Six

WHY THE DEVIL HADN'T HE ASKED QUESTIONS SOONER?

Because his life had been such that he'd come to expect the worst, to the extent that he raged and railed and fought rather than sit back and act sensibly.

At that realization, Trev halted in midshout. Mick was heading toward him, stallion in hand, looking at him as if he had taken leave of his senses—which for all intents and purposes, he had.

They hadn't found Laurence's body.

He was a fool to believe that meant a thing, but without a body, there was a tiny chance that Laurence still lived.

"I'll be right back," he shouted at Mick.

He couldn't ride about looking like a macaroni. Not if he wanted answers. He strode quickly back to the house.

The petite artist was nowhere to be seen. He didn't know whether to kiss her for helping him or bellow at her for trying to make an idiot of him. Had she deliberately told him to ask about the grave, knowing there wasn't any? What insidious game did she play? At the moment, he had too many other things on his mind to fret over a woman's intentions.

He didn't have time to wash out the powder and pomade, but he threw off the lace and heels and found good stout boots and a sensible cravat. The men he needed to see would care more about what he had to say than whether his linen had frills.

The gallop to the coast gave him entirely too much time to think. He gave Rex his head and tried to concentrate on not running over any stray pedestrians. He fed his physical restlessness by urging Rex to jump hedgerows rather than wait for doddering sheep to cross the road. But once the stallion began to slow, Trev had plenty of time to berate himself.

Why had he so blithely accepted the news that his cousin had died at sea? Because he'd lost good men that way, perhaps. Because the earl and his accusations had driven all else out of his head. Because everyone else in his life had died. The fact remained, Laurence had been as good a sailor as any Trev knew and a strong swimmer. They'd learned together as boys. Even if he had somehow managed to lose his craft at sea in a storm, he knew how to stay afloat.

And if Trev remembered anything at all of the tides off this part of the coast, Laurence's body would have washed ashore by now.

He'd sent his own ship to Holland to trade Jamaican rum for fabrics and gewgaws, but it would return soon. He longed to see the *Pirate Lass* in the harbor, to feel the wind in his hair and smell the salt of the sea. But he had a duty on land now.

By nightfall, he was riding into the coastal village he remembered from his youth.

Brighton hadn't changed greatly over the years. It was still a sleepy fishing village that might wash away with the next storm. Trev had seen the like in countries from here to the West Indies. He tied up his horse at the end of the street near the sea, noting the tavern he remembered being here had apparently tumbled out with a tide. Instead, he entered a nearby inn beneath a swinging sign so cracked and faded that the paint could no longer be read.

He waited until his eyes adjusted before scanning the dusky lobby and locating the smoke spilling from a room down the hall. Sweeping off his hat, he followed the smoke to enter the tavern. The stench of sour ale and unwashed bodies filled his nostrils, but it was an honest smell and not the perfumed masquerade of London.

He located the table at the back where the locals watched

him with varying degrees of interest. At this time of day, they were only gray hairs too old to go out with the fishing boats. Spotting a nearly bald man with a pipe, Trev strode across the worn wooden floor, ordering a round of ale for the table as he did so.

"Nick," he greeted the pipe smoker. Looking closer, he nodded at a wiry man with features the wrinkled nut brown of a winter apple. "George, it's good to see you hale and hearty."

Nick chuckled and gestured toward a bench. "Heard ye were home, lad. Wondered if ye'd remember us."

"How could I forget?" Straddling the bench while the round of ale was delivered, Trev waited through the introductions of the rest of the men, slowly recognizing other faces from his youth. But it was Nick and George who had taught him to sail.

As the bartender departed, they waited on him expectantly. Trev took a deep draught to wash away the dust of the road and gather his thoughts. He was comfortable here, as he was not in the elegant salons of London.

"I wish to hear all you can tell me of the day Laurence died."

The old men nodded sagely. It was George who answered first. "He was out in that yacht of his, the one he'd had painted red and called the *Sea Queen*."

"He wrote me of her," Trev replied. "Sturdy, not a racing yacht, because his new bride worried for him."

"Ain't no way he could have turned it over," Nick agreed. "Mayhap a whale caught him, but he never went far from shore. Always came in when the weather went bad."

On known ground, Trev didn't leap to conclusions but studied all angles of the problem. A brief squall, an underwater ledge, a large shark, anything might overset an unwary sailor in a small craft. "Were any of you here the day it happened?"

"We all were. It was the week of the summer fair that Duke Harry arranged. Booths and actors and jugglers—it was a sight to see," said Nick.

"The ladies wore their finest, and the children raced about underfoot as if it were Christmas. Yer cousin brought his lady and the little girl. They stayed the night with the Wesleys."

George took a deep drink of his ale as if this speech had dried him out.

One of the men less well-known to Trev continued. "The viscount didn't get to the shore often with his lady breedin' and all. He told us he'd take the *Queen* out on a last sail before dry-dockin' her. He was thinking of selling her, he was."

"He'd never sell the *Queen*," Nick argued.

"His lady hated the sea. Right squeamish she is," George returned.

"Gentlemen." Trev held up his hand to halt the diversion. "Just tell me what happened that day."

"He couldn't get away until about sunset. The fair was closing up and everybody headed home. That's the last we saw of him." Nick's voice was rough with grief.

"That's it? No sudden storm? No whale beaching on the tide? No loud explosions?"

"And no body washed ashore," George finished for him. "We been wondering when someone would ask us about it, but the lady cried and carried on so when he didn't come back, didn't no one dare say nuthin' to her."

"The yacht?" Trev asked.

"Washed up in pieces over the next few days. There was a storm the next day. He mighta run out of wind and been caught in it."

Trev heard the doubt in the speaker's voice. "Laurence could always find the wind if he had to blow it himself."

The others nodded in agreement.

"The lad could whisper up a wind and tack that boat to port as pretty as could be." Nick sat back and puffed his pipe.

Trev looked from face to face. They held something back. He frowned and slammed down his mug.

"I learned my trade from you, gentlemen. You needn't keep your lips closed around me. I've held my peace all these years, haven't I?"

Nick and George exchanged looks and shrugged. George spoke first. "There's been no moonrakin' hereabouts in many a year, but that's not to say a boat or two don't still go out in the dark of a moon."

In other words, the village no longer lured unsuspecting ships to the rocks with lanterns, but smugglers still worked their trade. Trev had accompanied the smugglers on a trip or two in his youth, although Laurence had very properly stayed home.

Laurence had always accepted the responsibility of being the heir to an earldom and had behaved accordingly.

With the same wild streak possessed by his father, Trev had always behaved as was expected of him—which was to say he'd never behaved at all.

"And was it the dark of the moon the night Laurence disappeared?" he asked, a lump of hope forming in his throat and threatening to stop his breathing.

"It was," George agreed.

"And the tide here still washes everything ashore what goes down upon the rocks," Nick confirmed.

The yacht had washed ashore. Laurence had not. Trev kept his burgeoning hope from his face as he'd learned to do over the years. "I don't suppose you could give me any names?"

"The free traders aren't from hereabouts these days, lad," one of the older men said. "They stop here to sell their goods when the weather is right, but it's not like the old days."

Trev heard the regret in his voice, but he was glad the village no longer relied on the trade. He disagreed with the tariffs that made smuggling profitable, but a criminal trade attracted dangerous men. Smuggling had never been a safe proposition when strangers stepped in.

"Do you know where they might hail from?" It was a wild shot that smugglers might know anything of Laurence, but he would try anything.

"We're old men, lad," George said sadly. "The young 'uns wouldn't tell us if they knew. They think they invented the trade all themselves."

"You will try to find out what you can though?"

They all nodded solemnly. Trev ordered another round, thanked them, and strode off, his mind whirling like a spinning top.

Laurence might be alive!

If he were alive, why hadn't he tried to reach his wife?

His body hadn't washed ashore, and he was a strong swimmer.

The yacht had wrecked, and it had been three months since he'd disappeared.

Laurence could have swum the wrong way on a moonless night. Sharks and stray tides could have carried him away. No one knew better than Trev that the sea wasn't to be trusted.

It didn't matter if he was on a hopeless quest. He couldn't relax until he'd covered every possibility. He strode for the harbor, his mind now ticking like a precision clock.

⁓

"He did what?" Christina asked in horror as Sinda blocked out a color on her canvas.

She'd set up her easel again since Sir Trevelyan had taken himself off so precipitously.

"He tries to be stoic as a gentleman should, but his Spanish blood tells. He's a veritable tempest beneath that cool exterior." Not bothering to repeat her story of being manhandled, Sinda shifted her position for better light from the window and layered in the russet of her background. She shivered inwardly as she remembered the results of the pirate's tempests and prayed he never discovered she was the artist for whom he hunted.

"It is men who lose their temper who end up murdering their loved ones," Christina pointed out.

"It is men who coldly plot for gain who start wars and murder thousands," Sinda countered. "At least one knows where one stands with Sir Trevelyan." If one wasn't lying to him, that was.

"You like him!" Christina crowed. "Sinda, you are mad. You are a mild rabbit and he's a dangerous wolf. You are seeing the figment of your imagination and not the real man. Papa said Sir Trevelyan thundered and growled his way through the lords as if he owned them all. And you just admitted he *carried* you clear through the house!"

"He can be quite intimidating," Sinda agreed. "I daresay that is part of the reason he has fared so well in his profession.

Melinda told me that he was captured by a navy impressment gang when he was but fourteen."

"Fourteen!" Scandalized, Christina sat down on a bench. "How dreadful. Even if his grandson was illegitimate, the earl should have helped him. Why did he not?"

"I don't know. I've not met the earl. I wonder if our mothers have?"

"If you so much as ask, they will be down here on the morrow," Christina warned. "Sir Trevelyan is not for you."

"Of course not. I was just curious." Sinda stepped back to sight the lines she'd sketched earlier, then added another daub of russet. "I cannot sense evil as Felicity does or see auras as you do, so I must learn about people the hard way. The neighbors gossip. They say Sir Trevelyan was a wild child."

"If I remember rightly, Laurence married young, while we were still in the nursery, but from the few times I've seen him, he was always a quiet sort. I suppose Sir Trevelyan could have led him astray if they grew up together. That might have outraged the earl."

"That was my thought. This manor once belonged to Sir Trevelyan's father, according to Cook, who has worked here forever. Lord Rochester's parents perished of smallpox when he was young, and the earl was a widower with no interest in raising a small child. So the boys grew up here under the tutelage of Sir Trevelyan's parents."

"If he had both parents, how could he be illegitimate?"

Sinda frowned and dipped her brush in linseed oil. "I'm not privy to more than gossip and speculation. Sir Trevelyan is very exotic looking. His mother was Jamaican. It's whispered her mother was of mixed island blood, not aristocratic at all. Her father may have been a Spanish aristocrat, but the earl despised Spain. So Trev's father kept the marriage secret until he returned to England with wife and child. It's all very romantic, but not very clear. I just know that a carriage accident orphaned him at fourteen while the boys were off at school. The earl stepped in when they returned from the funeral, and Sir Trevelyan disappeared into the navy shortly after."

"I can make discreet inquiries, but if our mothers hear a

whisper of it…" Christina rose from the bench with grace despite her pregnancy.

"I know, I know." Sinda waved her away. "Thank you for stopping in, but I am fine. Melinda is a bit of a damp rag, but she'll come around. If you do not wish to reveal me, you had best go on. Duchesses do not gossip with artists."

"This masquerade is quite silly." Christina's skirts rustled as she headed for the orangery door. "You should simply move in with us. We have walls enough to start your own gallery."

Sinda looked up from her canvas to give her daring cousin a fond smile. "It may come to that someday, but right now, I am thoroughly enjoying my freedom. I never knew how liberating it would be not to have to change gowns a dozen times a day and smile at visitors when I would rather paint. I can be anyone I want to be and sketch all night and day if I like."

"That, I understand. I'm glad you've come to Sommersville. We just need to find a better way to visit each other."

With a wave of her hand, Christina departed. With a tug of gladness that she had such understanding family, Sinda returned to her painting.

She would need a *very* understanding family should they ever learn that she was determined to unravel the mystery that was Sir Trevelyan Rochester.

Seven

IN THE GLOOM OF EARLY EVENING, A WEEK AFTER HIS VISIT with Nick and George, Trev stopped in the orangery to study the canvas Lucy had been working on. Large blocks of dull colors covered the lively pencil sketch he'd seen last. He searched the canvas for some sign of a cat or kitten, but he couldn't even see a dog in these odd chunks of color.

He supposed the lines might show through in better light, but when the light was good, the artist was here, and he stayed away.

He wasn't certain he needed the distraction of a woman who tempted him in so many ways that he couldn't sleep nights.

He needed to be certain Lucy Jones had naught to do with Lucinda Pembroke.

He had hired men to hunt for the duke's missing daughter, but they'd found no more trace of her than he had. How could she have caught the Sussex coach without anyone seeing her?

Far more likely that she'd had a ship and a lover waiting.

But he could not let go of the mystery of why a duke's daughter would paint him as a murderer for all the world to see. His grandfather had to have arranged it somehow. He just needed to find her and learn why.

He carried his candle back to the front of the house where the butler waited. "Good evening, James. Have the ladies dined comfortably?"

Trev was grateful the older retainers in the household remembered him. The new maids scurried out of his way, but James had looked supercilious ever since he'd known him as a footman in his youth. Trev took that look now as a sign of acceptance.

"Good evening, my lord."

Trev bit his tongue about the title. Apparently James had already transformed his loyalty from Laurence to the man he considered the new viscount.

"Miss Charity has asked if you might visit the nursery before she goes to bed, my lord."

Since none of the maids dared come near him, James was left to do messenger duty, it seemed. Trev nodded. "I'll check on her when I go up." He felt comfortably paternal saying that. He, who had once given orders to blow up ships, now craved the simple duties of reading a book to a child.

He took the stairs to the nursery and knocked. The woman who answered had graying hair and a grandmotherly plumpness that should speak of the wisdom of age, but she gazed on Trev with a baleful eye. "Miss Charity has gone to bed," she informed him coldly.

He'd spent years of his life intimidating more formidable opponents than Miss Plum. Looking over her head, he called, "Charity, are you awake?"

"Yes, Cousin Trev. Would you read me a book? Papa gave me one all about ships and Mama won't read it to me."

As if he'd turn down a request like that! Trev focused his evil eye on Miss Plum, who skittered out of his way. Triumphant, he carried his candle through the schoolroom to the chamber he and Laurence had shared as children.

White eyelet adorned the poster bed that had replaced their more Spartan counterpart. Dolls instead of sailing ships lined the shelves. But the little girl propped against the pillows had Laurence's fair hair and blue eyes, and Trev could deny her nothing.

"I trust your papa gave you the very best book on sailing," he said with a sternness the child laughed at.

"Papa said you have a ship like this." She set the picture

book within the circle of light from her bed candle and pointed out a topsailed schooner. "Where is it now? May I ride on it?"

"It is on its way to London right now." He was impatiently awaiting a message from London saying the *Lass* had arrived. He was torn between sailing with the crew in search of Laurence and staying here to oversee the estate. He knew far more about ships and searching than he did about sheep and farming, but one was the past and the other his future. "One of these days, if your mama permits, I will be happy to escort you aboard."

"No child of mine will ever set foot on a ship," a faint voice whispered from behind him.

"Mama!" Charity held out her arms for a hug.

Not looking at him, the frail viscountess entered. With her velvet dressing gown trailing the floor and her hair tucked beneath a cap, she didn't look much older than a child herself except for the burden of the belly preceding her.

Lady Rochester had never before voluntarily appeared in his presence. Trev tried to look harmless, but he felt like a Spanish galleon in a harbor of fishing boats.

"Papa promised to take me sailing," Charity insisted, bottom lip trembling.

"Ships are far too dangerous." The viscountess finally lifted her shadowed eyes to Trev. "You do us no favors by reminding her of things she cannot have."

"Ships are no more dangerous than horses. I lost my parents in a carriage accident caused by runaway animals." The grief at their loss still ached deep inside his soul. "Would you have me go about on foot?"

She looked away. "I would have you go in any way I could."

Trev shut his eyes as the pain of rejection lanced through him. He would *not* let her wounded gaze and frailty affect his goals. "This house was once mine, madam. You do *me* no favor by reminding me of what I cannot have." Throwing her own words back at her, he brushed past and out the door, down the stairs, and into the night. He'd soak his wounds in rum.

After merrily lighting as many lamps as she pleased, Sinda studied the canvas on the easel in the cottage's front room. She did not very much like painting still lifes, but she was restless and needed some outlet in the evenings. She missed the energy of her sisters and cousins running in and out, giving her subjects galore to record on paper or canvas. She almost missed going out of an evening to the theater or a concert of chamber music. They had provided ample inspiration for her art, even if they did mean hours spent away from her easel.

She simply needed to adapt to her new life. She studied the bowl of autumn flowers and pinecones on the table. There was something missing in the composition. Well, she could add it later when she thought of it. She wanted to see the pictures appear under her fingers. The story in the painting intrigued her more than the craft involved.

She had the urge to splash a big white sail and the deep blue sea across the canvas, but she resisted. Her father had a yacht, and she'd sailed on it a time or two, but the yacht didn't match what she saw in her head. She needed to stick with subjects she knew. It was far too dangerous to let her imagination rule her hands.

She blocked out the background for the flowers, but the colors dissatisfied her. So did the lighting. She wanted blue. And sunlight.

Leaving the oil to dry, she rummaged in her box for her colored chalks. Chalks were for children and amateurs, but they were all she had a mind for tonight, it seemed. She'd made several miniatures in her notebook of the dogs playing in the garden. Perhaps she could transfer them to her large sketch pad.

With lamps still blazing, she settled on her settee to indulge in playful colors. She had the blue sky appearing under her fingers when a knock rapped at her door. She nearly leaped from her seat in startlement.

No one came to her door at night. Had something happened to Christina?

Alarmed, she threw down her pad and raced to open the door.

Sir Trevelyan stood there. Or leaned there. He swayed slightly in surprise as the door opened, then grabbed the door-jamb to steady himself. "May I come in?" he asked politely.

He hadn't worn powder and pomade in his hair today. A black strand spilled loose from his queue and over his neck-cloth. Whiskers shadowed his angular jaw—not enough to hide the thin white streak of a rapier scar on his cheek. His jabot had come undone, and as usual, he'd not fastened his coat or vest.

The wells of loneliness and anguish in his eyes caused her to step back and allow him in.

"Are Charity and Lady Rochester well?" she asked, keeping the moment as proper as possible given the total impropriety of inviting a man into her home unchaperoned.

Of course, living unchaperoned was already improper. That's why she called herself *Mrs.* Jones in the village. Artists and widows had freedoms dukes' daughters never knew.

"The lady is stubborn, bigoted, and a royal nuisance, but fine." His voice didn't slur as he entered her front room and looked around.

She had thought the cottage quite spacious until he filled it. His head brushed the beams, and his shadow cast her settee in darkness. He smelled of strong ale, sandalwood, and raw male. It was the *male* part no doubt that was encouraging her to do foolish things.

She snatched her pad up and gestured. "Have a seat, sir. Might I bring you some coffee?"

"Trevelyan. Trev. Call me Trev. No one else will." He stared at her lone chair as if he didn't know what it was doing there. Or what *he* was doing there. "You have coffee?"

"I do. Sit. I will stir the fire."

He didn't sit. He locked his hands behind his back and studied her canvas. Sinda fled. She wanted to feel worldly and sophisticated, but mostly, she felt young and flustered.

Her cousin had hired someone to cook two meals a day and dust and sweep the cottage. Beyond that, she was on her own.

Always observant, Sinda had studied servants over the years. She knew how to bank or stir a fire. She could prepare tea and hot chocolate, but she preferred coffee. So she'd learned that simple task as well, and the familiar process steadied her hands.

She heard Sir Trevelyan moving around as she worked, and her heart pounded nervously. Had he discovered her identity? If so, he hadn't lopped off her head the instant she'd opened the door. That was promising.

He wasn't wearing a sword. That was even better.

He was drunk. And in pain. Curiosity won. She carried cups and accessories in on a tray, shoving aside her still life to set the tray on the table. Sir Trevelyan—Trev—was studying an unfinished sketch she'd pinned to the wall. Just the image of his broad back in front of one of her drawings had the power to tug her heartstrings. She wanted to know what he thought of it.

"I will be right back with the coffee." She retreated to the kitchen where the coffee had begun to boil. Why had no man in London appealed to her as this one did? Was it because she'd spent months last winter unknowingly painting his portrait, so she thought she knew him?

If so, that was silly. She knew no more about the man than she knew the king. Actually, given her father's reports of his sovereign's activities, she probably knew the king better.

She poured the coffee into a sturdy pewter coffeepot scavenged from the duke's manor house and carried it to the man waiting in her front room. She didn't know if curiosity was a vice or a virtue, but she was beset with it.

"Sir… Trev, would you take a seat, please? You loom over me so, I fear you will haul me off my feet and carry me into the night." Holding the hot pot with a folded towel, she waited for him to accept that the room had only one piece of furniture upon which he could sit.

Not sitting, he eyed her with sardonic disfavor. "I did not think you feared anything, madam." He took the pot from her and nodded toward the cushioned settee.

Just like that, he usurped her control of the situation. Irritably, she swept her skirt aside and took one side of the seat. "If you are to be Trev, then I must be Lucy," she corrected him primly. "But only in private. Did you come here tonight because you thought me fearless?"

He poured the dark brew for both of them and handed her one of the thick porcelain cups. "I came here on the vapors of alcohol to see if you are friend or foe." He poured another cup for himself and sipped it black.

"As far as I am aware, I am neither," she answered. "I am merely the artist painting your family's home. Despite your appalling manners, I have attempted to be polite. I shall endeavor to continue doing so if it is your coin that will ultimately pay for my time and talent. That is the way of the world."

His eyebrows drew down in a thick line over his nose. "You talk like a man."

Startled, Sinda laughed out loud. "Thank you. My mother would not be proud to hear that, but I sound much like her. We are a practical people." With odd and often fey abilities, but she had no reason to mention that. She enjoyed her anonymity. Back home, her suitors watched her as if she would turn them into frogs. Being known as a fey Malcolm had as many drawbacks as being a duke's daughter. She would dearly love to explore a man's reactions to her as merely a woman, except this was not the man on which to experiment.

Sir Trevelyan's frown went away, and he nodded with some understanding. "My mother was like that—a cross between a brigantine and a schooner. She could sail over men with the sheer force of her will or slip past them unawares. I'd forgotten that about her."

"I prefer the invisibility of a schooner. If you will not sit beside me, could you at least take the hearth pillow? There is not enough room in here for me to slip past you and you are blocking my harbor."

He glanced down at the small pillow upon the low hearth, then to the comfortable settee on which she was ensconced.

Sinda regretted saying anything. He might be foxed, but his gaze focused amazingly well on her. She was afraid to look down and see if her kerchief had come loose from her bodice.

With the careful precision of the drunk, he lowered himself into the seat beside her without spilling a drop of coffee. "Are you going to jump up and run away now?"

She heard sadness more than a taunt in his question. She sipped her coffee before speaking. "Are women in a habit of running from you?"

"Not until lately. Apparently English women are more faint of heart than I remembered."

"Or you are growling and misbehaving more than usual," she countered. "English women prefer a pretty face and a charming smile as much as any."

"Lady Rochester does not," he said gloomily. "She would see me to perdition even if I were to produce pearls of wisdom and diamonds of grace."

"She thinks you murdered her husband and mean to steal her home. Be grateful she does not run you through with a sword."

"That is one way to look at it." Relaxing, he leaned against the cushions and sprawled his long legs across the braided rug. "I learned last week that the sea never gave up my cousin's body. He has no grave."

The emotion in his voice forced her to look at the man. He showed no expression but stared into his cup as if waiting for answers to appear there. "I am sorry. I did not know about his grave," she whispered abjectly. "It must have been a dreadful homecoming to hear such news."

He shrugged. "I did not kill him, you know. It is a sorry state when everyone believes the worst of a man because of a foolish painting."

Was he toying with her? Did he know she'd painted that portrait? Did he suspect?

It was bad enough that his knee brushed her skirts, making her aware of physical desire, without adding suspicion to the mix. Nervously, Sinda sat up straighter so their shoulders wouldn't touch. She might be technically innocent, but she wasn't ignorant. Trevelyan exuded raw power, and she could picture intimately the anatomy of his musculature beneath his tailored garb. Line drawings of muscles in books did not begin to compare with the powerful, sensuous play of the real thing.

"Perhaps people believe there is little difference between a privateer and a murderer," she answered, then bit her tongue. She had no practice at private conversation with a man.

"There is a great deal of difference between killing men at war and murdering for greed," he growled. "And I never killed a man except in defense of my life or that of others. The king *knighted* me for killing his enemies."

"You are aware this is not proper drawing room conversation?"

"And this isn't a proper drawing room and there's nothing proper about my presence here," he agreed. "Shall I leave?"

She knew she should say yes. He was merely drunk and feeling hurt because his cousin's widow disliked him. Because all England believed him a murderer. *Because she had painted him as one.*

"We are from different worlds. We cannot be friends," she pointed out truthfully enough.

"I doubt that either of us belongs in any world the other recognizes." He stood and, taking her cup, set it and his on the table.

Startled, she made the mistake of looking at him. Desire burned like hot coals in his eyes.

He took her hands and drew her up, and she didn't stop him. The hardness and strength of his grip held her paralyzed.

"This is the only world we need right now," he murmured.

Before her muddled mind could make sense of that, he pulled her hands behind her back and drew her against him, so her breasts brushed his shirt and his heat enveloped her.

Then he lowered his lips to hers, and the world as she knew it went away.

Eight

SHE HAD NEVER BEEN KISSED

Startled by the heat and pressure of Trevelyan's mouth, Sinda fell into the pleasure of it without another thought. The odor of ale no longer assaulted her, but the male scent of his skin was new to her, an erotic aroma all its own. His whiskers burned, but his mouth…! The sensation was overpowering, and she jerked her hands free of his grip so she might clutch his arms to steady herself. With his strength to brace her, she could lift herself more fully into his kiss, and she shuddered as his tongue brushed along the seam of her lips.

Trevelyan wanted more, she could taste it, but she wasn't ready to give up this unique experience yet. She felt his muscles bunch and tighten beneath the expensive fabric of his coat as she pressed closer and offered her mouth more fully. He was trying to be cautious with her, but desire melted them together into a new potion heady with promise.

He wrapped his arms around her waist and tilted her completely against him. She ached with the need to touch more of him, but she couldn't release his mouth. She drank in the flavor of her coffee as he nipped small kisses at the corners of her lips and his embrace tightened. She stood on tiptoe so they fit perfectly together, and he groaned as her hips pressed into him.

He removed his mouth, and his dark gaze fastened hungrily on her. "Lucy…"

The world stopped spinning, and she shoved him away. *He didn't know who she was.* Panic fluttered in her breast. This had to stop.

He tried to hold on to her, but Sinda escaped, backing across the room and holding up her hands to ward him off. "Please, I think you should leave."

He looked as if he might protest. For a moment, pain and anger flickered behind his eyes, but then he recovered his impassive expression. He stepped forward to take her outstretched hand and bowed formally over it, then turned it over to press a kiss to her palm. "My regrets if I have caused you any undue distress, madam."

Back straight, he departed, the door closing behind him as if he'd never been.

Sinda wasn't certain she would ever breathe again. She stared at the palm he'd kissed, waiting for it to go up in flame. She could feel his kiss all the way up her arm.

She felt his kisses in parts best not mentioned.

He thought she was *Lucy*, a widowed artist. He didn't know she was the woman who had condemned his life to scandal and woe.

Not that it should matter, because she shouldn't have been kissing him in the first place. She was a good girl, not a wanton widow available for soothing his hurts. She'd never allowed her suitors to steer her into dark corners. She'd never tasted stolen kisses.

Probably because she'd never been stirred to do so.

Why did Trevelyan have to be the one to stir her? Had taking one rebellious step from her family plunged her into a morass of sin? How had that one portrait turned her life so completely around?

Shaken, she blew out her candles, picked up her coffee tray, and returned it to the sink. She washed out the cups as if that would wash away all evidence of what she'd done.

But her body told her differently. It ached for an act that she might never know. Thinking she might not marry had never bothered her until now, when confronted with the physical actuality of what she would miss. She loved kissing.

She still didn't believe the societal obligations of being a proper wife and mother were what she wanted. She'd rather lose herself in her work than cater to the needs of others.

She would simply never kiss a man again, she decided, and then she would not suffer from this ache of longing.

She doused the heat burning through her with cold water, donned her long flannel nightgown, and crawled into her cold bed, vowing to avoid Sir Trevelyan Rochester forevermore.

❧

Sir Trevelyan Rochester had an entirely different view of the evening. Tugging off his jabot and gazing into his cheval glass, he burned for another meeting with the lovely schooner who had dodged him so neatly.

Her rejection had hurt at first, until his head had cleared and he realized she had responded to him as vibrantly as he had to her. She was young and simply being missish. Perhaps he was her first encounter since her husband. "I'm a hunter by trade," he told the glass, flinging his neckcloth across a nearby chair. "And she's a prize worth chasing."

"Sir?" Manchester, his valet, carried in a pitcher of hot water for washing.

He wasn't used to servants sneaking up on him like that. Vaguely irritated to have his pleasant reverie interrupted, he shrugged off his coat. Manchester put down the pitcher and immediately stepped in to help him.

"How am I supposed to tell if a woman's truly missish or just playing coy with me?" he demanded, for lack of anyone better to talk to. He wished Laurence were there. Or even Mick. Mick wouldn't know the answer, but he'd at least grunt intelligibly.

"I'm sure I couldn't say, sir," Manchester replied.

"I'm sure you couldn't," Trev concurred dryly.

Remembering the avid way Lucy's lips responded to his, the way her plump breasts pressed into him, the way her eyes shone with wonder when she looked at him… hell, he'd sink for that look alone. "Is there anywhere about that I could purchase the kind of frippery that would please a lady?"

"Certainly not, sir. The viscountess orders a few things from the mercantile in Sommersville because the duchess does, but London is the only place for true fashion."

"The duchess?"

"Of Sommersville, sir. The duke has an estate some distance on the other side of town." Shaking his head in dismay, Manchester brushed at the coat Trev had soaked in dust and ale and perspiration all day. "You should leave your card."

He had a vague recollection of an old duke and duchess several miles up the road. They'd not entertained much and certainly hadn't entertained a rough young lad like himself, not with the taint of his mother's blood and his noble grandfather's disapproval.

Dismissing unknown and inaccessible dukes, Trev pondered the lovely artist. She was a beautiful young widow living unchaperoned. She'd invited him in as if it were a natural thing to do. He had to believe propriety didn't apply to her.

"I need a steward who knows more about farming than I do." And who would give him more leisure to pursue the artist. The demands upon his time by the estate and his shipping business didn't allow for the kind of dedicated pursuit for which he was famous. Or infamous.

He should check on how the earl fared. It had been over a month since the ugly scene at his grandfather's when he'd had to knock down the butler to visit the sickroom. He hadn't bothered visiting on this last trip to London. He'd been too infuriated by the refusal of Parliament to acknowledge his claim. He'd feared he would kill a footman or two out of frustration.

Maybe the old man was conscious by now. Trev really wanted his grandfather to be aware when he finally presented a formal petition in Parliament to have his name legitimized. Having to name him heir would give the bastard another apoplexy.

If he returned to London, he could find the finest gewgaws to tempt a timid artist.

"I need to check on my ship," he said aloud. "Pack a bag for London. I'll leave in the morning." He hoped the *Lass* had returned to port in his absence. He was impatient to start a search for the smugglers who might have seen Laurence last.

Besides, if Lucy Jones was playing coy, he could teach her that two could play that game. Absence might make the heart grow fonder.

Sinda woke to a cold wind, a pounding headache, and a sensation of loneliness so deep that she wanted to weep from the pain of it. She drew the covers around her shivering shoulders and looked to see what window she'd left open. She winced as the action jarred the pain in her head.

She never had headaches. Whatever on earth had caused this one? Forcing her eyes to focus in the dim gray of morning, she peered at her window from beneath the blankets. Why would she have left it open at this time of year?

It wasn't open.

She closed her eyes and sank back into the pillow. She was still cold, but there was no draft. She must have been dreaming.

Exhausted, as if she'd spent the night awake instead of sound asleep, she drifted into slumber again.

She woke to the smell of bacon frying. Bridget must have arrived, and she hadn't heard her. She never stayed in bed this late. Hastily, she threw her feet over the side of the bed, and the pain in her head shot straight through her. She gasped and rocked on the bed's edge, holding her brow in hopes the warmth of her hand would eat through the agony.

Her hand. The memory of the prior night seeped slowly past the ache, and she flushed in embarrassment. How could she have been so blind? Trevelyan had come here not as a friend, but as a man who wanted a woman and thought she was available. Stupid, stupid, stupid.

She forced her legs to hold her long enough to stagger to the washstand. No more coffee for her at night if this was the result. She was never ill. Her mother didn't believe in illnesses, or so she said. The Duchess of Mainwaring was terrifying enough to scare off the slightest cold. Sinda missed her dreadfully. Perhaps she ought to go home.

But going home meant giving up, and she wasn't a quitter. She had promised the viscountess a painting of her home, and she wouldn't back down—even if it meant hiding from Trevelyan. Besides, she liked it here, if Trevelyan would just go to the devil. If it weren't for him, she could invite her sisters down or visit Christina more often.

Of course, that would mean giving up her lovely anonymity. She wasn't quite ready for that yet either. She studied her henna-dyed hair in the mirror. It seemed quite odd to see herself without the spun silver of childhood, but she thought she looked older this way. More mysterious. A woman of the world.

Sinda snorted at that. If last night were any example, she would never be a woman of the world. From now on, she'd never open her door after sunset.

The headache gradually receded as she dressed. The delicious aroma of frying bacon and boiling coffee encouraged her to hurry. She was very bad at dressing her hair, so she pinned it however it would go and pulled a cap over it.

"Good morning, Bridget," she called as she hurried down the stairs, still stuffing stray lengths of hair inside her cap.

"Mornin', missus," the cheerful maid called back. The mother of ten, she had a brisk way about her that efficiently set the cottage to rights in a matter of moments. "That's a fine drawing ye done last night. My man used to sail on a ship like that. It's a grand sight to see."

Ship? Sinda halted at the bottom of the stairs, suddenly afraid to go farther. She couldn't draw ships. She had a distinct memory of deciding to sketch… What had she been about to sketch? Trevelyan had knocked on the door and interrupted. Perhaps she had drawn something that reminded Bridget of a ship?

Feeling foolish at her fears, she swept into the front room to see if the oil of her still life had dried yet.

The still-life canvas was propped against the wall. On the easel sat a completed chalk drawing of a man working the lines of a small sailing ship in what appeared to be a sudden squall. Gray gusts of clouds swept the sky, the canvas billowed, and the figure in the rigging wore no coat or hat, as if the day had been a warm one.

In the rigging. Sinda abruptly sat down on her settee and stared. She couldn't have done that. She knew utterly nothing of ship rigging, yet this drawing showed the intricate pattern of ropes and sails and knots. She could almost feel the cold wind in her hair.

The draft from a window that wasn't open.

As curious as she was terrified, she stood up and examined the drawing closer. She could see very little of the man's face. The sails and the clouds dominated the sketch. She could catch a glimpse of the ocean beyond, as if the drawing were done from below. The man wore a linen shirt and dark breeches, but she could not tell their quality. He had broad shoulders and long legs and possessed an aura of both tension and assurance. She could see Trevelyan in the daring pose.

Perhaps the pirate had returned and placed this sketch here for some reason. It wasn't as if anyone in the village ever locked their doors. Anyone could have walked in.

That was foolish denial. Every line and stroke looked like hers.

Almost unconsciously, she scanned the lower part of the drawing that showed a glimpse of the ship's deck. Her heart plummeted as she found a cat asleep in a coil of rope, verifying what she already knew. The cat looked like the kitten Belinda had found after the portrait of Trevelyan was done.

She'd sworn she would never draw another portrait. And so she'd sketched a landscape—with a man in it.

In her sleep.

That simply was not possible, but the icy fear in her heart forced her to cover the sketch and carry it upstairs to the attic where no one would ever see it. She would have no more scandals blamed on her. She didn't wish to draw that kind of attention to herself ever again.

She had to pray she wasn't going mad. There could be a simple explanation for the drawing. She'd wait before leaping to any conclusions.

But instead of walking directly to the Willows that morning,

Sinda took the back lanes and cut across fields to the manor belonging to the Duke of Sommersville.

Now that the harvest had begun bringing in cash, the new duke had ordered reparations to the older parts of his home. Scaffolding engulfed the stones of the castle towers on the left side of the drive. Carpenters worked diligently on a new entrance to the charming Tudor manor that tied the castle to the new mansion on the right.

Sinda knew her cousin preferred the center portion of the house, but she preferred not to be seen and talked about by the construction people. She slipped around behind the mansion in the direction of the servants' entrance. To her satisfaction, she found Christina puttering in the medieval knot garden.

"Help," she whispered, taking a seat on an ornamental bench in the sunshine.

Christina looked up and smiled widely. "Sinda! How wonderful to see you." Mud coated the hem of her old gown as the duchess pulled herself to her feet and came to sit down beside her. "Have you decided anonymity has lost its thrill?"

"No, I fear I may need it now more than ever." She wasn't even certain she should be worried, but the collective Malcolm wisdom might soothe her fears. "Did you feel anything… different… when you began to see ghosts?"

"Different?" Christina wrinkled her nose and thought about it. Not often given to thinking, she didn't try for long. "Not that I remember. I just see ghosts as more distinct auras than the auras I see around living people. Why?"

There was no sense in disguising her concerns from Christina, who had probably already read her aura and knew she was worried. It was just a matter of which worry to express. Shy of mentioning men, Sinda stuck to the topic only a Malcolm might comprehend. She related the morning's strange experience.

"I really don't know when I paint something prescient," she continued, presenting her argument first. "I suppose, if I knew, I wouldn't paint it."

Christina nodded in understanding. "Like Felicity, who

wears gloves so she won't feel the pains other people have experienced."

"Precisely. Not all our gifts are useful, and sometimes they can be destructive or dangerous. It might be far better if we had none at all."

"Oh no!" Christina looked horrified. "If I couldn't see ghosts, I couldn't have helped Harry restore his estate. And even though it was painful, Felicity helped Ewen and others. Last I heard, she healed a child who wouldn't speak by telling the mother that the person who killed the girl's pony had threatened her. It's just a matter of finding a use for our gifts. Have you painted something dangerous?"

"I don't know. It was merely a ship with a man in the ropes. Could I have simply drawn a dream?"

"You've never wakened to a headache or cold drafts before?"

Sinda shook her head.

"Does the sketch look as if it may hold secrets?"

"I have no way of knowing. I sketch all the time, night and day. Very few of my sketches contain prescient elements. I am still not convinced people aren't seeing things in my work that aren't really there. I'm not at all convinced that my romantic horseman is a portrait of Sir Trevelyan running away from the site of his cousin's death."

"It's possible that everything you sketch has something prescient in it but few of them are identified," Christina said, looking off in the distance. "We often don't know what we are capable of."

"Do not tell me that. I would have to give up drawing entirely!" Sinda said in horror. "That would be akin to cutting off my fingers."

"You could learn to use what the pictures tell you," Christina pointed out. "That's what your gift is meant for."

"Even the goddesses couldn't predict that a man existed on earth who looked just like my portrait," Sinda protested.

"Perhaps you should marry."

Sinda stared at her lovely, occasionally bubble-headed cousin in horror. "Why?"

Christina smiled knowingly. "Other than the usual reasons?"

Sinda flushed and tried not to remember last night. "The usual reasons have naught to do with strange sketches appearing in my front room."

"They might." Christina sent her an odd look.

Sinda feared her aura was giving her away, but she steadfastly refused to admit that she had never been kissed before last night.

Christina spoke without need of encouragement. "It wasn't until Harry and I… married and became more intimate that I came into my full gifts. And now that I'm carrying…" She indicated her belly. "I can do things I've never done before. I have even talked with people beyond the grave who do not normally haunt the house. I spoke with the vicar's mother yesterday."

Sinda stared at Christina with wide eyes. "The vicar is as old as Methuselah!"

"And his mother is dead." Christina nodded in agreement. "She told me that Mora needs help, although she couldn't quite explain why. I didn't say my gift is always useful."

"Mora?" Sinda couldn't think of a more independent, self-sufficient person than the vicar's daughter. She sighed. "I don't suppose talking to ghosts involves headaches and cold drafts?"

"No, not that I've noticed." Christina patted her hand. "Shall I send for Aunt Stella?"

"No, not yet. This could very well be… just a disturbing incident that will never be repeated." With determination, Sinda rose. "I'm sure it won't happen again."

Especially if she stayed well away from Sir Trevelyan Rochester. If physical intimacy increased Christina's abilities, that kiss could very well be the source of her nightmares.

Nine

FROM THE PARK IN THE CENTER OF A SQUARE OF ELEGANT London town homes, Trev gazed up at the imposing edifice of the Duke of Mainwaring. It was midmorning, and the only life stirring appeared to be the maid scrubbing the front steps. No light or movement could be seen behind the blank windows.

"You could always spark the maid," Trev said nonchalantly to his companion.

Mick studied the maid and shrugged. "Too young for the likes o' me. I'll do better chatting up the lads in the stable. Not that they're likely to know much unless the lady has returned."

"It would help just to know that. I heard nothing of it in the coffee house last night." No one of importance had spoken to him, but he had found a corner where no one knew his phiz. He'd read the newssheets and listened to the gossip for hours. He saw and heard no mention of Lady Lucinda Malcolm Pembroke. He didn't know if that meant no one was concerned about her or if she had returned home so there was no reason for worry.

"Sure you don't want me to come with you?" Mick asked, regarding his employer with misgiving.

"No, best to keep you free to rescue me should they heave my battered carcass into jail." Trev offered a grim smile. "You know how to find my lawyer."

"I don't like this," Mick muttered. "You should just leave the old vulture alone and go on about your business."

"What business should I go about?" Trev asked with a shrug. "I can't find a wife if all London thinks me a murderer. And I can't buy another estate while Laurence's needs my aid. And the *Pirate Lass* isn't in port yet. Might as well get my jollies checking on the old buzzard."

Knowing how they'd spent these last years, Mick just grunted. Breaking into an earl's stately home could scarcely be called hair-raisingly dangerous compared to tracking and trapping outlawed pirates.

Trev watched Mick cross the road and slip down an alleyway in the direction of the mews behind the duke's house. Servants would talk more readily to other servants than to him.

Swinging his walking stick, he set off down the street to his grandfather's home. The distance wasn't great, and he had time to spare. He could inquire after the earl's health.

The Earl of Lansdowne's London home was not nearly as imposing as the duke's, but it was respectably genteel on a quiet street of wealthy homes. Trev assumed the inhabitants had estates elsewhere and only opened these smaller houses when Parliament was in session.

By all rights, he should have been raised here and offered the honorable life of aristocracy to which he'd been born. Instead, as a lad, he'd had to fight his way up through the ranks of the navy after his impressment. The fury in him had won his first ship and the letter of marque when he was but twenty-one. He wasn't at all certain that he regretted having the silver spoon removed from his mouth, but he regretted the loss of family and friends and the scars on his soul from his life of violence.

For that, the earl would pay.

He studied the mansion but saw no more signs of life there than at the duke's. He was hoping he'd arrived early enough to find the staff scattered about their duties. His mistake on his last visit had been to come to the front door like a gentleman.

Ignoring the high steps to the locked front entrance, Trev surveyed the street and, seeing no one, slipped down the narrow stairs to the basement kitchen. As he'd known it would be, the door had been unlocked to let out servants on their morning tasks.

Several mob-capped cooks and maids stared as he walked in, but he traversed the kitchen boldly, swinging his stick as if he did this every day.

No one crossed his path until he climbed to the ground floor main hall, where a startled footman challenged him.

"Just come to check on my grandfather, you know," Trev drawled with the arrogance of a man accustomed to having what he wanted. "Don't bother showing me up, old fellow. I know the way."

And he did. His parents had brought him to London on several occasions, and they'd stayed here. Unable to tolerate the presence of his son's foreign wife and the mongrel she'd borne, the earl had departed the instant of their arrival, but Trev knew which chambers belonged to the bastard.

At the time, the earl had simply been an inexplicable black cloud on his youthful horizon, scarcely rating a second thought. He'd led a sheltered existence back then, thanks to his loving parents.

Whistling nonchalantly, Trev took the stairs to the next floor. Nothing had changed over the years. The house and its contents had grown older and more decrepit along with his grandfather. He heard the butler panting up the stairs behind him as he strolled down the corridor. He really didn't want to hit the man again. The servants had undoubtedly sent for a constable by now, but he didn't mean to linger until one was found.

He shoved open the big double doors to his grandfather's chambers and crossed through the outer parlor. A maid laying a fire in the hearth dropped her kindling. The portly, bewigged butler burst in behind him and hastened to block Trev's path, raising a poker. Trev twirled his walking stick, nodded at the maid, cast a pointed glance at the upraised poker, and veered around the stout old man.

"Sir, I insist that you leave."

"Bugger off, Jonesy." Trev addressed the man as he had as a youth. "I just want to see if he's alive and not a carcass hidden up here while his solicitors pick his bones clean."

He opened the inner chamber door quietly. He wouldn't

mind giving the old man another apoplexy, but he wouldn't lower himself to the earl's level by doing it on purpose.

His eyebrows arched in surprise at the unexpected sight of his grandfather sitting up against the pillows, being spoon-fed gruel by his manservant. Without his wig, the old man's bald pate had a waxen sheen and his once-plump features had shriveled to a fraction of their formidability, but his scowl remained unchanged.

The man in the bed spat and sputtered at the sight of Trev, drooling gruel from a corner of his mouth. He lifted a frail fist and pounded the bedcovers, but despite his obvious fury, he could not leap from the bed to strike down his unwanted visitor.

Trev had seen men laid flat by strokes. He knew the symptoms. The chance that his grandfather would ever walk again was slim but possible. Just as he had once felt no hatred for the earl, he felt no sympathy either.

"Good morning, Grandfather," he said cheerfully. "Glad to see you're awake. It's much more entertaining to have a conscious opponent. Just thought I'd let you know that your solicitors are not tending Laurence's affairs. His widow faces starvation. You wouldn't want that, now would you? She could be carrying your heir, you know."

The man in the bed jerked and partially raised his fist to swat ineffectively at the covers.

"He does understand me, does he not?" Trev asked the frozen valet. "I wouldn't wish my message to go wasted."

"He understands… sir," the valet replied warily.

"Excellent." Trev made a formal bow. "I'll see myself out. Get well soon, my lord. We have a great deal to talk about."

Spinning on his booted heel, Trev marched out, past Jones and the staring maid, into the upstairs corridor, where several terrified footmen held kitchen knives and candlesticks and shivered in their shoes as he passed.

"I'm leaving now," he told them amiably. "Next time, perhaps you'll let me in the front door."

Not that they would, he knew with bitterness. Not while the earl lived. They had their positions to protect, and he didn't envy them their tasks.

With a brisker, angrier stride, he took the front steps down to the street. Perhaps he ought to go back to Jamaica. His mother's family was still there. The solicitors would eventually find some distant relative to take over the earl's estates if Melinda did not bear a boy. Unfortunately, since Melinda had been dowerless, that would mean she and her children could be denied their home. And since the earl would consider her a failure if she did not present an heir, he was quite capable of such maliciousness.

Trev couldn't let Laurence down like that. He had to look after his cousin's family, or he could never live with himself. It was as simple as that. If he had to fight the earl and a whole contingent of lawyers and Parliament itself to see they had what they deserved, he would.

People dodged out of his way as he stalked down the street. Perhaps he had learned to scowl as fiercely as the earl. That would be enough to scatter demons.

There was more activity now, dairy carts and fishmongers traversing the cobblestones, cooks hastening to market for fresh produce. The scent of bacon cooking watered his mouth. He'd eaten at his hotel, but it wasn't the same as waking in one's own bed, anticipating a morning over coffee and newsprint, and dining with one's own family.

He hungered for that life even more than he hungered for food, but it was an old hunger, one that had gnawed his guts for almost two decades. He could survive a few more months while he straightened out his affairs.

Autumn had turned the trees in the park colorful reds and golds. He'd missed the changing of the seasons he remembered from boyhood. He leaned against a stout oak trunk and enjoyed the brisk cool air while Mick completed his errand.

To Trev's great satisfaction, two carriages drew around to the front of the Duke of Mainwaring's mansion, and an explosion of silks and laces spilled out the front door and down the steps.

He recognized the matronly duchess in her powdered hair shepherding her daughters into the waiting vehicles. Several of them looked old enough to be the missing Lucinda, but none seemed quite the right height to match his fading memory of that night.

As he'd been informed, every one of them was fair, with hair in shades from palest yellow to darkest gold. Some were short and plump. Others were tall and skinny. Some had curly hair and the youngest had straight hair halfway down her back. The older ones wore their hair pinned under hats, but blond tresses curled at their napes.

He hoped Mick had discovered something about the missing one because he couldn't separate wheat from chaff. A man's head could spin off his neck just watching the lot of them giggling and talking and crushing petticoats into the carriages. He wasn't entirely certain why they didn't spill out the other side, there seemed so many of them, although he supposed there couldn't be more than half a dozen.

He tried to picture Lucy amid these others and failed. Her hair had a reddish cast that didn't fit in. She possessed a quiet grace that didn't seem to match these chattering, active females. And she'd invited him into her home, as a duke's daughter would never do. She couldn't be the missing artist.

As the carriages pulled away, Mick left the alley and crossed the street.

"Well?" Trev demanded, turning toward the hotel and his horse.

"She ain't returned far as they know, but none seem to think that's odd. Seems the women in the family have knacks for odd behaviors, and they look out for their own. There's a whole passel of 'em, cousins and whatnot, older as well as younger. She could be with any of them."

Trev couldn't be everywhere at once. He had to put the goal of finding Laurence above his search for a missing artist.

"I could hire someone to inquire on them all," he said, thinking aloud.

"Could take months. There's at least one in Scotland, another comes and goes from Bath, and one's right down where we are in Sussex. I couldn't keep them all straight except that they're married to powerful men. It's not a family to tangle with lightly."

In Sussex, with the red-haired artist. He tucked that information away for later perusal. "And?" Trev heard the doubt behind Mick's words and waited.

Mick hesitated, then, looking like a man who'd swallowed a frog, admitted, "They're said to be witches."

Trev hooted so loudly that passing strangers turned to stare.

"Witches? The British Empire sails the seven seas, but its inhabitants still believe in witches? By Neptune, did you see the chits? They're all blond faerie sprites who no doubt melt in rain. *Witches?*" He hadn't heard anything so funny in ages, and he roared in laughter, enjoying the joke and the day and Mick's outrage.

"Well, I reckon it takes all sorts," Mick grumbled. "They say the missing lass painted a portrait of the late prince in his coffin before he died, and she painted Bonnie Prince Charlie with blood on his hands before he entered Scotland. There's other, even more fanciful tales. The lads believe them."

"Of course they do," Trev agreed genially. "It's a defense women use if they're at all smart. Convince the world that they have charms or beauty or powers or intelligence far beyond the common mold so others will hold them in respect and keep their distance. It's not as if they can wield swords."

"Aye, but that doesn't explain the paintings," Mick said stubbornly. "They show things she can't have known, like babies what ain't been born—or conceived—yet."

Trev halted and held Mick at a distance with his walking stick. "So you believe Lady Lucinda painted me in England at the time my cousin died when you know for yourself that I wasn't there?"

Mick scowled. "That don't mean she's right all the time. But she painted your likeness without ever seeing you. That's odd enough."

He had a point. Nodding, Trev resumed walking. How the devil could the artist have painted him so accurately, right down to the scar on his cheek? That was not normal.

But witches? He grinned. Perhaps he would peruse a few more coffeehouses this evening while waiting for his ship to arrive. Armed with this new knowledge, he could stimulate some entertaining tales if naught else.

⁓

With Sir Trevelyan gone the better part of this past week, life had been relatively peaceful, Sinda decided. She'd done her best to wipe the man and his kiss from her mind and immerse herself in her art.

Gazing at the spaniels sleeping in front of the sunny windows of the orangery, Sinda fought the urge to add a patch of pink to one side where a child's dress should be. Charity wasn't sitting there. She would not paint the child, no matter how strong the urge.

Perhaps if she simply painted a puddle of fabric from her gown as if the child were hiding amid the greenery…

No, most certainly not. The dogs, the lovely windows and ironwork, nothing more. She longed to paint the viscountess in the blue salon, but she would not do that either. An image of the dead viscount dripping seaweed was bound to appear beside her, and she could not bear it.

She smiled at the sound of childish footsteps hurrying down the aisle, grateful for the distraction. She stepped aside so Charity could see how the painting progressed.

"Oh, I can see Davida's tail!" she exclaimed, bouncing up and down. "Why can't I see her nose?"

"Her nose is a different set of colors that I haven't mixed yet. I'm laying on the mahoganies and umbers today." Noticing the child carried something in her hand, Sinda pointed her paintbrush at it. "What are you playing with?"

As if she'd forgotten she held it, Charity held her toy up for inspection. "Sir Trevelyan said I might have it. It has little dollies, but they are very small."

Sinda took what appeared to be an ivory tusk elaborately engraved with dozens of little figures up and down the length and on all sides. The work was intricate, detailed, and must have taken weeks. Ink had apparently been worked into the engravings to make them more visible.

"Did your cousin Trevelyan tell you where he found this?"

Charity took back the tusk and studied the drawings. "He said this one is almost my aunt. Isn't she pretty?" She pointed at the image of a lady in a long gown.

Almost her aunt? What on earth did that mean? "She's quite lovely. You should take very good care of this. It is extremely rare and valuable."

"It's good to know you think so," a deep male voice intruded. Sinda almost jumped in startlement. "Sir Trevelyan!"

Instead of his usual plain colors, he wore a cobalt-blue coat over a gold-embroidered buff vest, topped with an elegant waterfall of gleaming white linen that set off his dark features to such perfection she almost swooned.

"Mrs. Jones," he answered mockingly. The glitter in his dark eyes questioned her formality when they'd been on a first name basis before he left.

"Your mother is asking after you, lass," he said to Charity. "And I brought a little surprise from London. Why don't you run up and see what it is?"

"A surprise? You brought me a surprise?" Transported with delight, Charity flung herself into Trev's arms.

The expression of wonder and joy on his face was so raw that Sinda forgot her vow to stay away from the man. She watched as he hugged her, then gently sent the child on her way. He didn't turn back to Sinda until Charity was out of sight—and his face had recovered its earlier noncommittal expression.

"I brought you something too." He picked up a box he'd dropped during Charity's impetuous hug. "The shop said an artist could use these."

She ached to take the box. She loved surprises and adored the creative possibilities that a new color or brush could produce, but she would not be obligated to this man. Ever. She locked her hands behind her back to keep them from temptation.

"That is very kind, sir, but you should not. I am a servant here. It wouldn't be proper."

"No one else can use them but you. They would go to waste. Besides, if I am paying for your work, I wish to see you use the best materials."

He looked so very innocent when saying this that Sinda

knew he lied. She narrowed her eyes and studied him. "I cannot be bought, you know."

He grinned. "I thought as much, but it doesn't hurt to try. And you would have thrown jewelry or perfume in my face."

She wanted to laugh aloud at his audacity, but she shouldn't encourage him. "You are a scoundrel, but buying a gift for Charity was thoughtful of you. She's so lonely right now, you will make a friend of her for life." As she spoke, she accepted the box and cut open the strings with the small knife she kept among her artist's tools.

"I hope so," he said with seriousness. "Laurence was my friend for life. I would have Charity know she has the same in me."

Even though she had the box open, Sinda glanced up at his tone and saw the naked sorrow on his face. There wasn't any way she could believe this man had murdered his cousin.

To hide her confusion, she glanced back inside the box.

"Lapis lazuli," she cried in delight at the shimmering gem nestled inside. "I cannot grind this! It would be criminal. No art supply shop would give you a polished gem to grind!"

He poked his big finger into the box, moving the tissue aside. "There's a bar of lapis for grinding beneath. And some other colors they said are popular. But the blue was so very pretty and reminded me of your eyes, I could not resist."

He'd noticed her eyes? He thought they were the color of lapis lazuli?

Compared to her more glamorous sisters and cousins, she knew she was merely pleasant to look upon. Her suitors didn't quote poetry about the blue of her eyes. No one had compared her eyes with the brilliant pigments she used in her work. Or bought gems to match them.

Before she knew how to respond, Trevelyan set the box aside. He caught her elbows in his hands or she would have swooned of a certainty at the heated look in his eyes and the firm grip of his fingers. The faint scent of sandalwood surrounded her. She knew she ought to pull away, resist, but his expression, his presence, was so compelling, she could merely stand fixed to the spot, waiting to see what would happen.

Without a word, he showed her the response he expected as his lips closed over hers.

Ten

SHE KISSED LIKE AN ANGEL.

Trev struggled with his lust so as not to scare her away, but the melting eagerness of her mouth undid him.

As a young lad, he'd learned about the pleasures of the flesh in hard ports with hard women. In the years since, he'd never sought the luxury of innocence or respectability, so he had no measure of comparison and no standard of behavior. He simply knew the lovely widow felt like heaven in his arms, and he would do whatever it took to keep her there awhile longer.

The humidity of the orangery and the scent of lemon tree blossoms created a Garden of Eden, and Lucy Jones was the Eve his soul craved. She filled his arms with warmth and life, and he wrapped her tight in hopes of more. He smiled at her prim kiss and licked her lips just to feel her shudder with the desire coursing through them both.

He ran his palms along the lush satin concealing her bare arms. When they reached her slender shoulders, his fingers brushed the crisp starch of her kerchief. He tugged, and the linen came loose from her bodice. His hand cupped her bare nape.

He was rewarded with a gasp at the intimate contact of flesh on flesh. Like the pirate he was, he took advantage of her open mouth to plunder the treasure within. His tongue swept in to conquer—and he nearly went up in flames at the shocked, vibrant response of her fingers digging into his arms as she raised up on her toes for more.

"Cousin Trev!" a child's voice shrieked, shattering the sensual cocoon he'd woven around them. "Help! Pirates!"

Lucy leaped from his arms, her hand flying to her swollen lips as she stared at him, wide-eyed.

Trev didn't think it was fear so much as wonder he saw on her face, but Charity's shrieks were enough to conjure abject terror. Reluctantly turning from the temptation of Lucy's loosened kerchief and unpinned tresses, he scooped up the child running down the aisle.

"Pirates are on ships, goose," he informed her. "And if you yell like that too often, people will think you cry wolf. Do you know the story?"

But even as he asked, he could hear the shrill cries of the women of the household. With a frown, he thrust Charity at Lucy. "Look after her."

Trev had a suspicion of what had sent the maids into hysterics, and joy rang in his heart as he hurried through the back of the house to the front.

"Cap'n!" a familiar voice shouted over screams and wails. "Tell 'em to bugger off, will ya?"

"Caleb, you great dolt, you could have sent word from the inn instead of terrifying the women with your gruesome phiz!" Arriving in the front hall to see half his crew milling about, Trev pounded his first mate on the back.

In truth, his hulking first mate boasted the visage of a Greek god but the manners of an ape. Caleb held one of the footmen by the back of his coat, dangling him above the polished foyer. Trev's hard slam against his mate's shoulder released Caleb's grip, and the footman scurried out of reach. With the servant free, Trev shook hands with the motley assembly stinking up the elegant mansion and muddying its polished halls with their shoes.

From the wails in the salon, he assumed the viscountess had swooned—again—and her guests were trying to rouse her. He hoped that distressing tendency was a product of pregnancy.

The butler had frantically summoned all three footmen.

The last to arrive was still buttoning his jacket as if just roused from bed. The newly released one stood behind the others. Staring wildly, they blocked the entrance to the salon and their mistress.

Trev rolled his eyes at the standoff between his men and the servants. His crew hadn't been able to resist seeing how he lived any more than the women could resist screaming at their presence. What the devil would he do with the two halves of his life?

The attention of his crew shifted to someone behind him, and by the way they drooled, Trev knew who.

"You might suggest that your friends repair to your study while I see to Melinda," a soft voice suggested.

Bemused at having his question answered without asking, he glanced down at the slight figure who had followed him despite his orders otherwise. She had tucked her kerchief back in, but wanton waves of warm strawberry silk fell about her shoulders. She still managed to look the picture of virginal innocence as she studied the rough men studying her, and his heart skipped an interested jig.

Charity clung to Lucy's hand, but the child was no longer screaming, thank Neptune. Trev's crew quit cursing to straighten their shoulders, and even the footmen barring the door attempted to look more manly. Lucy lingered in the doorway, appearing more feminine than Venus with her dreamy eyes assessing the situation. His uncouth friends fell silent in awe.

Her suggestion was an excellent one. Get the men out of here and away from the ladies. "Come along, lads. Now that you're here, I'm proud to see you. I've some rum you'll fancy." Pulling Lucy and Charity aside with an oddly proprietary gesture, Trev allowed his rough and tumble crew to precede him down the hall.

He didn't know if he should see to the viscountess, apologize for the intrusion, or order the servants to fetch drinks, physicians, or tea. The clash of his two worlds left him spinning.

"Rum at this hour is a bad idea," the soft voice chided.

"Why don't you have Cook send up coffee and mutton pie to fill their stomachs first? Hurry before they frighten any more maids."

Trev studied Lucy in amazement. He had chosen his crew partly for their ability to instill fear in men far larger and braver than she. He would have to ask sometime why they did not frighten her.

"Apologize to the ladies for me," he ordered in the same manner as she had done to him. It seemed natural enough, as if they were in this together. He liked having a partner with whom he could share his problems.

Holding Charity, Sinda watched Sir Trevelyan stride briskly down the hall after his noisy companions. A man who could command an army of villains with just a word was a dangerous man indeed.

With the child on her hands, she couldn't think of the things he'd done to her just moments before, but she knew she would dream of them. She could feel his tongue slipping past her throat to tickle her heart, and desire surged.

Rather than acknowledge what he did to her, she hurried into the salon where the viscountess had evidently been entertaining the neighbors. She breathed a sigh of relief at the sight of the vicar's daughter attending to Melinda's prostrate form on the sofa.

"James, if you would," Sinda murmured to the butler, "have Cook send up a hearty meal for Sir Trevelyan's visitors, and pots of coffee." Remembering how the large one had stared hungrily at her, she added, "And have the footman, instead of a maid serve them, if you would."

As if accustomed to taking orders from itinerant artists, the stately butler bowed. "Yes, my..." He looked momentarily confused, then finished properly, "Madam."

Accustomed to the "my lady" he'd almost said, Sinda scarcely noticed his confusion. Holding Charity's hand, she swept across the room to the ladies fanning their faces and collapsing against the high backs of the damask chairs. "Mrs. Flanagan, Miss Flanagan, it's a pleasure to see you. Lady Rochester is overexcitable these days, as I'm sure you understand."

She smiled conspiratorially at the ladies, who regarded her with mixed astonishment and suspicion. She did not normally put herself forward, but the occasion seemed to require it. "Charity, why don't you run up to the nursery and fetch those lovely drawings you made yesterday? I'm sure the ladies would love to see them."

Ever observant, Charity hesitated, but Sinda winked at her, and she beamed. With a curtsy, she ran off.

"Shall I send for Lady Rochester's maid?" Sinda asked the vicar's daughter. The young viscountess didn't seem healthy, and she was worried about her.

"Melinda, sit up, you have guests," Mora scolded in response to Sinda's concern. "You didn't used to be so spineless."

Sinda thought the jaws of the two guests dropped to their chests, but Mora's pragmatism had the desired result. The viscountess struggled to sit up against the pillows, then paled as a roar of male laughter traveled down the hall. She steadied herself enough to smile faintly. "Well, that was a surprise."

"That Sir Trevelyan has friends?" Sinda asked with a hint of exasperation. She didn't know why she defended the man. He was obnoxious, overbearing, and a confirmed scoundrel. But beneath that crudeness was a man who loved Charity and wooed with gifts of paint.

"Under the circumstances, that he has friends *is* a trifle surprising," Mora agreed. Although her words were tart, she said them with a tone and expression of forbearance.

Unlike the others, Mora knew Sinda had painted the oil that had cast Trevelyan into disgrace.

Perhaps she should return to London and try to save his reputation by declaring that Trevelyan hadn't been at the seashore that day, but no one would believe her no matter how much she protested. They believed her paintings, not her.

"I think they are his crew," Sinda said in response to Mora's comments about Trev's friends. "Mrs. Flanagan, Miss Flanagan, it was good to see you again. If all is well, I will return to my work. Lady Rochester." She dipped a curtsy, intending to depart.

Before she could make good her escape, male boots echoed

on the floor outside the salon, and the viscountess shrank back against the cushions. Biting her tongue against a surge of unruliness, Sinda waited. She recognized the impatient tread.

"Just came to see that you're all right," Trev announced, entering the room with the brashness of a bull in a china shop.

Sinda admired the broad expanse of linen revealed by his unbuttoned vest and rakishly askew neckcloth, but the ladies all collapsed against their chairs again. Their eyes were agoggle as they fanned so rapidly she was surprised the draft did not blow the pictures from the walls.

"I apologize for my crew, but I'd left word that I needed to see them," he explained, coming to an abrupt halt at his obviously unexpected reception. Or lack of it.

His dark gaze flashed with annoyance at the women, who did little more than nod faintly at his apology. His fingers furled and unfurled as he apparently sought some other means of reassuring his cousin's wife and friends that they were not about to be run through with rapiers.

No civilized gentleman would expose his linen to respectable ladies. It was difficult not to imagine the manly chest beneath the thin cloth when he stood there with legs spread and arms crossed as if he commanded a deck, his unruly black hair streaming down his back. Despite the elegant clothes in which his valet had attempted to dress him, Sir Trevelyan still appeared large, swarthy, and intimidating.

Not until that instant did Sinda recognize his problem. Trevelyan seemed so strong and self-confident that she had assumed he was being obnoxious on purpose or out of deliberate defiance. Now she realized that he had no idea of the effect of his uncivilized informality on society. He truly was as out of place in elegant drawing rooms as a darkly erotic Caravaggio oil painting in a lady's boudoir.

It wasn't her problem, but she couldn't resist helping the man any more than she could resist assisting a kitten stuck in a tree.

Boldly, she stepped in front of him and curtsied. She could feel the immediate removal of his gaze from the other ladies to her bosom. She'd correct that faux pas at another time.

"How good it is of you to reassure us, sir. Mrs. Flanagan was quite weak with fear, but she and dear Miss Flanagan held up bravely for the sake of Lady Rochester. Your friends are quite imposing."

His eyes narrowed at her elaborate and silly speech, but not a fool, he took his cue from her. Nodding curtly, he hastily buttoned his vest at her pointed look, then stepped past her to the ladies Flanagan.

"My apologies again, ladies, if my friends frightened you." He took Mrs. Flanagan's plump palm and bowed over it. "You are so kind to look after my cousin-in-law in her time of need."

Sinda left the Flanagans simpering over the handsome scapegrace. She assumed Mora was still casting daggers at him, but she hadn't the backbone left to linger. She was a trained observer, not a participant, and all this playacting left her exceedingly unsettled. She needed the quiet of the orangery and her work. Trevelyan was on his own.

❦

He could do this, but he didn't want to.

Trev listened to the horsefaced woman's simpering platitudes while his mind's eye followed the slender artist's progress through the halls. How soon could he pry himself away from duty to follow her?

Not soon enough, he deduced.

Lucy Jones had looked at him as if she could see right through him. And she had. If she hadn't stepped in and forced him to mind his manners, he no doubt would have bellowed his irritation at the foolish fainting females and left them weeping in terror.

He was a graceless lummox, and he knew better. He'd simply spent too many years in the company of rough men—and women—to break the habit of outswaggering, outshouting, and outdrinking his companions to prove his superiority.

He had to relearn the rules of civilization so he could outsimper, outdress, and outgrace society's finest. Biting back a grin at that thought, he turned his attention to his hostess and the demon imp who called herself a vicar's daughter.

"My lady, my sincerest apologies for my uncouth companions. They've saved my life on many an occasion, so I value their friendship, but I will try not to visit them upon your patience again. If you will forgive me?" He bowed deeply over Melinda's frail hand.

For a change, the viscountess accepted his apology without a murmur. He counted that as a step in the right direction. The little witch of an artist had been right—flattery and polish were the key.

The little witch.

He almost barked his laughter as he remembered Mick's warning. He might start believing in witches if he met any more women as perspicacious as Lucy Jones.

"Of course, Sir Trevelyan," Melinda replied faintly. "Your… friends must be welcome here."

Trev studied his cousin's widow with concern. She couldn't be any younger than Lucy, but her wide eyes and dainty chin reminded him of a child's. Grief and pregnancy had left dark circles beneath her eyes. He was a beast to impose himself on someone in such delicate health.

"If you would prefer, I can remove myself to the inn where you will not be alarmed by further surprises," he suggested, although he would rather carve out his heart than leave this house he called home.

She looked tempted, and he held his breath. The vicar's daughter squeezed her shoulder, and the lady sighed and glanced down at her wedding rings.

"I have been told you are doing all that you can to see to the duties I have neglected," she murmured. "Laurence would be appalled if I should show you any less welcome than he would. I hope you will forgive my faintheartedness." Her fear of him was still obvious, despite the polite apology.

He wanted to shout, "I didn't kill your husband!" at the top of his lungs, but he'd learned that lesson. He merely bowed, nodded at the guests, and with a few murmurs of farewell, escaped.

He glanced longingly down the corridor to the orangery, but the loud shouts of argument from the study warned he'd neglected his crew too long.

Standing between two worlds, knowing he no longer belonged to either one, he wanted nothing more than to set sail for the unknown.

He glanced in the direction of his new horizon. He knew where to find her when the time was right.

Eleven

SINDA AWOKE THE NEXT MORNING AWASH WITH SUCH anguish that she wished to rip out her heart to be rid of it. Her head hurt, and she cried into her pillow, so scared and lonely that she couldn't leave the bed. She, who had never known misery a day in her life, wept with sorrow.

She wrapped her arms around her pillow and hugged it, and the memory of strong arms rocking her seeped through her anguish. Eagerly, she grasped the image, calling up the reassuring scents of coffee and sandalwood. She sought the excitement of heated lips on hers and burrowed deeper into the blankets. Desire flowed through her, replacing anguish with restlessness. She wasn't entirely certain which was worse.

Groggy with the lingering effects of a headache, she threw aside her pillow and swung her legs over the edge of the bed. She sat there, bracing her head in her hands. She'd drunk no coffee and had naught to blame for this pain.

She was exhausted. And there was chalk on her hands.

She stared at the telltale blue beneath her fingernails. The last time she had woke in such misery…

This would not do. Taking a deep breath, she washed in the cold water on the washstand. She would go downstairs and fix some coffee and toast and feel better shortly. Bridget had said she couldn't come in today.

She'd kissed Trevelyan yesterday and had chalk beneath her fingernails this morning.

She didn't want to go downstairs.

But she refused to be a coward. She could face whatever awaited her. She just prayed it didn't involve blood and coffins.

She dressed slowly. The October weather had turned cold, and she donned a quilted and embroidered petticoat beneath her taffeta gown. She should have packed woolens. She dallied over choosing her warmest stockings. If she wanted to stay here through the winter, she would have to buy more coal to keep a fire burning in the bedroom or she would wake to ice in the basin.

Concentrating on normal housekeeping matters helped. She had never thought it would be so pleasant to have her own home. Perhaps if she apologized very prettily to her father, he would restore her allowance and let her remain here.

Or banish her to Northumberland upon her mother's orders. One never quite knew where one stood with the duchess.

She went to the kitchen first, to stir the fire and start the water boiling. Once that was done, she had no further excuse to procrastinate. It wasn't as if anything disastrous had come of the last drawing.

Having made up her mind, she strode briskly to the front room, threw back the curtains, and turned to the easel.

As she feared, a new chalk sketch rested there—a sketch she had no memory of having drawn.

She wanted to tear it up and throw it away without looking at it, but curiosity held her in its grasp. She had to look. She turned it to the morning light from the window.

The sea was still there, but reserved for a small corner of the scene. This sketch seemed to depict a calm, sunny day. Flowers spilled from a pot on a cottage front step in the background, and the subject seemed to be warming himself in the sunlight.

She'd drawn a man again. This time his features were visible, but she did not recognize them and could not tell if it was the same figure as before.

She studied the angle of his head as he bent over a rope. She thought it might be the same man, but it was hard to tell. He was still a fisherman, at least. Rough hands worked at the strands of jute he wrapped into a single thick rope. He sat with legs over the edge of a dock, his head covered only by a red kerchief. A square of white that might be a bandage peeked from beneath the scarf. His ragged coat lay on the planks beside him. He did not wear the vest of a gentleman. The worn linen of his shirtsleeves billowed in a breeze off the water, and a strand of fair hair escaped his kerchief.

There was no blood or coffin in either sketch to give warning of imminent disaster. She didn't know any fishermen. She had no one to warn of anything. What should she do?

She would fetch Christina. Perhaps ghosts had done this through her hand. The style was her own, and the kitten hunting behind the rope was a good indication that her fingers had held the chalk, but the topic and the means… Christina would know if the cottage had ghosts.

Hurriedly, Sinda drank her coffee and ate her toast. Grabbing an apple from a basket on the table, she wrapped in a warm mantle against the morning chill and set off across the fields to the Duke of Sommersville's sprawling mansion. She did not think it a wise idea to go anywhere near Trevelyan and the Willows until she understood what was happening to her.

When she arrived, she realized she should have brought her paint box so she could pretend to be there to work. It was too early for Christina to be out playing in the garden. She would have to go to the door and knock. Did artists go to front doors or servant doors?

She didn't care. She marched up the steps to the new wing since the old one was covered in scaffolding. She pounded the heavy knocker and waited, praying Christina was up and about.

The footman appeared startled to see her, but she had remembered the pencil stub and notebook in her pocket and had them in her hand.

"I am Mrs. Jones. I've come to make sketches of Her Grace's pets," she announced. "I am expected."

The servant left her in the front salon and hurried off to the upper story. Sinda thought she heard voices above, but it was a very large, echoing house. The late duke had not finished furnishing this wing, and Harry, the new duke, was more interested in stabilizing the old structure than working with the new—probably at Christina's behest.

To her surprise, male boots clattered down the marble stairs instead of Christina's lighter tread. She rose hastily as Harry, the Duke of Sommersville, strolled into the room, his hair rumpled and his normally immaculate attire disheveled.

"You'll have to come up," he greeted her with a grin. "The babe and Christina are having a disagreement this morning, as they have had every morning this past week."

"If she's not feeling well…" Sinda hated to bother her. Living in a family of women, she knew all about morning sickness, although she thought it might be a trifle late in Christina's pregnancy for it.

"She assures me it is just my son asserting his opinion, and that he is wrong and she is right. I don't ask questions."

Harry's eyes danced with joy, and Sinda wished she had a husband who so thoroughly enjoyed her company that he didn't mind morning sickness or disagreeable unborn babes. A man like that would almost be worth keeping.

But there were very few men so accommodating or agreeable. Harry was one of a kind, and he was Christina's.

Sinda followed Harry up the stairs and down long corridors to the old Tudor part of the mansion. She could hear Christina loudly arguing with someone, but Harry didn't hesitate. He threw open the double doors to the family sitting room and gestured for her to enter.

"I don't think she'll be pleased to see me right now, so I'll leave you with her. Tell her I'll see her when she's ready to break her fast."

Tugging his neckcloth back into place, Harry winked and strode off.

Sinda approached the door to Christina's chamber. She and her cousin were of a similar age and had always been close, but Christina had been a married woman for six months or so now, and she was a duchess. It did not seem quite proper to pop in and out of her rooms as she had before.

Christina flung open the door before Sinda could knock.

"Good, it's you. If Harry asks me one more time if I would

like a little tea, I might have to fling a cup at him. I like Harry much too much to wish to be unkind to him."

Still wearing her dressing gown, long, blond hair spilling down her back, Christina swept back into a bedchamber littered with odd objects, old journals, and drawings. She rummaged through the pages on a secretary desk until she found what she wanted and waved the letter in front of Sinda's nose.

"Our cousin Ninian says she does not remember arguing with her son before he was born, but he is an Ives and far more understanding. Did you know her son has mastered the trick of levitating balls?"

Sinda had learned long ago there was no use in talking to Christina when she was in full rant. She obediently took a chair in the corner and let her cousin pace the floor, although she rather thought the poor child in her belly would be a shaky pudding if Christina waved her arms about much more.

"*My* son thinks I ought to eat peas and carrots. You know I detest peas and carrots. He is going to be just like Harry, just you wait and see. I want a son who levitates balls, but I have one who directs my digestion!"

Sinda bit back a smile. There was no sense in encouraging her, but Christina did have a way of making one's troubles look meaningless. "You are certain you carry a boy, then?"

"Only a male would tell me to eat peas and carrots when what I really want is hot chocolate and crumpets." She sat down at her dressing table with a noticeable thump. "Soon he will be telling me that I can no longer explore the Roman ruins because they're too dangerous."

"Exploring a field in winter could be dangerous for someone unbalanced by pregnancy." She didn't know where that had come from. She'd never tried arguing with Christina before. Her newly red hair must be affecting her brain.

Christina looked up in surprise. "You take his side! Shame on you." In one of her abrupt about-faces, she stopped ranting to examine her guest. "You have a new color in your aura. Something is happening to you. Did you sleepdraw again last night?"

Sinda clasped her hands to keep from fretting at the chair

arms. "Another fisherman. He is splicing rope. I have never seen anyone splicing rope. I do not even know how rope is made."

"The same fisherman?"

"Possibly. I can see his face this time, but I don't recognize it." Sinda waited, hoping Christina would have some amazing insight that would reassure her she was not losing her mind.

"I see ghosts and you see fishermen. I'm sure we would make amazing dinner conversationalists if people believed us." Christina swung back around to face her mirror.

"Perhaps I ought to go home," Sinda suggested tentatively.

Christina waved a careless hand in the air. "Only if that's what you wish to do. Since I've had no demanding or terrified messages from your mother, I assume she has figured out where you are and has decided you're safe here. You're not harming anyone." She studied Sinda's reflection in the mirror. "Although you may harm yourself if you sleeppaint too frequently. You should take naps during the day."

"Does your son tell you that?" Sinda asked dryly.

Christina's eyebrows soared. "Do you think he might? Perhaps I am carrying a physician."

"A Malcolm physician?" Sinda would much rather discuss the child than herself. "That makes as much sense as anything. Although he may have some difficulty fitting his medical duties in with his duties as a marquess and heir to a dukedom." Sinda was quite willing to play this game of *What If?* to distract her thoughts from her own troubles. Malcolms had so many strange talents that they spent many a rainy day guessing what they could do.

Christina grimaced. "Another good reason why we shouldn't have boys. Combining male responsibilities and duties with our sensitivities could drive a person to madness." Christina stood up to pull a gown out of her wardrobe. "I want to see your drawings. Help me with these fastenings and I will call a carriage. Harry insists that I not walk to the village these days."

"You are what? Five months along? Walking is hardly a difficulty. But the day is chilly and there is no sense taking a cold."

Christina cocked her head and studied her again. "Definitely changing. The old Sinda would simply have agreed with me."

"The old Sinda slept soundly all night."

"The old Sinda didn't steal kisses from a pirate." Christina held up her trailing hair so Sinda could fasten the hooks of her gown. "Did you steal more kisses yesterday?"

Sinda flushed but before she could reply, a hasty knock on the door startled them both.

"Come in," Christina called. "It's my new maid, Sally," she whispered to Sinda. "She frightens easily. Don't say *boo*."

The young maid tiptoed in and widened her eyes at the sight of the duchess nearly dressed. "Oh, Your Grace, you should have called me—"

"Never mind that. Did you bring us a message?"

Sally's eyes widened even more, if that were possible. "Matilda said as I was to tell you that the king's men have come to visit His Grace."

"King's men?" Obviously surprised, Christina swept toward the bedchamber door, her hair still tumbling down her gown. "On what business?"

"I'm sure I cannot say, Your Grace." Sally backed against a wall, out of the way of Christina's petticoats. Accustomed to the eccentricities of the duchess, she did not blink at Lucy's presence.

"Perhaps you should allow your maid to put up your hair before you rush down there," Sinda called after her.

Christina scowled but obediently returned and sat down. "A cap or something quick, please."

"They say in London the ladies curl their hair in front," Sally murmured now that she had an audience she perceived as supportive.

"The ladies in London wear red heels and trip over their own feet as well. If you come near me with curling tongs, I'll fling you from a window."

Sinda snickered. That sounded like a distinctly Harry thing to say. She wasn't at all certain husband and wife were good influences on each other. She glanced nervously at the door.

She knew her father sponsored a regiment. Surely he would not send soldiers to collect her?

She waited impatiently for the maid to pin her cousin's hair into respectability. Christina's gown was an old one, designed for gardening, but Christina wore it like a duchess. Sinda sighed in awe as her cousin swept from the room as if she were wearing a crown.

Harry's shouts carried all the way up the stairs. Christina increased her pace. Sinda held back, clasping the banister. Anything that made genial Harry shout could not be good.

Two red-coated soldiers marched out the front entrance. The stately butler slammed the door after them. That the butler had deigned to come into the front part of the house to see to their guests spoke volumes. The entire household must be on alert. Sinda shivered in her shoes and waited until she saw Harry stalking down the hall before she dared to step further. If the soldiers were after her, he hadn't turned her in.

Catching sight of Christina on the stairs, Harry stopped and visibly relaxed his expression from one of anger to amusement. "They have not come to take me away yet," he called up to them. "I suppose that means debtor's prison does not await me."

"Your aura is still angry, Harry. You cannot fool me. Why were they here?" Hurrying down the steps, Christina stopped in front of her husband, held his shoulders, and reached up to kiss his cheek.

Sinda sighed in appreciation of this loving exchange. She was glad Christina had found a man who endured her irritating ways. Could there possibly be a man out there for her as well?

And why did she wonder such a thing? Until now, she had rejected the idea of having a man of her own. Until now…

Harry glanced up to Sinda and waited for her to reach the foyer so he need not shout. "They are looking for Sir Trevelyan. It seems his grandfather has charged him with murder, and they wish my help as magistrate to apprehend him."

Sinda drew in a breath of shock. "That's *mad*," she cried.

Before anyone could stop her, she lifted her skirts and flew out the door in a furious flurry of petticoats.

Twelve

SINCE LUCY HAD ADMIRED THE CARVED IVORY HE'D GIVEN Charity, Trev carried a better piece of work down to the orangery as a peace offering of sorts. The artist had run away yesterday just as he'd feared, and he'd tried to do the gentlemanly thing of staying away from her cottage last night.

But her lure was too strong. She'd handled his crew and the ladies with admirable aplomb. He couldn't have managed it without her. Perhaps if he told her so, that would constitute flattery and she would be appreciative…

Bearing gifts and honeyed words, he entered the orangery and immediately knew she was not there. He couldn't smell the scent of lilacs and lavender that she carried with her, and the air did not vibrate with her intensity. Just as he had a sense of where he was when at sea, he knew when Lucy was about.

He fought his way through the greenery just to prove himself right. Her oil stood covered, her paints and brushes neatly cleaned and put away. She had not been here at all today.

Had he frightened her away forever? If so, Melinda would never forgive him. The viscountess was still convinced that he would put her into the street once he had the legal right to do so. He could strangle his grandfather for that alone, without considering all the other reasons the old man should choke on his own bile.

It was his duty to fetch the artist back. Laurence would

want his wife to be happy, and this late in her pregnancy, she needed serenity, not turmoil. He needed Lucy here to provide it.

Tucking the ivory into his pocket, Trev plucked trailing orchid stems and bunches of small, frilly white flowers to create a bouquet. He'd sent many of these specimens back to Laurence from his journeys. His cousin had enjoyed using his botanical knowledge to label them and write scientific treatises on the exotic flora of the West Indies. He wished his cousin were here now to tell him which flowers would be best for wooing wary ladies.

Trev rummaged beneath a garden bench until he found a vase, pumped water into it, and jabbed the flowers into the opening. The result was not quite so elegant as when he'd held them in his fist, but they were flowers. He could wish for ones the blue of her eyes, but he didn't think such a color existed anywhere in the floral kingdom.

Feeling foolish, he summoned a carriage instead of his stallion. No point in going about in public carrying flowers like a lovesick milksop. Mick could keep his trap shut.

"Heard the little artist made even Caleb behave," his driver said as Trev climbed into the carriage bearing the bouquet and a basket of scones he'd swiped from the kitchen to add to his booty.

"The clowns nearly fell over their own feet when she walked in," Trev replied grumpily. He didn't want to share Lucy with his crew. "And if you say another word, I'll send you sailing with them."

"Sent them off again, did you?" Unconcerned by the threat, Mick spoke through the open hatch into the carriage as he clicked the team into motion. "What be they carrying this time?"

"Nothing. I've sent them looking for someone." Trev leaned over and slammed the hatch shut. No sense in letting the entire area know he was insane—or pathetic—enough to believe his cousin lived.

He prayed Laurence lived, more so every minute. Although he desperately wished he could discuss botany or anything else with his cousin, it was Melinda's grief that would have him setting sail again. He could not bear much more of her sleepless eyes.

Rather than contemplate the dark side of his duty, Trev tried to picture Lucy Jones in the front room of her cottage, applying her talented fingers to some sketch on the easel he'd seen in there. He'd seen no cats in her house or in her drawings. Surely she wasn't the lying Malcolm who had caused the scandal. She treated him as if he were a man to be admired, and he craved that regard right now.

Despite his lack of polite manners, he would find his way around Lucy's timidity in lovemaking. He could teach her a great deal once she let him. Perhaps at some future time she would gift him with the story of what kind of husband had left her so naïve.

The carriage halted before the modest brick cottage the artist had taken. This late in fall, only a few daisies bobbed in the garden. A rowan shed leaves in his path as he walked up the steps. A faint wisp of smoke curled from the chimney, but he saw no other sign of occupation.

Holding his silly bouquet and a basket on his arm, Trev knocked, trying not to think of the way his stomach clenched as he waited for Lucy to open the door. As a youth, he'd held a passion for a few women who were not the sorts one brought home to mother. Since then, he'd acquired better taste and had held several ladies in high esteem, but he'd never craved them as he craved the mysterious artist.

When she did not answer the knock, he frowned at the village street. Few people were about at this hour. Could she have gone shopping?

The chill wind dipped the orchid blossoms in his hand. He had a vague idea that they shouldn't be exposed to cold. He damned well didn't want to take them all the way back to the house if she wasn't here.

Perhaps he could surprise her with them? Did women like surprises?

After knocking a second time and receiving no response, he tested the door latch. The door opened without hesitation.

He could set the flowers and basket on the table, find some paper, and leave a note. Or let her curiosity drive her up the road to find him. He liked the notion of having her come to him.

He slipped inside the front parlor. The day was overcast, but the curtains were open. He could see enough in the gray light to find the tea table and set his gifts upon it. He tugged the ivory from his pocket and added it to the basket so she would suspect it came from him.

A drawing on the easel beckoned. She'd been working on a bowl of fruit the other night, but this didn't seem to be the same piece of work.

Going closer, he frowned at the sketch of a man on a dock. What did she know of docks? It wasn't as if she could see one out her front window.

He moved the easel into the light and nearly choked on a rapid intake of breath as he recognized the subject. *Surely not.* He must be hallucinating, imagining things that he desired but that couldn't be.

He lifted the sketch and carried it to the glass. *Laurence.* It had to be Laurence. He hadn't seen him in nearly twenty years, but there was the nick on his brow that he'd received in a fall from a tree, smaller now than Trev remembered, but in the same location. There was the fair hair, the blue eyes, the cleft chin that so resembled his own. They'd had very little else in common in the way of looks except that chin.

And the man in the portrait was left-wrapping the rope. Not one man in ten wrapped from the left.

Did this mean Laurence was alive? Had Lucy seen him? The hope welling in his heart over a foolish painting was frightening. Did his grandfather, for some perverse reason, hold Laurence hostage somewhere? And if this painting was the real thing, what the devil was his cousin doing looking like a poor fisherman, with calluses to prove it?

Trev thought he'd lost his mind until he noticed the small kitten hunting behind the stack of rope. A kitten. The telltale sign of the artist Lucinda Malcolm Pembroke. Lucy Jones.

The pain at her treachery immediately ripened into fury so

hot that he could have ripped the cottage down with his bare hands to find the lying, conniving witch.

She had to be in league with his grandfather to have carried this perfidy so far. What had they done with Laurence? He didn't know what he would do once he had his hands on her—

A knock on the door distracted him enough to realize his fingers were about to tear the precious sketch apart. Carefully, he set it back down and glanced out the window.

Soldiers!

Given the artist's sudden absence and the extent of her betrayal, there could be only one reason for soldiers to have arrived on the doorstep while he was here. They'd been sent for him.

They must have seen him through the window at the same time he saw them. He heard a shout, and a boot kicked the front door.

Without second thought, Trev dashed for the kitchen and the back door, cursing his stupidity in taking a carriage that announced his presence to all the world instead of the stallion that could have carried him away faster than any could follow.

A musket fired over his head as he dodged clothing on a neighbor's line. A small child screamed, and a woman raced from her door to scoop him up. Another musket fired, this time right past his shoulder.

Bloody damned soldiers. Muskets weren't a gentleman's weapon. Where were their swords? Where was his? At home, damn women to Hades.

"Halt, in the name of the law!" the soldier shouted after him.

Ahead, two more soldiers raced down the lane, lowering their muskets to firing position. Between him and them were more clotheslines and women and children. Muskets were notoriously erratic in firing. He could use the clotheslines to hide his escape through one of the cottages into the street where Mick might have the carriage ready, but the cottages could be filled with children and old people whom the inexperienced young soldiers would trample in their haste to follow.

He couldn't do it.

With the bitter taste of gall in his mouth, Trev halted and spread his hands to show he had no weapon.

❧

Part way down the duke's drive, Lucinda stopped in midflight. She had come on foot. It was a mile to the village from here, and another mile to the Willows on the other side. She needed a pony cart or horse to get her there faster. Perhaps if she warned Trevelyan in time, he could escape to his ship before the soldiers found him.

She would not even consider that she was helping a murderer escape. Trevelyan was not a murderer. She believed that with all her heart.

Harry, bless him, had followed her down the stairs and had already shouted at a servant to bring a carriage around.

"You can't go with me, Harry," she told him. "If you have a horse or pony cart to spare, I would greatly appreciate it. But you're a magistrate. You can have no part in this."

"I have far more reason than you. I'm an officer of the law. You are nothing to the man. Your mother will turn me into a toad should I let you become involved. Now, go back inside and keep Christina company while I see what I can do."

"Christina must be far more patient than I ever gave her credit for to put up with you," she replied with exasperation. "Do as you must, and so will I." Turning, she started back down the drive, leaving Harry to fetch horse or carriage or stay behind. She had a feeling that honest Harry would not be of much use to Trev now, and she refused to sit at home and wait to find out.

On foot, she could take some shortcuts that a carriage couldn't. The soldiers were on horseback, but she hoped Trevelyan wasn't at home or that the soldiers must report elsewhere for new orders now that Harry had turned them down. She had to hope. Hysterical weeping wouldn't help.

She stepped off the drive at the sound of wheels and a horse galloping down the drive. Harry might have the best grooms in the world, but they couldn't have harnessed a team so quickly. She looked up as a pony trap halted beside her.

Christina climbed down from the cart. "It's not much, but it will be faster than walking. Harry will be right behind you though. Be careful."

Unable to find words, Sinda hugged her cousin and climbed into the cart. The pony was off and trotting with only a feather lick of the reins.

She had no idea why she had suddenly decided to go into the business of rescuing arrogant pirates, except that she felt guilty for being the cause of his trouble.

She saw no soldiers on the road between Harry's manor and the Willows. She took a farm lane instead of traversing the busy village streets. Perhaps the soldiers didn't know of this route. Perhaps she was ahead of them.

She chewed her bottom lip and urged the pony to trot faster when they came in sight of the manor. How would she find Trevelyan? She scanned the countryside but saw no sign of redcoats. Or the pirate.

She felt as if her fear had become a small boulder in her stomach as she reached the Willows and pulled the cart around to the stable. A carriage was waiting in the courtyard, harnessed and prepared to go. Maybe he'd heard already? With relief, she pulled the cart to one side and waved to the carriage driver. "I must speak with Sir Trevelyan. Is he here?"

Did she mistake, or did the driver look grim?

"Be ye here to help him or harm him?" he demanded.

Alarm immediately replaced her momentary relief. "Help. Have the soldiers come already?"

"They caught him in town. They're taking him to Brighton." The driver narrowed his eyes as Sinda leaped from the cart. "Do ye know summat that will help him?"

A groom had come running to take the pony's reins. Without a moment's hesitation, she gave them over and tugged on the carriage door. "Maybe. I won't let him believe he has no friends."

She needed both hands to hold her voluminous petticoats. Managing to pull herself up without the steps was awkward, but she couldn't wait until everyone agreed whether or not she should go.

"You have some way of getting him out?" the driver demanded.

"That depends on a great deal, does it not?" With a strength she hadn't known she possessed, she tugged herself inside. Finally receiving a signal from the surly driver, the groom slammed the door after her, and the carriage bolted down the drive as if demons were upon it.

She grabbed a handle and held on.

She had absolutely no idea what she could do, if anything at all. She just knew Trevelyan needed someone to stand at his side, and the viscountess couldn't possibly do so.

She had a powerful family. Perhaps they could help.

They would certainly be on her trail the instant they heard what she was doing. Even Christina couldn't keep this escapade a secret.

Thirteen

LUCINDA LEARNED THE DRIVER'S NAME WAS MICK AND THAT he had once sailed with Trevelyan in the West Indies. It was difficult to talk with him through the hatch while the carriage barreled down country lanes, hitting ruts that sent her flying against the roof. At this pace, they ought to arrive ahead of the soldiers.

She thought Brighton might only be ten miles or so further south, but she had no idea where prisoners were held once they got there. She should have waited for Harry. She should have done a lot of things, but she hadn't.

She should have told Trevelyan who she was.

Not that it would do much good now. If his grandfather had chosen to charge Trevelyan with murder because of her silly painting, the earl was even madder than she. Did he have some other evidence that she didn't know about? If so, wouldn't it have been the talk of the town?

One of the horses lost a shoe before they'd gone more than a mile from the village. Sinda wanted to take the other horse and ride on, but the surly driver refused. He insisted they turn around and find a blacksmith. Terrified Harry would stop her, Sinda considered hiding inside the carriage, but she had left home without a farthing on her. If she must be frustrated by this delay, she would put it to good use.

While Mick saw to the horses, she slipped down a back lane to her cottage. She had some leftover bread and meat that could serve as luncheon. She hadn't been paid for any of her work yet, so her purse was thin.

She hurried into the front room to find a basket to carry her meager luncheon in and halted in her tracks at the sight before her.

A marvelous bouquet of orchids in a cobalt blue vase lay turned on its side on her table. Water dripped slowly to the floor and onto a spilled basket of scones and... She stooped to pick up the long thin rib of ivory covered in etchings. Trevelyan had been here. He'd brought her flowers and gifts.

From the looks of things, the soldiers had found him here.

Sick at heart, she gathered the flowers back in their vase, grabbed the basket of scones, and left the rest of the room as it was. The soldiers had trampled her drawing, but a piece of paper meant nothing to her.

A man like Trevelyan meant everything, not just to her, but to the viscountess and Charity and all who worked at the Willows.

She would not stop until she'd done all she could to prevent injustice. If revealing she was the portrait's artist would help, then she must do so.

He'd brought her flowers. She could weep with the unfairness of it.

Once the horse was shod and watered, they returned to the road. The sky grew gloomy, until she could scarcely tell if it was night or day. Despite the darkness, Mick drove like a man possessed. The road was unpaved, and the carriage poorly sprung for speed. She feared the wheels would splinter in the ruts, and even so, it seemed hours before they saw town. By the time they arrived in Brighton, she was exhausted, bruised, and terrified. She hadn't thought this through at all.

The immensity of her folly had finally started to sink in. She had acted on reckless impulse, without a single thought in her head. She never did things like that. And for what? Because she liked a man's kisses?

Or because she'd spent an entire winter painting his likeness on a canvas and had fallen in love with her dream?

Looking at the dismal building to which Mick took them,

she doubted that her name would help much. She knew enough about the law to guess this small jail held men until they could be tried by the circuit judge in the quarterly assizes. She had a vague notion that more serious crimes had to await a royal judge in a different court. She had no idea who the judge was or when the next court would be held. To whom could she give evidence before then?

Helping Trev seemed impossible.

Mick leaped down from the driver's seat and opened the door for her, pulling out the stairs so she could climb out more gracefully than she had gone in. She shivered in the chilly, salt-scented wind off the ocean. Her mantle was too light to protect her.

"Perhaps they'll let you see him, lass," Mick said in a more kindly tone than his sharp one of earlier. "Tell him I sent word to his crew. It might be days, but we'll be ready when he is."

She was too frozen in fear to question. She nodded and stared at the unsightly wooden door of the building looming over her. Brighton seemed a very small village, and this was a small prison compared to those of London. She heard no moans or cries from the occupants. Trevelyan had been knighted by the king. Surely they would treat a man of position with care?

"Will there be soldiers inside?" she whispered.

"Aye, I imagine so. The earl will have called on one of his colonels to make the charge. He must have recovered his speech. You don't have to go in if you don't want to. I can take you to an inn, stable the horses, and find my way back."

She didn't have enough coin for an inn. Harry could arrive any minute. She ought to wait for him, but she felt personally responsible for this atrocity. She would simply ask to see Trevelyan and tell him he had friends.

With a sigh of relief at that plan, she tugged the hood of her mantle closer and walked up the stairs to the terrible door. Should she knock or just walk in? There wasn't a knocker. Taking a deep breath and almost choking on the stench from the gutter, she turned the door latch.

The smells inside weren't much better than those outside. Cheap tallow candles hissed and sputtered against the gloom, joining their stench with that of pipe smoke, body odor, and the fouler smells of a privy. A rotund, balding man sat at a battered desk, masticating a meat pie with his mouth open.

Lucinda tried not to gag as he looked up. The real world was considerably more depressing than the pleasant one her parents had wrapped her in. "I was told that Sir Trevelyan Rochester was brought here. Might I see him?"

The man snorted inelegantly and took a swill from his mug to wash down his pie before replying. "And who be you?"

Well, there was the problem in a nutshell. Did she announce that she was Lady Lucinda Pembroke, daughter of a duke, artist of the painting that had incriminated Trevelyan? The guard would either laugh himself silly or call all his comrades to share the jest. In her simple gown and quilted petticoat, with her hair tumbling about her shoulders, she hardly looked like a duke's daughter. And Trevelyan would probably kill her with his bare hands if he found out.

Perhaps it would be easier to tell him if he was behind bars. Once he calmed down, he would know what to do with the knowledge.

She folded her hands and tried not to let her voice quake. "I am Lucy Jones, a friend of the Viscountess Rochester. She wishes to see how he fares." Just a faint hint of aristocracy to impress him.

The man at the desk snorted again. She thought him very much like a pig she had seen once. His bulbous nose needed to be a little blunter, perhaps, and he should have hooves instead of hands. That wasn't very nice of her. She should save her imagination for her drawings.

"You can take him back his supper. He threw it at the last man who went back there. Shouldn't bother again, but it might be worth the entertainment. We don't get many claimants to earldoms here."

With difficulty, he maneuvered his wooden chair away from the desk and dragged his bulk to his feet. "Ain't got no fancy trays. Take the pie what's left and that mug there." He nodded toward a pewter mug and a brown-paper-wrapped package. "I'll show you back."

Wondering if the man had intended to eat Trev's supper if she hadn't arrived, Sinda clenched her teeth to keep them from chattering. She took the greasy parcel and the heavy mug and followed the jailer through a dark hallway lit only by a few flickering lamps. She should have brought Mick. She saw no soldiers in here, no one respectable at all.

But other women must do this. She could do anything they could. If she meant to live on her own, she must not rely on her father's name. Independence had its price.

They passed several doors with small windows and bars, but no sounds came from behind them. Perhaps Brighton did not have very many prisoners. That was a relief at least.

"Lidy to see you, then," the jailer announced, pounding on one of the doors. "Make yerself presentable."

Gripping the pie until the juice ran down her wrist, Sinda waited for the jailer to unlock the door and shove it open. Trevelyan didn't belong in this black hole. He belonged in the sunshine with the wind in his hair as she'd painted him.

The door opened, but it was too dark to see within. She hated stepping in blindly. "Trevelyan?" she whispered hesitantly.

"You!" A hand shot out, gripping her wrist and tugging her inside. The mug fell to the floor and splashed her skirt and petticoat with ale.

Sinda bit her tongue as he flung her to one side. She could see Trevelyan's tall, broad-shouldered silhouette against the lamp in the corridor, but she could not believe anything else she saw. He raised his fist and swung so rapidly at the clumsy jailer that she could not quite catch the connection between his action and the jailer's grunt. Only when the man's bulky body crumpled to the floor did she fully grasp the significance.

"Did you come to taunt me in my prison cell?" Trev growled, grabbing her wrist again and jerking her toward the open doorway. "Did you think me some tame pet to come at your call so you might put a leash on me?" He slammed the cell door on his jailer and turned the key in the lock.

Keeping his harsh hold on her wrist, he raced down the

hall. Sinda had to run to keep up or fall and be dragged along. She had no idea what madness had come upon him, and terror prevented her from thinking on it. Speech was well beyond her.

No soldier leaped out of the night to stop him. Heart pounding, she tripped and almost fell on her skirt, but fearing what this madman would do, she caught herself in time. He stopped at the door she had first entered and peered around it. Apparently satisfied with what he saw, he dragged her outside.

"Bless you, Mick," he cried as he ran up to the carriage. "Take us west. I'll tell you when to stop."

Mick did not appear the least startled at his employer's mode of arrival. He climbed into his seat as Trevelyan threw Sinda into the carriage and jumped in beside her.

The carriage was jolting down the road before she realized she still held the crumbled pie in her hand. In a state of shock, she stared at the mess oozing between her fingers rather than face what had just happened.

"Did you come to gloat or to verify that you had accomplished your goal before reporting to my grandfather?" he demanded.

So furious he could only see the tight ball of his rage, Trev tore the parcel from Lucy—no, Lady Lucinda's—hand. It stank of onions and grease, but he was too hungry to care. He'd walked fifty miles pacing his cell and storming at the fates and treacherous women. He sank his teeth into the oily crust and tore off a hunk with all the finesse of a starving dog with a bone.

He had to do something with his hands or strangle her.

When she said nothing, he glared through the early evening gloom. She was daintily dabbing at her hand with a lace handkerchief. Lace. How many itinerant artists could afford lace? Why hadn't he paid attention?

He'd been a fool for the first pretty face to cross his path. That made him more furious still.

"Will you just sit there and pretend innocence?" he asked, rebelliously wiping his mouth with the back of his hand like the crude sailor he was. "Did you think me so dull-witted as to fall for your charms and never question? What the devil have you done with Laurence?"

That brought her head up with a snap, he noted with satisfaction.

"Laurence? The viscount? What have *I* done with him?"

"You drew him. I'd recognize him anywhere. You must have seen him. When it comes to that, how the hell did you paint me without my knowing it?"

She dropped her messy handkerchief on the carriage floor and fretted at the edges of her mantle. "When did I paint the viscount?" she asked with an odd quietness.

"*Drew.* Not painted. Chalks. On your easel. Did no one mention that they caught me inside your house today? I thought that a lovely piece of irony. If you planned it that way, I cannot see how."

Remembering the sick fool who brought her orchids and scones and all his hopes, Trev curled up tight inside himself as he had done for years. He'd actually begun to believe that he could come home and find peace and welcome. Had he not learned his lesson once? What would it take to get it through his thick head that he didn't belong here?

But he could still help Laurence. He'd find out what sort of treachery his grandfather had committed this time, return Laurence to his home, and then he'd leave. But this bitch would pay first.

Her voice shook a little as she replied. "The sketch on my easel? You saw that? The fisherman?"

"That's no fisherman!" By Neptune, he wanted to leap across the seat and strangle her. Instead, he pried open the hatch to shout at Mick. "Take us to George's place. Do you remember it? Just north of the road?"

Mick responded in the affirmative. Assured that he had the means of escape in hand, Trev returned to studying the dainty miss across from him. He finished off the meat pie and licked his fingers. He would kill for a mug of ale right now. Or an entire cask. Kicking the basket on the floor, he hauled it to his lap and uncovered his offering of the morning—scones, still uneaten. He lost his appetite.

"If you tell me where to find Laurence, I'll send you back to your father, no harm done." He thought he meant that. He wasn't entirely certain. He hadn't planned any of this, and he was still too shattered by her betrayal to think clearly.

"Why, so you might murder your cousin of a certainty? Perhaps your grandfather means to protect him."

Her cold aloofness was no more than he deserved, but Trev wanted to rip the roof off the carriage with his bare hands or choke her until she saw reason. Except neither action would get him what he wanted. "Then he should be protecting Laurence's unborn heir as well, and he's not doing much of a job of that. Give over. The viscount means nothing to you. Where is he?"

"I never met Lord Rochester," she said frostily.

"You drew him!" he shouted, his rage soaring up the scale to cataclysmic. "He was splicing rope left-handed, just as he always does. He has two moles beside his left eye. It may have been twenty years since I saw him last, but that was Laurence. I'll say this for you, Lady Lucinda Pembroke," he said her name with a twist of scorn, "you are a far more talented artist than you are seductress."

She flinched, drew her hood more tightly around her face, and turned to look out the window. "I draw what I see in my mind." She held her chin high. "I do not expect you to believe that. People believe what they want to believe, I have found."

"You draw what you see in your mind?" he asked in incredulity. "And you see Laurence? Just like that. You see the Viscount Rochester, heir to Lansdowne, as a fisherman on a dock?"

"I did not know his name. I saw a fisherman, that is all. Just as I did not know your name when I painted you at the fair. You were in my head and came out through my fingers. That is what artists do. They create."

"Aye, and this is what pirates do, kidnap and plunder," he said with a sneer. "And murder, if my grandfather is to be believed. I was no pirate before, but what have I to lose now? I'm already found guilty without need of a court of law. You will tell me where to find Laurence or become my first victim."

"People believe my drawings are predictions," she whispered in a voice on the edge of tears. "Perhaps your cousin decided he preferred to become a fisherman rather than deal with affairs of state. I do not know. I cannot say. I am only the artist."

"You are telling me that sometime in the future my cousin will become a fisherman?" he asked incredulously.

"I am telling you only that I drew what was in my head. Beyond that, I know nothing," she said.

He could hear the tears and pain in her voice and every ounce of his sinful soul wanted to believe her. Fortunately, he had recovered enough of his mind to see her for what she was. Stark, cold logic pushed aside his fury and took command.

"Whatever my grandfather is paying you, I will pay you more. I am worth a fortune. Ask what you will. Just tell me where to find Laurence."

She ignored him.

"Does my grandfather blackmail you?" he asked with false patience. "Is that how he persuaded you to paint that portrait of me? If so, I will find whatever he is holding against you and I will destroy it. Just name your price."

She said nothing.

His fury began to overtake his icy coldness. He wanted to shake her, to rattle her as she had rattled him. He couldn't allow it. He had to plan and scheme and beat the earl at his game.

But he couldn't prevent one final furious plea from escaping his tongue. "What have I ever done to you to be condemned to this fate?" he cried.

She turned and looked him square in the eye. "You have not believed in me. Until you do, we have nothing further to say to each other."

She held her silence until they arrived at George's tiny fishing cottage beside the sea sometime after the sun had set behind stormy clouds. She even held her tongue when he gave his old friend and Mick their orders.

She did not speak when he sent the men off with the carriage and left them alone. But her eyes screamed obscenities when he finally tied her wrists together with his linen jabot and roped her to the bed.

Fourteen

"YOU CANNOT DO THIS!" SINDA CRIED, STRUGGLING WITH THE bonds of linen around her wrists while Trevelyan tied a rope from the jabot to the iron bed behind her. Her alarm verged on hysteria at his proximity, at her imprisonment, at the thought of spending a night in the company of a pirate who had apparently reached the brink of sanity.

"What, you need the privy again? Or do you need silk sheets to sleep on?" he asked sarcastically. "You can have anything you want simply by telling me where to find my cousin."

"For all I know you sank your cousin and his yacht just as the earl says!" She tugged futilely at the rope, fighting tears. To think she had believed in him, had felt guilty at his imprisonment! She had believed a wretched vase of flowers meant his innocence.

Her accusation hardened his expression. "All I ever wanted was to come home and live in peace with my family. You and your scandal-mongering art have driven me to this villainy."

With a tug to verify the rope would hold, Trevelyan turned his back on her—which was good, because she didn't have a response to his desperate cry for peace. She'd run away from home to protect her own family from her art. She had never wanted to harm anyone. She had wanted to *help*…

She'd betrayed herself by becoming a mush-minded fool who thought her dream had stepped out of a painting.

Trevelyan removed his coat, and she was presented with the sight of the fine broadcloth of his vest straining across his shoulders as he lifted a tankard of ale on the table. He didn't have a gentleman's vanity about his thick black hair. Mussed and disheveled, it was held back by a dangling ribbon. A single tendril curved around his square jaw. The shadow of his beard gave him an even more piratical aspect.

The cottage was a farmer's hovel with one room and an attached shed for cattle. A crude table, two chairs, and the iron bedstead served as furnishings. The owner had gone off with Mick on some mysterious errand of Trevelyan's. Neither man had showed her much sympathy. She didn't think they'd bring rescue.

Despair threatened to overwhelm her. What had made her think that she could play with wolves and not get bit? Just because Trevelyan Rochester dressed the part of a gentleman and spoke with charm didn't mean that he'd changed his nature. Privateers were dangerous predators, not pets.

"You will regret this," she said quietly, knowing he wouldn't believe her in that either. "My mother will find you and my father will have you hanged, and all because I wanted to help."

"Don't count on it." He sat down and poked at the fire with a stick. "I sent Mick west with the carriage to give the soldiers a merry chase. George will find us different transportation by morning. We'll be on my ship before they learn they've followed a false trail."

Sinda wiggled to push the pillow behind her and leaned back against the headboard. "My mother does not need soldiers to find me. I know you do not believe me, and you will regret that. For Charity's sake, I am sorry."

"For a lot of reasons, so am I. You'd better get some sleep while you can. We have a hard journey ahead of us." For a moment, holding his mug and staring blankly at the fire, he looked as shattered and lonely as she felt. Then he deliberately erased all trace of expression and sat back in his chair to drink.

She didn't want to know where he was taking her. He'd crushed all her foolish fancies, and she had no illusions left. She didn't know if she wished to live in a world without dreams.

Scooting down in the bed, she turned her back on him to settle uncomfortably into the mattress. Why had she drawn Trevelyan's cousin in her sleep? If she only had a better understanding of her gift, could she find her way out of this situation? If the viscount was still alive… Was that possible? Or had she drawn Trevelyan's dreams instead of her own?

❦

In the flickering lantern light, Trev warmed his boot soles at the fire and tried not to look at the sleeping figure on the bed. He wouldn't sleep this night anyway. His brain burned as if afire, with just as much use. All his thoughts went up in smoke.

Ale and exhaustion had abated his fury. Lady Lucinda's dignity and pride had increased his confusion. He could see no reason for her to hate him enough to condemn him to a murderer's fate. His grandfather, on the other hand, had every right to fear him now that he'd returned. There had to be a connection, but he wasn't seeing it.

He had to keep her in his sight until he uncovered the source of the mystery. She had *seen* Laurence. It could have been before his cousin's death, he supposed. The sketch might be an old one. But why the fisherman's attire?

Smoke and mirrors. He didn't know how she did it, and until he found out, he wasn't letting her go.

He could either try to sleep or drink himself into a stupor listening to her toss and turn in the corner. He didn't have to look to see the spill of her red hair across the pillow. Red. He'd thought Malcolms were fair. What was one more mystery to add to the others? At least she no longer denied her identity.

Lady Lucinda Pembroke, daughter of a duke. How she must have laughed at him when he'd arrogantly kissed her! He, a mere knight with a besmirched reputation, had dared steal kisses from a woman whom all the princes of Europe could court. Why wasn't she married and blessing some lucky man with her huge dowry and a pack of children?

Best not to drink too much ale or he was likely to ask her. Making a blanket of his coat, he settled on the floorboards before the fire. He'd spent years sleeping on the hard deck of a ship in blustery wind and tropical heat. It would do him good to be reminded of how far he'd come. And how much the old devil owed him.

He didn't know how long he'd dozed when he heard the first moan. Years of living on the edge brought him instantly alert. He lay still, seeking the sound of horses outside. He didn't expect George back until dawn. Did he have visitors?

Weeping. Devil take it. She was awake and weeping. He hadn't thought her the sort to cry. He tried to ignore her and go back to sleep, but she tossed and turned as if she were attempting to free herself. She couldn't. His skill with knots prevented that. He steadfastly kept his back to her. If he didn't see her, he could remember she was a traitorous temptress and not the innocent…

He flinched. She wasn't a widow. No wonder she didn't know how to kiss! He worked his way through a litany of curses in three languages while she tossed and moaned and wept. He'd lived too long among harlots and liars and didn't know how to recognize a maiden when he met one.

He could assume she was a rich man's spoiled wanton of a daughter, except he hadn't heard a breath of scandal about her. Or at least, not a breath of scandal outside her artwork. She was no libertine. So how had his grandfather persuaded her to his will? Did she really believe him a pirate out to steal the earldom?

That would be just like a silly miss, fighting for truth and justice when every man of the world knew no such thing existed.

Giving up on sleep, he carried the dying lantern to the bed. She twisted her head back and forth, and her hair flailed the pillow as she struggled to free herself from the bonds imprisoning her. He expected her to be glaring at him with loathing, but her eyes were closed and tears stained her cheeks.

He had given her nightmares. He had plenty of nightmares of his own. He wanted to condemn her to the same hell as his grandfather, but he couldn't help believing she was ensnared in something she didn't fully comprehend.

He was perfectly aware that he was letting a pretty face sway him. And innocent kisses. And a reserved smile combined with a quiet pride. And if he thought too hard on it, he would cut her bonds and let her go.

Instead, he blew out the lantern and sat down on the bed's edge. He soothed her brow with his rough hand. She quieted, as if seeking the source of the touch, but he thought she still slept. When she began moving restlessly again, he reached beneath her to cup the nape of her neck and massage it lightly. That did the trick. She lay still, and the moans stopped. Within minutes, she was breathing lightly.

He sat there awhile longer, enjoying the silk of her hair falling over his wrist, the satin softness of her skin beneath his fingers, the light womanly fragrance that drifted around him. If he were a real cad, he'd light the lantern again and watch the rise and fall of her breasts beneath her dainty bodice. He could hope the linen had worked loose so he could see even more.

The problem with being a cad, though, was that the consequences were hell, right here on earth. She'd twisted his head around enough without adding the obsession of physical hunger. Hands-off was the best policy.

But his hand lingered, lightly stroking, until he was certain she slept.

Physical hunger wasn't something that could be denied by even the coldest, most logical mind in existence.

❧

"Aunt Stella!" Christina, Duchess of Sommersville, cried in relief as the older woman stepped down from the carriage in all her London elegance, as if she'd left a ball to arrive here at dawn. "Thank goodness you are here. Sinda has run off with Sir Trevelyan!" There was no point in hiding the matter. Her aunt knew everything that happened within the family sooner or later. The fact that she had arrived all the way from London almost immediately after Christina had sent word spoke volumes.

"Has she, now?" Stella, Duchess of Mainwaring and Lucinda's

mother, drawled with heavy irony. "Is that what the imbeciles are saying?"

Christina bit her lip and waited to be told what had actually happened. Harry had already given the soldiers a severe dressing down over allowing a dangerous prisoner to escape. He'd gone off to prepare a search last night and ordered Christina to remain here, but she couldn't, not while Lucinda might be in some danger. She couldn't believe her quiet cousin would aid Sir Trevelyan's escape as the soldiers were saying.

"The duke has summoned the family," Stella announced, "and is having the yacht prepared for launching. Where is that husband of yours? We haven't time to wait."

Christina brightened at her use of the word *we*. "I'll send for him. I'll have Cook prepare a luncheon to take with us. You know where she is?"

For the first time in Christina's life, her regal aunt looked as uncertain as any mother whose chick had strayed. "Not for long," she murmured.

❦

Sinda's head hurt when she woke, and she was stiff from lying in one position all night. She could scarcely have drawn any more troublesome sketches while she was tied like this, so she supposed the headache was from fear and cold. Although sleeping in a corset couldn't have helped.

She could hear someone moving about, but she wasn't ready yet to face the reality of yesterday's nightmare.

"George brought us breakfast and our cart is waiting. If you don't wake up now, you'll go hungry for the rest of the day."

Although her back was to him, she could sense Trevelyan standing over her. She wanted to tell him that tying her up was senseless since she could scarcely punch him in the face, as he had the jailer. But she was too terrified of his looming presence and anger. She simply clenched her teeth and held still while he released her hands. She was dreadfully aware of the masculine aroma of his unwashed body and the rough hairs on his wrist and fingers as he worked the knots on her bonds. When he stepped back, she rubbed her wrists and refused to look beyond his boots.

If she were really lucky, her mother would have called in not only Sinda's half brothers, but also her cousins' Ives husbands and all *their* brothers to locate her. Trevelyan would be fortunate if he wasn't drawn and quartered by day's end.

Thinking that wicked thought, she staggered from the bed, used the chamber pot behind the screen of bedding he'd erected for her, and washed as best as she could. Not feeling much better, she attempted to right her hair with her few remaining pins; then holding her chin high, she emerged to take a seat at the table. Her taffeta gown was crushed beyond repair, but that was the least of her concerns.

Trevelyan hadn't shaved, and his jaw was even more heavily shadowed with beard than it had been last night. The one recalcitrant strand of his hair hung down in his face, and his eyes appeared sunken from a bad night's sleep. He looked like she felt.

And still her insides stirred with desire at the handsome sight of his cleft chin and high, rakish cheekbones.

Garbed in tight breeches and billowing shirt with no neckcloth, Trevelyan was a more virile man than she'd ever seen at her breakfast table. His presence filled the tiny room. She could scarcely touch a bite with her painful awareness of his proximity—and of the scabbard he'd strapped to his waist. The cart he'd mentioned had apparently come provided with weapons. The sword made their escape all too real and dangerous.

"Why is your hair red?" he asked abruptly, standing beside the fire and sipping the strong brew he called coffee.

"Why is your hair black?" she taunted, stabbing at her eggs.

"I'm fortunate it isn't gray by now. Have you decided to tell me where I might find Laurence?"

"In Davy Jones's locker, I believe is how you say it." She tore off a piece of cold toast.

"Right. And perhaps you found his body when it washed ashore and had it mummified so you could keep it in your closet and bring it out to sketch on idle evenings." He stabbed the fire, burying the burning log in ash. "Finish up. If we mean to catch the *Pirate Lass* at the next port, we'll have to hurry."

"The *Pirate Lass*?" she inquired.

"My ship. The crew's been sailing the southern ports. They should be nearby."

Could her mother find her if she was on a ship? The duchess might know where she was, but even Malcolms couldn't fly. Sinda swallowed the rest of her coffee and debated bringing the tin cup down on the vile man's head, but she thought the cup more likely to dent than his head.

When she dawdled, he grabbed her elbow and all but dragged her toward the door. She fancied he could break her in half if he chose to do so. She wasn't silly enough to think she could fight him, hampered as she was with skirts and petticoats and corset.

She wouldn't give him the satisfaction of asking where he thought he would sail to. She feared he would say the West Indies.

And a tiny, traitorous part of her wanted to go.

Billowing gray clouds filled the autumn sky, blowing a blustery wind across the landscape. She shivered inside her light mantle, but she wouldn't beg or plead for anything.

"Mick thinks you come from a family of witches," Trevelyan said conversationally as he lifted her into the crude wagon waiting at the front door. "He thinks you'll turn me into a toad."

"Tell Mick he has nothing to fear," she replied sweetly, crossing her hands in her lap and staring out over the barren countryside. "You already are a toad."

He chortled grimly as he climbed up and took the reins. "In the Americas, they have what is called a horny toad. That would be me. None of this kissing a frog to find a prince business for my kind."

She suspected there was some meaning behind *horny toad* that she didn't comprehend, but the description seemed ugly and appropriate enough to her just as it was. "Princes are highly overrated anyway," she said haughtily. "Most croak like toads in my experience."

"And being the daughter of a duke, you know a lot of princes. Have I raised the ire of one and that is why you make my life a living hell?"

"Why, thank you for the compliment." She fumed and forced herself to gaze about her as if her only interest lay in the passing countryside. "Most people think of me as shy and retiring. That you think I have the courage to annoy a pirate is quite flattering."

"Shy and retiring?" He hooted a disbelieving laugh. "I know society contains a lot of fools, but I did not think them blind as well. Name me one woman of your acquaintance who would have followed me into that rat-infested jail."

"My cousin Christina, the Duchess of Sommersville. My cousin Ninian, the Countess of Ives and Wystan. My sister—"

Trevelyan waved a hand to cut her off. "I see why Malcolms are called witches," he said dryly. "I might as well have a flight of stubborn women as well as soldiers on my trail. My life has been exceedingly dull of late."

"And you think kidnapping me will improve your lot? You need only leave me at the nearest inn, and my family will disappear from your life."

"If they are so good at locating people, they may find my cousin, and then I will let you go. Not before."

"I don't believe they have much incentive to find him, and I'm not certain they can find nonfamily members. Our gifts are a trifle ambiguous at best and unpredictable to say the least."

"Painting a man you've never seen isn't ambiguous—if I believed for a minute that you didn't possess some portrait from which you copied. I simply don't understand *why* you would do such a thing."

"Evidently I was bored and wanted to see a man condemned to hang," she replied in the same dry tone he'd used. "Once I've accomplished my life's mission, I suppose I must marry a frog and settle down to producing tadpoles."

He choked on what might almost have been laughter. She didn't turn to see. She was furious that he wouldn't believe her. Silly of her to think a man might understand her gift, especially when she barely understood it herself.

She pulled her notebook and pencil from her pocket and began making furious strokes across the paper. She remembered every detail of that first chalk fisherman. The rigging was a trifle difficult to duplicate with pencil alone, particularly while jolting over a rutted country lane. She cursed as her hand slipped and flew off the page, but doggedly, she kept on.

"Do you think to draw a picture of me to put on a reward poster?" he asked with interest. "Or a cartoon for the newssheets?"

"I have naught better to do than teach a fool." If she truly was drawing the viscount, she wished the earl's soldiers hadn't interfered, so she might have drawn more over time. It would be marvelous to know that Lord Rochester was alive. Drawing someone alive instead of dead for a change was an appealing prospect.

Trevelyan patiently steered the cart through back country lanes, following some direction only he seemed to know, while she scribbled in her little book. The sun was high overhead by the time she finished. Letting her mantle hood fall back to her shoulders, she ripped off the page and handed it to her captor without a word.

He took the page and studied it as he urged the ancient mare past a herd of milling sheep. Sinda thought he would crumple it and fling it away with scorn. Instead, he tucked it inside his coat pocket.

"Did you just make that up?"

"No, it is a copy of a chalk sketch that I hid in my attic. I know nothing of sailboats. I woke up and found that sketch on my easel the day after… after you visited. I do not know the man or how the sketch came to be, but there is a kitten in the corner that resembles one of mine."

She waited for him to laugh or call her a liar. She fully expected it. She had done all she knew to convince him of her gift and could do nothing more.

"The rigging is a special one that Laurence had developed for his yacht," Trevelyan said coldly. "He sent me a sketch when he was having the boat built. It very much appears he's preparing for a storm."

"I thought as much," she said quietly. "The day looked blustery, much like today."

"Or like a *summer* cloudburst," he agreed.

The viscount's yacht had gone down in summer.

Fifteen

If his timing was right, Trev hoped to meet the *Pirate Lass* at the fishing village of Hastings, *east* of Brighton, while George led the soldiers west. Of course, if everything went wrong, as fate frequently seemed to decree, his grandfather would have already learned of the *Lass* and have had it boarded by the navy under some pretext.

In either case, he had to go into Hastings to find out. He couldn't see much of the village as they approached, just the main road into town and the usual assortment of horses and pedestrians. The harbor would be visible once they reached the summit of the hill.

The village could be teeming with soldiers looking for him or, if his companion were to be believed, exploding with scores of her noble family, ready to maim and murder.

He cast a glance to Lady Lucinda sitting with shoulders straight beside him. It had been a long, cold day riding over ruts on the wooden seat of a farm cart. A delicate lady should be wilting with exhaustion or whining for a halt. Instead, her dreamy gaze alighted on every detail of the countryside. Occasionally she produced her drawing pad and sketched some aspect that interested her. Despite her pensive demeanor, he had no doubt that she could tell her family the precise roads he'd traversed. Her confidence that they would come for her was so great that she hadn't even attempted to escape.

The drawing folded in his pocket nagged at the back of his

mind. He doubted there was another rigging like Laurence's anywhere in the world. He could understand her remembering the sail positions if she'd seen the yacht cruising across the water, but the rope positions? Even he couldn't have done that with ease.

The man in the rigging hadn't worn a kerchief to hold back his hair. The man who looked like Laurence in the second sketch had. Did that mean anything?

He would drive himself mad with wondering. Instead of answering all his questions by finding the missing Lady Lucinda, he'd only opened an entire Pandora's box of new ones. And in so doing, he was losing his certainty that she had plotted with his grandfather, or that she knew more about Laurence's whereabouts than he did.

It would be far easier to stay angry with her if she would sulk or nag or behave less than the lady he'd admired from the first. Instead, she quietly sketched and otherwise pretended he didn't exist. That was probably what got his back up the most—he wanted her to be as aware of him as he was of her. Every hair on his body prickled when she moved.

"I saw a soldier enter the tavern," she said aloud, jarring him from his reverie, "and unless your ship is the size of a fishing boat, I don't believe it's here."

He'd made both observations at the same time she had. Damn, but his luck was against him, as usual. He'd hoped there wouldn't be enough soldiers to search both east and west.

In this raw weather, the *Lass* may have been delayed. In that case, he would have to lie low here, possibly for days, until it arrived. Or perhaps his crew had scoured the town earlier and sailed on already. He'd know once he had the opportunity to ask around.

For the moment, keeping the lady away from the soldiers was his goal.

Trev steered the cart into a break in the hedgerow, stopping beneath the thick branches of a beech. A heavy overhang of gold leaves prevented them from being easily seen from the road.

The lady looked at him warily, as she should have been

doing from the first. That he'd finally succeeded in making her fear him didn't assuage Trev's ill humor.

"They'll be looking for you as well as me." Without another word of explanation, he tugged off her hood and gathered the wavy masses of her hair in his fist. She froze, which suited his purpose perfectly. The beauty and softness of her hair presented the same temptation as a willing woman to a sailor home from a six-month voyage. He would prefer to indulge in this with the luxury of time, in front of a fire, with a bed waiting, but that wouldn't happen.

Enjoying the sensation of burying his fingers in her fine tresses, he braided her hair with a few deft twists and tied it with the ribbon from his own hair. Then, wrapping the plait into a knot, he pinned it up at the back of her head so it couldn't be seen. He hated to let loose the lovely mass of strawberry silk, but her gaze shot daggers at him already.

He jerked the mantle hood up again. "They're less likely to notice you this way. Unless you wish to spend the night in jail with me, keep quiet and stay invisible."

"Me? Why would they put me in jail?"

"Because you helped me escape. Soldiers don't ask questions. They follow orders. They're not any more likely to believe you than I am."

He hoped that gave her something to think on as he urged the horse down the road and into the courtyard of a respectable-looking inn. Mick had brought the coins Trev kept at the house for an emergency. He wouldn't be short of funds for a long while. In his experience, money wrought miracles.

But money wouldn't buy Lady Lucinda's silence. He was coming to understand the steel backbone she concealed behind that demure dress.

"Not a word out of you or a great many people could get hurt today," he warned.

He didn't linger to be cut down with her dagger gaze. He halted the cart in the inn yard and swung her down from it. Flipping a coin to the boy who ran up to take the reins, he caught her elbow and steered her through the mud and muck to the door.

The innkeeper rushed up, wiping his hands in his apron and darting worried glances from Trev's sword to the woman at his side. Trev calculated that their wrinkled and dusty clothes combined with Lucinda's regal grace raised questions in the poor man's mind. His unbound, unpowdered hair was not that of a gentleman's, but he might pretend to be a merchant.

"Our carriage turned over some way back, a bad rut and a broken axle. But my wife is in a hurry to meet her family in Dover, so we've borrowed a cart and march ever onward." He added a hint of disapproval and sarcasm to his voice. "Have you a room so we may repair ourselves and rest before setting out again in the morning?"

"Yes, sir, of course, sir." The innkeeper darted another hasty glance at Lucinda hidden in her mantle. "Shall I send up baths and dinner?"

"If you would, please. We left our luggage with the carriage and our driver. I don't suppose you have a modiste or tailor who might provide fresh clothing?"

The lady jerked her arm from his grip. Perhaps she objected to sharing a room so publicly, but after they'd already spent one night under the same roof, another would make little difference. Her father could only shoot him once, although he didn't think Her Royal Highness would appreciate the distinction.

"We have both, sir. I'll send for them at once. Let me show you to your room." Nervously, the innkeeper led them upward, out of the bustle in the lobby. As he unlocked a door, he cast a glance over his shoulder. "There been soldiers here looking for a man what sounds a lot like you," he whispered.

Good loyal man of the sea, Trev decided. Probably stored smuggled rum in his cellars. He rewarded him with a gold coin and a jovial nod. "Met up with some earlier. Some scalawag out of prison, eh? I'll lop off his scalp should I meet him so we won't be mistaken again."

"I just don't want any trouble," the innkeeper warned.

"And none there'll be. I'll come down later and present myself if I must." Trev laughed with the arrogance of men like his grandfather, sure of their places in the world. "But I think

I'll keep my lady to myself. Wouldn't want her sharp tongue to lash the lads, would we?"

"Only drunken louts feel the lash of my tongue," the lady in question said in a pleasant tone with a posh accent.

The juxtaposition of sweet tone with tart words startled the innkeeper into backing away from a domestic dispute. Trev almost laughed aloud as the man scurried down the stairs.

"Probably not well done of you, my dear. He'll remember us. But it did move the prying gossip on." Throwing open the door, he dragged her inside and shot the bolt behind them.

She threw back her hood, and the sun hanging low in the sky outside the window caught on fine strands of ivory amid the strawberry of her plait. The contrast of the black ribbon against such beauty seemed a sin, and Trev wanted to pull it out. That wasn't all he wanted to do, so he kept his hands in his pockets and waited for the promised lash of her tongue.

"You are tempting fate," she said in a soft voice that fell short of accusatory. "You intend to go down and taunt the soldiers. That isn't very wise. Yours is a distinctive visage. And I have no desire to be labeled a trollop."

He leaned his shoulders against the door and crossed his arms. "We need a place to rest for the night, and I must learn if my ship has come and gone. I have no choice but to be bold."

Sinda turned away from his arrogant stance, unfastening her mantle but not yet removing it. With her skirts brushing Trevelyan's boots, she was entirely too aware of the close confines of the room and their proximity to the bed.

"You have choices," she reminded him. "You simply choose the most direct ones. Yours isn't a secretive nature. I could see that when I painted your portrait." Of course, she had probably been imagining the man she had wanted him to be and not the man he was. She'd loved the idea of a laughing cavalier. She had not realized he was a reckless pirate.

"You painted me on a white horse wearing red ribbons," he complained. "That isn't bold. That's foppish."

She had rather imagined the subject of her portrait had chosen the horse and ribbons for his lady's favor, but she wouldn't tell him that. It had taken her a long time to realize she lived in a world of her own imagining and not the real one. Faced with the facts, she was uncertain how to go on. Should she run away? To whom? The soldiers? That sounded more unpleasant than the man who at least treated her with some degree of respect.

"Forgive my female fantasies," she said dryly. "Had I known you were a pirate, I would have painted a black horse flying a skull and crossbones."

"I've caught several ships that flew a pirate flag. Had you ever met the occupants, you would understand why I don't appreciate the comparison," he said gruffly. "You might as well make yourself comfortable. I won't be leaving until the servants have all come and gone."

She wasn't sorry if she'd insulted him. He'd accused her of outright treachery. She drifted to the window overlooking the village street below, wishing she could go back to last week when all she thought about was the kisses of a laughing gentleman who made her heart spin. "You could send one of the servants down to the harbor to ask if your ship has been here. Do you know where it would have gone next?"

"They're sailing along the coast from London to Cornwall, asking after Laurence and smugglers. They'll stop in any harbor they spy."

She was aware of him moving about the room. She heard his scabbard rattle against a wall. She didn't want to imagine how he would look raising a sword to soldiers. She feared she would paint blood and caskets of a certainty then.

"Your crew is looking for the viscount?" That surprised her. His voice took on a new note of surliness, as if he were embarrassed by his admission. "His body never washed ashore, although the tides in that harbor brought up his yacht. My cousin was a good sailor and a strong swimmer. I have to hope."

He continued to look for his cousin, even though he stood to inherit—or at least control—a fortune and a title. A most unusual man. No wonder her sketch had sent him into shock.

A knock on the door warned their dinner had arrived.

Sinda desperately wished for a bath first, but not with this man hovering in the background. And, if she sent him out, he would end up taunting soldiers. She shouldn't care, but she did. She could not give up her silly fancy that he was her dream come true.

She turned and watched as a maid transferred their dinners to the small table beside the fire. Before they could sit down to sate their hunger, a seamstress arrived. Under Trevelyan's impatient glare, the woman jotted down a few notes and scurried off without taking measurements. Sinda couldn't imagine what sorts of clothes might be available at such short notice, but anything would be preferable to the wrinkled, soiled taffeta she'd slept in. It still stank of the ale from the prison.

"I could lock you in and go down to the tavern," Trevelyan suggested after everyone had departed.

"Excellent idea," she said. "Take my clothes with you when you leave so the soldiers or my father will find me naked when they arrive." She didn't know when she'd developed such a tart tongue, but the words sprang naturally from her mouth. She didn't even flush with embarrassment when he grinned and looked her up and down appreciatively.

"I'll gladly stay and help you undress, if that is your will."

She flung her mantle over the bed that separated them. "My will would be that I'd never met you, never painted that wretched portrait, never knew you existed!"

"I'm not willing to go that far," he said. "I could wish the portrait to perdition, perhaps, but I'm not sorry I met the artist." He turned to face the mirror, jerked his jabot into place, and, realizing he had no means of keeping his hair back, looked about for a solution.

"Here." Sinda pulled his ribbon from her hair and held it out. Her heart tripped like a hammer at his words, but she refused to read any meaning into them.

She simply couldn't ignore him. Nobody could. His essential life force blazed like the sun, filling the confined space with energy, electrifying her nerves.

Trevelyan came forward, crushing her outstretched hand along with the ribbon. From the heated look in his eyes, she thought he might kiss her, and she held up her free hand to halt him. "Eat first. I would not drive you from your meal."

He hesitated long enough that she thought she might go up in flames beneath his regard. His hand was rough and brown against hers. He hadn't bathed, but his male scent wasn't unpleasant. It just reminded her that he wasn't a perfumed gentleman of society. He finally thought better of whatever had been going through his head, took the ribbon, and backed off.

"I will admit to hunger. If you will join me—" He gestured toward the table.

She returned to watching the street from the window. "I would like to be prepared when my family arrives." She didn't say it gloatingly. She didn't think she meant it that way either. But she drew some satisfaction at his silent grimace. Let him worry as much as she.

"You'll not want them to find you." He took a place at the table. "I've told the innkeeper we're married. Your father will hold a gun to my head and march us both off to a vicar."

Sinda considered that, then shook her head. "Christina's father is like that. Mine is more of a politician. He'll consider all the ramifications first. Then, if he determines you are wealthy enough to bother with, he may agree to a marriage in name only, take you for every farthing he can, and lock me up in a tower."

"The English aristocracy and pirates have a lot in common, it seems." Unfazed, he stabbed his beef and dug in.

"You could leave me here and go on," she suggested. "I do not much mind being locked in a tower. I've spent most of my life isolated as it is."

"You hold the key to my cousin's disappearance. I'll let you go the day my life's blood pours into the street."

"Well, I'm certain someone will arrange that sooner or later." Shrugging, she did her best to ignore him. The thought of Trevelyan lying cold and lifeless in the street gave her chills.

She tried not to look at the bed and wonder if he planned to tie her up again.

Sixteen

UNABLE TO BEAR THE EXQUISITE TORMENT OF WATCHING—OR listening to—Lady Lucinda bathe, Trev left her alone with the tub and locked the door behind him. He wished for his loyal crew so he could post a guard, but he'd have to take his chances. Or go up in a bonfire of lust wishing for what he couldn't have.

He had debated shaving so he would appear a gentleman or leaving his beard to hide the telltale scar. The beard had won for now. He could make up a story of waiting for his valet, anything rather than linger longer in the chamber with the lady.

He found a corner in the tavern where he could keep his back to the wall and watch all arrivals. He didn't doubt that soldiers would come back one more time before calling it a night. He could remember a night in Tortuga a few years back when a Spanish crew came through hunting his blood, and Raw Patty's son had escaped prison to seek revenge. He'd sat in a corner like this playing one against the other, feeling powerful and clever. He'd escaped into the bed of a willing woman while the men had burned the tavern down, and he'd called the day a success.

Maybe he was getting old, but he wasn't interested in burning any taverns tonight. The maid brushing her bounteous bosom against his shoulder and breathing down his neck didn't hold much appeal either. He tried to summon an idle pat on her ample backside but barely grazed her skirts.

His mind was too thoroughly fixed on a slender redhead in the room above. His nose was still out of joint because he'd thought a widowed artist too beneath him to marry, and now the tables had abruptly turned. Not that he wanted to marry the treacherous lady, he reminded himself. But he disliked being thought beneath the dignity of a duke's meddlesome daughter.

It was justice, he supposed, if he was in the mood to be fair minded, which he wasn't.

He wished he dared trust her. She had a quick mind and an inner strength that he needed on his side. But she'd lied to him on so many levels that he wouldn't trust his own judgment, much less hers. He was almost relieved when the redcoats finally walked through the door. Here was a concrete problem that he could manage.

He was probably three times a fool to tempt fate, but he hated hiding as if he'd done something wrong. If he had to wait another day for the *Lass*'s arrival, he didn't want to spend it suffering the torments of the damned alone in Lady Lucinda's company. He wanted the freedom to move about.

Both soldiers ordered tankards and leaned against the bar to look around.

Trev made a show of gentlemanly boredom, squinting at his pocket watch, sighing with resignation, and impatiently shoving it back into his vest. Tapping his fingers, he nursed the dregs of his ale, then slammed the empty tankard back to the table and eased out of his booth.

As he'd hoped, the innkeeper appeared in the tavern doorway, anxiously twisting his apron in expectation of trouble. His gaze darted to Trev unfolding his height from the booth, then back to the young soldiers trying to look dangerously alert. They all wore swords.

"Aye, there you are, my good man," Trev called to the innkeeper with the jovial accents of a London merchant. "Has the seamstress finished with my lady yet?"

"She just left, my… sir," the innkeeper replied with confusion, glancing to the soldiers.

Trev kept his evil grin to himself. If the innkeeper wanted

to think he was a lordling disguised as a merchant, that was fine with him. He reserved his impatient glance for the slim soldier stepping in front of him, blocking his exit. "What? I've talked to you fine folks earlier. I'm eager to get to my wife. She's a sharp tongue on her when she wants, but buy her silks and laces and she's sweet as can be. I want to take advantage of the opportunity."

The village men at the bar chuckled and turned to watch.

The soldier couldn't be more than twenty. His downy cheeks reddened, but he stood straight and held his hand at his sword hilt. "A word with you, sir. Your name?"

"Puddin' an' tame, ask me again, and I'll tell you the same." Trev crossed his arms and played to his audience. He'd spent a lifetime in taverns like this, knew the game well. He'd wager the soldier was some rich man's younger son with too much schooling and too little education in the realities of life. He wanted to pat the tad on his tawny little head. "Now I ask you, do I look like a prison escapee?"

"Yes, sir, you do, sir," the soldier responded bravely as his comrade stepped up beside him. "We'll have to ask you to come with us."

Trev roared with laughter and slapped the man on his back. "That's rich, it truly is. Barkeep, buy this pair a round. They ain't never been married, I see." He swept his hand to take in the grinning onlookers. "Now I ask you, good fellows. How often is it that your wives are willing and waiting?"

The men hooted and hollered and slammed tankards on the bar.

"And what real man goes off to talk with a bunch of nose-in-the-air lobsterbacks when he has a willing woman in his bed? If you've aught to say to me, say it now, boys."

"Don't stand between a man and a jolly rogerin'!" a wit at the bar called.

"Does a bloody murderer buy his wife silks?" another shouted.

"Leave the man alone. You'll catch him later when he's weak and grinning silly," an older fellow advised. "Come along, then, and drink your ale like good boys. Ain't no murderers around here tonight."

The tavern maid eased up to the soldiers and handed them their mugs, brushing teasingly against them as she did. The younger soldier reddened even more.

"I'll be upstairs, tending to my business, boys." Trev slapped them on their backs again. "Follow us to Dover if you like. I'll be happy to hand over my harpy of a mother-in-law if you're truly dedicated to ridding the countryside of nuisances."

The crowd at the bar roared at this jest. They jostled and shoved and surrounded the soldiers, cutting Trev out so he could make his escape.

Stepping down the hall out of sight of the tavern and its merriment, he lingered in the shadows beneath the stairs. To his relief, the boy he'd sent down to the port materialized. Removing a coin from his purse, Trev held it up and raised his eyebrows quizzically.

"She's been and gone, sir," the boy whispered. "Scoured the village yesterday and sailed with the dawn."

"That's a good lad. If you've ever need of anything, you know where to come."

"Aye, cap'n." The boy tugged his forelock and disappeared into the shadows again.

Trying not to curse, Trev strolled up the stairs, whistling.

The *Pirate Lass* had already sailed up the coast. He'd have to head west where Mick had gone—smack into the full force of the earl's regiment combing the countryside for him.

⤜⤐

Trevelyan strode through the bedroom door wearing a black scowl that had Sinda regretting her decision to don the nightdress the seamstress had brought. It was of a lawn so fine that one could see through it, and she'd been unable to resist the pretty rose ribbons with flowers painted on them. She'd wrapped a blanket around her so no one could see the gown except herself. That had seemed practical at the time.

It seemed unutterably stupid now. She should have donned nightdress, her old gown, and the new dimity, then wrapped the quilt and blanket around her, hit the seamstress over the head, and fled. She wasn't very good at this prisoner business.

She tried to stay out of the way as Trev stalked up and down the narrow chamber. She half expected a black cloud to form over his head and produce torrents.

He didn't even appear to know she existed. Perversely, she wanted to stand in his path and shout "Look at me! What do you intend to do with me?" But she wasn't *that* stupid.

Instead, she escaped to a corner, pulled out her notepad and pencil, and began to work. When she realized she was drawing Trevelyan, she hastily scribbled out the sketch and threw the pad on the table.

She had never seen Trevelyan as the cool, collected gentleman he portrayed for others. She had always seen the passion bubbling inside. There was eagerness in the way he snatched at life with long, limber fingers. Fire lit his eyes with curiosity and intelligence, and brash recklessness marked his stride. But tonight all that fire and energy smoldered in a dangerous cloud that she feared might combust if ignited by the wrong words.

"Use the bed," he ordered, startling her from her waking fantasy. "Leave me the blanket for the floor."

"I prefer to remain where I am." She was dropping from fatigue but refused to submit to the indignity of being bound to the bed again.

"Get into bed or I'll put you there." He said it matter-of-factly, without looking at her. "I'll not have you ill from lack of sleep. You're nodding off as it is."

He'd noticed? She could have sworn he'd forgotten her existence. "I won't be trussed and bound like a Christmas goose," she insisted.

"You'd rather I stayed awake pacing the floors? I can promise lack of sleep won't improve my humor."

Impasse. Sinda struggled with her dignity. "I'm not going anywhere. Did I leave when you were down in the tavern?"

"I could have seen you if you had tried. I'm trusting you not to scream for soldiers. That's as far as it goes. Climb in bed. I want a quick bath before the water turns to ice."

Heat flooded her cheeks. She glanced at her hands clasped in her lap, anywhere but at the man filling the other end of the room. Of course he wanted a bath. How foolish of her to think she was the duke's daughter, entitled to hot baths and clean sheets whenever she pleased without thought to others. He'd ordered the bath for himself as much as for her.

"Don't tie me," she begged. "I cannot sleep when you tie me."

"You slept last night. I cannot promise I won't hurt you if I have to fight you. Be sensible and go to bed."

She didn't want to be sensible. She wanted to scream and beat her fists against his chest. Clenching her teeth, she sat down on the bed's edge.

Trevelyan stopped in front of her, his long coat and legs blocking her view of the room. She held her gaze on her hands as he wrapped his jabot around her wrists. The linen was soft and didn't hurt. It was simply the distrust that gave her pain.

She was aware of his coiled tension and didn't dare examine the placket of his breeches directly in front of her as he knotted the rope to the linen.

If anyone learned how she'd spent these nights, she would be ruined. She would have to marry him, share a bed and the secrets of marital intimacy. She was half tempted to ask him to go ahead and ravish her, so she needn't worry over it any longer.

But she knew that was her base nature speaking. Her father wouldn't force her to bed a pirate. Children came of marital relations, and she wasn't prepared for that. Logically, she knew she should run as fast and hard from this man as she could go.

She scowled as he fastened the rope loosely to the bedpost. Had she been brave, she would have bitten him where it would hurt.

As if sensing her rebellious thought, he backed away, but not before she took note of the swelling arousal beneath his breeches. A maiden shouldn't notice that, but she had an eye for anatomy. She'd observed many things she shouldn't have.

Of course, men were likely to respond to any available female. Sinda shrugged off the blanket and let it fall to the floor for his use, exposing the lovely nightdress. Let him see what he was throwing away by treating her like a thief. Her breasts swelled beneath his hungry gaze.

With a growl, Trev flung a sheet over her before retreating to the screen and the tub.

She turned her back on the room rather than watch his clothing appear over the top of the screen, but she couldn't close her ears to the sound of water splashing as he bathed. The bath had to be chilly. How could he stand it?

He scrubbed briskly, and she heard him toweling off within minutes. Served him right if the bath was cold. Did he don the clean breeches and shirt the seamstress had brought? Or would he sleep in nothing rather than wrinkle them? She refused to give in to curiosity and look.

She heard the door open when he was done, and she held her breath. Would he leave her here, alone and helpless? She heard voices, and the door shut. Terrified, she lay there a little longer, listening for some sound of him.

When she could not tolerate the silence any longer, she turned over to scan the firelit shadows. He chose that moment to walk back in.

He wore only half-fastened breeches with his shirt untied. The dishabille was more seductive than if he wore nothing at all.

Sinda tried not to gasp aloud but assumed she failed when his dark gaze flew to the bed. She drank her fill of the sight of all that lean musculature. The open linen revealed that he was bronzed all over, with a curly V of hair between the hard swells of his chest. She almost sighed with regret when he turned his back on her.

"They will clean our clothes by morning." Without another word of explanation, he set a chair by the fire, propped his bare feet on a second chair, and effectively shut her out.

She wished she'd eaten more at dinner. She was so hungry her insides ached.

She had a grave suspicion that food would not assuage the ache.

Biting back a groan, she rearranged her hands so she could turn her back on temptation. She *hated* the man. She would do well to keep that in mind.

Her dreams that night were of cold and loneliness and frustration.

Seventeen

Lady Lucinda's scream toppled Trev from his chair.

He hadn't intended to fall asleep, but he must have been wearier than he realized. He hadn't thought he'd ever sleep again after seeing the lady's wide-eyed approval of his state of undress.

Approval, he snorted, picking himself up off the floor, rubbing his bruised tailbone while the lady whimpered and struggled in the bed. He'd no doubt given her nightmares.

Even in her sleep, she fought him when he tried to calm her down as he had on the prior night. She clawed at him and whipped her head back and forth until he feared she'd injure herself. He sat down on the bed and lifted her into his arms, but she started to scream. She'd have soldiers up here in a minute. Impulsively, he covered her mouth with his and hugged her close, silencing her in the only way he knew how.

Her lips tasted sweeter than the wine she'd drunk for dinner. He swallowed her scream and filled her mouth with his tongue, savoring the delicious moment he had never expected to experience again.

She froze, and her screams died in her throat. Not satisfied with just having her gossamer-clad body against him, he stroked her side, enjoying the soft give of her curves. Trev had thought he would explode when she'd defiantly dropped the blanket earlier. Without layers of corsets and petticoats, she exposed a luscious body created for seduction. This might be the only time he'd ever be granted the opportunity to touch her natural suppleness.

She moaned in pleasure, and he tenderly kissed her mouth, using his tongue to draw out hers. She arched into his embrace, offering her breasts to him, and, lust-starved wretch that he was, he accepted. He cupped a ripe mound in his hand, molding her softness to his fingers until she wept with the need that also raged through him.

Her eyes were shut. He told himself he was merely feeding more pleasant dreams than the one that had woken him. But if he did not stop soon, he'd have her back against the mattress while he sprawled on top of her. More than sprawled. More than on top of her. He had to fight his own hand to keep from untying the ribbons of her nightshift.

She whimpered in protest when he tried to lower her to the bed. She grabbed his arm and resisted when he released her. For a slender thing, she knew how to put up a fight. The bed ropes creaked and a crooked post at the foot of the bed rocked up and down against the wooden floor. Anyone listening would envy his bed play, a thought that didn't ease his agony.

He finally gave up and arranged her in front of him on the mattress. Wrapping his arm around her, kissing her nape, Trev urged her into the curve of his body. She settled into some semblance of slumber, although she occasionally whimpered until he kissed her again.

His loins raged with a fire that kept him wide awake into the early hours of dawn.

⤜✦⤐

Sinda woke with perspiration pasting her gown to her skin and a heavy hand splayed across her breast. A headache prevented her from reacting rashly to the odd sensations even when she realized who held her.

She hadn't counted on her family being so slow to find her. Two nights with the pirate could be ruinous—not just to her reputation, but to her physically. She wanted Trevelyan's hand to come alive and do more than touch her.

She didn't feel ravished. In fact, she felt in dire need of ravishing. The longer she lay there, the more her breasts swelled and the place between her legs ached for completion. She desperately wanted the man holding her.

Trevelyan snored lightly in her ear. She tried to wriggle away, but he pulled her more firmly against him. His big body filled the bed, holding her trapped between him and the wall. With her hands bound, she couldn't even pry his fingers off her breast. Her nipple had puckered into a tight peak begging for encouragement.

She wanted to hate him, but her traitorous body knew nothing of logic. It wanted the pleasure of a man's hand.

She kicked her heel backward and was rewarded with a shin. Trevelyan snorted and readjusted their position but did not wake.

She tried elbowing him, but his arm over hers was too strong. She only succeeded in waking his fingers to ply her breasts until she thought she might scream with need.

She curled up tighter in an attempt to protect herself, and her bottom rubbed against his hips. He moaned and licked her ear.

She shot straight up, nicking his nose with her head—

Sending Trev sprawling backward onto the floor.

Without an ounce of guilt, she glanced down at his expression of shock. "Touch me again, and I'll carve your intestines out your nose."

He spluttered. He covered his bearded face with his hands, and his broad body rocked back and forth in what she suspected were spasms of laughter. She didn't care. He was out of the bed, and she could breathe again.

"Stop that silliness and untie me," she commanded.

He stomped his bare feet on the floor and roared. She didn't think he appreciated the seriousness of the situation.

"The chamber pot is on the other side of the room, and I cannot reach it," she informed him coldly between his gales of laughter.

That sobered him fairly swiftly, although a grin still fought at the corner of his mouth as he propped himself on one elbow.

"Good morning to you too, Your Royal Highness." White teeth gleamed against bronzed skin. "It's good to know you rise so cheerily at dawn."

"Don't be facetious. I'm in no mood for it. Will you cut me loose and quit grinning like a bumpkin?" She held out her hands.

"Do I detect the faint trace of frustration?" he chided, tugging the knot so it pulled free in a single move. "That can be corrected, I assure you. The bed may not be wide, but it's soft, and I'm more than willing."

Seriously annoyed that he understood her mood even better than she did, Sinda resisted punching him as he deserved. It was embarrassing enough using the pot while he stayed in the room.

"I need my petticoat," she exclaimed in dismay some moments later when she decided to dress rather than reappear in her flimsy nightdress.

"The maid will return it with our breakfast. If you'll come out from behind there, I'll move the screen and feed the fire."

"I can't come out! I have no clothes!"

"You have clothes," Trevelyan pointed out. "You have no undergarments. I'm rather enjoying that turn of events, so don't tempt me to keep it that way."

"You're a pig, a pure, unadulterated *swine*!" Exhausted, frustrated, and still bearing the remnants of a headache, Sinda shoved the screen aside and flounced into the center of the room wearing only her new nightshift, with her hair streaming down her back. "I cannot think how I believed you would be good for Charity. She is no doubt prostrate with grief for no good reason."

He winced, then covered the weakness by inspecting her from head to foot with a knowing leer. "For a *widow*, you are looking quite angelic this morning, my dear."

She flung a pillow at him.

He caught it and flung it back, hitting her upside the head far more accurately than she had him.

Startled that any man *dared* treat her in such a manner, Sinda stared at his smirking grin. Then, with a fury she could never remember experiencing, she beat him solidly about the chest and shoulders with the sack of feathers.

Grinning, legs braced and hands on waist, he let her pound away until she swung too hard at his head. Then with a simple twist, he disarmed her and flung the pillow across the room. "Feel better now?"

"No. I still want to kill you." She grabbed a blanket from the bed and wrapped it around her when a knock sounded at the door.

"I was beginning to think you hadn't the spine of a jelly-fish," he countered, opening the door to let in the servant with a steaming breakfast tray.

Furious, Sinda stalked for the open door, heedless of her lack of clothing. Trevelyan caught her before she crossed the floor, dragging her off her feet with the sweep of his arm.

She struggled and kicked, much to the startlement of the maid. Trev merely grinned.

"My wife would like her undergarments back," he said with an aplomb that seemed to declare this explanation enough of their behavior.

The maid bobbed a curtsy and hurried out, closing the door behind her.

"There are soldiers down there itching to throw my hide behind bars and ask questions later," he murmured in her ear. "Unless you wish to join me there, I suggest we behave with a little more decorum."

"If they put us in separate cells, I'm quite inclined to accept." She tugged free of his grip the instant he returned her to the floor, but she wasn't as certain of her response as she tried to sound. She really didn't want to be locked away in a damp and smelly prison. She'd seen enough of that horror the other night. She needed sunlight and color the way other people needed air to breathe.

What was taking her family so long?

"Tell me where to find Laurence, and I'll personally deliver you to your family's doorstep," he promised.

"Don't tie me to the bed, and I'll no doubt draw his hiding place in my sleep," she countered, although she had no such confidence that his cousin was even alive much less that she could draw him.

"I'll do that once we're aboard ship and you cannot escape." He drew a chair to the table and began uncovering dishes.

"Aboard ship?" she asked in dismay, realizing he was still set on carrying out his threat. Sinda couldn't think of anything more horrible than being trapped forever aboard a ship of men, separated from her family by an ocean of water.

He didn't even look up. "Of course. My grandfather and all his soldiers can't touch me aboard the *Lass*. Mayhap I'll take up smuggling until the old man dies and leaves me in peace."

"I thought your ship wasn't here," she whispered, when actually, she had given it very little thought at all. She had assumed her family would have found her by now.

"And it's not," he agreed. "We'll need to find new disguises and go looking for it."

⤜≈⤏

"She is gone." The imperious matron stepping from the carriage glanced disdainfully around the fishing village of Hastings.

"Harry has not come out yet to tell us so, Aunt Stella," Christina protested. "This is the best inn in town. You said so yourself. We have made very good time." Good time given that they'd apparently had a later start than the missing couple and had to stop for the night west of here. It was nearly noon now.

"She is gone, and that dreadful wretch of a pirate has her. I detest Lansdowne, but he may have a point about that grandson of his." Stella, the Duchess of Mainwaring, looked grayer than her years as she gazed about the inn yard. "Sinda is too gentle a child to fight a man like him. He will ruin her."

"You have taught her to be strong, Aunt Stella." Watching the inn door for some sign of her husband, Christina added, "She left of her own free will."

"She's a child. She knows nothing of these matters."

Sinda and Christina were much of an age and certainly not children, but Christina refrained from correcting her distraught aunt a second time. They were all worried, and it did not help to argue among themselves.

She brightened as her husband dashed down the steps looking handsome and confident as always. Harry extended his elbows for both ladies to take.

"Your instincts are excellent, Duchess," he cried triumphantly. "The pair we're tracing left at dawn. I'm certain it's them, and according to the innkeeper, they're heading for Dover. Let us rest and have some coffee while I misdirect a few soldiers. I think they will come to us more readily once the earl's men are gone."

"They aren't going to Dover," the duchess corrected crossly. "They have changed direction *again*. Send word to the duke's yacht in Brighton to watch out for them, and if any of those Ives boys show up, tell him to ride to the next westward port."

Christina and Harry exchanged glances. The "Ives boys" were grown men with wives and lives of their own, but if Aunt Stella said they were on the way, who were they to argue? After all, the soldiers in the inn hadn't realized their prey had slept right beneath their noses.

Aunt Stella had.

~

"I do not even know how to put this on," Sinda grumbled from the other side of the cloth draped across the interior of the caravan.

"I'll be happy to help you," Trev said cheerfully, sitting on a trunk and bouncing his boot up and down as he scanned his latest acquisition. The caravan couldn't compare to the *Lass,* of course, but for cruising land instead of sea, it had several advantages. Not that the lady would agree. She might have run off with the Gypsies if he hadn't held on to her.

"No, thank you," she said irritably. She threw back the curtain and stepped out. Her strawberry tresses fell over a drawstring neckline that slipped over one shoulder the instant she moved. The colorful dirndl skirt dragged the ground, and she had to hitch it up to keep from tripping on it.

Trev sat back to admire his handiwork. He wished the skirt were shorter so he could see her toes, but the Gypsy who'd previously worn the clothes had been a tall, imposing woman, not a faerie sprite like his captive.

"I am the wrong color for a Gypsy," she complained, tugging the blouse back in place only to have it slip off the other side.

"But I'm not." Enjoying the sight of fair shoulders and glorious sunset tresses, Trev stood up. His head nearly grazed the roof of the caravan. "My swarthy complexion may as well serve a purpose. Let people think I've kidnapped you for your lovely red hair."

"It's blond," she muttered, pulling the offending locks behind her and hastily braiding them.

"Would you argue that day is night as well? I can see it with my own eyes. It's red."

Sinda stamped her foot and glared. "It's blond. All Malcolms—except Leila—are blond. I *dyed* it. So if red is your fancy, you can forget about me. I'm a plain, boring, washed-out blond."

She stalked past him and out the door. Stunned, Trev stood there a moment longer, readjusting his thinking. She'd lied about her name and position and her knowledge of his cousin. And now even her *hair* was a lie?

Right now, given everything he knew, if she told him two and two were four, he wouldn't believe her.

He ran down the steps after her, fearful this time he'd driven her hard enough to run away. He should have known better. She wore no shoes, and she'd halted not feet from the wagon to nurse a stubbed toe and send him a scathing look.

"The boots were too big," he pointed out. "And your slippers are too elegant. Stay in the wagon and you won't hurt yourself."

"My toes are *cold*. I wanted the fire. What do we do for warmth at night?"

Trev tried not to grin too widely. She wasn't stupid. Her maidenly mind simply hadn't learned to think like his lust-starved one yet. "You can wear my boots at night," he assured her solemnly.

To his amazement, she burst into tears.

"Lucinda, look, I—"

Ignoring his proffered hand, she raced past him and back into the caravan. She slammed the door, and he heard the distinct sound of the bolt sliding home.

Well, he guessed that told him his place in the scheme of things. He didn't enjoy feeling like one of the pirates he'd trapped and captured. Pirates were cruel men who thought that what they wanted was more important than the wants and needs of their more civilized brethren. All he wanted was peace and family.

So how the hell had things got so out of hand?

Eighteen

SINDA ROLLED UP ON THE PALLET TO ALLEVIATE HER CRAMPS and wished she were home with a hot brick. She hadn't thought things could get worse until her flow had started this morning. Now she was not only humiliated and ruined, but in pain. If things deteriorated from here, she'd simply have to kill Trevelyan and hope his grandfather offered a reward for the deed.

She could hear her captor harnessing the horses and whistling. Maybe she would kill him simply to stifle his unrelenting energy. That would teach her to paint laughing scoundrels. From now on, she would paint only dignified gentlemen who would know a lady in distress when they saw one.

No, she wouldn't. She intended never to paint another portrait in her life, especially if they were going to come alive and step out of the canvas like this one had.

The big-wheeled cart rocked into motion as she huddled beneath the blankets. At least the bedding was clean. It had been drying in the sun when Trev had come upon the Gypsy encampment. He must have offered his weight in gold to persuade them to part so easily with the sturdy caravan and its contents.

She should be grateful she didn't have to sit upright on a wagon seat beside him. Just because she liked his mellow baritone and appreciated his acute observations didn't mean she enjoyed his company. How had her cousins arranged to find such agreeable men when all she had come across was a pirate who thought her a silly, snobby liar?

Gradually, the rocking motion of the cart eased her into sleep. To dream...

⌘

Sinda jerked awake when the cart halted. Cold, with an agony in her belly as well as in her head, she was too miserable to weep. She huddled under the covers and willed herself back to sleep, but sleep wouldn't come.

She needed something hot in her stomach, and she needed to find clean rags. Perhaps she could tear up the pink dimity with the red dancing figures that Trevelyan had bought for her. If she were to dress as a Gypsy from now on, she wouldn't be needing a decent gown.

Grumbling bitterly as a means of ignoring her pain, she eased to a sitting position. But as she tried to stand, her bare toes encountered a loose pencil, and she stumbled and had to grab the wall to keep from falling.

Pencil. Her pencils had been in the pocket of the gown she'd removed. Had she made another sketch while she'd been asleep?

The inside of the wagon was too dark to see. Stumbling across unfamiliar territory, she ran her fingers along the wall where she remembered noticing a small opening that must serve as a window or vent. Finding the latch, she drew it open and pushed on the panel.

The sun had almost set. A breeze carried the scent of the sea, and in the distance, she thought she heard the pounding of waves against rocks. Of course, the pirate would take them to the coast. She would be fortunate if he did not haul her to Jamaica or France.

The faint square of light gave very little illumination, but she examined the floor as best she could. The open notebook was white against dark, so she found it before the pencil.

Heart pounding, she carried it to the opening. Trev had a fire going already, but the distance was too great to cast much light upon the pencil lines. The sketch didn't offer as much detail as chalk, but she could discern the outline of a fishing dory. No complicated sails or rigging this time. Just a simple rowboat, a net with a few fish, and a man's hand sorting through the catch. A hand wearing a signet ring.

She wanted to rush out and show the image to Trevelyan and ask if his cousin wore a ring like that, but she had lost her impetuous trust of him. He wouldn't believe that she hadn't done the sketch from memory. It would only convince him that she knew something she did not.

Shivering, she hid the notebook in the pocket of her gown again. It wasn't as if the sketch showed where his cousin might be, if it was the viscount's hand she had drawn.

Could she concentrate on envisioning the setting before she went to sleep? Would she draw the viscount's location then?

≈∞

Trev's mother had never been the fretful type, determined to instill guilt in him for his youthful transgressions. After nearly half a lifetime of plotting revenge against his grandfather, he hadn't developed much of a conscience either.

But when Lady Lucinda descended from the wagon on shaky knees, looking pale as the whitecaps on the water, he experienced a searing jolt of guilty conscience.

Before he'd torn her from the comfort of her home, she'd been as blithe as a daisy. He'd taken joy in her smiles and admired her serenity.

In the course of a few short days, he'd turned the lady into a bitter virago with drawn features and a listless pace. Perhaps the heavens were telling him he didn't deserve a good woman, peace, or family. He'd sowed a life of destruction and now reaped the result.

He had to remind himself that she was only good when it came to lying, mischief making, and plotting intrigue against him. The question was—*why*?

He hurriedly set a low stool before the fire and offered her a tin mug of coffee. She accepted both gratefully, warming her palms against the hot metal and sipping slowly.

"Where are we?" she finally asked.

"On the coast road. I'm hoping the *Lass* will wait in Brighton for me. They should have heard the rumors of my escape by now."

"I don't suppose you'll leave me there for my family to find."

He ought to, he supposed. But the memory of her portrait of Laurence was too strong. She was lying to him for a reason. He couldn't afford to let her go.

"I can leave word for your family that you're well and safe," he conceded. "But you're the only link I have to Laurence. Until you admit—"

"I cannot admit what I do not know. I draw what is in my head. How it gets there is inexplicable even to me. You will be sorry to make an enemy of my family. It is far better to work with them than against them." Her claim held no anger or challenge, just sadness.

"I am already sorry to make enemies of them, but you leave me no choice." He handed her a plate of fried bacon and eggs.

She looked at the food as if it were fried ants and toads. "Do you have a bit of toast? I'm not hungry."

"You wish to starve to death so I might have that sin on my hands as well?" He whacked a thick slab of bread from the loaf he'd bought with the other provisions from the Gypsies.

"I don't wish to starve. I'm just not feeling well, and hot grease won't ease me. A little porridge might be nice, but toast is fine."

"You don't feel well? Are you ill?" he asked in alarm. "Should I find a physician?"

She slanted him an indecipherable look. "It's nothing a physician can fix. I'll be fine in a few days, although I don't suppose the Gypsies sold you old linens while you were buying out their camp, did they?"

He'd spent the better part of his adult life around men, but he wasn't entirely ignorant of women. Just a little slow. Chewing his bacon, he added up her outburst of tears, her unusual anger, her lack of appetite, and eventually reached the appropriate conclusion. *Damn.*

"I'm sorry. I wish the hell this all hadn't happened." Leaping up, he hoisted himself into the caravan by brute strength rather than take the stairs.

Sinda contemplated walking off into the night, but she hadn't the energy. Or the foolishness. The dark was filled with dangers she had no weapons to combat. Whatever she might think of Trevelyan, he had not offered physical harm. She'd prefer to live long enough to have her family nail him to a wall.

She was just starting to wonder if he was some kind of sorcerer who had cast a spell to prevent her mother from finding her when he emerged from the wagon again, his hands full of white linen strips.

She hadn't realized how much her lack of basic hygiene had bothered her until she was swamped with relief at this precious gift. "Thank you," she murmured in true gratitude as she took his offering. "Where did you—"

But examining a scrap of rare lace still dangling on one corner, she knew. "Your shirt! And jabot. You shouldn't have, Trevelyan. You'll need them to look like a gentleman if we ever—" Another realization had her stumbling to a halt. He no longer had the means to bind her wrists. She didn't know what to make of that.

He waved her concern aside. "I have the Gypsy's shirt." He lifted his arms and flaunted the black satin that clung like a second skin to his broad shoulders and wide chest. "It suits me well, don't you think?"

It suited him much too well. With his long black hair, swarthy complexion, and tight black breeches, he looked like the King of Gypsies. She ought to be frightened, but he'd just handed her her heart's desire without word of the cost to him. Despite appearances, the gentleman had some modicum of decency.

"You need a gold earring to complete the look," she suggested.

"You think so?" He tugged his earlobe and flashed a white smile against the evening gloom. "Perhaps I'll become a land pirate. I think I'm suited to it."

"I think experience has taught you how to do it. That does not mean you're suited to a pirate life." Or perhaps she was remembering the portrait and not seeing the man. She was too tired and confused to know.

His grin disappeared, and he returned to his seat by the fire. "I don't seem destined to have a home, so I might as well enjoy the life I've been given."

He was a large man, dressed all in black and looking like every villain she had ever imagined. And she was silly enough to see a lonely man looking for a home. Perhaps she'd better eat her eggs. She was obviously light-headed.

"You could have hired lawyers instead of escaping prison and kidnapping me," she pointed out. "That is what a normal, civilized gentleman would have done."

He shrugged. "I've done things my own way for too long to conform easily to society's methods. I hired lawyers in London and all they've done is take my money. I thought I wanted to be a gentleman, but if that means rotting in jail while my grandfather cackles, then I was wrong."

"You could have escaped prison and left me," she insisted. "You are behaving rashly."

Stubbornness set his jaw. "You know something. You are the only hope I have of solving my problem. I did not murder my cousin."

"I don't believe you did. And I don't believe a court of law would accept my painting as evidence. You have but to present your argument to a judge, and you would be free."

"No, I wouldn't." He flung his empty dishes into the frying pan. "My grandfather is terrified I have come seeking revenge. He'd use his authority to see to it that I rotted in prison until I was mad, then he'd have me brought before a hanging judge. At very best, he would trump up enough charges to have me transported. In his mind, the embar-rassment of my mixed blood makes me no fit company for decent Englishmen, so he would feel no guilt at all. He tried to be rid of me when I was a harmless child. He knows I'm no longer harmless."

"You were never harmless," she said dryly, adding her dishes to his, trying to imagine this man as a frightened boy and failing. "Now that he is ill, he must see that he has no other heir. Perhaps he would overcome his objection to your mother's heritage. At least you aren't French."

"Oh, I'm quite possibly French as well as Spanish and perhaps even African. It's a different world over there. A man or woman is judged by what they make of themselves, not by their origins." He shrugged. "Although in these last years since the British have occupied many of the islands, they have tried to create the same prejudices as here."

Oddly enough, she wasn't horrified by his admission. If his mother's mixed blood had made him into this bold, passionate man, she was more fascinated than appalled. "I still think your grandfather acted out of anger at your father's rebellion and expressed that anger upon you. He might have learned to regret his hastiness if it had not been for my wretched painting."

"If he regretted anything, he would not have believed me capable of murdering my cousin. It's an old fight, and I'm tired of it. If I could just find Laurence and return him to his home, I'd happily sail away and leave the earl this wretched island." He rose to carry the dirty dishes to a nearby stream.

"How do you propose to find your cousin when he's probably dead?"

Trevelyan clattered the tin plates angrily. "I will sail up and down the coast and terrorize the populace until someone tells me what I want to know."

Sinda thought he was quite capable of carrying out that threat, but his soul would shrink to the size of a nutshell if he did.

Knowing she ought to help him with the dishes, feeling too achy to try, she climbed into the wagon and curled up on the pallet, not caring where the pirate would sleep.

Trevelyan entered sometime later and quietly slipped a hot rock swathed in rags between the covers.

She moaned in gratitude and, wrapping around the warmth, fell asleep.

Not wanting to disturb her and no longer possessing a soft binding for her wrists, Trev sprawled on a blanket in front of the door and kept his sword near at hand. The next day would be long and difficult, and he needed more sleep than he'd had the night before.

Grappling with the dilemma of what to do with the lady, he drifted into slumber.

He didn't know what woke him or how long he'd slept. He simply turned over and knew Lucy wasn't in bed. She hadn't left the wagon. He could hear her moving about. Cautiously, he lay still while his eyes adjusted to the dark.

A square of night sky appeared in the narrow aperture high on the caravan's wall. Pale moonlight formed a puddle on the floor. A shadow rustled in the clothing hanging from hooks on the wall. Was she dressing?

She would have to climb over him to escape. He wanted to see what she was up to. He wanted to understand why a beautiful, high-born lady with the world at her feet would create this hell he'd plunged into. It made no logical sense. He thought he'd heard regret in her voice when she'd spoken of the painting earlier. Or was that wishful thinking?

Instead of dressing, she carried something to the puddle of moonlight and sat down.

Relaxing now that he could see her, Trev stretched out to watch. She hadn't changed from her Gypsy clothes, but she didn't seem aware of the blouse falling down her arm. Instead, she seemed intent on what was apparently a drawing pad in her lap.

He'd seen her scribble on the paper these past days. As he'd observed before, she was amazingly talented. In a few swift strokes, she could capture the twists of a strikingly shaped tree or the feeling of wind in the clouds.

What the devil could she be sketching in the middle of the night? Was she creating messages for her family that she was hiding under rocks, unbeknownst to him? Was that why she was so confident they would find her?

Torn by curiosity, he waited patiently as she worked over the sketches. He couldn't imagine there was enough light for her to see what she was doing. Her own shadow covered the notebook, but she didn't seem to notice. In the darkness, he couldn't discern her expression. He could only sense her hand moving surely across the page.

Her teeth were chattering by the time she'd tucked the pad

back into her clothing. The night was cool, but not so chilly that she should be freezing. Trev watched as she returned to the pallet and wrapped up. He was eager to find her sketch once she slept.

She rolled restlessly in the blankets for a while longer, her teeth still chattering. He didn't know how late it was, but he couldn't bear for her to become ill in his care. He rose and threw his own blanket over her. She snuggled deeper into the warmth, but she still seemed to be trembling. She didn't acknowledge his presence.

Frowning, he slipped outside and tested the rocks of the fire. There was still some warmth in them. He carried in one of the larger ones to place at her toes. She was rubbing her head as if it hurt, but he thought she relaxed as she stretched her feet to feel the heat.

He wanted to climb in beside her to keep her warm as he had the night before, but he didn't trust himself. She looked too frail lying there bundled in blankets, and he remembered her pain of earlier. She wouldn't welcome him.

She settled down more readily than she had last time. Perhaps binding her hands had caused her unrest.

Perhaps not being able to sketch had caused it.

Unable to resist his curiosity any longer, Trev slipped to the taffeta gown hanging on the wall and rummaged to find the deep pocket she kept her treasures in. Her Gypsy skirt didn't have a slit where she could tie a pocket. He would have to fashion something for her.

He carried the notebook to the moonlit vent, but he couldn't discern what she'd drawn. How could she have seen what she was doing?

Amazed, he carried the paper outside and started a small fire. Once he had it blazing, he positioned the page so the light fell upon it.

He continued staring long after his eyes absorbed every line and his brain translated what he saw. He just couldn't accept it. Perhaps he was dreaming.

In a few astoundingly accurate strokes, she'd created a sketch of Laurence's expression as he gazed off into a distance that did not fit onto her notebook. Trev could see the laugh wrinkles of his cousin's eyes, the moles beneath what appeared to be a scarf around his head—and the deep, abiding sorrow in his eyes.

Trev wanted to weep. With a few pencil strokes, she'd brought him to tears. The woman was a witch. Not the kind who made potions and magic spells, but a witch just the same. No wonder rumors flew about her family. No one had the right to be so talented.

Or strange. *How* had she done this? Laurence hadn't stood there in the caravan, posing for her sketch. It wasn't even a pose. It was as if she'd captured a real life moment and transferred it to paper. In the dark. In her sleep.

Before the fire died, Trev started at the beginning and turned the pages of the pad to examine her other drawings.

Trees, birds, houses—all the normal things he'd seen her draw. Here was the sketch of Laurence she'd showed him earlier. He hadn't believed that one, had fastened on the rigging instead of the marvel of the subject.

He reached the page before the last and the signet ring leaped out at him. The design on the ring would mean nothing to anyone—except Trev.

The insignia showed a stylized tree of life—the family crest of Trev's non-English mother. Trev had sent the ring to Laurence for his twenty-first birthday because the earl had been in a snit and denied Laurence the Rochester signet to mark his coming of age.

When had Lady Lucinda seen Laurence's ring?

Nineteen

SINDA WOKE THE NEXT MORNING FEELING COLD AND TIRED and resigned. It was as if she'd given up on something vital and become a numb automaton. She didn't like the sensation at all.

Dazed, she sat up and held her swirling head. Uneasily, she glanced around, but she had no easel here, no chalks, no canvas. Her gaze drifted to her gown containing her notebook, but she resisted looking.

Trevelyan hadn't bound her hands last night. She might have done anything. She didn't want to know what she had done. She was beginning to think she didn't know herself at all, and she hated feeling lost.

Her tormentor wasn't here, for which she was grateful. He'd left a bowl of water that was still warm, and she performed hasty ablutions. There was no mirror or brush, just a simple comb. She dragged it through her hair as best she could, then sought her shoes. No more going barefoot for her, no matter how inappropriate the high-heeled satin.

Since she had no intention of asking Trevelyan to carry out a chamber pot even if there was one, which there didn't seem to be, she hurried out into the cool dawn to the shrub near the creek she'd found last night.

Trevelyan was sitting beside the fire, sipping coffee, but she succeeded in ignoring him long enough to do what she had to do. By the time she was done, she was feeling a little more herself. She sat on the stool beside the fire and accepted the coffee he handed to her.

He seemed to be regarding her strangely, but she needed the heat of the coffee before she could summon the strength to care.

"How are you feeling this morning?" he asked politely.

"Cold. Stiff. Annoyed," she answered curtly.

"Tired?" he suggested.

Exhausted beyond words. She had her answer, but she wasn't ready to discuss it. She shrugged in reply.

"You said you drew your picture of Laurence and his ship from memory." He chose his words carefully.

"No. I said I drew what was in my head." She reached for the bacon he'd set aside to cool. She had a feeling she would need the nourishment.

"I caught fish. It will be ready soon." He indicated the golden fillets bubbling in the pan. "Do you always see pictures of my cousin in your head?"

The fish looked delicious. The topic was more dangerous. From beneath her eyelashes, Sinda studied Trevelyan's expression. She could see nothing on his face, not even curiosity. Sitting on a large rock, he wore his black satin shirt and draped his arms over the knees of his tight doeskin breeches and knee-high boots. With his hair recently washed and pulled tight and his sword at his side, he looked the part of ruthless pirate as he reached for his coffee.

"No. I never see your cousin in my head." She crunched the bacon noisily. She wouldn't even contemplate hoping he would understand. If she couldn't, how could he?

He nodded and sipped from his tin mug. "You just wake up, and the sketch is there?"

"Exactly." He must have seen her sleepdraw. She wondered what she'd done this time, but the heaviness of the problem weighed her down, and she didn't ask.

"So you see Lawrence in your sleep?"

"Apparently." She cut a slice off last night's bread and placed it on a stick to toast over the fire as she'd seen him do.

"I sent him that ring," he said, apropos of nothing.

"If someone saw it, could they identify him?" she asked, trying to sound unconcerned. He'd seen her notebook then, seen her other drawings. Anxiety gnawed at her. What had she drawn last night?

"Only if they knew Lawrence and recognized it. It's not an English seal. In the sketch you drew last night, he looked lost."

He handed over the page he'd apparently been staring at all night. Sinda took it and recognized the expression on the face of the man in the drawing.

"He's given up." She wasn't certain how she knew. It had something to do with how she'd felt this morning. Numb. Lost. Hopeless.

"Do you think that's how he felt last night?"

She shrugged and traced her finger over a cloud in the picture. "Last night, last month, next year. I have no way of knowing, although mostly, people see predictions of the future in my work. I tried to quit painting portraits to avoid the scandal they cause." She supposed that was why her mind took over in her sleep.

"He seems to be wearing a heavy sweater. That could indicate it's not summer."

"Or that he's in Scotland." She flipped the page back to the ring, relieved that Trev was attempting to approach the problem sensibly. She pointed out a small detail. "Are the fish in this net of any significance?"

"I'm not a fisherman by trade," he replied with a shrug, "and it's been years since I fished in England. I could ask some friends in Brighton. We need to move on."

She nodded and accepted the plate of poached fillets he offered. He'd given her heated stones and remembered her inability to eat grease. He'd ruined his best shirt for her. She doubted if any of that offset kidnapping, but if he could believe in her sketches…

She didn't dare hope. It was asking too much. Even she didn't fully believe they meant anything. She simply wanted him to understand that the sketches were unintentional. She nibbled the fish and let the delicate flavor occupy her.

"There's honey for the bread." He offered the pot sitting at his feet.

She accepted the sweet on her toast. Some of the numbness from last night must still be with her, because she couldn't hate Trev this morning. He looked as ragged around the edges as she felt. The angular lines of his face seemed to have grown deeper crevasses overnight. His eyes looked haunted and full of regret.

"I'm a Malcolm," she tried to explain. "My younger sister Belinda talks to animals. My cousin Ninian reads emotions. Simple things, really. My cousin Christina talks to ghosts."

"And your mother?" He rubbed at the wrinkle on his forehead.

"She knows where people are."

"Then why isn't she here?"

"It isn't a precise science any more than my sketches are. That is the problem with our gifts. We know more than we should, but interpreting what we know is up to the observer. Had you not recognized your cousin, I would never have known my sketches meant anything. My mother probably knows our direction, might even know what road we took. She can't know how we're dressed, and she's not a witch. She can't fly. She has to follow us like any ordinary person."

He nodded, deep in thought. "I had a first mate once who knew our direction without need of the stars. And a cabin boy who knew when whales would blow before we saw them. The world is full of mysteries."

"My cousin Ninian says they are instincts that most of mankind has buried too deeply to rely on. It's hard to trust instinct when common sense says they're impossible and unreliable."

"Your drawings are more than instinct." He still used no emphasis, as if he merely spoke his thoughts aloud.

"Yes. Malcolms…" She hesitated, uncertain how to phrase what Christina had told her. "Our instincts are apparently extraordinarily sensitive to…" She gestured helplessly. "I cannot explain clearly. I drew the first portrait of your cousin the night you came to my cottage."

That brought his head up sharply. Black eyes studied her

with the same focus and intensity as a hawk's. A strand of hair fell over his forehead, somehow humanizing his sculpted features. "I kissed you that night." Warmth returned to his voice.

She tore her gaze away from him and stared at the fire rather than see what was in his eyes at that memory. Or let him see what was in hers. "Yes."

"I didn't kiss you last night." He stalked the perimeter of the concept, exploring the boundaries.

"No." She couldn't, wouldn't explain his effect on her.

"But I was nearby. We're aware of each other."

"That's a polite way of putting it." He didn't tread the next step, thank the goddess, although she suspected he would grasp it quickly enough. If just his kisses and proximity inspired sleep drawings, what would an exploration of their deeper desires lead to?

He darted her an interested glance, then pulled his curiosity back to more polite ground. "That's a dangerous admission. I trust you will not explain it to other men."

"I have no way of knowing if it works with other men or even if it works with you. I'm just making an observation."

He nodded and rose abruptly. "We'd better be going."

Did he believe her? Or was he just humoring her? What would he do now? She had hoped if he believed that she didn't know where his cousin was, he would let her go. Too late, she saw he couldn't possibly let her go if there was some chance her sketches might lead him to the viscount.

For the first time, she allowed herself to wonder if the viscount could be alive—and if she held the clue to finding him.

Helping Trevelyan clean up and pack away their supplies, Sinda rubbed at the aching knowledge she'd tried to deny. The sketches were meaningless to her, but not to Trev. He truly believed his cousin could have survived the yacht acci-dent. He wasn't the kind of foolish man who believed what he wanted to believe and disregarded the rest. He thought there was some chance his cousin lived, and that she could help find him.

If they could find the viscount, Charity and her mother

could stay at the Willows. They could smile again. The unborn babe would have a father.

And the earl couldn't put Trevelyan in prison on trumped-up murder charges.

She glanced at Trevelyan speculatively as he climbed to the driver's seat. She debated climbing up with him or remaining in the back.

He'd admitted he was *aware* of her. In the same way she was *aware* of him. It was more than awareness. They both knew that.

She shivered. She was attracted to a buccaneer who might sail off upon the tide. She ought to run for her life, to save herself the grief of an attraction that could never be acted on.

But if there was any chance her sketches might find the viscount, could she deny him that knowledge?

❧

Trev drew the caravan to a halt in a copse of trees not far from a low-lying bluff near Brighton. In his barbarous youth, he'd visited the seaside village frequently enough to know his way around. In the decades of his absence, the Channel had dug deeper into the coastline. There had once been a cottage not far from this spot, but it had apparently slid into the sea during one of the many storms that battered the coast.

Uselessly admiring the scenery when he was so close to port and possibly his ship was not what he wished to be doing right now.

From this viewpoint, he scanned the sprawling fields around the village for soldiers, but they weren't likely to be parading about like a military troop. They would be in town, shuffling from tavern to tavern, questioning all and sundry. To take the open road into town would be to draw attention to himself.

He'd done it last time, but he didn't think his companion appreciated his daring. He cast a glance to the woman sketching in her notebook. She'd chosen to sit with him after she'd napped following the midday meal. If she'd sleepdrawn, she hadn't shown him the results, and he was reluctant to badger her. She had to be exhausted if she never slept a night through.

She finally noticed that he wasn't moving on, and she put down her pencil. "We're there," she stated without question.

"Near Brighton, yes."

She thought about that a minute. "But you're afraid to take me into town and afraid to leave me alone."

He twisted his lips wryly. "That sums it up nicely."

"Would it help if I promised not to run away?"

"There are too many dangers for a woman alone. It's not safe to leave you here." He stared at the horizon, knowing the sea was just over the next hill. Life had seemed so much simpler when all he had to care for were his ship and his men.

"Gypsies are often tinkers, are they not? Could you drive us into town, pretend to be a tinker, and stop where you wish to ask questions?"

"I could, but it's dangerous. I'm known there. It's difficult to hide this phiz of mine, even when I'm garbed so fashion-ably." He indicated a feather she'd given him that he'd stuck in the ribbon binding his hair.

"Wrap a scarf around your head like your cousin has in the sketch. Your beard hides your scar and looks very Gypsy-like. I will remain in the back. If you're quick, it might work long enough to find out what you wish to know."

"I only need drive close to water to know if the *Lass* is there. Boarding her is the difficulty." He thought about it and decided he had little choice.

Leaping down, he helped her into the back of the caravan, rummaged for a colorful scarf, and hid his hair under it. "The road is rough. It will not make you sick?"

"It's a fine time to ask," she answered tartly, curling into a sitting position on the pallet.

"I know. I'll never be a gentleman. But sometimes there are advantages to being a less civilized man." He pressed a kiss to the top of her head. Her hair smelled of lilacs.

He stepped away quickly and smiled at her wide-eyed shock. "I do appreciate your forbearance, and I will attempt to disentangle you from my troubles as quickly as possible."

He didn't know precisely what he meant by that, but he returned to the horses with a lighter heart. He didn't know when he'd made the decision to believe her, but he had. It was hard not to after watching her performance last night.

She hadn't run away or screamed for soldiers even when he'd treated her rudely. She'd offered wise advice and had come to his aid when it couldn't be expected of her. His lust-muddled mind refused to believe the lady would work with his grandfather.

Flowers and flattery, he remembered. He'd have to provide her with both. There was little enough he could give her in exchange for her aid.

He drove the colorful caravan along a wandering lane rather than the main road. Approaching town, he noted the changes the sea had made to the village he'd once known.

The shacks that had once clung to the seaside were gone, along with half the beach. He'd already learned that the tavern he used to stop at with George and his fishing buddies no longer stood at the lane's end, leaving a crumbling bluff in its place.

He turned the horse uphill to the inn where he'd found George on his last visit. The tall, narrow houses that were crammed into the lane blocked any view of his ship.

He took the back entrance to the stable yard of the Black Lion and parked behind the privy. The wagon's bright paint had been spattered by enough mud and dust to make the conveyance appear derelict should anyone glance at it.

He stuck his head in the door to check on his passenger. "Are you all right?"

Her strawberry tresses gleamed in the weak sunlight from the window. "I am fine. Be quick. I do not want to have to go looking for you."

"Bolt the door. This is not the best of neighborhoods," he warned, oddly warmed by her words. It had been a long time since a woman had cared if he returned safely.

He listened for the bolt before he strode across the stable yard to the back door of the inn. If his grandfather had offered a reward for him, he was taking his life in his hands by appearing in public where he was known.

He shouldn't know anyone in the kitchen. Donning what he hoped was a Gypsy tinker smile, Trev stepped into the steaming kitchen.

A scullery maid stopped her scrubbing to stare. The cook turned, caught the girl staring, and swatted her to return to work. Then she came after the intruder with a wooden spoon. "Out, you thievin' Gypsy! Be gone with ye. I'll not have the likes of ye poisoning my trifle."

Trev made a sweeping bow. Flowers and flattery, he reminded himself. Probably worked on womanhood of all walks of life. He produced a yellow bud he'd stolen from the yard and flashed his teeth. "I see a lady of your great skill does not need the services of a lowly tinker. There is nary a pot that does not gleam with polish!"

That was a great lie. The pots he could see were blackened, covered with grease, and stacked haphazardly on every available surface. When the cook only sniffed suspiciously at his offering, he lay the flower on the dirty table and lifted an old pie pan beside it. "But I could mend the hole in this if my lady wishes. And for each repair a customer pays for, I will mend a pot of yours for free if you will but let me speak my services to your guests."

"What would the guests be needin' with a tinker?" she demanded, although the idea of free pot mending had obviously caught her interest.

"I can mend watch chains, shoe a horse, fix a bridle," he asserted. "I've a lady whose hand I would win if I can earn enough to buy her a gold ring. Would you not help the course of true love?" Trev thought he might be entirely too good at this when the stout cook actually looked at him approvingly.

"There's none out there but the infirm and useless. You should sell your services to the wealthy. But you're welcome to try—for the price of mending that pan." She crossed her doughy arms triumphantly.

He contemplated whacking her over her dirty cap with the pan and striding past into the inn, but he smiled ingratiatingly instead. "Of course, my fair lady. Let me just find my tools."

Instead of going out the back door, he strode briskly

through the kitchen and into the corridor leading to the front of the inn. The cook screamed blasphemies after him, but he wasn't much concerned. He simply wanted to avoid soldiers.

He peered into the lobby before entering. No redcoats graced the benches. Neither did anyone else. He could hear voices coming from the tavern in back where smoke rolled out in choking clouds. It wasn't quite sunset, so the fishing boats wouldn't have come in yet. But the old men would be gathering to wait for them.

He eased down the secondary hallway and nonchalantly leaned against the wall, glad for his dark clothes. Few were likely to notice him hovering in the shadows.

He adjusted his hearing to detect the closest voices and listened for a familiar one.

"Aye, the earl's even sent the lobsterbacks aboard the *Lass* to wait for him. Ye'd think we be in France, for a free man to be treated such!"

Trev recognized the voice as that of Caleb, and his heart sank.

His grandfather had stationed soldiers aboard his ship.

Twenty

TREVELYAN STRODE FROM THE INN AND SKIDDED TO A HALT with a frown of disapproval. Sinda glanced up from her sketching, then handed her drawing to the young girl waiting for it. The maid gaped in awe and exchanged a hair ribbon for the hasty caricature. Sinda told herself a caricature wasn't the same thing as a portrait, and the result had seemed safe enough.

The maid glanced at Trev, giggled, then putting her head down, ran back in the direction of the inn, holding the sketch to her meager bosom as if it were the crown jewels.

"You shouldn't be out here." He went to the horse's head and began dismantling the harness.

"I had to use the privy and the maid saw me. I thought offering to trade a sketch for a ribbon was very Gypsy-like." She raised her eyebrows at his activity but refused to question. He did not appear to be happy with whatever he had learned inside.

"You will have every maid in the place out here with ribbons. And the men will follow. Before I know it, they'll want you to dance for them. I think I've attracted enough trouble as myself without creating it under another guise. I have a room for the night. Let's hurry to it before anyone else finds you."

"I thought you bought the caravan so we wouldn't have to stay in inns," she protested, climbing down from the seat without his aid. She'd hated being left out here alone, wondering what was happening inside.

"The *Lass* is in port, but there are soldiers aboard her. I have to find a way to join my men and pry the soldiers off. You may as well have a decent bed to sleep in while I do."

He wasn't looking at her. Instead, he leaped into the caravan and came back out with his sword strapped to his side.

She cringed at understanding that he anticipated combat. "We are not far from Sommersville. You could take me there," she suggested, hoping to save him from himself.

Leading the horse toward the stable, Trev snorted in an ungentlemanly fashion. "And I could leave you here to find your own way back without risking my neck. Don't think I haven't considered it."

She could see no way that this episode could end happily. The soldiers or her family would find them, and there would be the devil to pay. Perhaps if she slipped off and found some means back to Sommersville on her own, the explosion wouldn't be too loud.

Except nothing had really changed since she'd run off to help Trevelyan. She was still responsible for the painting and the murder charge. And now she knew she might hold the key to the viscount's whereabouts. How could she desert Trev knowing that?

"What will you do now?" she finally broke down and asked. It wasn't like him to be surly.

"The only soldiers in town are on my ship, so the inn is safe enough for us. Some of my crew are here. We'll work something out." He left the horse with a stable hand, who stared at Sinda and Trevelyan as if they were a puppet show stepped from the stage.

"It would be better if you were not seen with me," she murmured.

He shrugged and led her through a side door and up the back stairs. "There are no other guests. No one will see you. Even the soldiers grew bored with the tavern. The town is dying. Or dead. Half of it has fallen into the sea."

"Christina tells me that's changing." She gazed at the room he brought her to, a private room with a decent-sized bed and a window overlooking the street below and the sea beyond. No fire burned in the grate, but it was still a warm day, despite the breeze off the water. "Some physician wrote a book a few years ago about sea-bathing restoring health, and it's all the rage to come here and try the waters. I believe that's a hotel going up near the beach."

He snorted in disbelief. "The water stinks of dead fish and sewage. They may as well bathe in the gutters of London. I'll fetch our clothes."

She wandered about the room, picking things up and putting them down again. She supposed it would be nice to sleep on a mattress instead of a pallet, to have a chamber pot again, and a maid and a bath. But oddly enough, she rather missed the intimacy of their private copse and the caravan with no one else about. Not that she had showed Trevelyan that she preferred his company to that of others. That would be foolish and dangerous.

She'd never been quite so unsettled inside herself before. She'd always been content to do as her sisters or parents wished and spend the rest of her time drawing and painting. Now that she had none about to tell her what she should do, she was adrift.

She ought to run away. She really ought. Trevelyan was leaving her openings to do so. Perhaps he secretly wished her gone.

But she had something he very much wanted—her drawings.

He must be as torn about what to do as she. She had no real reason to trust him or to help him. So why was she lingering?

He knocked briefly and opened the door without waiting for her to call out. He'd removed his scarf and donned his long blue vest and coat over the black satin shirt—open necked, with no neckcloth. The effect was distinctive, and she had to drag her gaze away from him. His scabbard protruded through the vent in his long coat.

"I don't know if this is what you need, but I bought you something." He held out a brown paper-wrapped parcel. It was too large and stiff to be clothing.

"For me?" she asked, startled.

"In apology, for tying you up. You had nightmares those nights, didn't you?"

She flushed at his knowing how she had slept. It was highly improper. Everything they did was highly improper. She accepted the package and tore it open. "A sketch pad!" She tore the paper faster and a box dropped at her feet. "Chalks! Oh, bless you." Resisting running up and hugging him, she sat down on the floor to open the chalk box and to stare in delight at the bright new colors. Her fingers already itched to apply them.

"I hope they are what you need. The mercantile had only just ordered them at the request of a lady taking sea baths for her health. It seems your cousin is correct about the folly of Londoners." If he had hoped for hugs, he hid his disappointment well. His voice sounded quite pleased with her reaction.

"Duchesses seem to know these things," she murmured, half to herself as she toyed with a brilliant aquamarine and wished she could take an easel to the beach.

"Duchess? I thought she was your cousin."

"Christina *is* my cousin. Cousins are allowed to marry dukes. You'd like Harry. He tried to steer your grandfather's men away from you." She looked up. "We could go to Harry. He would help."

Trev shook his dark head firmly. "I will not involve anyone else in my fight with my grandfather. It is not your family's place to do so."

"Probably not, but that's never stopped them before." Heedless of her Gypsy skirt, she leaned over and brushed the aquamarine across the sketch paper. Excellent quality. Ideas bloomed.

"Your family hasn't arrived," he said carefully, as if breaking bad news. "Caleb is below, keeping an eye out, and he's seen no one."

She barely heard him. A crab had taken shape on the sand, and she needed the right shade of peach to reflect his shadow. And gray, for the rocks. She had only been to Brighton shore once, but the picture was firmly wedged in her mind.

"I'll leave you to it, shall I?" Amusement tinged his voice. She didn't hear the door close after him.

∽

"When does the tide turn in the morn?" Trev demanded of his first mate.

Having left the lady happily entertaining herself, he felt safe in seeking out his crew. He prayed she wouldn't run, but he no longer wished to hold her captive. The desire to protect the lady and his need to save his cousin tore him right down the middle.

"If we send a messenger to say I've been seen leaving town," he continued, "will the soldiers follow me? I don't want to hurt anyone if it can be avoided. These fellows are as much victim of the earl as I am."

Caleb looked mulish. "They act as if they own the *Lass*, demanding victuals we ain't got and pokin' fun at the way we talk. I'd as soon heave them over the side and be gone."

Caleb was a good sailor, but he was young. Trev rubbed his brow. "I don't want to sail with them aboard. Go back tonight and act suspicious. Whisper to the crew, make preparations to set sail, get the soldiers worried. Come morning, I'll have someone set up a hue and cry on shore. You'll have a boat prepared to row in. Argue with the soldiers if they say they want to row in with you, but let them have their way. Do you understand?"

He did. Trev could see it in the way Caleb's blue eyes lit like the sun on the sea. The scheme was tricky. He could envision a half dozen ways it could go wrong, but he saw no other choice. He had to take sail or be captured.

He had no intention of turning to Lucy's aristocratic family in hopes of aid. They would chew him up faster than an angry jaguar. He could scarcely blame them.

He'd had a meal sent up to the room and hoped Lucy remembered to eat it. He had to make some decision tonight about whether to take her with him or not. He longed to. Her sketches could lead him to Laurence faster than questioning every smuggler along the coast.

But she was a maiden. There might be some chance her family could hide what she'd been doing these last nights. He'd left her untouched. He didn't know how much longer he could do so. She might not understand what drew them together, but he would end up teaching her if they stayed in this close proximity.

He ought to be noble and let her go.

At the thought, his spirits fell through the floor.

Trying not to think why that might be, he finished his ale and sent Caleb off to carry out his orders. If he was really lucky, Lucy would be in bed, and he would only have to get through one more night. In the morning, he'd assign someone to see her home.

The inn was dark and empty as he strode up the stairs. He could get a good night's sleep without fear of soldiers banging on his door by sunup.

Perhaps Lucy could ask her duke to look after Laurence's estate. He could send a purse back with her to keep Melinda in comfort for a while longer. That would be a worthy end to this escapade. Not the one he wanted, of a certainty, but he was trying to shed his uncivilized veneer and act as a noble English gentleman.

He unlocked the chamber door and let himself into the unlit room. No fire was set in the grate, and he bit back a nasty taste of fear. Lighting a candle, he held it high.

Lucy had fallen asleep on the bed, fully clothed. Gazing about, he smiled at the sheets of chalk-covered paper that littered the floor. She'd apparently meant to lie down for only a minute before finishing one of these.

He examined each sketch carefully, looking for some hint of Laurence in them, but she had only filled the pages with seaside scenes. There were several places where she'd begun to draw something and scribbled it out. In this dim light, he couldn't discern what was beneath her hasty crosshatching.

He gathered up the papers and stacked them on the table beside her barely touched food. She hadn't unlocked the door to let in the maid to pick up the tray or light the fire. His lovely artist might starve to death without a keeper.

That thought depressed him. She wasn't his. He had no right to see that she ate or slept properly. That belonged to her family. They had taken far better care of her over the years than he had these last few days.

Removing his vest and jacket, unstrapping his sword, he tried not to look at the vulnerable form curled upon the bed. He started a small fire in the grate to take the chill off the room. Then he pulled the blanket around her as best as he could. He contemplated removing her shoes, but the ribbons on her slippered ankles tempted him too much. He envisioned holding her delicate feet in his big hand, and the image nearly crippled him with longing.

He set a comfortable upholstered chair near the fire, moved a wooden one to the right distance to prop up his long legs, and used his coat as a blanket. One more night of this, he told himself. One more night of hard chairs and floors, and he could be in his bunk on the *Lass*. Alone.

He wouldn't think like that. That's how he'd got himself into this mess in the first place, believing it would be better to be with family than to be alone. He had to remember that family was the reason he'd nearly died beneath the hatches of an English man-o'-war.

A woman's cry ripped him from a sound sleep some hours later. Nearly bashing his head on the fireplace as he leaped from the chair in search of his sword, Trev caught himself on the mantel when the cry faded. He wrapped his fingers around the sword hilt and scanned the chamber.

The fire had gone out. Only the dim light of the moon illuminated the room. Anxiously, he searched the bed, but the slender form he'd left there had disappeared. If he thought it was possible for a heart to physically leap from a chest, his performed that feat as he searched the shadows and found nothing. Had he dreamed her cry?

In relief, he released the sword upon discovering Lucy at the table with the sketch pad.

She'd found the chalks and leaned over the table, sketching furiously, with strokes that covered the large surface of the paper. She plucked chalks from the box just as if she could see their colors. He was eager to see the result, but remembering how he'd found her on prior nights, he debated the wisdom of letting her continue.

She didn't seem to be shivering this time. She wasn't crying. Perhaps letting her work was safest. Tying her up had certainly been a bad idea in retrospect. He still hated himself for having done so.

He stirred the embers in the grate to warm the room. She'd discarded the blankets. No wonder she woke up shivering. Her Gypsy skirts weren't much warmer than a nightshift. He wanted to fling a blanket around her shoulders but he'd been told waking a sleepwalker was dangerous.

She was shivering by the time she laid down the chalks an hour or so later. Trev caught the chair and pulled it out of her way, fearing she might trip over it. She swayed and put a hand to her head, and he swallowed hard, not knowing if he should reach for her. He longed to so badly he figured it was his own desire driving his urge and not her need. She made her way back to the bed on her own without any trouble.

He craved a glimpse of the sketch, but he crossed the room first, pulling the covers securely over her so she didn't catch any more of a chill than she already had. She lay as one dead, not noticing. Her braid had come partially undone, and wisps curled about her face and across the pillow. He wondered about their real color and wanted to brush them off her cheeks but bit back the urge. She wasn't his to hold, he reminded himself fiercely. She was fine. She was sleeping.

He turned away from the bed, lit a candle at the fire, and raised it over the sketch.

Laurence sat on the stone stoop of a very small cottage crammed in among a dozen cottages just like it. A bedraggled Michaelmas daisy bloomed in a clay pot beside the stoop. He wore a knit cap over his head, as if the wind was chilly. Trev couldn't tell, but it looked as if he had a scab or scar peeking out from beneath the cap's edge. His cousin seemed to be bent over an object in his lap, examining it intently.

Trev leaned closer, trying to discern the shadowed items just beyond the artist's eye. He thought the largest might be a leather purse. And the bit shining between his cousin's fingers might be a gold piece. From the look of determination on Laurence's face, Trev thought he may have decided on some course of action. That look was far better than the earlier one of despair.

His cousin appeared weathered and weary. His clothes were that of any poor fisherman anywhere. But other than that, he seemed hale and hearty. Trev took comfort in that.

The setting was still anonymous, but there was more of it this time. He was glad he'd purchased the largest pad of paper he could find. Someone might identify the lane of stone houses and the wall in the background. He had the vague recollection that Michaelmas daisies only bloomed in fall. Did that mean this scene had taken place recently? Or a year from now?

Behind him, Lucy whimpered and the bed clothes rustled.

Dropping the sketch, Trev whipped around. She had wrapped herself in a cocoon of covers and pulled them over her head. Now she seemed to be fighting them, struggling against their binding.

He blew out the candle so as not to disturb her more. Then he crossed the room to untangle her from the blankets.

When he had her head uncovered, she sobbed and buried her face in the pillow. The sound broke his heart. He didn't know for whom she wept or why, but he couldn't bear to hear her sorrow. Should he wake her?

He hated to do that too. Steeling himself, he sat down upon the bed's edge and hauled her into his arms. She shook with the force of her sobs, and he cradled her closer, murmuring senseless words of comfort.

She seemed to settle down at that. Her sobs lessened, but her shivers began again. She moaned and shook until he could no longer resist but lay down against the mattress, wrapped her firmly in blankets, and pulled her into the curve of his body.

Perhaps if she was no more than a mummy in his arms, he could survive this one more night. With her sweet-scented hair against his face, he curled himself around her until she stopped shivering and slept soundly.

He might never sleep again, wondering how she fared after he was gone or how he would survive without the magic of her presence in his life.

Twenty-one

SINDA WOKE TO THE COMFORT OF STRONG ARMS WRAPPED around her and the sound of church bells in the distance. It was Sunday, but she didn't think she'd make it to church today.

The shivering she was accustomed to suffering upon awakening lately had disappeared with a furnace blast of body heat. Even the headache had lessened. On the whole, she felt so *normal* that she wanted to kiss someone.

She didn't know how she could feel normal with a man in her bed, a big heavy man whose arm held her pinned and who smelled mouth-wateringly wonderful. Smiling at her foolishness, she untangled the blanket and turned carefully so as not to wake him.

Trevelyan uttered a soft snore but did not wake as she perused his handsome face. Except to trim the roughness, he still hadn't shaved, and his beard colored his jaw in black bristles. She studied his mouth with interest. She always had difficulty drawing lips, but his were curved and sensuous, not too thick or thin, just right for kissing. She could draw them easily.

She could kiss them even more easily. Without giving it much thought, she leaned over and planted a soft kiss on his temple. When that didn't wake him, she kissed his nose, and then daringly, his tempting mouth.

The dastard was waiting for her. He caught her firmly in his embrace and opened his mouth beneath hers and swept her breath away.

His whiskers scratched, but she didn't notice that after his tongue teased her lips open and his heated breath mixed with hers. At the same time, she became aware of how intimately her breasts were crushed against his brawny chest. She gasped at the thrill, and Trev rolled her over against the mattress to more comfortably plunder where he might.

The delight of his kiss stole away any fear she might suffer from his heavy weight propped over her. She wrapped her fingers around his muscled arms and eagerly accepted his kiss. Returning it with her own, she learned the pleasures of his mouth on hers, experienced the excitement of her blood coursing through her body and pooling deep within her. Her breasts began to ache for his touch, and she arched upward, wordlessly pleading.

Abruptly, Trevelyan shoved away, gasping as he rolled off the bed to escape her. With a groan, he staggered into an upright seated position on the floor and plowed his hands into his hair, propping his elbows on his knees.

"You unman me," he muttered.

Sinda scrunched up her eyes and tried to puzzle that out while the cold air of reason flowed over her, cooling her overheated desires. "I would not call your kiss unmanly."

He snorted. "Nor gentlemanly, but that's not what I mean."

"Then what do you mean?" She felt like weeping. His kiss had felt so right. Why had he stopped? Had she not done it right? Did he not like her as she liked him? More than liked him, though she wasn't ready to admit that. She simply wanted to explore these physical sensations more. She was twenty-two years old and this was the first man she'd ever wanted to kiss.

Trev scrubbed his face with his hands. His expression was a study in dismay and affection that she might try to capture on paper for the rest of her life and never succeed. She wanted to caress his jaw, but she had used up all her boldness for the morning.

He didn't have the same reservations. Leaning toward the bed, he brushed the tickling hairs from her brow and cupped her chin with a touch she thought might be loving. From this hard man, it was nothing short of amazing, and Sinda stared, wishing she could read his mind.

"I cannot remember the last time anyone kissed me awake," he murmured. "I cannot remember a time when someone held me in their arms without expecting coin in return. There, now have I embarrassed you?"

She blushed. She could feel the warmth in her cheeks. She wanted to reach out to him again, but something in the steely look of his eyes prevented it. "You deserve better," she said.

His smile was tender, but he stood up just the same. "I doubt I deserve any more than I get. I'm sending you home this morning. I cannot justify keeping you any longer."

She ought to rejoice, but sadness swept over her. "Where will you go? What will you do?" She sat up and adjusted the Gypsy blouse, keeping the blanket around her.

He lifted one of her papers from the table and carried it to the daylight from the window. "I will look for this town and my cousin." He glanced up from the sketch to her. "Will your family accept your absence or should I go with you and do the proper thing?"

She almost choked as she took his meaning. Her eyebrows must have swept upward because he smiled wryly.

"I know I'm no prize," he said, "but I would not wish you to suffer for my actions. I'm a wealthy man. If my grandfather has his way, you could be left a wealthy widow."

Sinda flung her blankets away and stood up. "*Dolt!* Fool! You are a prize any woman would desire. Do not throw yourself away because of an old man's fear of dying. Besides, you want a peaceful home and all I bring with me is scandal— although the gossip that follows me about might be fitting justice for your depredations. Did you know they call me the *Prophetess* behind my back? I once had lovesick maidens lining up at the door because I drew Cupid hovering over a dancing couple who later married." She snatched the sketch from his hands and studied it, all too aware of her lack of undergarments and the nearness of the big man beside her.

Rather than argue, he pointed out the pot of flowers in the drawing. "These bloom in fall, do they not?"

"They do. But it could be next fall for all I know. I painted you before you arrived. If gossip is to be believed, I usually paint what hasn't yet happened." She wanted to lean back against his broad chest, feel his arms wrap around her, warm herself in his heat, but she resisted. She didn't have the right to ruin his life any further.

She had sketched last night, and she hadn't woken with a raging headache this morning. What did that signify?

"I could not bear it if he's lost for another year. I still hope I'm getting closer." Trev turned away to stir the fire.

"What if I keep drawing him?" she demanded. "How will I let you know what I have seen in the sketches?"

He shrugged. "I will find some way. You will return to London and your life there. Your family will see you have a handsome husband to make you forget these past days. It's what I would do if I were they."

"I like it in Sommersville," she said stubbornly.

"It's not likely they'll let you stay there. I have to catch the tide out this morning. Why don't you wear the pink gown we bought the other day? I've scarcely seen you in it."

"You didn't carry in my petticoats." Frustrated, knowing she shouldn't hold him back, she paced the room. "I'll need to go to the caravan to dress."

"That can be arranged."

She thought he strained to sound amused. "I need a brush. I imagine I look a sight."

"Oh, you look a sight, no doubt." This time, his amusement was real and coupled with admiration. "Let me comb out your hair before we go down."

She sat, and Trev carefully unraveled the braid he'd made yesterday, combing with gentle strokes as he worked. She was amazed that this powerful man could have any interest in acting as her handmaiden, but his strokes were as sensuous as caresses. Her skin prickled in anticipation as he carefully held the hair close to her scalp to ease out a knot. She wanted to relax and enjoy it, only she was too aware that she might never see him again.

She wanted to know more of his touch, not forget it. Or

him. Asking to go with him was a dreadful thing for a lady to do. He would be horrified if she were so bold, and she would be mortified if he refused her.

"Pack your bag and we'll carry that with us," he said after braiding her hair and fastening it with the ribbon she'd earned with her caricature. "I'll gather your sketches."

"What will become of the caravan?" she asked, nervously gathering her things. Her Gypsy clothes were wrinkled beyond redemption from having slept in them, but she couldn't wear the taffeta or the dimity until she had petticoats to hold them off the ground.

"I'll leave the cart with some old friends who live around here. Perhaps I'll come back as a Gypsy some day. Keep an eye on the road for me."

She supposed if that was the life proscribed for her, she could wait for him to return like that. If she thought he would return. The excitement of living alone as a widowed artist palled now that she knew what it was like to share her days with a man like Trevelyan. Now that he grasped what she was, he took her seriously and didn't laugh when she suggested the impossible. There were so many things she would like to talk with him about, so many things she wanted to know.

She would run mad if she thought too hard on it. It wasn't as if these last few days were normal in any way or that she had enjoyed them. He'd tied her to a bed, for pity's sake.

She glanced at the bed where he'd held her and kissed her so thoroughly, and she knew there were worse things than being tied to a bed.

"I'll wait," she said with determination.

She sensed his steady stare but continued packing. She was really not the rebellious sort, she reminded herself. What he was telling her was the proper thing to do. She had no argument against it. She simply wanted to scream and shout and protest for no good reason.

Holding her tongue, minding her anger, she snapped the case shut, straightened her shoulders, and prepared to depart. Forever.

Trev watched her march out the door ahead of him and

held back a sigh of admiration. The top of the lady's head reached past his chin only when she wore heels. She couldn't weigh more than eight stone, soaking wet. Her wrinkled blouse kept sliding off her slender shoulder, and her colorfully striped skirt had wrinkled in the back to reveal the delicate turn of her ankle. And she looked every inch an aristocrat.

He had tasted the hunger on her lips this morning, felt her loving eagerness, and it had nearly broken him. If he could imagine a future with her waking up in his embrace every morning, he'd fight two armies to keep her.

But she needed her family and her home and her art, and he couldn't stay here with a murder charge hanging over his head.

He could sail away and wait until his grandfather keeled over. By then his lawyers ought to have proved his legitimacy. He could ask her to live with him in his cousin's home, but that could be a decade from now, and he didn't think she'd appreciate sharing a home with Melinda.

He had to do this as a proper gentleman would. So he tucked the memory of the first loving embrace he'd known in years into the back of his mind to cherish later. Gently brushing a straying hair from her brow, he kissed her cheek. Before he could let her startled look lead him astray, he escorted her down the back stairs toward the side door and the caravan.

At the sight of the massive man blocking the exit below, Trev nearly dropped the sketch pad he held beneath his arm. The giant uncrossed his ankles, lifted his shoulders from the wall, tucked a whittling knife away in his coat pocket, and straightened to his full towering height as soon as they came into sight.

Trev's hand itched for the sword at his side, but he would have to drop the valise in his hand to grasp it. He stayed in front of Lucinda to shield her.

The giant looked them over, took note of the sword hilt, crossed his arms, and waited.

Stand off. He couldn't strike an unarmed man. Before Trev could decide whether to use his tongue or fist, Lucinda peered around him.

"Aidan! Whatever are you doing here?"

The intruder relaxed his stance a fraction. "I wondered if you'd acknowledge me," he answered frankly. He turned his gaze back to Trev. "Do you deserve my fist down your throat?"

Her family had finally found them. Not knowing whether to feel relief or regret, Trev met bluntness with bluntness. "For kidnapping her, yes. For more than that, no. You have arrived opportunely. I was about to send her home."

The man called Aidan looked properly dubious. "Aye, and that's what they all say when caught. Perhaps I'll be taking you to the duke to have that discussion."

"My father, or Harry?" Lucinda demanded, brushing past Trev to confront her relation. "There isn't time for either. Trevelyan must reach his ship and sail with the tide before the soldiers find him."

She reached for the pad beneath Trev's arm and swept out the sketch she'd done last night. "If you wish to be helpful, you can have everyone search for this place and this man. That's the viscount. We think he's alive."

Without blinking an eye, the big man took the sketch, studied it, then glanced from Lucinda to Trev. "The soldiers landed moments ago. They're on their way up the hill."

Trev cursed under his breath and grabbed Lucy for one last kiss. She wrapped her arms around him as if she wouldn't let go, and he soaked up this memory for savoring later too. Her sweet curves rested against him trustingly. Her fingers dug into his back, and her mouth opened beneath his. He wanted nothing more than to sink into her embrace and never leave again.

The giant cleared his throat, and Trev hastily set her down again. "You're safe with him?" he demanded, indicating the stranger.

"Take me with you," she whispered, ignoring the question. "Please. I can help you find your cousin faster. You can clear your name. Then we'll have time…"

She didn't have to explain. Trev could see the same hope in her eyes as he knew was in his. Even though he wanted to say *yes* more than he wanted anything else in the world, she asked the impossible. He couldn't drag her down with him.

He looked up to her kinsman, not even knowing the man's full name or relationship. "It's too dangerous. I can't do that to her."

Lucy clung defiantly to his coat. "It's my choice. I'm a grown woman, not a child who doesn't know better."

"Her mother spent the night in Sommersville," Aidan contributed. "She'll be here this morning."

"Aidan, please!" She faced the giant. "There must be some way. Those sketches will help us find the viscount. Trev needs me!"

"Lucy, don't be ridiculous," Trev intervened. "I have to go. If I'm quick, I can gain the ship before the soldiers know I've gone."

She turned on him fiercely. "*Sinda*. My family calls me Sinda. Aidan can stop the soldiers. My mother can turn them into frogs. Let us go, now!"

She fled for the door as if wolves were at her heels.

Sinda. He hadn't even known her real name. *Sinda.* Somehow, it seemed singularly more appropriate than simple Lucy.

Not about to let her out of his sight, Trev grabbed her bag and faced the impassive giant waiting with upraised brow. If her family didn't stop her, why the hell should he?

"I don't know what kind of family she has, but tell them…" Trev glanced after *Sinda*'s retreating back. "Tell them whatever the hell you like. I won't let a prize like that go."

Leaving Aidan with the sketch she'd drawn last night, Trevelyan loped down the hall and out the door, chasing the dawn of a new day.

Sinda darted behind the stable and down the alley, straight for the sea as if she knew where she was going. He prayed fervently that was the case, because she'd turned his head around so far and fast that he couldn't see himself coming or going.

Twenty-two

SINDA STOPPED TO CATCH HER BREATH AND PUZZLE OUT THE best way of reaching the ship without being seen. She hid behind the last of a row of crumbling warehouses where there was an abrupt drop-off and the water just below her. She couldn't quite see the main road to the beach but knew it had to be in front of the buildings where the soldiers were.

Not even breathing hard, Trevelyan caught up with her. Carrying both bag and sketch pad, he couldn't reach out and grab her, although from his voice, she wondered if he might like to wring her neck.

"Have you run mad?" he whispered hoarsely, scouring the scene from his greater height. "Your family is right here, ready to welcome you back to their bosom and safety. Return while you still can."

"The soldiers will be at the inn door," she said, easing farther along the brick wall so she could see the road in front. "How do you propose we reach your ship? In that rowboat?"

"You have no idea what it's like to travel by sea." Tucking the pad under the arm holding their bag, he caught her elbow and dragged her toward a path at the edge of the bluff. "One night on board ship, and you'll regret it. It's no place for a lady. I can still leave you below and you can return to your family after the soldiers have gone."

She jerked her arm away and scrambled down the rocky path, holding her Gypsy skirt away from her high-heeled shoes. She'd left her petticoats in the caravan. She regretted that. She regretted naught else. "My family would return me to a society that considers me a freak and reads dire predictions into everything I draw. I ran away from them for a reason."

That shut him up for a minute or two. Or the rocky unevenness of the path claimed his concentration. It certainly claimed hers. Scrambling over rocks hadn't been her intention.

A pebble slid from beneath her toes, and she flailed her arms to claim her balance. With his one free hand, Trev grabbed her waist and hauled her back against him. "Let me go down first so you'll fall on me." He lifted her behind him.

She did feel somewhat safer with his wide shoulders and sure-footed stride in front of her. He made it look easy. She took a deep breath and climbed down more carefully. She hadn't realized how tense and rushed she'd been until he'd accepted her flight. Or at least quit arguing.

She stared in dismay at the drop-off where the path had washed out several feet above the beach. Trev leaped to the rocks below with the sureness of a mountain goat. Would he leave her stranded here?

"You ran away from your family?" he asked, dropping the bag and paper and reaching his arms up for her.

She sighed in relief at his acceptance. If she were to follow him into hell, she supposed they had much to talk about. Since Trev didn't seem to be inclined to talk about himself, she would have to show him how. She shoved off from the edge, trusting him not to drop her.

He caught her by the waist, enveloping her so firmly that she feared she would never breathe again. Just as abruptly, he set her down, grabbed their bag, and hastened toward the rowboat and the man waiting beside it. Now didn't seem the time to answer his question.

"Caleb!" she cried in recognition as the burly sailor came to attention.

He grinned, touched his cap, and turned to his captain in inquiry.

"She can help us," Trev said sharply.

Before Sinda knew what he was about, he swung her into

the rowboat. She was going with him! She hadn't really been sure he would take her. Silent in delight—and terror—she settled where Trev placed her and tried to be unobtrusive. She scanned the shore but didn't see any soldiers racing to halt them.

Trev grabbed the oars and Caleb shoved them off, leaping in at the last minute before a shout rose on the bluff.

"Get down," Trev ordered.

Sinda ducked as far down in the small shell of a boat as she could. Someone threw a canvas over her, and she nearly asphyxiated at the stench of fish rot.

An explosion shattered her eardrums, and she quit breathing until she heard the steady pull of the oars on the water and Trev's curse. The unhealthiness of her hiding place no longer concerned her. For the first time, she recognized the real danger of this adventure.

The soldiers could kill Trevelyan before he even stood before a judge!

The men in the boat didn't seem concerned by the sound of musket fire. They merely exchanged curses and pulled harder, negotiating the tide and currents with expertise. She sensed a change in pace as they approached the waiting ship, and the explosions no longer split the air.

"You can come out now," Trev murmured sympathetically, tugging at the canvas. "They can't see us here."

She looked up at the ship looming over them. They had rowed to the far side, out of sight of land. She gazed in trepidation at the rope ladder dangling above her head. She truly hadn't thought this through at all. Gulping, she turned to Trev, who wasn't smiling.

"Shall I have Caleb row you back?"

"No." She tried to sound sure. "Just tell me how to climb that thing." The overlong Gypsy skirt would be a hindrance. She tugged the back hem between her legs and tucked it into the front of her skirt as she'd seen Christina do for tree climbing.

Once she had her skirt arranged, Trev lifted her up. "Put your feet on the first rung and hang on where you can. I'll be right up after you."

The rope was painfully rough against her palms, and her slick-soled shoes wanted to slide, but she managed to cling to the swaying ladder while Trev swung up behind her.

"Halfway there already," he said cheerfully. "I've got you now. Just hang on where I place you, and you won't fall."

She clenched her teeth to keep them from chattering, told herself this was the adventure she had wanted, and followed his instructions. It didn't help that a man's body pressed against her from top to bottom, reminding her of all that she had invited by this impetuous action.

Callused hands reached over the rail from above to wrap around her elbows, and Trev's strong arm lifted her up from below. In a flurry of loosened skirts, she was hauled on board like so much excess baggage. She didn't have time for embarrassment before Trev climbed up and hugged her triumphantly. Then with a hand at the small of her back, he shoved her into the waiting hands of a boy who couldn't be much older than sixteen.

"Take her below," he ordered. Then turning to his men, he bellowed, "Let her rip, boys!"

A cheer went up, the creak of an anchor winch pierced the ears, canvas rose and slowly filled, and the *Pirate Lass* swung toward open sea.

❧

Trev stayed on deck for as long as he dared, glorying in the feel of wind in his hair and the freedom to sail where he chose. He was at home here, as he had not been on shore. Perhaps it had been a mistake to return to England.

He watched his men scramble to their tasks as Caleb took the helm. They were rough men, but stalwart and loyal. They knew their duties and performed them well. He had sent them on a merchant journey to Holland and back without him. Without a Spanish galleon to chase, he was superfluous. The old feeling of restlessness tumbled back as if he'd never left.

This was the reason he'd pursued new challenges. With a grimace, he reflected on life's perversities. Chasing warships hadn't been enough for him. He had to crawl under the skin of his grandfather for fun and kidnap a duke's daughter for amusement.

And now that he'd let himself think about her, he had to wonder what Lucy—*Sinda*—was doing with herself right now. There was one who found amusement wherever she was. She'd probably littered his cabin with sketches and hadn't noticed his absence—the very opposite of a weeping, clinging vine like Melinda.

Now that his thoughts were thus engaged, he wouldn't be a man if he didn't picture Sinda on his bed and remember the heat of the kisses they'd shared. Had she been a wanton widow, he'd picture far more than that. But she was a damned duke's maiden daughter, and he was a fugitive. His mother had taught him better, even if he liked to forget that when he could.

In a froth of frustration, he threw himself down the companionway, then stomped through the dining cabin to his private quarters in the forecastle. He'd had the ship built to accommodate his height, but he still had to duck to enter.

Holding the latch as he stepped inside, he absorbed the wondrous scene awaiting him.

Sprawled across the royal blue velvet covering his bed, Sinda industriously detailed a bit of her chalk drawing with such intent that she didn't seem to notice his entrance. She'd apparently been kicking her legs. Her Gypsy skirt had hitched up around her stockinged knees. She'd removed her mud-splattered shoes, and he could see her slender ankles and the hole in her stocking heel. Her wavy hair wouldn't remain in the long braid he'd fastened for her, and fine twists of it fell about her cheek and forehead. She scarcely looked fourteen, a child playing with a new toy. He felt like a cradle robber.

Until she put the finishing touches on her drawing and sat up.

Trev's knees nearly gave out from under him, and he swiftly closed the door and leaned against it. Between the impact of her bold, inquiring gaze and the curves of full breasts revealed by the loose shirt, he stiffened into full arousal faster than he ever had as a youth. It was embarrassing for a man his age to lack control.

"Do you have any idea what you do to me when you sit on my bed like that?" he growled. He might as well make her aware of how things stood if she didn't already know.

"No, but I suppose I'll find out. Shall I take a chair?" She slid her legs off the side of the bed, and the skirt rose higher.

Trev took the chair. It was closer to the door. Hot coals burned in the brazier. He assumed she'd bewitched Will, the cabin boy, as well. A kettle bubbled over the heat, but coffee wasn't what he had on his mind. "Are you still running away from your family?" he inquired. That statement had preyed at the back of his mind since she'd made it. "Is this your way of getting even with them for some imagined wrong?"

She looked at him in puzzlement. "Of course not." She tugged her skirt back in place until it covered her toes, but she kicked her feet back and forth, uncovering them again. "I ran away so as not to hurt them." She wrinkled up a nose that had gained a few freckles over these past days. "And because I wanted to be free to draw without everyone looking over my shoulder, wondering what disaster I would portray next."

"And here I am, looking over your shoulder, waiting to see what you'll sketch next." Gloomily, he stretched his legs out and admired his boots rather than look at her.

"Well, I've already hurt you, so that seems only fair."

He couldn't help it. He had to look again. Sinda had her hands on the bed's edge and was leaning forward in an earnest attempt to explain. But his male brain could only register the intriguing valley revealed by the low cut blouse and the knowledge that no corset embellished all that lovely fullness.

"Trevelyan?" She studied him quizzically, then, following his gaze, looked down. With a fast-spreading blush, she abruptly sat up and pulled the blouse back. "Go away and I'll change."

"Not for my benefit," he drawled, crossing his arms and admiring the way the thin cotton pulled taut over tempting curves when she held it tight like that. "You do realize this is not a floating hotel and we must share this cabin?"

She pulled her legs up and sat cross-legged, glaring back at him. "I am not a total lackwit. We have been sharing a room for several nights, if I remember correctly. Do you regret that you will not get much sleep?"

He grinned. "If I did not know you so well, I would believe that was an invitation." He held up his hand in warning. "Don't fling the pillow. Feathers aren't easily come by at sea."

She returned the pillow to the bed, averting her gaze. "If I invited, would you accept?"

Stunned, he sat there without a decent thought in his head for a full minute before he processed the question with something other than his lower parts. "I would be hard pressed to say no," he admitted, "but I would have to, so don't ask, please. You are far too young and unworldly to understand what you offer."

The glance she sent him was full of the same frustration that he felt.

"I understand far more than you think," she answered frostily, "but I would not burden your conscience any more than necessary. Understand this though—I will not be returning to the 'bosom of my family' as you put it. I am trying to come to terms with the fact that my gift is such that I must live alone from henceforth. I am not entirely certain how I will go about it, but my family will support whatever decision I make. Eventually. So think of me in terms of an independent woman and not a marriageable duke's daughter."

He rolled his eyes heavenward. "Oh, certainly. I'll do that. Cad that I am, I always bed independent maidens who leave their families. I've a litter of bastards spread across the islands to prove my prowess. Excuse me, my lady, but I think I have a sailor to flog."

With controlled anger, he slammed the chair aside and strode out.

The instant the door closed, Sinda drooped. She had tried very hard to be brave and look to the future instead of the past. Instead, she had insulted the man who could take her forward.

She supposed she wasn't meant to share her life, however briefly, with a man. She simply did not understand the way their minds worked. She had thought about this quite hard while he was above, setting the ship to sail. She had enjoyed their kisses this morning. She had wanted to release him from any sense of obligation. He had seemed quite interested. What had happened? Did he think he would be saddled for life to a woman who could only bring him embarrassment and pain?

Did she really care what he thought? If she meant to live alone, she didn't need a man in her life anyway. She'd help him find his cousin and return to her art. She would paint every dog and cat on Christina's estate if she liked. And every tree and bush.

She picked up her sketch pad and chalks and, avoiding the bed this time, sat on the floor by the fire. The rolling motion of the ship presented something of a challenge to her drawing, but she'd learn to accommodate it.

Perhaps she ought to draw Trevelyan after all and see if the picture told her of his future.

Fearing to see his fate, she determinedly set about sketching the kitten in her head. Kittens were safe.

Twenty-three

TREV SUPPOSED HE COULD HANG A HAMMOCK AND SLEEP AND eat with his men, but he simply couldn't bear to abandon Sinda all evening. He tried to tell himself that was because she was likely to come looking for him and cause a scene, but he didn't believe his own lies.

The aroma of Cookie's jambalaya permeated the entire ship by nightfall. His cook was showing off. Meals on board would be reduced to salted fish and hardtack soon enough, but in the last weeks of simple English fare, he'd missed his cook's exotic stews. Mouth watering, Trev succumbed to the lure of the woman and food waiting in his cabin.

Entering, he discovered his desk had been converted into a crude easel. Sinda had stacked books to hold the sketch pad upright against the bulwark, but she wasn't working in front of it. He scanned the small cabin. His desk chair had been moved so Sinda could sit with her feet on the brazier with a book in her lap.

A book. He didn't have many books. He glanced at the ones holding up her sketch pad. His ship's journal wasn't among them.

"Did no one ever tell you that journals are private?" He reached for the tankard of ale Will had left on the table and drank deeply.

"Really?" She closed the book and peered around the chair back. "I thought they were meant to be informative. You don't write much in yours though. I can't read these things with all the abbreviations."

Thank Neptune he kept his private thoughts in code.

Trev slammed the tankard back on the table and steeled himself to resist temptation. Sinda chose that moment to rise and tug her blouse back up her shoulder. His head immediately emptied of anything except the desire to pull the damned garment over her head and fling it into the fire. He was in for a long night.

"The abbreviations show the ship's latitude and longitude each day." He tried to concentrate on the conversation. "What made you think journals were for reading?" He remembered his manners long enough to hold out a chair at the table for her.

"My family keeps journals, except mine generally contains sketches instead of writing. We try to keep a record of our discoveries. We once had a library dating back hundreds of years, but it was lost a century or so ago. My cousin Felicity has been tracking it down."

She took the chair and spread out her Gypsy skirt as if it were a silk gown and petticoats. She demurely waited for him to be seated while examining the exotic fare set before them.

His pleasure at introducing her to the foods of his late home in the islands settled some of his restlessness. He scooted his chair up to the table and dished a generous portion of the shellfish and rice onto her plate. "Cookie must have restocked his herbs while the ship was in London. He used to cook for the French governor in Louisiana until there was a misunderstanding involving a woman and a knife and he departed the colonies rather hastily."

Her reaction was one of interest rather than alarm, he noticed. He watched as she speared a bit of fish and chewed it with enjoyment before responding to his provocative statement.

"I trust he has found better means of controlling his anger since you still keep him about. A man with a bad temper and a kitchen full of knives wouldn't last long around here, would he?"

Trev relaxed. She behaved as if all around her was her

own private oyster to explore and that danger didn't exist. Or perhaps she trusted him to make it safe. He liked that notion. "We slammed him over the head with his pots a few times until he learned to give up brandy. He can even make biscuits taste like ambrosia when we've been at sea for weeks. He just needed to control his drinking problem."

"I believe one of my sisters has a posset to be given to those who overindulge. It's said to cure them of ever doing so again." She sampled more of the stew and hummed in pleasure. "This is truly delicious. I've never eaten anything quite like it."

"Living at sea where food must be culled from the surroundings, one learns to create strange combinations. Tomatoes are rather hard come by though. Are you familiar with them?"

She lifted a chunky red piece from the dish. "Ninian uses them in her medicinals, and Dunstan has experimented with them in his greenhouse. I've never tasted ones like this."

"I'm glad you enjoy it." Trev thought all his blood ran south when she licked a bit of sauce from the corner of her mouth with the tip of her pink tongue. She blushed when she caught him staring and properly used her napkin.

If he didn't know better, he'd swear she was provoking him on purpose. She hadn't the experience for seduction, yet her innocent actions boiled his blood and left him in a state not conducive to rational thought.

She was his for the having.

He desperately tried not to think of that. Circumstances had forced them into physical proximity. That did not mean he should take advantage, especially since he did not know what the future held. A man did not bed the daughter of a duke lightly. That was a sure way to lose his head, as well as everything else he hoped to gain.

More important, he didn't think he could bed her without keeping her. He'd recognized that when she'd offered herself it was on a temporary basis, as if she didn't consider him good enough for marriage. Which, given his lack of education and upbringing, he probably wasn't.

Unfortunately, it wasn't his head doing the thinking while

he watched Sinda sip her wine, dab her luscious lips, and smile winningly at his jests. When she laughed, her head fell back to reveal the slender column of her throat and the full thrust of her breasts. The loose blouse continually fell off her shoulder, and he imagined kissing the creamy flesh revealed, pushing the cloth down her arm, and kissing deeper until she surrendered all.

He couldn't stir from his chair if he tried.

She glanced overhead as the anchor winch creaked and the ship leaned slightly to port. "What are they doing now?"

Trev shrugged. "There's a fishing village on a point that looks ripe for smugglers. We're sending in a few men to make inquiries. I wish I hadn't given that sketch to your family. My men might use it to look for similar houses. Who is that Aidan person anyway? I feared he might rip my head off my neck." That thought cooled his ardor somewhat. She had a family more powerful than the earl's and could probably see to it that he disappeared without a trace.

Impatiently, she brushed a strand of hair from her face, finished the last bite on her plate, and reached for her glass. "No one is entirely certain who Aidan is. We seemed to inherit him when my cousins married into the Ives family. Christina swears there is a trace of Malcolm in his aura, but that's impossible. Malcolms only have girls. With some rare exceptions," she admitted. "He does seem to turn up at the strangest times, so I suppose one must wonder."

"You will have to draw me a family tree sometime. Do all of your female relations carry the Malcolm name even though they are married?" Trev thought he might be a little drunk because he honestly cared about the answer. She had this immense, elusive, extremely aristocratic family that he would do best to avoid if he wished to keep his head, but the idea of family drew him like fish to bait.

"It is part of our marriage contracts that the Malcolm name always be included. It is the easiest way to keep track of all of us, I suppose."

He ought to be on deck, directing his men in their search, but he seemed to be glued to his seat for no good reason other than admiring his companion's sunset tresses and charming blushes. And her hair wasn't even really red. He could tell now that the red had started to fade to its natural color. "All of you? How many of you are there?"

She wrinkled up her brow in thought. "I do not know precisely. Both my aunt and my mother have had more than a dozen of us between them. I had another aunt who died young, and as far as I'm aware, Ninian is her only child. But our grandmother had several sisters. I'm sure my mother could tell you more, but I've only met a few of them once or twice. They're the Northumberland and Scots branches. They cling to the old ways, and I have the feeling they do not approve of our more modern society."

"Over a dozen girls?" Trev tried to wrap his muzzy thoughts around such a cavalcade of riches, but his mind had only one direction. "No brothers?"

"Oh, we have lots of half brothers and half cousins—the marquess and the earl and the spares. They are older with families of their own, but we could summon an army if needed." She said it with perfect innocence, blinking her sea-blue eyes at him as she set her glass down. "And my older sisters are all married to wealthy men of power. I think the Malcolms could form a dynasty if King George would merely step out of our way. We look out for our own."

Trev choked on his ale. He was a dead man.

She folded her napkin and set it beside her plate. "So with an army of relations at his command, by morning Aidan will have sufficient copies of my sketch drawn to cover all of the south part of England. If those cottages exist, my family will find them."

He nearly slid off his chair in relief. "I had rather thought your family story would come to an uncomfortable end," he murmured.

She beamed mischievously. "I rather thought that's what I intended."

He laughed out loud from relief and at the unabashed impudence of her reply. "You are too wicked for mortal man!" he crowed. "No wonder you set London on its ears."

"Oh, I am not like this in London," she assured him. "I think it is the red in my hair. It affects my brain. I have never teased anyone before."

"You are much too good at it to be inexperienced." He finally dragged himself out of the chair and offered his hand to her. "And if I do not return to my duties, I may be trapped in your spell and never leave again. Are you comfortable here?"

Sinda clung to Trevelyan's strong brown hand longer than she should. He radiated such confidence that she hated to let him go. On her own, she had no spirit. In his company, she came to life. She did not know why this was so and wished to explore the oddity further, but she could see he was eager to escape.

Reluctantly, she released his grip. "I am very good at entertaining myself. I wish I could be of more use to you though."

"If your family is out searching for my cousin, then you are of great use to me already," he said. "Go to sleep and see if you draw something else interesting."

She brightened. "I could do that, although I would rather be able to tell myself to draw what you need to know. I wonder if that is possible?"

"That last drawing showed Laurence with a cut or scar upon his forehead. Go to sleep thinking about that and see what you dream. But I think I would rather you waited until I was around before experimenting on something that might be painful."

"Painful," she repeated, sitting on the bed's edge and thinking about it. "I usually have headaches when I wake after drawing the viscount, except this morning it was not so bad. I wonder if that has anything to do with the scar?"

His brow drew down in a formidable frown. "If dreaming gives you headaches, I forbid you to sleep. Would you like to come above for a while?"

Sinda smiled at his silliness. "I have to sleep sometime. But it is early yet, so you are safe for now. Go on. I shall be fine." When Trev stalled with fists at his narrow hips and a mulish expression on his arrogant face, she called on the confidence he'd given her. "You have rice in your beard. Do you intend to stay bushy now that you're not hiding?"

He grabbed a napkin and stalked off muttering and wiping his perfectly lovely whiskers. She itched to sketch him in his beard before he shaved it off, but hell would open before she risked a portrait again, especially of Trevelyan. She'd learned her lesson well.

But the sleepwalking drawings had been more helpful than harmful. If she could find the viscount, all could be made right again and perhaps Trevelyan wouldn't fear her family any longer.

She hoped that was the only reason he didn't wish to make love to her. She'd hate to die an old maid who never knew the pleasures of love.

Flipping through her small notebook to memorize all she'd drawn so far, she tried to concentrate on the viscount's brow. He'd worn nothing to cover it in the first sketch, so he'd been unharmed then. He wore a sailor's kerchief in the second, but the square of white beneath might be the first sign of injury. The sketch of his hand wasn't helpful. The small sketch of him staring into the distance showed the scarf again, but she couldn't discern a bandage. Did that mean the cut had healed? Or that the bandage was simply smaller than the earlier one?

She quickly drew last night's sketch from memory. There were the same daisies and cottages from the earlier drawing. His breeches looked a little more worn. He was wearing his coat and a sweater. He had a leather purse in his lap, as if he were counting his coins. Bent over as he was, it was difficult to tell if she'd drawn a bandage or a scar, but there was certainly something there beneath his knit cap that hadn't been on his brow in the first drawing.

Pondering these nuances, she climbed in beneath Trevelyan's blankets and plumped up his pillows. She was in a man's bed. The intimacy of it gave her ideas she shouldn't entertain.

Her monthly flow was usually brief, and if she remembered the lessons in her family journals, the likelihood of pregnancy immediately after was small. Perhaps in a night or two, she could learn the pleasures her older cousins and sisters had already experienced.

She was supposed to be concentrating on the viscount, not Trevelyan.

Dutifully, she summoned the images of the various sketches, studied the viscount's visage, concentrated on the cottages. She'd never really applied her mind to her instincts before. She wasn't entirely certain it was a wise idea—but she would do anything in her power to free Trevelyan from the unfair charges laid against him.

❧

"There's none as knows the place or the man," Caleb said, returning the sketch after clambering on board. "We'd need to spend more time ashore to find out about the trade."

Trev shoved the sketch into his pocket and contemplated the little village clinging to the spit of rock. "We could get ourselves shot inquiring too closely about smugglers. I'll leave that to George and them on land. He'll send word down the coast if he finds out more."

"The coast of England is mighty long," Caleb said doubtfully.

"I've the rest of my life and nothing better to do until the earl sticks his spoon in the wall. Let's set the sails and keep heading west looking for stone houses."

"Aye, aye, Cap'n." Caleb swaggered off to give the orders and claim the wheel.

In the light of the rising moon, Trev studied the village with his eyeglass until it was out of sight, wishing he could catch a glimpse of a stone cottage with a pot of Michaelmas daisies in front. Life would be much simpler so.

He'd have to write Melinda and his lawyers, set up some means of keeping the estate running in his absence. Having Sinda's powerful family to aid him in this would be welcome, but he didn't have her confidence in her family's willingness. He'd handle it himself.

Catching the deck on either side, he swung down the companionway and entered his cabin, trying to pretend he was only interested in the pen and paper in his desk and not what his fascinating guest might be doing.

She was sleeping—in the middle of his bed.

Torn between sharing the bed with her as he had at the inn and spending the night in an agony of lust, he turned on his heel and went in search of a hammock to set up in the cabin.

Leaving her alone was out of the question. She'd be walking the decks at midnight.

How long did he dare keep her before he must give in and return her to her family?

Twenty-four

WITH HIS HAMMOCK STRETCHED ACROSS THE CABIN, TREV awoke the instant he heard Sinda's bare feet hit the floor. The cabin was black as pitch, but the nightshift he'd bought for her in Hastings gleamed white against the dark. It couldn't be warm enough.

Keeping half an eye on her as she located her paper and chalks, he swung out of the hammock to throw more coal on the brazier. When she curled up on the bed with pad in hand, he gently dropped a blanket around her shoulders. She didn't seem to notice.

She was frowning but not shivering. He wondered if her headaches were some manifestation of whatever Laurence had felt or was feeling even now, but he had no way of knowing. The whole experience was too otherworldly to grasp. He simply knew that he didn't want her harmed by whatever was happening.

She cocked her head, as if waiting for some signal. Did she know he was here?

Trev hesitated. Should he interfere? Would it be better if he pulled her back to bed in hopes she would sleep? Or would it be like the nights when he'd tied her up, and she'd tossed and turned and cried?

He couldn't bear to hear her cry again. Slowly, so as not to frighten her, he sat behind her and drew her back against his chest, capturing her long, wavy hair between them. She relaxed as if it were the most natural thing in the world, and he had to fight an almost giddy grin. Whatever her opinion of him when conscious, the duke's daughter trusted him when she was asleep.

"Can you draw the town where Laurence lives?" he murmured into her ear. "Perhaps a tavern sign? Does he go to the tavern?"

She cocked her head again, studying the pad in her hand. Propping her bare feet on the bed, she created an easel of her knees and began to draw. Trev wrapped his arms around her waist to better support her and tried not to hold his breath as the picture unfolded.

Not that he could see much in the meager light from the coals. He doubted that Sinda could see anything either. That was how he knew she was sound asleep. Her fingers went unerringly to the box of chalks, finding the colors without looking. Could some spirit be directing her?

Had he not seen it with his own eyes, he would think anyone quite mad who told him about this. But he knew the woman in his arms was saner than most people, intelligent far beyond the common mold, and as far from an hysteric as it was possible to get. She was just blessed by magic.

He had heard about the voodoo the slaves practiced in the West Indies, had seen things too strange to believe. He knew he ought to fear this woman and her mysterious talent, but there wasn't any room in his heart for fear. She'd filled it with wonder instead.

She had the page nearly complete when she startled him with an obscene expletive and flipped the paper to a blank sheet.

She slashed at the paper with her chalks, drawing angry dark lines. Her fingers jerked, and she pressed so hard, the chalk broke. She didn't stop. She sat straight up, put her feet on the floor and covered the paper with fast, furious strokes, balancing the pad on her knees.

When she was done, she shoved paper and chalks to the floor and turned to crawl back into the bed. Or at least, Trev thought that was her intent. He seemed to be in her way.

He fell backward and let her crawl over him. She nearly unmanned him with her knee. He groaned and twisted to avoid worse damage, and her knees slid to the mattress, straddling him. Warm, sweet-scented woman enveloped him, and his body responded. She hesitated, and he held his breath.

He exhaled in relief when she slid to one side. While he would have gladly made love to her, her choice would be much sweeter if she made it while wide awake. She curled up beside him and sank into exhausted slumber. She wasn't shivering, but he curled around her anyway. The sketches would still be there in the morning. He didn't want her to be alone tonight.

He didn't want to be alone tonight. Something strange was happening to him, opening long-closed doors in his heart, and this fey spirit in his arms had much to do with it. He ought to be afraid, but he wasn't.

⁂

When Trev awoke in the morning, Sinda was standing in the center of his cabin, a piece of paper in her hand and more lined up at her feet. She had draped a quilt over her nightshift, but her feet were bare. Pillow creases reddened one of her cheeks, and her hair waved and spilled down her back and over her shoulders without regard to ribbon or braid. She didn't seem aware of her disarray. She looked so enchanting, he wanted to just lie there and watch her.

He'd thought she hadn't noticed his awakening, but as soon as she found a place to lay the sketch in her hand, she announced, "The sketches are in order."

Was he supposed to make something of that remark? Propping himself on his forearm, he leaned over the bed to study the exhibit she'd arranged. There was the rigging, the rope, the ring, the purse, and a new one—Laurence hoisting sail on a small fishing boat, his hair blowing in a strong wind.

Hair blowing. Trev sat and picked up the last sketch. It clearly showed Laurence's brow marred by the long gash of a nearly healed scar near his hairline. Behind him, a coastline curved, neatly indented with a wall that almost hid a row of small stone cottages.

He studied the progression of portraits again, and something like excitement burned beneath his rib cage. "He has no scar in the first drawing."

"He covers up a bandage in the next," she agreed. "I tried concentrating on your cousin's forehead before I went to sleep. My head didn't ache when I woke up."

Trev jerked his gaze up. "Is there some relation to your head and Laurence's?" he asked as she echoed his fear from yesterday.

"When I drew that first sketch, I woke up freezing with a great pain in my head. But he's not hurt in that sketch." She puzzled over the copy she'd made of the original. "But in these last two, the pain has been fading, just as the wound apparently has."

"I would not read too much into that," he said cautiously. "You may just have become accustomed to the practice."

"Perhaps. But I think I am drawing these in sequence. The first seems to be the summer since it shows the yacht intact."

Trev picked up the next sketch of Laurence splicing a rope on an unidentified dock. "But this is of autumn, isn't it? There are the daisies you said came out then."

"But the plant is compact, has only one stray bloom, and many buds. It could be early September, about the time you arrived in London. It appears as if he's recovering from the blow. If the injury happened in July when the yacht went down, the wound must have been a serious one for it to take so long to heal."

"That's nonsense," he protested, desperately wanting to believe his cousin had survived the yachting accident but not daring to accept this tale cut from whole cloth.

"If we follow the sequence, he's fishing to earn a living," she continued as if he hadn't interrupted. "He's saving his coins. The daisies have gone past their full bloom in the picture with the purse. That could be the end of September. But what I don't understand is why he stays there. Surely he need only send word to the earl and someone would fetch him, wherever he is."

"Not if he suspects my grandfather tried to kill him," Trev said.

She shot him an impatient glance. "It's you Lansdowne wishes to kill, not his heir. My fear is——" She studied him closely, as if to be certain he was ready for her next thought. "I fear the blow to his head may have damaged his mind. My cousin Ninian has nursed patients who have never fully recovered their wits after a severe blow."

They both stared at Laurence's head in the latest sketch. It was a very large scar.

Trev grabbed the new sketch and carried it to the porthole to study. Pride and excitement overcame his imaginary fears upon noting an additional feature. "There's a tavern sign with a picture of a black unicorn! The lettering isn't distinct, but I'll wager it says the Black Unicorn. If we show this around, someone might recognize that piece of coast. We're going to find him!"

Triumphantly, he swung around and caught Sinda up in his arms. "Last night while you were sleeping I told you to draw me a village and a tavern, and you did!" he crowed. "You listened. You heard me while you slept!"

She flung her arms around him and kissed his neck. "It is you, then. You're the reason I'm sleepdrawing. You are a very scary man, sir."

"We can be scary together." When she lifted glowing eyes to his face, he lowered his mouth to claim hers, ignoring a knock at the door. Her lips melted beneath his, and her body bent pliantly in his arms.

Abruptly, she caught his jaw and pushed his head back. "You shaved! You look like a new man." Before he could reclaim her, she scrambled to escape his embrace and retreated to wrap the fallen quilt around her shoulders, glancing nervously at the door.

Cursing whichever of his men dared intrude, Trev paced up and down a few times until his flagpole lost some of its stiffness, then flung the door open. Will stood there, holding a breakfast tray of steaming dishes. Growling in frustration, Trev let him in to arrange the table.

"Caleb says as there's another port ahead and we'll be anchoring soon," the boy said, darting curious glances between the two of them.

"Tell Caleb we have a new sketch he needs to show about. I think we're getting closer." Trev handed the precious piece of paper to the boy before remembering that Sinda had drawn two pictures last night, and she hadn't shown him the other. He waited until Will was gone before he studied his fascinating companion.

She was seated at the table in her nightdress, pouring their coffee as if she were in her family parlor. There was nothing inhibited about his lovely artist. *His*. He snorted. Even had he the temerity, how could he make it so with all these damned interruptions?

He should probably be glad the boy had saved him.

"You drew two pictures last night. Where is the other?" He had come to trust Sinda, he realized in amazement, but he was still wary of her gift. She'd been furious when she'd sketched that last. Had she deliberately hid it from him?

Head bent, she stirred her coffee. Trev thought he might explode with fear and frustration while he waited, but he wouldn't push her. She had to trust him too, and it wasn't as if he'd given her a lot of incentive to do so. He took a seat and accepted the coffee she handed him, prepared just as he preferred it, with a spoonful of sugar and no cream.

"It may be that my concentrating on your cousin's brow and your asking me to draw the village produced some aftereffect," she admitted. "My gift, such as it is, is not precisely logical."

Trev waited. He'd learned patience in his profession. One didn't chase after pirate ships and win. One waited, setting up ambushes in order to save as many lives as possible. He didn't want to ambush her. He simply wanted to know everything about her, even if it took a lifetime.

She sighed. She grimaced. She set down her spoon, stood up, and located a balled up piece of paper that looked as if it had been jumped up and down upon. Trev accepted the crumpled sketch and carefully smoothed it out on the table.

It depicted his ship near what appeared to be Brighton. The sketch might have been of yesterday, except black clouds loomed overhead, and the assembly on the bluff wasn't soldiers but a handsome group of women dressed in fine gowns and men in expensive wigs, hats, and embroidered coats.

With a lump in his throat, he carried the sketch to the porthole. Despite the angry slashes of clouds and wind-filled sails, she had drawn sufficient detail for him to recognize himself standing stiffly in the *Lass's* stern. His gaze traveled to the crowd on shore and found Sinda's tear-filled features with ease.

"You drew us," he murmured in wonder. He didn't want to invent a story to go behind this. He didn't need to. There was enough similarity in the features to recognize her father in one of the men and Aidan in another. Her mother, the duchess, could be recognized by her formidable figure alone. This was her family around her.

"I quit drawing myself years ago," she murmured unhappily. "There was always a black cloud hovering around me when I did."

"Well, the cloud is *above* you in this one." He tried to sound cheerful as he returned to the table, but even he could see what the sketch was about. She was waving him farewell. He tried very hard not to put too much significance into it, but he was failing badly. He didn't have to let her know that. "Does this mean if I sail away, the cloud lifts?"

"And goes with you? How charming." She stabbed her eggs. "Throw it away. It's trash."

"It's confusing," he said with equanimity. "If we believe your sleepdrawings are of the past while the things you paint during the day are of the future, then what is this one?" He folded it and tucked it into his pocket. If this was all he had of her to take with him, he would treasure it.

She frowned, her attention caught by the puzzle. "I would say it meant we were wrong and that my sleep drawings are of the future, but the yacht was destroyed, and I drew it whole, so that had to be the past. I think my gift is singularly useless."

"Very definitely not," he insisted. "I cannot believe you

would draw Laurence if he were in his grave. You have given me hope where there was none. That's not useless. It means I'll keep looking instead of giving up. And if he lives in that village, we'll find him. You will have given Melinda and Charity a gift beyond compare if we can return him home."

She said nothing, which was better than what she could have said. Her gift wasn't useless. It was terrifying. He hadn't the foolishness to tell her that his sailing away in the sketch didn't mean he'd leave forever. The black clouds were very convincing, even if he hadn't seen the anger and fury with which she'd drawn them. Or the tears running down her face.

Trev studied her bent head with a pain in his heart. What had he done to her in his self-absorbed insistence on locating his cousin?

"Did I ever tell you of Jamaica?" he inquired, diverting the gloom that had permeated the cabin. "My mother has family there. It's a beautiful island. If you enjoy drawing flowers and birds, you would love seeing it."

She dabbed surreptitiously at her eyes with her napkin and turned an attentive expression to him. Trev thought he'd never seen anything more beautiful than those sea-blue eyes, and he fixed them in his memory—just in case. She made him feel as if he had things to say that were of great importance. The wound in his soul that had never healed began to knit when she was around. He wanted to be the man he saw in her eyes.

"Tell me about your family," she urged.

And he did, discovering with amazement that he missed the exotic family he'd located once he had a ship of his own. "My mother's name was Alegra de la Fuente. Her father's family was Spanish and owned a sugar plantation until the English conquered the island. Her maternal grandmother was the daughter of an Englishman and a tavern maid, a native islander of mixed blood. My grandmother inherited one of the English plantations and married a French sailor." He hesitated, waiting for her to grimace at his motley heritage. Instead, she appeared to hang on to his words as if he painted a fascinating oil.

Relieved, he continued. "My father was on a botanical

expedition when he met my mother. Many of the plants in the orangery came from his explorations. The island and its society is all very colorful and exotic. Their homes are spacious and open, unlike anything you will see here. And they welcomed me without any of the prejudice of my father's world."

"Your mother must have been a fascinating woman. I wish I could have met her," Sinda murmured. "She would be as proud of you as her family must be. When I painted you, I could see that your heritage gave you a strength no other man I knew possessed. I think I halfway fell in love with you right then."

Shattered by her revelation, Trev spoke the first words to reach his tongue. "You loved me because I wasn't English?"

She grinned, that impish grin he adored so much, and the twinkle returned to her eye.

"Or because you were canvas and couldn't break my heart."

Laughing, he threw back his chair and reached for her. A man could resist only so much temptation.

Twenty-five

TREV'S KISS WAS EVERY BIT AS DELICIOUS AS SHE REMEMBERED. Sinda savored the roughness with which he grabbed her, the hunger of his lips, the way he gentled his grip when she came into his arms. She responded with all the love and desire inside her.

Love. She finally understood what it meant to love, and joy bubbled and rose in her. She'd found her soul mate.

She loved this wounded man with his rages and his laughter, his strength and his vulnerability. He was maddening. He was marvelous. She could spend a lifetime listening to him, following in his footsteps, observing the world from his perspective—if he would only let her stay by his side.

And she knew he wouldn't. Couldn't. She had finally seen her own future in her drawings, and heartbreak was written all over it. She had to let him go eventually to find the peace and family he desired—the peace she couldn't offer with her predilection for scandal. The peace he could find in the West Indies where his grandfather wouldn't haunt him. She'd heard his love for his foster home in the tales he told. He would be happier there.

The anchor had lowered while they were eating. Now, she heard shouts as the men returned and linked the rowboat to the hull. Any minute now, his crew would intrude. She couldn't let her fears deny whatever pleasure she might have now. She would grab every moment she had with him, hold on to it, take the most from it, and the future be damned.

They hadn't dressed yet. Trev had worn his breeches and shirt to bed so as not to embarrass her, but she wore only her nightshift, and she could feel the way his body changed when they embraced. Holding his powerful shoulders, she stood on her toes to rub against him and was rewarded with his moan of pleasure inside her mouth.

He nibbled her ear and down her throat, slid his hand between their bodies, and cupped her unfettered breast. Desire spiraled through her, making her dizzy with the need for more. He treated her with the respect one gave precious porcelain, as if he feared she would break—or that she would tear away from him at his unseemly exhibition of desire. Instead, she met his hunger with her own, digging her fingernails into his back to seek better purchase so she might experience the thrill of matching her tongue against his.

Taking her response as permission to continue, he played her aroused nipple until Sinda thought she might go up in flames. She considered climbing up his tall form until they toppled backward on the bed. She needed him on top of her, around her, inside her, blanketing the flame consuming her.

A knock pounded at the door, and this time she was the one to ignore it, frantically pressing into Trev so she could imprint his body along her own. Any interruption might signal the last time she saw him.

"Cap'n!" Caleb sounded excited. "Cap'n, I think we got him. We know where to go!"

Trev shuddered and held her close. Sinda buried her face in his shoulder and tried not to weep. He desperately wanted to find his cousin. She couldn't hold him back, but letting him go was the hardest thing she'd ever done. Biting her lip, steeling herself, she shoved away. "Go. See what he's discovered," she whispered, grabbing a blanket and covering herself.

Trev's dark eyes watched her with both joy and sorrow before he turned and let himself out the door, closing it behind him so she might have her privacy.

She wouldn't cry. She didn't know what the crew had found out, didn't know if this meant they must part. There might still be time together, and she refused to be the kind of weeping female that Trev disdained. She would be strong, like he was.

She had emptied their valise yesterday, hanging the dimity he'd given her so the wrinkles might fall out. She still had no petticoats, but she couldn't go ashore dressed like a Gypsy. The taffeta she'd worn the day he'd escaped had been designed to show off the frills of her petticoat and was open in front, so the dimity would have to do. She wasn't much of a seamstress, but she found Trev's sewing kit and sat down to hastily tack the hem up a length so she wouldn't trip upon it. Then she cut a slit in a seam to reach the pocket she removed from her taffeta so she could carry her notebook.

By the time she was dressed, she could tell the ship was in full sail again. She could entertain herself in his cabin, but she longed to see Trev in his element.

No one stopped her from traversing the small dining cabin and climbing the stairs. The ship tossed and rolled more than it had the other day, so she assumed they were heading for rougher seas. The motion didn't bother her. She clung to the railing and looked around with one focus, and that was the man she found standing at the helm.

If he were Neptune risen from the sea, she wouldn't be surprised. His powerful hands held the wheel, and he wore only the shirt and breeches he'd slept in. He stood barefoot and uncoated in the chilly wind with his face upturned, absorbing the elements and feeding their energy into his ship. She would swear they flew over the waves by the strength of his will alone.

That was nonsense, of course. The instant Trev saw her, he yelled at Caleb to take over, and he bounded across the deck to wrap her in his wet grip. His shirt was soaked.

"We're in for a squall. Take a good look now because you'll not be able to come above shortly," he yelled against the wind and salt spray.

"I don't need to see the water to know it's there. Come below and put on something warmer." She clung to his waist as if she were a strumpet or his wife. She didn't care what the men thought her.

He flashed one of his wide grins but obeyed, helping her down before swinging down without touching a step. It was very obvious this ship was his and he knew every inch of it.

"Miss me already?" he teased, draping his arm over her shoulders and steering her toward the cabin.

"I'll not swell your pride any more than it already is. Tell me what they found." She swept into the cabin and picked up his vest.

She turned to hand it to him, but he'd ripped off his wet shirt and flung it across a chair. He stood there half-naked, drying his chest with a towel as if she were not even there.

She'd never seen a half-naked man. She had to pry her mouth shut and try not to sit down too abruptly. He was magnificent. Far better than the engravings she'd admired in books. His torso was wide shouldered and slim waisted, with a fine line of dark hair symmetrically dividing his broad chest. The pronounced muscles were even better than the anatomy books depicted.

The desire to paint him tore through her with the fire of lust.

Sitting on the bed's edge, she hugged his vest to her as he turned and bent over to rummage in a chest for a dry shirt, giving her a clear view of what his vest and coat normally hid. His breeches molded to a very pleasing posterior.

She was the next best thing to speechless by the time he straightened with shirt in hand. He gave her a puzzled glance but shrugged the linen over his head without questioning.

"Caleb found some fishermen in town who recognized your drawing and the Black Unicorn," he announced. "It's in Poole. The coastline there is a smugglers' haven. The town has a well-protected harbor and a wall around it. You can see a portion of it in your sketch. Asking questions there could cost us our heads, but the drawing will ease the way."

She didn't know whether to be elated or afraid, but Trev's joy knew no bounds, and she decided not to throw a damper on it. "How long will it take to get there?"

"We're not far. We're riding into a squall, so that will delay us, but if the harbor is sheltered, we'll be safe enough once we arrive." Shirt and vest on, he scooped her off the bed and hugged her. "We're going to find him!" he cried in joy. "And then all will be well."

He kissed her soundly, set her down, and grabbing his coat, ran back to the cold and wind above.

Sinda collapsed on the bed after he was gone and hugged her knees. Joy warred with despair, and she could do no more than rock back and forth with the ship and pray fervently that all would go as he believed.

≈

The storm struck before they reached port. Trev took the helm and gave the order to *heave to*. He'd weathered hurricanes but never while carrying a treasure as priceless as the one below. This was merely a squall, but he'd not have Sinda thrown about heedlessly because he raced against time. Laurence had waited this long. He could wait another day.

With soldiers scouring the coast for the *Lass*, Trev didn't want to appear in port until he was in a position to sail out quickly. A three-sided harbor like Poole was a trap for a fugitive ship. They'd have to weather the storm at sea. It was nearly midnight before he was satisfied with their position.

Ascertaining that the sails were safely lashed and that the anchor held, Trev handed his duties to the mate on watch and went below.

He wasn't certain what to expect when he entered. Above, the wind howled and rain struck the deck. The *Lass* heaved up and down with each rolling wave. He doubted Sinda had any experience of a storm at sea. He regretted leaving her alone, but her safety and that of his crew were paramount.

She'd intelligently doused the lanterns and brazier. The cabin was icy cold and dark. He couldn't hear her, so he hoped she slept. He couldn't bear not knowing. Bolting the door so it wouldn't fly open in a draft, he crossed to the bed.

"Thank the goddess!" she whispered, before launching herself into his arms.

Surprised, Trev caught the soft bundle of enticing curves thrown at him just as the ship lurched. Unbalanced, they toppled into the tumble of covers that was his bed.

"I know you deal with storms all the time and you're very good," she said senselessly, clinging to his sopping vest. Her breath caressed his frozen skin as she pulled at his wet clothes.

Trev's mind put bed and woman and *good* together and traveled down wanton paths that didn't involve storms. He had an armful of eager woman telling him he was very *good*. What else was a man to think? Before he could react, she snuggled closer and completed her thought. "But I was terrified you would be blown overboard."

Still flying high on the joy of weathering the storm, Trev couldn't control his shout of laughter at his own expense. So much for his pride-inflated fantasies. "You're good for me, lass," he murmured.

"Do you mean that?" she asked, going quiet in his arms.

Startled by her intensity, wishing he had light to see her by, he brushed a cold finger over her warm cheek. "Aye. You bring me joy and hope and make me believe that anything is possible. You show me there are still good people in the world."

He could almost feel her smile as her busy fingers returned to working the buttons of his wet vest. He was soaking the bed as well as her. As the ship rolled and tossed in the increasing wind, he tried to sit up and shrug out of his coat, but she wouldn't let him. He couldn't say that he objected to her warm hands against his personal garments. It had been a long time since he'd had an eager woman, except this one thought she was being *helpful*.

"I was afraid I was a handicap to everyone around me," she confessed. "I scared off my sisters' suitors, you know."

He chuckled and kissed her cheek before catching her busy hands. "London is full of puling milksops. Real men conquer fire. Only fools fear it." He swung to sit up with his feet over the edge of the bed and jerked off his coat and vest. Despite the cold and wet, he was hot and hard under the influence of Sinda's feminine proximity. The air around her was laced with the scent of lilacs, and he feared he'd dig his hand into her hair and haul her against him if he stayed too close. The wind howled, and he wished he could do the same.

"And you're a man who conquers fire," she said in admiration. "I hadn't thought of it like that. It takes a reckless man not to fear the unknown."

"I like to think I have more wisdom than to be reckless," he protested, but her admiration soothed his soul. Her talented fingers peeling his wet shirt upward inflamed his ardor. She'd have him inside out and upside down if he was not—

She was *seducing* him.

Amazed, he let her draw his shirt from his back, wondering just how far she might go.

She was a *duke's daughter*. A maiden. He was a man on the run.

But tomorrow, he would find Laurence, and the earl would have no case against him. Tomorrow, he would be a free man. And Sinda would be a ruined woman in the eyes of the world. Ruined enough to accept an untitled, uneducated sailor for a husband?

She was accepting that fate without protest. More than accepting. She was flinging herself joyfully into it.

Tearing off the shirt she couldn't quite tug over his head, Trev shifted to tenderly stroke her hair and marvel at the gift she meant to bestow upon him.

"Sinda," he cautioned as her fingers trailed up his chest and his heart took up a dangerous tattoo. "You don't know what you're doing to me. You're a beautiful woman, and I desire you more than life itself."

"I rather think life is what lovemaking is about," she whispered, bending her head to press a kiss to his chest, narrowly missing his nipple.

Trev sucked in air so swiftly he thought he'd keel over. He reached to hold her back, but his fingers clasped the supple softness of her arms through the thin nightshift and wouldn't let go. The small part of his mind that was still functioning said he would do right by her as soon as he found her family…

The rest of him merely pulled her into his lap, clasped her against his chest, and plundered her mouth.

She responded vibrantly, hugging his neck, meeting kiss with kiss, entwining her fingers in his hair as he did hers.

Heat spread everywhere she touched, and he wasn't aware of wind or cold. The constraints of his wet breeches reminded him soon enough of what he did.

"I wouldn't take you like this," he protested. "A lady should have silk sheets and feather beds and—"

She covered his mouth with kisses and ran her hands over his chest. "Then I'll not be a lady," she said decisively. "I see no advantage in it."

She was fierce in her challenge, and he wanted to laugh out loud in delight. The demure lady and quiet artist were disguises that concealed the passionate woman beneath.

He grasped her shoulders and pressed her down against the mattress, trapping her with his weight. He captured her wrists and held them above her head so he could savor the taste of her delicate skin and spread kisses without interference. With each new depredation, she wiggled and gasped and nipped his nose and surged against him, demanding more.

Trev feared his breeches would cut off all circulation in his lower parts, but before he unbuttoned them, he would make certain of his claim. Transferring Sinda's wrists to his left hand, he used his right to free her breast from the dainty lawn nightshift. While the ship rolled beneath them, he lifted her breast until he could taste the rosy crest with his tongue. He licked, and she moaned low in her throat. Granted that measure, he wanted more, and he finally indulged his desire to drink deeply at that sweet fount. The nipple pulled taut, and she cried out and arched into him. The answering response in his loins threatened to cripple him.

"I have spent my life taking prizes and keeping them. I do not give up what is mine once I claim it, Lady Lucinda," he said, reminding her of who she was and who he would always be.

"I vow to love, honor, and take thee in equality from this day forward," she responded fervently. "But if you do not let me touch you soon, I'll pull every lovely hair from your head."

The word *love* startled him, but her threat made him laugh. He stood and stripped off his breeches.

The wind roared. The ship bucked and rolled. And Trev had never felt so free and happy in his life.

He'd come home.

Twenty-six

Sɪɴᴅᴀ ᴅɪᴅɴ'ᴛ ɴᴇᴇᴅ ᴛᴏ ᴘʜʏsɪᴄᴀʟʟʏ sᴇᴇ Tʀᴇᴠᴇʟʏᴀɴ ᴀs ʜᴇ lowered his heavy weight beside her. His image—all the images impressed upon her these last weeks—were permanently etched in her mind's eye. The difference now was that she could touch what she saw.

It was almost frightening knowing that the broad-shouldered rogue with the rakish scar and sensuous mouth was about to take possession of her and teach her what it was like to be a woman. But the man was so much more than the portrait that she wasn't afraid.

The powerful hand that she'd painted holding a stallion's reins now slid her nightdress up. He still held her wrists above her head, and she felt her disadvantage as his hand stroked her leg and along the curve of her bottom. She could do no more than whimper with need.

"Open for me," he murmured, sliding his hand between her thighs to show her what he meant. She parted her legs for him, exposing her vulnerability, trusting him. While his mouth sucked her breast, making her ache with desire, his finger slipped inside to excite the ache more. Startled, she raised straight off the bed, driving him deeper. Overwhelmed by a myriad of strange and wonderful sensations, she quivered and tried to hold still.

"Liquid fire," he whispered approvingly against her ear before continuing to smother her with kisses, distracting her from his roaming hands.

He released her wrists. Propping himself on one forearm, he cupped her jaw and drank deeply of her mouth while his thumb caressed her hardened nipple. She was dizzy with so many sensations at once that she forgot the ship, the storm, and everything except her need for this man and what he was doing to her.

"You smell like spring," he murmured.

With the powerful grace of a large cat, he rose to his knees, moved over her, and spread her legs wider. He was naked above her, and she was within minutes of losing her virginity. The hair on his muscular limbs brushed her sensitive skin, reminding her this was very real.

She moaned in protest when his hand abandoned the sensual tune he played upon her breast to slide beneath her hips. He tilted her until a thick brand seared the sensitized flesh between her thighs. She was open to him and could do no more than gasp and grab the powerful arms on either side of her as he inched deeper.

The ship rolled, and apparently conscious of her every sound and touch, Trev shifted his weight so he did not ride her so fully. Instead, his fingers returned to the secret place between her legs to tease and dip and seduce forth the moisture there.

"I apologize. I do not mean to frighten you, but I'm a starving man. In my haste, I fear I'll hurt you," he said with regret.

With his ministrations, a hollowness opened inside her, aching to be filled. She had just vowed to share herself with this man, and she feared this would be her only opportunity. She would not let timidity stop her now. "It's worth the hurt," she whispered, pushing into his palm.

Trev chuckled and returned to apply his kisses to her mouth. "Pleasure first," he whispered.

And pleasure it was. His kisses roamed southward to take command of her breasts. From that message center, heated orders traversed her nerves to the place where Trev's knowing fingers exploited them well. Her insides swelled to the point of explosion, and when she heard herself cry *please,* she didn't recognize her voice.

He slipped another finger inside, and she writhed as a will other than her own took possession of her.

She was outside herself, seeing it all from above with eyes that didn't require light. There was Trev's muscled back, his flesh dark against her paleness. Her tousled hair spilled across the pillow, rippling as she tossed her head. She hadn't realized her legs were so slender next to the length of his muscled ones, where their limbs created an eight-pointed star against the sheets. The urge to paint him in all his glory returned, but it had no power against the other urges pinning her to the bed. Her fingers clung to Trev instead of reaching for her chalks.

Her physical body cleaved to the man who held her. Her nails scratched his chest and shoulders as she tried to force him to hurry. Her legs spread wider and bent upward in invitation. But the infuriating man merely chuckled and murmured reassurances and plied her with his fingers until she knew she would burst with the pressure. Her inner eye closed, and she surrendered to the building rapture of his touch.

When she thought she must surely come apart if she did nothing, she clasped his hard maleness and dared an exploratory stroke. With a primal cry, he finally lost what little control he'd struggled to maintain. He drove his fingers deep inside her, riding her back and forth until she grabbed his hair, screamed, and shattered in his arms.

Instantly, Trev covered her, and a thickness pushed into the passage where his fingers had been. Sinda jerked with the shock of invasion, and with the force of powerful muscle, he pulled back. He gasped from the effort of it, and a lock of his hair fell forward to caress her face.

"Don't stop," she murmured.

He hesitated, but nature took its course, and he surged forward with the roll of the ship. She cried out again at the strangeness and the fullness of the intrusion. He halted, but he did not leave her. To her wonderment, once she adjusted to their joining, she experienced only the joy of filling and none of the pain. She wanted to give him the ecstasy he'd given her.

He was large, but with her urging, he hesitated only briefly before repeating his thrust, this time fully breeching her narrow passage and settling in to the hilt with a groan of pure joy. Stretched to the limit, Sinda eased his way by wrapping her legs around his hips. With a roar of relief, he pulled back, and with a mighty surge, he drove deep inside her again and again, until he spilled his seed with a trumpeting cry.

This time, there would be no child of their joining, Sinda knew. Unless she found some way to keep him, there would never be a child. She had given him her vow of faithfulness.

She didn't let her momentary sadness ruin the pleasure. Trev stayed within her, stiffening again as he pressed kisses along her throat, and she sighed with delight. She was complete. For the first time in her life, she felt whole. And grounded. Her body possessed the same power as her mind. Now she understood what her sisters and cousins had told her about.

"This is all I've ever wanted," he murmured into her hair, "the peace and welcome of loving arms, and someday, a home and family of my own."

For the first time, Sinda allowed a blossom of hope to unfurl inside her heart. "I'll be happy to grant your dreams if you'll take away my nightmares," she whispered back.

"You have a talent for passion, my lady," he said. "Let us explore that tonight."

He received no argument from her. Threading her hand through his thick hair, Sinda drew his head down for her kisses. If this was to be the only night of love she would ever have, she wanted to take all she could from it.

Trev had spent enough nights without sleep to know they normally left him heavy-headed and sluggish the next morning. When the storm lifted at dawn and he left Sinda's arms, he was as light-headed and giddy as a boy.

He took the helm with a huge grin on his face. He'd like to dwell on the glowing beauty of the woman he'd left below, or the things she had allowed—nay, *encouraged*—him to do last night. But he hadn't totally lost his senses. Tonight would be soon enough to revisit those pleasures.

Today, he meant to find his cousin.

As soon as possible after that, he would return triumphantly to London, clear his name, and ask Sinda's father for her hand in marriage. He didn't much care if the duke refused him. He would ask only out of politeness and respect. Sinda was of an age to do as she wished, and pirate that he was, he had no intention of letting her go.

He wouldn't let even the specter of Laurence's injury deter him. Sinda's sketches had convinced him his cousin was alive and well and functioning normally. He believed her sketch, mad though it seemed.

"Maybe we should anchor the *Lass* here and go in by land?" Caleb asked, eyeing the natural harbor ahead with doubt.

"Maybe we should, but we won't." Trev scanned the port with his glass. "There's no navy, no ship to match ours. We'll be faster in and out this way."

Lowering the glass, still looking over the harbor, he recognized the instant Sinda appeared on deck behind him. Electricity crackled across the ship. The sails flapped harder, the waves rolled smoother, the men laughed louder. And the scent of spring enveloped him.

"If you find your cousin, where will you go next?" she inquired without preamble, slipping her hand into the crook of his elbow. He loved the way she accepted the change in their relationship so naturally, as if it had been inevitable.

She was his. Pride swelled in him, a pride that had been stolen nearly twenty years ago, a pride that had been battered and beaten but had never quite been lost. And she gave it all back to him, whole and better than ever. He might not have title or education, but a woman as talented and beautiful as this one had deemed him worthy of her.

With tenderness, he brushed her wide, pale brow and admired her long-lashed eyes when they smiled up at him.

She'd braided the short hair in ribbons about her face so the tendrils framed her face instead of blowing in her eyes, and she'd fastened the heavy length in back with a red scarf. Trev thought she looked a colorful faerie sprite as her ribbons waved in the breeze and the sun sparkled through the silver-gold showing through the red dye of her hair. The sun's rays were stripping the red. Her disguise wouldn't last much longer.

"We'll sail to Brighton and ride back to Sommersville to deliver Laurence home," he answered promptly. "Then we'll be off to London."

"Could you not have Caleb row your cousin ashore in Brighton while we stay on board and sail to London?"

He shot her a wary look. "Why? I cannot be charged with murder if he's alive."

She released his elbow to lean over the rail and watch the village of Poole grow closer. "Because I've drawn the future and don't like what I see."

Relieved that it was only her skepticism that bothered her, he circled her waist and pulled her against him. "We make our own futures. Your work can be interpreted many ways. Perhaps it is only one of many possible futures."

She leaned into him, her ribbons caressing his face. "I can accept that far easier than I can believe the future is predestined."

"Good. Will you go ashore with me?"

She hesitated, then reached to stroke his jaw. "No. You are more likely to come back safely if you know I'm here."

She was right about that. He kissed her boldly in front of his crew, then ordered the sails trimmed. He scanned the village with his glass as they sailed into the harbor, praying for a glimpse of his cousin.

If all went as planned, he was about to introduce Sinda to his family.

❧

Sinda stayed on deck and watched the whole time Trevelyan was ashore. The storm had blown off on a brisk breeze. The sun peeked out from behind scurrying clouds, and whitecaps dotted the water. The village sprawling along the curve of the harbor appeared interesting. She borrowed Trev's spyglass to look for the portion she had sketched.

She thought she found it. There was the small jetty where the viscount had spliced rope. She didn't see the flowers, but it was late in the season. There were several stone cottages. Any cottage could have been the one she'd drawn.

She watched as Trev and his men questioned the curiosity seekers who came out to greet them. Trev stood head and shoulders above the crowd, if not always in height then in the way he carried himself. She could never mistake him for anyone else.

The scar on his cheek whitened as the villagers spoke, and she quickly scanned the horizon for soldiers, for fear he'd been warned of their arrival, but she saw no danger.

She bit her bottom lip as Trev's long strides carried him away from the villagers, along the harbor road toward the cottages. She knew him so well now that she could read his mood from the way he walked. He wasn't happy.

"It's cold out here, my lady," Will said, coming up beside her. "You ought to be below. Cookie said he'd send up tea."

Sinda tugged her mantle around her and raised the glass again. "Thank Cookie and tell him to wait until the captain is aboard. If there's whiskey, he may wish to have that on hand."

"And for the viscount?" Will asked eagerly. "I ain't never met a viscount."

Sinda watched as Trev entered a cottage and came back out wearing the expression of a haunted man. Her sketches had been wrong. She'd encouraged him for no good reason. Grief welled within her. "I don't think you'll be meeting him today," she told the boy. "I'm sorry."

Her imagination burned with images of last night. Her fingers craved the challenge of painting the rippling strength of Trev's back. She longed to capture the pleasure and sensuality they'd shared. Once upon a time she would have retreated to her oils and canvas to paint her dreams and to forget the pains of reality.

But Trevelyan was her dream as well as her reality, and she could not escape his anguish. Instead of going below to her chalks, she waited for his return. How had her sketches steered him wrong? What would he think of her if his cousin was not alive? She couldn't bear to consider the possibility that he might have lost his only interest in her. She knew that since she loved him, she would eventually have to leave him to find the peace he craved, but not yet. Please... not yet.

The instant he climbed on board, she ran to him. Trev draped his arm over her shoulder and led her back to the companionway.

"Tell me," she demanded. "Was I all wrong? What happened?"

Will rushed into the cabin after them, carrying a tray of tea and whiskey. Trev barely acknowledged the unusualness of the decanter on a tea tray but poured a swallow of whiskey into a teacup and drank.

"Thank you, Will." Sinda sent him out and shut the door, eyeing Trev's stark features with anxiety. Had she given him false hope? She would hate herself forever.

"They recognized the man in the sketch," he finally said, pouring another swallow of the liquor but adding tea to it.

Sinda wanted to collapse with relief but forced her hand to take a teacup instead. She had drawn someone recognizable at least. She hadn't been totally wrong. "And?" she prompted.

"They don't know who he is."

She sank into her chair but didn't touch the tea. "I don't understand."

He straddled a chair, crossed his arms over the back, and buried his forehead against them. "They will not say how the man in the portrait arrived, just that he was seriously injured in an accident last summer."

"But it is him, is it not?" The viscount *had* to be alive. She couldn't bear Trev's anguish if he weren't. Now that she had accepted that her gift, she wanted her drawings to be right or all this scandal would be both purposeless and harmful.

"When he woke, he did not know his name," Trev said heavily. "You were right. His mind is damaged. If it is him."

She wanted to jump up and down and rip the story from him, but she sipped her tea and waited. Odd, she had never really been of this world until Trev had taught her to reach out and feel, and now she had all these emotions and didn't know how to express them appropriately.

"How damaged?" she asked as steadily as she could.

"He remembered nothing." Trev rubbed his brow and sat

up straighter, reaching for his cup. "He kept to himself once the injury healed. They said he fished for a living."

"Where is he now?" She had a dozen other questions, but this one was paramount.

"They don't know." He threw back the mix of tea and whiskey as the sails above caught the wind. The ship rolled and sped before the breeze, but he didn't seem to notice. "They won't talk of the trade. They just say he went out the other night and did not return with the others."

A pall of dread fell over her, and Sinda froze beneath the cold weight of it. "He went out with *smugglers*?"

"So it seems." Trev rubbed his eyes and didn't look at her. "Laurence was the most upright, law-abiding man I ever knew. I don't know whether to believe it wasn't him or that his brainbox has been so damaged that it may as well not be him."

They were sailing away from Poole—leaving all hope behind. Sinda shook her head in disbelief. "You're giving up? You'll take their word for it and accept he's gone?"

He set down his cup and finally met her gaze. "I'm not giving up. I'm going back to Brighton, to my friends who promised to look into the smuggling along the southern coastline. I need names. Then I'll post a man in Poole and take you home."

Sinda shivered at the firmness of his declaration. If his grandfather wouldn't accept him, he had nothing to lose. He was about to set sail after smugglers. Instead of giving him the family and peace he craved, she was sending him off to war again.

"You're about to return to privateering, aren't you?" she asked quietly.

He snorted and stood up. "With no letter of marque from the king, I'd be a pirate if I stopped a ship to search for Laurence. We can hope it won't come to that." He walked out.

∽✤∾

That evening, Trev didn't return to the cabin. Sinda understood what was going through his head. Without proof his cousin lived, he couldn't clear his name, couldn't return to shore—couldn't offer her a home. And he offered no opportunity to argue, although she could have told him that she fully intended to make her own home rather than cause pain and disruption in his.

As much as she'd soaked up the sweet words they'd exchanged last night, she knew she could never really be his wife. She could not even begin to imagine how Melinda would react should Trev take a wife who might draw a scandalous portrait showing a member of her family dying. And Charity was far too young to be saddled with an aunt who painted the impossible.

But that didn't mean she and Trev couldn't have each other now.

As the night deepened and he still didn't seek the solace she could temporarily offer, her understanding turned to wrath. She could not spend the rest of her life waiting and observing as she had all these past years. She wanted to *live*, and Trev was the man with whom she wished to share this part of her life.

And he wasn't even giving her a chance to present her case.

In a fury so great she was surprised that thunder did not crackle over her head, she gathered up the paper and chalks he'd bought for her and marched up to the deck. He wasn't at the helm, but acting on unerring instinct, she located his dark silhouette leaning against the rail.

He wanted to go forward to a home and a family, but he was turning his back on the future to follow a path forged in the past. Perhaps she wasn't being fair, but she wasn't feeling fair right now. The only man she would ever love had some idiot idea that he was doomed to forever live alone and insisted on being noble and honorable and taking her home without looking for any place of compromise in between.

Trev didn't turn around as she approached. For that, Sinda whacked him on the back of the head with the sketch pad.

He lifted his hand to his head and turned to stare at her quizzically. Now that she had his attention, she took the precious box of chalks and flung them as far out to sea as she could. They barely made a sound as they hit the waves and sank.

Before he could stop her, she heaved the paper over as well. "There. If you can give up your dreams, so can I." Without another word, she stalked back to the cabin.

Stunned by such wrath from a dreamy-eyed woman he thought incapable of it, Trev followed her down, but the bolt slamming home showed him the foolishness of arguing. He could shout at the door, but what would he say? She was right.

He sprawled on the bench in the dining cabin and contemplated hunting for Cookie's supply of rum, but he didn't think it healthy to let a woman in a rage roam freely. How long would she keep the door bolted?

He didn't want her to give up her dreams. Or her art. Or him, for that matter. But she belonged on land, with her family, and he didn't. It was as simple as that.

He stared at the door, willing it to open. He could take her to Jamaica, he supposed, but that felt like running away. He refused to let his grandfather win. He had to fight to stay here where he wished to be. He couldn't let Sinda get caught in his war.

Would she have nightmares tonight without her paper to work on?

He wanted to take away her nightmares the way he had last night.

Maybe she was so tired she would fall asleep and not wake. But then, what about tomorrow night, after he'd taken her home? And all the nights in the future?

She had to trust him to win this war and come back to her.

Maybe he should have told her that.

Invigorated with that thought, he rose and slammed his fist against the door. "Let me in!" He had no desire to make a laughingstock of himself before his men, but if it came down to it, he'd kick the door in before he'd let her keep him out.

He heard no sound of the bolt's removal. The door was good solid mahogany. Fine, then. He pounded some more, and when he received no response, he lifted the bench seat in the dining hall and rummaged among the tools there. Finding what he sought, he lifted the hatchet and carried it to his door. "I have something to say to you, Lucinda Pembroke, but I'm not about to stand out here and shout it. If you don't open the door, I'll hack it down!"

He didn't hear a rustle. With a curse at the destruction to his lovely ship, he lifted the hatchet and prepared to smash it into the door near the bolt latch. As he began to swing, the bolt rattled. He stumbled to prevent hitting her or the door, banged into the mahogany with his shoulder, and fell into the room when Sinda jerked the door open.

If he stayed around this surprising woman for long, he'd be battered head and foot—unless he remained one step ahead of her.

Wide-eyed at his ungainly entrance, she stepped aside. Trev flung the hatchet to his desk and unable to find the words he wanted, lifted her from the floor, and kissed her, kicking the door closed in the process.

He kissed her as if he were a drowning man and she was his last breath. He kissed her until she quit struggling and wrapped her arms around his neck and fed his need with her own. He drank deeply of the nectar of her desire, filling his empty soul with all she offered—the promise of the home and family and love he'd never known. She made him feel as if he deserved all of that and more. She made him feel larger than life and capable of saving the world.

"I'll come back for you," he promised, ripping his mouth from hers long enough to speak now that he remembered the words. Before she could argue the point, he carried her to the bunk and made his case in the only way he knew how. He kissed her senseless again.

She placed her hands on either side of his face and refused to release him as she returned his kisses. His hands found better things to do. Leaning on one elbow, he ripped at her laces and shoved back fabric until he could find her breasts. She moaned against his mouth as he cupped her nakedness. She had the most perfect breasts he had ever encountered, firm and full and the ideal size for his palm. He could spend the rest of his life admiring their perfection, except he needed to do more than admire.

Wrenching his face from her sweet kisses, he suckled her

nipple, loving the way she cried out and gave herself fully to the experience. His breeches grew tight as she dug her hands into his hair and arched higher, begging for more. Of all the men she could have, he was the one she chose. He would see that she never regretted the decision.

Slowly, savoring every inch of skin uncovered, he stripped away her clothes. Inexperienced, she attempted to do the same for him. He groaned when she spread her magic fingers across his bare chest, and he ripped the shirt off so she might touch him more easily.

"The scars," she murmured. "How did you acquire so many scars?"

They were worth every minute of pain just to feel her caress them, to hear the concern in her voice. He nipped a kiss at her nose, then down her cheek, and to her bare shoulder. "Alligators, knives, and bullets," he said, applying the balm of her touch by grasping her wrist and running her hand down his chest. "A drunken seaman gave me my first. A pirate sword gave me my last. I earned my first ship with this one." He pressed her fingers to his ribs. "There'll be no more now that I have so much to risk."

"Someday, you must tell me all your adventures." She pressed a kiss to his rib, and Trev wanted to rip open his breeches.

"They weren't adventures. I survived. I had to kill the drunken navy man who thought I'd make a pretty toy. I had to shoot cannonballs into a ship full of men to earn my first prize." He felt compelled to tell her everything he was before she made the mistake of thinking him one of her gentle lordlings, but he continued kissing her, caressing her breasts, unable to let her go even as he warned her to do just that. "If you think me a pleasant interlude, we misunderstand one another."

"We misunderstand nothing," she whispered. "I spent an entire winter drawing you. I did not know the scars upon your body or your soul, but I knew *you*. Believe in my gifts, and do not mistake their significance." She ran her hands down his sides, to his breeches, and shoved the fabric over his hips.

"I believe in *you*," he countered, lifting himself long

enough to fight off the breeches, kicking them from the bed. Free of constraint, he covered her, holding himself up with hands on either side of her head. Her hair spread like rich silk across his pillows, and her pale body beneath his dark one seemed slight and vulnerable. "I believe you are a gifted artist, a wise woman beyond all understanding, and a faerie with magic in her fingers. You terrify me. And uplift me. I can't ask you to wait for me. But I cannot leave you alone as I should."

Her beautiful breasts gleamed like ivory in the moonlight from the porthole. Her legs parted invitingly, brushing against his. And all the blood left his brain and thundered into his lower parts.

"I will try to be all that you think I am," she said, raising her arms to draw him down. "And maybe a little more," she whispered against his ear as he sank deep inside her.

She was more, much, much more than he deserved. With a cry of surrender, Trev took her with him into the alternate realm of mystery where two people became one, two souls joined, and life formed.

Twenty-seven

Sinda woke to an empty bed next morning.

She felt Trev's absence in so many ways that she couldn't define them all. If he had his way, his absence might haunt her forever. But she couldn't stop him from searching for his cousin.

Feeling bereft and empty despite the words of promise they had exchanged, she donned her dimity gown and used Trev's brush to ruthlessly pull her hair into a knot that her few pins would hold. There was no evidence that her dreaming mind had attempted any further sketches, although she scanned Trev's desk for fear she might have usurped his pens or journal. Even the pencil and paper in her pocket remained untouched.

She prayed that didn't mean the viscount was dead.

Rather than contemplate the impossible, she went out to face the day.

She was learning the feel of the ship and knew before she emerged into the foggy morning that they were heeling into port. With a sinking in her stomach, she recognized the bluffs of Brighton. Trev was sending her home.

He had to know there would be soldiers waiting for him. If lashing him to a mast would help keep him at sea, she would, but she wasn't experienced with ropes and knots.

Perhaps she could hit him over the head with a belaying pin. She eyed the pegs that held the sails in place but couldn't figure out how she could sneak up on him with one. Or how she could persuade his men to sail away with their captain unconscious.

At least he had the sense to anchor out of sight of town. She could see the bluffs, but naught else. She watched as they loomed ever closer, returning her to the life she'd forsaken. She didn't know if she could go back to a quiet, observant existence after the joy of sharing Trev's adventure—and his bed.

Not that he was giving her a choice. She watched as he strode briskly down the deck in her direction. In his haste to be on his way, he hadn't shaved and had donned the clothes he'd left scattered across the cabin last night. He looked the part of pirate with coat off and sleeves billowing in the breeze. All he needed was a scarf wrapped around his black hair. A hank had escaped his queue and fell across his brow, just as in her portrait of him.

"I don't want to go home," she told him when he halted in front of her.

"We could be at sea for months. It's not a place for a woman." He brushed a straying curl from her forehead with a gentle hand. "If you wait for me, I will come back for you."

His voice held no inflection for her to interpret. The dark eyes above his angular cheekbones revealed no emotion. She would have liked a more romantic declaration, but Sinda knew him well enough to know his words said everything he knew how to say. He didn't believe she would wait or that he was worthy of her waiting. But she had vowed to love him, whether he was wrong or right. She might not be able to marry him or live with him, but she would always love him. She would fight her family to be there for him until he found the peace and family he deserved.

"I will wait," she said, "but you had better come or I'll hire a pirate and go looking for you."

A hint of laughter tilted his lips at that, and his eyes lit with admiration. "Advertise in the newssheets, if you would. I'll have someone watch for it."

She nodded and tears sprang to her eyes as he took her elbow and guided her to the rowboat and his waiting crew. This wasn't how she'd imagined their adventure would end.

"What if I sleepdraw more pictures of your cousin?" she asked, clutching his arm before they could put her into the boat.

Trev hugged her to him, pressing her head against his shoulder and resting his chin upon her hair. "Try not to, my love. You would do best not to think of me at all if I'm the one who stirred you into sleepdrawing. Perhaps once I am out of reach, you will rest."

"But I could help—" she started to protest before he cut her off.

"You have helped enough." Firmly, he pushed her toward the rail and the rope ladder.

He went down first, guiding Sinda as she followed. Caleb and Will came after them.

She refused to weep in front of his men. She pretended all was well, held her head up, and scanned the shore where they would land. The port had no dock. The bluff here wasn't much higher than the topmast, but high enough to conceal them from the village. She didn't know if Trev understood that he was not only rowing toward his friends and the enemy soldiers, but also her family. They would have had plenty of time to gather and station members at every port on this part of the coast. Even she couldn't predict what would happen next.

She would find out soon enough. As the boat landed on the beach and Will leaped out to pull it toward shore, two figures emerged from the shadows at the foot of the bluff.

She hadn't noticed earlier that Trev wore his sword. It had become so much a part of him that she thought of it as she did the scar on his cheek or the wind in his hair. She noticed when his hand wrapped around the hilt.

"No," she murmured, touching his sword arm. "You've met Aidan. The other is my cousin's husband, Harry. I've told you about him."

She didn't have time to explain further. The two men stepped up to help Will with the line as Caleb held the boat steady with an oar. Keeping a careful watch all along the bluff's edge, Trev stepped into the lapping waves and lifted Sinda into his arms.

He carried her ashore, not setting her down until she was safely on dry land. Warily, he turned to face the two strangers.

The towering dark-haired giant wasn't easy to forget. Trev read no menace in the depths of Aidan's too-knowing eyes. He turned to the shorter, fairer man who wore his rich clothes as if they were as much a part of him as a second skin. Trev wanted to dislike the fellow just for the casualness with which he carried his wealth, but the man wasn't even looking at him. He was admiring the ship.

Studying his adversaries, Trev missed the first part of Sinda's lengthy introduction but caught the last part. "Trev, this is Harry, the Duke of Sommersville, my cousin Christina's husband."

"Duke?" Trev thought his eyebrows soared. "You're the old duke with the castle?"

The blond man offered a genial smile and shrug. "My father was the old duke. We lost him and my brother last winter. I didn't have a chance to visit Lord Rochester before the accident, but I believe I remember both of you from childhood. I was barely out of the nursery at the time, but I have a vague memory of going to the village with my tutor upon occasion. You were the one everyone was always shouting at to come back, and Laurence was the one they always sent to find you. I was quite impressed with your intrepidness in escaping your servants."

The simple memory hit Trev with a punch that opened all the wounds he'd thought to heal by finding his cousin. He winced and nodded. "I climbed an apple tree once and when Laurence came to fetch me, I bombarded him with apples. He climbed up after me and fell and broke his arm. Most of our childhood was like that. You had an older brother, didn't you? I can remember persuading Laurence to hide in the hedgerows until we could jump out and startle his horse so we might rescue a marquess when his horse ran away." Probably one of his lesser rebellions against the society that scorned him, Trev realized with the wisdom of experience.

Harry swung his walking stick and studied him with interest. "Did you succeed?"

"Your brother was a better horseman than we anticipated. He caught me by the collar and hauled me home and dumped me on my father's doorstep."

Harry grinned. "A bit of a hellion, were you?"

"Still is," Aidan grumbled. "Let us depart from here before the soldiers find us." He turned to Sinda. "There is a bit of a climb up the rocks. Shall I carry you?"

"Over my dead body." Stepping in between Sinda and her relations, Trev offered his arm, blocking her from the two men while he lifted a questioning eyebrow to her.

She offered him the gentle smile he remembered from their first encounter in her cottage. It was a smile he associated with welcome and home. He desired nothing more than to take her back to that cottage and make passionate love to her and promise never to leave again. But he was a man of his word, and he couldn't make that promise.

"I will be fine with them," she murmured. "If you wish to find your friends, it might be better if you left me now."

Trev could almost hear the thoughts of the men behind him break into roars of outrage at the possibility that he might walk off unscathed after ruining her reputation. Women didn't understand the male code of honor. He shook his head with a smile. If he survived her family, he could survive his grandfather's soldiers. "I will escort you back."

She looked worried but didn't argue. Taking his arm, she faced her family with defiance. "The viscount is alive but injured. Trev must follow him. There isn't much time."

"There's time for him to meet your father," Aidan replied with confidence. "Would you have your mother and all the other females in your family ripping out our hair because we brought you back alone?"

Trev thought that an interesting viewpoint but didn't question it since Sinda instantly quieted. By Jove, she had *two* dukes looking out for her.

"Is there some reason you would rather I not meet your family?" he asked, voicing an age-old fear.

"Soldiers," she offered succinctly, almost making him smile.

"I'm the magistrate here, remember," Harry said, striding

toward the bluff, swinging his fashionable walking stick as if they traversed a street in London. "Your grandfather's men can only operate at my discretion, or so I shall tell them. I doubt they know the law any better than I do," he finished cheerfully.

"You're the magistrate and you don't know the law?" Trev was beginning to suspect he'd stumbled into a whole new world from the one of his childhood. His memory was embroidered with powerful English aristocrats who were the epitome of wisdom and education. He'd hated the idea of shaming Laurence with his appalling ignorance, but here was a *duke* admitting an astounding gap in his knowledge.

"It's not as if I were trained for the position," Harry said with insouciance. "But I have been informed that dukes are two steps below God, so I assume that outranks an earl and his soldiers."

"Which makes the rest of us pawns," Aidan grumbled from behind them. "I can understand the appeal of yon ship."

"You needn't interfere on my account," Sinda chided him. "Have Ewen and Felicity not finished the work on your castle yet?"

Castle? Trev tried to work his mind around the shabby giant owning a castle. Had he somehow stumbled into a looking-glass world where everything was the reverse of what he expected?

"They're better stewards than I," Aidan admitted grudgingly. "So I'm running Drogo's errands in Ewen's place."

Trev gave up on all the unfamiliar family names. He was fascinated by the notion of a clan that looked after each other the way this one did, but he had no right to expect Sinda's father to accept him as part of their aristocratic family.

Rather than take the beach and parade through town, the young duke led them up a fairly easy slope. He halted occasionally to offer his hand to help Sinda over a particularly rough section while Trev held her from below. He tried to memorize these last few precious moments with her hand in his.

No soldiers met them at the top, and he breathed easier. If

her family meant to send him back to prison, now would be the time to do it, while he stood defenseless. He was at their mercy. He'd left his men below to await his return.

"Do I dare ask how you knew where we would land?" Trev asked, eyeing the waiting carriage.

"Simple deduction," Aidan responded curtly.

"And a direct order from Sinda's mother," Harry concluded. "Never underestimate the power of a Malcolm."

"The deductive power," Aidan corrected. "Plus the power behind a dukedom," he added.

"Give over," Harry argued. "She knew where they'd be and had no way of deducing it logically."

"She knew they couldn't sail straight up to Brighton." Aidan climbed up to the driver's seat. "And behind the bluff is where the current is safest."

Helping Sinda inside the carriage, Trev sent her a questioning glance. She shook her head in response. "Aidan is an Ives and believes only in the power of logic and deduction."

"The women scare him," Harry whispered, climbing inside with them.

"Nothing scares Aidan," Sinda scoffed. "He's an obstinate oaf."

Charmed by the family argument, Trev settled back against the cushions and pretended all was well with the world—for a little while. He had the most beautiful woman he knew at his side, and she'd agreed to wait for him. He could pretend he had a bright future ahead of him—until his head rolled across the floor.

"My father, the Duke of Mainwaring." Sinda didn't curtsy to the regal man waiting in the downstairs parlor of the inn but held Trev's arm as if he were the duke's equal. "Sir Trevelyan Rochester, late of His Majesty's service."

Trev calculated her father was of a height with him and a few stone heavier. Beneath his elegant wig, the duke possessed the authoritative countenance of a man who judged all others beneath him, which was apparently the entire world except for the king and the prince. Trev had met the duke last on his London doorstep, in the light of torches. In the gray morning, Mainwaring looked younger than he ought, and Trev distracted himself by wondering if the Malcolms had potions to prevent aging.

"Is Mother here?" Sinda asked with the confidence of a woman who knew her place in the world. The certainty in her voice reassured him more than anything. If she was capable of standing up to her family, there was some hope for him.

"Your mother is upstairs with Cecily and Christina. You have caused them a great deal of concern." The duke frowned. "I suggest you go up to them while I speak with your friend."

Trev thought it might be more convenient if a hole opened beneath him and sent him straight to hell, but he smiled jauntily for Sinda's sake and bowed over her hand as if he'd simply brought her home from a concert. Pride allowed no less than supreme confidence. "I'll ask for tea to be sent up. You haven't eaten," he said.

He had no reason to believe the look she shot him was approving, but he liked to believe it was.

As Sinda left in search of her mother, Harry remained behind, whether as friend or enemy, Trev couldn't ascertain. Aidan hadn't come in from the carriage. Trev suspected he was a man more comfortable alone outdoors than inside with people.

With Sinda out of the room, Trev inhaled deeply and faced the outraged duke—not that anyone could tell that the duke raged behind his bland façade of an English gentleman.

"His Majesty knighted me for my service," Trev said boldly, taking the offensive. "I have accumulated sufficient wealth to purchase a small kingdom. I believe your daughter has developed an affection for me. I would like to ask for her hand in marriage."

Given that he'd ruined her, he could do no less than make an offer. He couldn't believe the duke would allow it, but he could hope.

The duke knotted his hands behind his back and rocked back and forth on his high heels. Trev assumed Harry was lounging against the mantel. Two dukes. Damn, but he had a knack for finding trouble.

"Did you find your cousin?" Mainwaring asked.

Trev didn't fool himself into relaxing at the man's casual tone. "A man who looks like Laurence has been living in Poole. He was last seen day before yesterday aboard a ship I believe to be owned by smugglers. That man was brought in injured this past summer and cannot remember his name."

"So if this man is actually your cousin, he cannot clear your name?"

Trev hadn't thought of that. He'd been so relieved to have reason to hope Laurence was alive that he hadn't thought further. Forced to look at it as others must, he clenched his teeth. "He's not dead. I was not in England when his yacht capsized. I had no reason to wish him harm. He is the best friend I have in this country."

"You stand to inherit an earldom if he dies and you prove your legitimacy in court," Mainwaring argued.

"I don't want the damned earldom! My grandfather saw to it that I was not raised to the life of an earl. I have no place in London or society or Parliament. I'm a sailor, a simple man. I want a home and a wife. Your daughter has agreed to be my wife." That was a slight exaggeration. She had said she would wait for him, and he was arrogant enough to believe that meant she would marry him. "I will find my cousin, show all the world that I do not wish him harm, and there will be an end to it."

"Your grandfather declared you a bastard long ago. He has charged you with your cousin's murder. He has recently appointed a distant cousin as guardian for the viscountess and her unborn child and ordered her to attend him in London."

"He will send her back to her family if she bears a girl," Trev said, horrified that Melinda's fears were coming true already. "Her parents have little or nothing but what Laurence gives them. The Willows belongs to Laurence. My grand-father cannot evict them."

"He can if Laurence is dead, the same way he took the estate from you after your parents died," Mainwaring said shrewdly.

Trev saw the hardness in the other man's eyes and knew the trap had been laid. Sinda had obviously inherited her intelligence and discernment from her father. He could walk out of here now, find Laurence, and pray Sinda would have him later.

Or he could stay and see what her father had up his sleeve.

As he'd already proved often enough, he wasn't a man inclined to walk away from trouble. "I have sent my credentials to Parliament to prove I am not a bastard, and I am not a murderer. My cousin is alive and I go to seek him now."

"I can call on a judge to have the murder charge rescinded and arrange for your credentials to be presented tomorrow. As immediate heir to the earldom, you could have the court appoint you guardian to your cousin's estate and family within the week."

Men like this did not grant his every desire for the sheer pleasure of it. Instead of feeling gratitude and relief, Trev waited to see from which direction the cannonball would strike. "In exchange for… ?"

"My daughter's happiness. You, sir, have admitted that you are not raised to society. You're a scoundrel who has kidnapped and ruined her, a privateer and a rakehell with a reputation that has followed you across the Atlantic. If you claim you can make her happy, I will label you a liar as well. She has been sheltered by her family all her life. If you know anything of her at all, you must understand why she must be sheltered. Leave her alone," the duke thundered, "and your case will be in front of Parliament by morning."

"If I have ruined her, then I have offered reparation," Trev answered incredulously, more concerned about Sinda right now than with the duke's incredible proposal. "Your idea of sheltering her is to return her to London gossip after she's been seen in company with me?"

"For all the world knows, she has been staying with Christina." The duke jerked his head at the younger man waiting by the door. "Harry will vouch for her. The artist from the village seen in your company has red hair. No one in London will believe she is Lucinda."

Trev swung on his heel to regard the younger duke. Harry didn't look happy, but whether that was at the ultimatum or something else was impossible to tell. Sinda's family could shelter her from scandal, give her the security he could not hope to offer even should he find Laurence—which he might never do.

His hope of marrying her died an agonizing death. He'd known it was the wrong thing anyway. His impetuous nature would always cause trouble.

He might agree with the duke that he made a poor husband for a delicate lady, but his stubborn nature refused to exchange Lucinda for the duke's crass blackmail. No matter how much he wished to protect the Willows, he would not have Sinda think he'd used her for his own gain.

Hand on the hilt of his sword, Trev glared at Mainwaring. "Lady Lucinda's happiness is all I care about. I do not need or want your aid. I suggest that you consult her as to what will make her happiest and act accordingly. I must bid you good day. The tide will not wait for me."

"Not so fast, young man!" the duke ordered with quiet menace.

Before Trev could ignore him and walk out, Aidan appeared in the doorway and Harry blocked his exit.

Trev spun around to confront Sinda's father. "You refused my offer. I leave your daughter here with you as requested while I go to find my cousin. What would you have of me?"

"Sinda's cooperation," the duke said with finality.

Twenty-eight

"THERE ARE SOLDIERS OUT THERE!" SINDA WHISPERED IN horror, glancing out the inn window of the spacious chamber her mother had taken. She'd hugged her family upon entering the room and immediately gone to check if she could see Trev leave. Two redcoats stood in the street below.

She wished her family hadn't brought Cecily. Her sister was too young to be involved in this argument. She spun around to face them. "What have you done with Trevelyan?"

"Not a thing that I'm aware of," her mother said with equanimity, settling into a chair. "Although I wouldn't object if they flung him into the ocean with his arms tied behind his back."

"Aunt Stella!" Christina admonished. "You haven't heard his side of the story. I think it's all very romantical."

"You're five months pregnant and thinking without your brains," the duchess replied implacably. "Sinda is a late bloomer who fell for a pretty face. Sir Trevelyan is a blackguard who took advantage of her innocence for his own purposes."

Sinda rolled her eyes, took a seat in the window so she could keep an eye on the soldiers, and removed her pencil and notebook from her pocket. "How very fair of you to judge a man before you've met him." She prayed Trev stood brave in the face of her father's equal fury.

"A gentleman would not have run off with you!" Stella, Duchess of Mainwaring, asserted.

"Perhaps I didn't want a gentleman," Sinda argued, smiling to herself. She definitely did not want the usual sort of gentleman. She wanted Trev.

"London is awash with rumors. They'll have the man hanged if he shows his face there again." Her mother dismissed Trevelyan as if he were no more than an aberration. "I have ordered up a bath so you might wash out that dye, and Christina brought your clothes." She nodded at a bulging portmanteau. "When you leave here, no one will know you're the woman who arrived with a pirate. With a little circumspect behavior, none of the rumors will touch you."

"So I might return to my ivory tower where you can hide me and my art from society? I don't think so, thank you." Sinda loved her mother, but even those who loved her had to admit that the duchess had a tendency to be domineering. It came from being the head of a rather creatively erratic family, she supposed, but they all had to learn to fly on their own sometime. She would continue hiding her portraits if she must, but not her landscapes. To paint only for herself was far too lonely.

"Have you drawn something while you were gone to tell us who killed the viscount?" Christina asked, interrupting before her aunt could say anything more explosive.

Relieved that someone was being sensible, Sinda answered, "The viscount was injured and has lost his memory. Trevelyan would be on his trail if everyone would leave him alone."

"How do you know? Does this have something to do with your sleep-walking drawings?" Christina demanded with excitement.

"Those drawings were of the viscount." Sinda ignored her mother's frown. "I've never seen him before, but Trev says the sketches are quite accurate. The last one I drew showed the village where he was staying."

Stella moaned. "And you believed him? You took *his* word that the man in the drawing is his cousin, alive and well?"

That startled Sinda, and she stared at her mother. "Of course I took his word. Why should he lie?" Which was a silly question. A dishonorable man would lie to protect his own neck. Trev wasn't a dishonorable man, but how could she convince her family of that?

Fury and frustration built. She did not possess the words to convince her family that Trevelyan Rochester was a man persecuted by his grandfather, a strong man who had survived despite terrible odds. Trev was a stranger to them, while the earl was well-known. She had only her gift as proof of the earl's treachery, and that was erratic.

She let her fingers fly across the page beneath her fingers and smothered the anger in her chest. Always, she had sat back and observed through family disagreements. She had no practice in fighting back because she'd never had any inclination to argue. She didn't have the ability now, only this pressure of unsaid words building inside her.

Acrimonious voices erupted in the hallway. Before any of the women could rise to discover the cause, the door burst open, and the spacious chamber suddenly teemed with large male bodies, physical energy, and fury.

Sinda sat frozen, watching an implacable expression form on Trev's bronzed visage the instant he recognized the room's occupants. Aidan had Trev's sword arm in a tight grip. Harry took a stance behind his wife, placing a reassuring hand on Christina's shoulder.

Sinda's father slammed the door. She'd always thought of him as a towering figure who'd marched through her life, casting aside all dangers, smoothing over life's hurdles for her. Now she saw Trev held his own against him, and she breathed easier. Her pirate was easily the most dashing, daring man in here. He would not let her family trample him.

Her fingers continued flying across the page, but her gaze remained firmly on Trev's handsome features, as his did on her. That he could concentrate on her in this maelstrom of loud and forceful people eased the pain in her heart. She waited.

"Find the viscountess," Sinda's father ordered, and Cecily jumped to his command. "Let us all hear this at once."

Trev jerked in surprise. Sinda raised her eyebrows and sought Christina.

"Melinda came to me," Christina explained. "She did not want to go to the earl in London, but she didn't know what had happened to Sir Trevelyan. She was so distraught, we brought her with us."

"What of Charity?" Trev demanded, startling the room's occupants. "Where is she?"

"With the nursemaid I hired for our son." Christina rested a hand on her slightly protruding belly.

Sinda tried not to chuckle as Trev struggled to stifle his curiosity about a woman who knew the sex of—and hired a nursemaid for—an unborn child. He was learning already that one did not question the beliefs of a new mother, especially a Malcolm. He merely nodded at Christina for her reassurance of Charity's safety. "Thank you."

"Aidan, for pity's sake, he's the grandson of an earl, not a noble savage. He'll not lop off anyone's head. Let him go," Sinda snapped, surprising herself. Trev was being reasonable. Why couldn't her family be? "How would you like it if Trevelyan grabbed your arm like that?"

"I'd like to see him try," the giant replied gruffly. But he released his prisoner and crossed his arms over his chest.

"Another time, perhaps," Trev promised, before turning to watch the door as slow footsteps approached down the corridor. "I assume the meaning of this will be explained? The tide will turn shortly, and my ship will be forced to leave me stranded."

The heavily pregnant Lady Melinda Rochester entered, leaning on Cecily's arm. Sinda's younger sister looked more fascinated than concerned about this turn of events. She helped Melinda into a seat near the window.

"Now, let us lay out the terms of our agreement so there is no question in anyone's mind," the duke ordered. "Sinda, this man has dared to ask for your hand in marriage."

She nodded politely at her father. Let him have his little drama. She didn't see marriage in her future, but Trev had done as was expected of a gentleman. She had anticipated no less. She fixed her gaze on Trev, flipped the page of her notebook, and began sketching some more, letting her fingers express what her words could not.

Accustomed to her nonreplies, her father remained unperturbed. "I have offered to bring the question of his legitimacy before Parliament so he might claim his rightful place and be named guardian of the viscountess and her children in the absence of his cousin. Will this suit you, Lady Rochester?"

Melinda looked terrified. She searched Christina's and Sinda's faces, then turned to Trevelyan. "You would not turn us out of our home?"

"You know I would not," Trev answered stiffly.

He might have told Melinda that Laurence was alive, but Sinda understood he wouldn't until he was certain of it himself. There was no sense in throwing the lady into grief again, especially now that she seemed to have quit weeping and was looking out for herself.

Sitting up straight, the viscountess tightened her jaw and turned to Sinda's father. "Sir Trevelyan has taken care of us well since his arrival. I trust him more than I do Lansdowne."

Sinda wanted to sing in triumph. She saw relief flicker in Trev's eyes. He had the family he wanted now, a family who trusted him. She would thank the goddess, but she didn't think her father was done yet.

"Excellent." The duke nodded approvingly and turned to Trev. "Do you wish to ask my daughter, or shall I?"

The pencil broke beneath Sinda's fingers as the tension between Trev and her father escalated. She was not going to like what she heard next. She glanced down at the drawing and bit back a gasp. Hastily, she flipped the page and tucked the broken pencil behind her back. Her mother looked at her with suspicion, but Trev's voice intruded.

"His Grace offers to trade his daughter's happiness in return for freeing me of the murder charge and supporting my cause in Parliament," Trev explained to his audience. "I have not accepted his offer because Sinda's happiness is more important to me than my own, and I would consult her. I can fight my grandfather and Parliament without need of anyone's help."

He said it so proudly and bravely that Sinda wanted to weep. He was an independent rogue, a man who took aid and orders from no one, and he was asking for her opinion at the expense of his future. She would love him for that alone.

She knew the basis of the argument without having it explained. Her father believed Trev unsuitable and had told him she would be happier if he would walk away. Almost any other man of her acquaintance would have cheerfully accepted the offer to escape the penalty of marriage.

If she truly loved Trev, she could give him everything he desired—freedom from the earl's tyranny and a life with his cousin's family—by telling him she could be happy without him. Except she feared it would be like a slap to his face if she said such a thing in front of everyone, after he'd behaved so nobly. She didn't want to hurt him.

She needed to remind herself of why she could never marry—to give her the incentive to send him away with a free conscience.

She flipped the page of the notebook back to the sketch she'd just completed. She understood clearly now why the black cloud had shadowed her self-portraits. She wasn't meant to be happy. But Trev deserved to be.

"I can be happy without you," she said so softly every person in the room strained to hear. "Go with my father to Parliament and clear your name so you might take care of your family."

She was fully aware that Trev stiffened at her response. She had spurned him just as his grandfather had done. She deserved to be struck for her cruelty. She waited for the frozen silence to shatter. Biting her bottom lip, she didn't dare raise her eyes from the evil horror in her lap, to the lesser horror she had just created in Trev's eyes.

She didn't want to watch his confident expression freeze over or see him escort Melinda from the room and never look her way again.

A babble of voices broke out around her, but she couldn't seem to hear them. Tears threatened to spill from her eyes as she stared at the abomination her fingers had unthinkingly produced: on the notepad, the battered and bloodied body of the viscount lay fallen in a trash-strewn alley while his murderers slipped away. They had their backs to the viewer, so she could not identify them. Thieves, she supposed. Thieves had murdered the viscount. Or possibly smugglers. That was why she no longer drew him in her sleep. Had his memory returned? Had they killed him because of what he knew?

But it was the second page that had forced her to give up Trevelyan, love, and her future in exchange for her father's offer to help. In the second sketch, she'd drawn Trev standing over his cousin, cudgel in hand, his expression of grief one she wished never to see in this lifetime.

She knew he had not murdered the viscount. She had drawn the villains, after all. But even she could understand the significance of the second drawing—and the future that her gift predicted.

Trev would be arrested for the murder of his cousin no matter what judge her father bribed—unless Trev was safely in London in the company of someone as powerful as her father until the viscount's body was discovered.

She could be happy knowing she was saving him, she supposed, even if it meant he would never want to see her again.

❧

"Tell me to my face that you never wish to see me again." In his anger, Trev disregarded the babble around him as he watched the slender woman in the window, the woman to whom he had trusted his heart and his future. Rage at her betrayal shook him back to the days when blind fury had ruled his life.

Did she not believe he could find Laurence and free himself? How could she so casually promise to throw away the vows they'd made? She sat there looking angelic, not a trace of emotion marring her lovely face as she sat with her hands in her lap…

Her hands were still. She had held a pencil earlier, and her fingers had flown across the page. That alone had reassured him that all was well. Sinda was being Sinda, ignoring the turmoil and escaping into the world she created. He adored the way she did that.

She wasn't ignoring the world now. She was right here with him, her fear so great that her back stiffened with the strain of it. Even her mother—disapproval oozing from every aristocratic pore—was beginning to look wary.

Before anyone could intervene, Trev stalked past both duchesses and Melinda to snatch the paper from Sinda's frozen fingers. He had to tug hard. She didn't want to let go. Her eyes were frightened shards of sky tearing into his heart as they pleaded with him.

"Stay with my father," she whispered urgently. "Every court in the land will believe him if he testifies that you cannot have done this. You have to think of Melinda and the children."

She released the paper, and Trev stared at the atrocity that had spilled from her unwitting fingers. He would prefer not to believe what she had drawn, but she had been right in all else.

Someone was about to murder Laurence. Or had already done so.

No, they hadn't done so. Not if he was standing over the body.

There was time to prevent the murder. He recognized the alley. Laurence had returned to London and was headed for the earl—straight through an alley frequented by the infamous St. James thieves. Laurence had not been in London this autumn to hear of their depredations.

"I know where this is." Dropping the paper back to her lap, he kissed her hair. "I love you," he murmured, although he didn't know if she heard through the uproar around them.

With no further delay, he swung around and rushed past the women. The men instantly blocked the door, and Trev whipped out his blade, slicing through the young duke's pretty coat buttons with a flick of his wrist. He didn't want to slay Sinda's relatives to save his own, but he'd damned well nick a few arms if it would get him out of here faster.

Behind him, Melinda screamed and kept on screaming. Someone had undoubtedly grabbed the notebook, and she'd seen the horror in it.

Sinda shouted "No, Trev! They will blame you. Don't you see…"

Unheeding of the hysterics, Trev raised a crooked eyebrow to Aidan, the biggest obstacle to his escape. "My cousin is about to be murdered, and I mean to prevent it. Do you move from my way or do I move you?"

Aidan cast a glance over Trev's shoulder. Trev could imagine the scene there, one duchess holding Sinda back while the other comforted Melinda. He pressed his blade tip into the sorry coat covering the other man's shoulder, slicing through to the vest below.

The two dukes had the sense not to make any sudden moves.

"You're as mad as all the rest," Aidan replied in disgust, stepping from his path. "The women bend you like willows."

Had he not been so furious, Trev would have roared with laughter. Willows bent but didn't break, after all. He was bent in more ways than one, but he wasn't broken.

He heard the shout as Sinda pulled free, but he would leave her family to catch her. He bolted out the door before anyone thought of other means to prevent his escape.

Boots pounded up the front steps. The soldiers downstairs would have heard the commotion. The duke was probably relying on the redcoats to stop him, but he had years of experience at avoiding traps. He'd noted the layout of the inn the last time they'd stayed here.

Without hesitation, he raced across the hall and to the first open door he found. A maid inside screamed and dropped a chamber pot. China shattered, but he had the window wide before the stench filled the room. Throwing his legs over the sill, he dropped to the overhang below, sword still in hand.

He heard shouts but saw no soldiers below. They'd catch on soon enough. Not waiting until they did, he slid to the lowest part of the arched roof and dropped to the ground.

He landed feet first. It was a damned long way back to the ship, and he didn't have a carriage at his disposal. He glanced around, noted three nags in the stable yard, and ran for the one that looked most sound.

Twenty-nine

"Sinda, no!" the duchess shouted as Sinda darted across the room.

Christina and Cecily had their hands full comforting the viscountess, who had grabbed the sketch from Sinda's hands and collapsed in a hysterical heap.

Holding her hands to her belly and moaning, Melinda looked as if she might give birth right there on the floor. Sinda was sympathetic, but there were people here far more qualified to help Melinda than she was. She would do better aiding the lady's husband and cousin.

Had Trev said he *loved* her? This wasn't the time to ponder the possibility.

Harry, her father, and Aidan had rushed out on Trev's heels. Sinda didn't know if they meant to stop or aid him. She simply calculated that the only person left to interfere in her decision was her mother, the grand dame of the Malcolm clan, the woman who could cast her into the streets if she so chose.

Admittedly, as she blocked Sinda's escape, her mother was a fearsome figure in towering high heels and elegantly coifed wig. With a single frown, she could intimidate generals and kings.

Sinda had never opposed her mother. The duchess always had the best interests of her daughters in mind, but in this, her mother was wrong.

"Let him go, Lucinda," Stella warned. "You have done all you can for him."

"If no one else will, I can stand by his side and declare his innocence. I can sail with him if he's forced to leave the country. He will need me." She didn't know what she would do if her mother attempted to physically stop her. Her mother was taller and heavier and once had the courage to break a parasol over the head of a thief. Sinda wasn't looking forward to a fight.

But she had no intention of letting Trev go without aid. She could hear the shouts of the men in the street below. Time was running out. She grabbed the portmanteau Christina had packed. It was heavy enough to use as a weapon.

"You would leave England and your family?" her mother asked in horror, grasping the significance of Sinda's choice of weapon and stepping back.

"I don't want to, but I will if I must. The chance is much smaller if you would let me pass." With all the confidence she'd gained these past days, Sinda swept past her stunned mother and out the door with all her worldly goods in hand.

She raced down the front stairs and out the inn door. To her horror, she saw Trev on a rearing horse, wielding his rapier to fight off soldiers attacking him with sword and musket.

Her father shouted commands that were ignored in the heat of battle. The soldiers would pay for their disobedience later, but at the moment, one of them was reloading his musket.

Before Sinda could scream a warning, Aidan caught the cur by his red coat, lifted him from his feet, and hurled him backward into the street. Harry grabbed the musket and pressed it to the fallen man's coat while Aidan grabbed the next man hindering Trev's escape.

They were helping him!

Sinda's elation crashed soon enough when she saw more redcoats racing down the street. Her family was merely clearing the way so Trev could escape to his ship—leaving her behind.

As if sensing her thoughts, Trev looked up in that moment, caught sight of her, and striking the rapier from the hand of the man clinging to his horse's reins, nodded at a wagon up the hill. The Gypsy cart!

All indecision gone, Sinda knew what she must do. Bypassing the battle raging in the street, she ran up the hill to the colorful cart with only a wooden block for brake and a horse to hold it in place. To her amazement, two old men scrambled from the back.

"Jump in, lass. We'll take you out of here. Trev will follow on his own." The balder of the two men held the door for her.

"No, no!" Dropping her bag out of the way, she gestured at the soldiers running up the street from the opposite direction. "Unharness the horse." She kicked the wooden block from beneath the right wheel and felt the cart lurch backward until the horse checked it.

They looked at her as if she were crazed yet leaped to obey her command.

She helped them unfasten the harness, then placed her shoulder against the cart as the men did after she explained what she wanted. With a shove, they sent the two-wheeled towering cart downhill toward the melee.

"Not bad for us old fellas," the balding man pronounced with glee as they watched the vehicle's rumbling progress.

Shouts of warning rang out below. Hands on hips, Sinda watched in satisfaction as all the men on foot scattered to avoid the top-heavy vehicle lurching from side to side, building momentum without a definite direction beyond *down*. "Thank you, gentlemen."

The wirier of the two cast her a sideways glance. "To make up for the way we let him treat you earlier," he offered in apology.

"Help him find the smugglers and his cousin, and I may forgive you." Understanding these were the men who had helped Trev escape, she could not condemn their loyalty to him. Instead, she lifted her bag to tie it to the Gypsy horse's harness.

Below, Trev took advantage of the confusion. While all else dodged the runaway cart, he flicked his rapier to disarm a soldier in his way and, kicking his mount into motion, raced past the careening cart and up the hill toward Sinda. Broad shoulders straining the seams of his coat, neckcloth flying in the wind, unshaven jaw clenched, he was magnificent.

"Help me up! Now!" she shouted at the old men watching the scene with delight. She grabbed the cart horse's reins and tried to climb up without benefit of saddle or stirrup.

The larger man kneeled down and gave her a step up. Casting propriety to the winds, she slung her leg over the horse's back and urged it into a canter before Trev could reach her. If she were throwing away her future and her family for the man, he'd better learn not to get in her way. Like it or not, she was going with him.

To her delight, Trev gave the rump of her horse another smack so it broke into a gallop to keep up with his. She clung to reins and mane and pressed her knees as tightly as she could into the mare's side. Her hairpins came loose and her hair flew into the wind. And joy filled her soul as Trev turned and grinned back at her, his hair streaming behind him.

Together, they raced toward the beach and the ship—arriving just as the sails caught the wind to ride the tide out.

"Too late," she murmured, heart plummeting as their only hope of reaching the viscount fled out to sea. "Can we catch them elsewhere? Where will they go?"

"They'll sail out with the tide and wait." Trev cast a glance over his shoulder. "Perhaps that's for the best. Your family will see the sails and think we've gone, but horses will take us to London faster."

She looked at him in disbelief. "You can't take a stolen horse!"

Without arguing, he rode his mount behind a crumbling fort where they were not quite so visible. To Sinda's dismay, he dismounted the stolen horse and strode toward hers. "I will not stay behind," she informed him, contrary to her earlier shocked objection.

"She's a Gypsy horse. She'll ride us." Without further ado, he swung up on the blanket behind her, keeping the reins.

Us. He'd said *us.* She was going with him. She leaned back against his chest and turned a beaming smile up at him.

Looking down at her, he frowned. "I have no idea what awaits us at the end of this road."

"Neither do I, but we will face it together," she said with assurance. She couldn't go back now, couldn't take the easy way and return to her safe little world. "It's my drawing that has brought us to this pass," she reminded him. "I can no longer keep drawing these things and not acting on them. I will stand as your witness."

He kissed her forehead in reluctant acceptance. With a snap of the leather, he sent the horse lumbering across the field to the London road.

In the distance, the *Lass*'s sails billowed across gray waves. Beneath the lowering clouds of an approaching storm, a colorful gathering of silk gowns and expensive frock coats stood on the rock bluff, watching the ship take to sea. Her family.

Her sketch had been wrong. Instead of standing on the rocks with her family, she was riding away with Trev. He hadn't left her behind. The ship had. She'd changed the course of her drawing. "I did it," she said, savoring the success of her rebellion.

Trev caught her chin and turned her head toward him, his eyebrows raised in question.

"I acted instead of observed," she explained.

Enlightenment appeared behind his dark lashes. "The sketch. You're not out there with your family, and I'm not sailing away."

"The scenes I draw don't have to happen," she agreed, waiting for him to grasp the significance.

"They're just one of many possibilities. The probable one, given the current course of action." He tightened his grip on her waist. "You can sketch the past, as you sketched Laurence. But if you draw the future, we can still hope to change it. We'll find him this time. He's only a day ahead of us, and he went the long way around, by fishing boat."

He said it with such certainty that she believed him. They were on course with her drawing. Trev could find his cousin. The question was, could he find him in time to save him?

The road to London led through Sommersville and past the Willows. They left the Gypsy horse in Mick's hands, exchanging it for Trev's powerful stallion and Melinda's mount.

"How long will it take before your family realizes we're not on that ship?" he asked as he threw Sinda into a lady's saddle and tied on her portmanteau.

He longed to leave her here where she would be safe, but she was right. He needed a witness. Mick would not be believed, but Sinda had two damned dukes and an entire family of powerful women who would testify in her favor—and thus his.

"I daresay my mother or Aidan already suspect," she warned. "Aidan may simply follow without raising an alarm. I cannot say the same for my mother. But my family would never desert Melinda, so they can't follow swiftly."

They took a trail across the fields, avoiding the obvious routes.

"Explain Aidan. Will he be able to catch up with us?" Would the man trust him or try to bring him down was the real question. Trev had seen the giant flinging the soldier into the street. He would excuse the action by figuring any honorable man would object to a musket against an unarmed man, except Trev hadn't been unarmed. The whole family was a mystery to him.

"I cannot explain Aidan. I don't think anyone can," she replied. "He has given his home over to my cousin Felicity and her Ives husband, and latcly he has been helping stabilize Harry's falling down castle. He comes and goes as he pleases, without word or explanation. I think he has no family, so he has adopted ours."

Trev thought he could understand that. He would gladly adopt Sinda's intriguing family and call them his own. He would live in Laurence's house and babysit if that was the only way he could have his home and family back. But he would never admit such a weakness.

"Then he will do whatever it takes to keep you safe," he said aloud.

Sinda threw him a startled glance, but he could tell she

accepted that judgment. As he accepted hers. Together, they had a chance to save Laurence.

Praying he wasn't too late, Trev urged their horses on. He knew where they had to be by nightfall.

He simply didn't know on which night.

～

"It must be past midnight," Sinda protested as they rode through a jam of carriages and sedan chairs on the new Westminster Bridge. "Why don't all these people go home?"

Trev knew she had to be exhausted, and he would give anything to deposit her in the nearest decent inn so she could rest, but he had to reach the alley he'd recognized in her drawing. He prayed he wouldn't find Laurence's body there yet. "Did you never go to Ranelagh or Vauxhall or a ball and arrive home in the wee hours of the morning?"

"I was not allowed in the pleasure gardens," she muttered, glaring as they passed the tangle of carriages and farm carts that blocked the bridge.

"Then I shall take you someday," he promised. They were almost at the alley. He didn't tell her that if his cousin wasn't there when they arrived, they must linger until morning. This was making less sense as the night wore on and he grew wearier. What possible chance did he have of being in the alley at the right time? Perhaps the thief he'd encountered when he'd first chased after Sinda kept regular hours and he could inquire, he thought sardonically.

"My mother fears that if I visit the gardens, I will see something lewd or unsavory and those kinds of things will occur in my paintings," she explained. "Apparently I need only sleep with you for murder to appear under my fingers."

Trev cast her a glance to see how she meant that. They'd stopped briefly for food and drink and to rest the horses. Sinda had braided and tied her hair in ribbons again, and looked more pirate lass or Gypsy than lady.

"I bring you in contact with less savory elements, admittedly. I am sorry." He'd had enough time to understand why her family had kept her sheltered. Everything she saw and felt, the people she met, no doubt even the songs she heard, became part and parcel of her unpredictable artwork. Give her pleasant surroundings and kind companions, and she might paint lovely things. Put her in contact with his fears and darkness formed.

"Would you prefer I not be aware of what happens to my cousin?" he asked, uncertain of his own answer to that question when looked at from her viewpoint. "That we not see what we aren't meant to see?"

"I don't know." Guiding her horse with expertise, she concentrated on dodging the crowd.

If they came out of this whole, it was a topic they must discuss, he knew. How could she continue to live with her visionary gift? She would have people looking over her shoulder every minute of every day to see what she might predict next.

For the moment, survival was uppermost in his mind. The streets of London were dangerous in broad daylight. At this hour, drunks and thieves lingered around every corner. He caught the reins of her horse and led her down a less-traversed byway.

"How can you know the alleys of London after you have been away so long?" she asked.

"They haven't changed that much since I visited London in my youth."

"You can identify an alley you haven't seen in almost twenty years?"

"I can when it's within a block of my grandfather's home. I used to run down it every day on the way to see what they had at the market. The West End of London is not so large that a small boy can't find his way around." Besides, he'd just been here a few weeks ago, chasing her. But he'd leave that explanation for another time.

"Do you think your cousin has recovered enough of his memory to find your grandfather's home?" She pulled her mare to a halt in the light of a torch from a nearby inn.

Trev halted beside her, studying the street for faces he might recognize—or villains carrying cudgels. "Perhaps he found his way there, and his murder is no accidental encounter."

She gasped at his insinuation. Trev had had a much longer time to consider the theory. It didn't hold water, but then, neither did anything else he knew.

Why, for example, would Laurence take a ship to London instead of straight home?

Thirty

"Much as I love you, my Lady Sin, I could wish you were a man right now."

Sinda heard the weariness in Trev's voice as they halted at the mouth of an alley so deep and dark she could not see its end. She smiled more at his name for her than at his jest. *Lady Sin.* She liked that. It sounded dark and exotic and romantic, completely unlike her.

Trev loved her. He had said it carelessly, as if he expected her to know it already, as if that one whisper amid chaos was enough. Or perhaps he said it to many women when they blindly followed him into trouble. Although his declaration caused her heart to beat with joy, now was not the time to indulge in romantic fantasies.

"Life might be simpler in some ways if I were a man," she agreed, "but it would be exceedingly less pleasant in others."

She thought he grinned at that, but the alley was dark and they had no torch. She hated dark, enclosed places. She took a deep breath to calm her nerves.

"Thieves inhabit this alley," he warned. "I could hope I chased away the last rapscallion it harbored, but there is always another to take his place."

A shout from the depths of darkness shattered any illusion that they might linger. Trev leaped from his horse, unbuckling his rapier.

"Hold the horses," he commanded, flinging the reins to

her. "If that's Laurence, the animals could trample him in the dark." He slipped into the shadows before she could protest.

He offered an easy excuse not to enter the frightening darkness. The horses were already nervous, shying at the slightest sound. The alley was narrow. She would only be in the way if she entered it. Instead, she could block the passage and prevent the villain's escape. Or run off and find help.

The sound of a *thud* and a dull moan killed any hesitation. She could not act the coward and let Trev come to harm. She slid off her mount and leading both horses, stepped cautiously into the alley. The walls on either side pressed in on her. She didn't think she could wield her valise as weapon with two horses in hand. She felt trapped. And terrified.

But she'd learned to overcome her timidity with action these past weeks.

Her eyes adjusted to the shadows and shapes scuffling amid the debris. Four men, she decided. She could see none on the ground, but it was very dark. Had Trev arrived in time to save the viscount, or were these all thieves?

"I told the last of you I met to find a new location before I returned!" she heard Trev shout. "You should have heeded my lesson."

His rapier caught a gleam of light from the alley's end, so she could identify him easily enough. He fought with a stout man who swung a wicked stick. She winced as Trev dodged a blow that would have been deadly had it connected. Beside him, a man nearly as tall as Trev but more slender grappled with a second man with a stick, holding his attacker's wrist to prevent him from using the weapon.

Before she could act in any way, the second thief tore his wrist free to crack his bludgeon across the slender man's head. Sinda screamed as the poor man sank to the ground. If it was the viscount, then he'd surely been killed despite their efforts.

Trev roared his rage and anguish. With an underhanded sword thrust, he disarmed his opponent, who screamed in pain and staggered backward, holding his side. Grabbing the fallen bludgeon, he swung at the slender man's attacker, causing the thief to double up in pain, then stumble into retreat after his bloodied companion.

Despite her terror, Sinda hurried forward.

On the floor of the alley the slender man groaned. Over him stood Trev, hardly winded, bludgeon in hand, just as in her sketch. Please the goddess, surely they had not come all this way only to lose him now?

She dropped to her knees in the debris without regard to her already bedraggled dress. "He took a nasty blow. If his brains were scrambled before, he'll have naught left of them now," she murmured. "Is it him?"

"Yes," Trev said curtly, kneeling beside her to test his cousin's pulse. "He's alive. We must get him to a bed and find a physician."

"My home is about half a mile from here," she said. "Can you lift him onto my horse?" The man on the ground lay still. She could see blood trickling down his cheek from a gash near his temple.

"The earl's house is closer."

Anger simmered in his voice, and Sinda didn't question as he lifted the fallen man. She supposed he must learn to deal with his family, although how he could recognize the viscount through the blood and bruises after all these years was beyond her. Love gave additional insight, she supposed.

Silently, she helped him balance his unconscious cousin in her saddle. Melinda's mare wasn't as tall or high strung as Trev's stallion, but it still took a good deal of strength to keep the viscount in place while they tied his arms around the mare's neck. Then Trev helped Sinda up behind his cousin to hold him in place while he took the reins and led them from the alley.

"You do not think the thieves will be waiting for us on the other end?" she whispered.

"Thieves are cowards. And idiots," he added with more exasperation than anger. "I've bloodied them. They'll run."

"Then it wasn't the earl's men who set upon your cousin?" she asked in relief.

"No, unless my grandfather has lost what is left of his wits and has hired the St. James thieves to hang about in alleys. How is he?"

She knew he referred to the viscount. The man lay slumped across the mare's neck, but he breathed. "Holding steady. Do not ask me to gallop with him though."

Trev offered a tired grunt of agreement. She prayed he hadn't been hurt. She tried to study him in the light of the few lamps they passed, but she didn't see blood.

"You saved him," she murmured. "All will be well."

"All will be hell," he muttered in return as they turned down a wide street of expensive townhouses. "I wish you did not have to witness this next scene."

"I would rather not have seen the last one," she said dryly. "I think I will need a lot of dark chalk."

He snorted in what might have been laughter; she couldn't be certain. If he could laugh at the idea of her staying up half the night slathering black chalk across a canvas to depict this scene, then he was still her pirate.

As they halted their horses in front of a dark mansion, a broad-shouldered figure stepped out of the shadows below the stairs. Trev instantly placed his horse between Sinda and the shadow, but she recognized the man approaching.

"Davy! Whatever do you do here?" she demanded.

"Aidan sent us to guard every house he thought you might go to. Is that the viscount?" He nodded toward the man stirring in front of her.

"Aidan again," Trev growled, swinging off his horse. "Does the man have elves and faeries at his command?"

Davy snickered. "No, just Ives. And Malcolms, but they're not so easily commanded."

"Davy is one of my Ives cousins-in-law," Sinda explained as Trev helped her down. "He can fetch a physician."

"I'm supposed to look after your safety," Davy protested. "And bring you home."

"That might be best," Trev said seriously, looking down at her. "You're exhausted. I have Laurence. I can send servants for a physician."

"I've seen you talk to servants," she scoffed. "Davy, fetch

a physician. Take these horses to a stable and give them oats. They've earned it."

Not allowing time for argument, Sinda climbed the stairs and pounded the door knocker while Trev and Davy lifted the viscount from the horse. She disliked waking people in the middle of the night, but there should be rejoicing once they realized who Trev had brought home.

It took several increasingly authoritative knocks to summon a candle in the window. She rapped with finality as Trev carried his cousin up the stairs. The viscount was not a small man, but Trev didn't seem to notice the burden. Sinda's heart wept at the tender care he used in handling his cousin. And to think people believed he would murder him!

The door opened a crack. "What is it?" a frosty voice asked.

"We've brought the viscount home and must send for a physician. Open quickly."

Trev didn't wait for a door to slam in his face. He had his shoulder against the panel and shoved it open the moment Sinda finished speaking. The startled footman leaped backward.

"Hot water and bandages," he roared, heading for the staircase. At least they weren't lined up to kill him this time, he reflected. "Someone to help with his clothes. Hurry up!"

"The viscount was set upon by thieves," he heard Sinda tell the anxious servant. "I hate to wake anyone. If you could tell me where the kitchen is, I could fetch water."

Trev assumed her voice of reason had more effect than his bellow since the footman replied fervently, "Praise the Lord! Is it truly him, raised from the dead? I'll fetch the water, milady. Don't know where the bandages is though. The scullery might."

Already on the next floor, Trev didn't hear how she answered that. He maneuvered open the door to the room Laurence used to occupy, and Sinda hastened after him to pull down the bedclothes. While he laid Laurence across the sheets, she scrambled for a candle and flint on the bedside table. She was more than his right hand. She was the other half of him.

"You shouldn't be here," he told her, pulling off his

cousin's boots, "but I'm grateful you are." Grateful, resentful, terrified, and elated, but he had difficulty explaining all that even to himself. He didn't want her to suffer the scene that would come next.

Laurence had to come first. Shattered by the changes wrought in his cousin's once-laughing face, Trev longed to turn back the hands of time. A long, pale scar gave evidence of a blow that should have laid any normal man dead. Calluses marred his hands. Red streamed down his face from the new wound.

But he was alive! The world had just become a far better place.

Dropping Laurence's boot, Trev straightened to brush a wisp of hair from Sinda's face and to peck a light kiss on her cheek. In the light of the candle she'd just struck, she appeared to be the guardian angel of his soul.

She smiled up at him as if he were her moon and stars, and he ought to feel ashamed, but he wasn't. "He's alive," he whispered, and she nodded her equal joy.

The footman and a scullery girl arrived with hot water, bandages, and looks of hope and fear on their faces. Sinda took the soap and cloth from them and began dabbing at the viscount's bloodied brow. Trev knew head wounds bled profusely no matter how shallow they might be, but as she uncovered it, this one looked deep. He couldn't bear to lose Laurence after just finding him. He wished the physician would hurry, but the chances of rousing one at this hour were slim.

"The lady is exhausted. Find her a room and bring her hot water," Trev ordered as the viscount moaned beneath her gentle ministrations.

"You won't be rid of me so easily," she said, shooting him a deadly glance. "Not after I've come this far."

"He's safe. I am surrounded by witnesses," he argued. "There is nothing you can do here that I cannot do better."

He thought she might slap him with the wet cloth, but she was grace personified under pressure. She merely took one look at his expression and returned to her self-appointed task.

He wanted to rage and tear his hair, but she remained unruffled and organized. Earlier, he had bellowed enough to wake the dead. She had murmured and kept the servants calm. He was terrified Laurence was dying. She reassured him with promises of physicians and aid. He couldn't survive without her.

"A gentleman sent this up, milady," the footman said, bringing in Sinda's portmanteau. "He said you might have need of it, and that... Ninian is on her way." He hesitated over the unusual name but apparently got it right, for Sinda nodded.

"Excellent, thank you."

"Ninian?" Trev demanded, picking her up and moving her out of the way after she started unfastening Laurence's vest.

"My cousin is a healer. Her husband is an earl and works a good deal with Parliament, so they're usually in town."

Trev noted with satisfaction that she hesitated about fighting him over undressing their patient. "Good, then help is on its way. Take your bag, wash, change clothes, rest. There is nothing further you can do here."

As if sensing he was attempting to be rid of her for a purpose, she lingered, but he'd used a voice of reason this time, not a bellow, and she responded. He breathed a sigh of relief as she took her bag to the anteroom that Laurence's valet would have used.

Trev did not fool himself into believing his grandfather still slept. Unless his physician kept him sedated, the old man would sleep lightly. If the apoplexy had left him partially paralyzed, it might take him time to find his way here, but sooner or later, the earl would be at the door. And Trev didn't want Sinda anywhere around when that happened.

He had no illusion of his grandfather's welcoming him with joy. He would be fortunate if the earl merely ordered him pitched down the stairs for daring to breathe the same air as Laurence. He wasn't certain he could keep his own temper.

Trev ordered the maid to fill the pitcher in the anteroom and prayed Sinda's cousin arrived with an entourage to take her home before the fireworks began.

He thought the potential for murder here tonight was still high.

∾

Sinda was grateful for the opportunity to wash and don clean clothes. She didn't wish to meet the Earl of Lansdowne wearing bloodied cotton.

After washing, she combed her wavy hair and fastened it into fresh braids, two shorter ones in front and several long ones in back. Feeling more human, she curled up in the blanket and fell asleep wearing only a fresh chemise and stockings.

A ferocious roar of rage and an answering bellow jarred her awake some time later. Blinking, Sinda staggered, then realized she was standing when her hand fell against a wall. She sat down abruptly on the cot and tried to orient herself.

The valet's room. Trev's grandfather's house. Angry shouts. She looked down at the hand still clenching the stubby piece of charcoal. She didn't think she wanted to see what she had just done. She wasn't holding her notebook so she had undoubtedly been vandalizing the earl's walls. Her head didn't hurt though. What did that signify?

She hastily washed the charcoal off her hands while the war outside escalated. Occasionally the shouts were interrupted by the sweetly feminine voice she knew was Ninian's. Sinda grabbed the bright pink-and-green striped gown she'd removed from her bag earlier and tugged it on. Hurriedly, she pulled the hooked front closed, covered the neckline with linen, and opened the door to the viscount's room.

As light spilled in, she was unable to contain her curiosity. She had used charcoal to draw on something, and the wall was the only object available. She glanced toward where she'd been standing when she awoke. Choking back a gasp at the scene depicted there, she ran out and slammed the door, praying no one else would see before she could clean it off.

The combatants in the outer room were so busy screaming at each other that they didn't even notice her arrival, although her cousin Ninian winked and returned to applying an herb compress to the viscount's temple.

Sinda could not believe this racket was good for the patient. Or for the combatants. The earl appeared to be turning purple, and Trev had his fist around the hilt of his sword.

She studied the earl before launching into an argument that was no doubt older than she was. Lansdowne's gnarled fingers clutched two massive walking sticks, not the polite slender kind but heavy carved ones that could be used as long cudgels. Except he obviously needed them for support. Every time he started to raise one and wave it, he stumbled and had to drop the stick back to the floor to steady himself.

She thought the earl might once have been as tall as Trev, but time and illness had not been kind to him. He was bony from his long convalescence. He hadn't bothered to don his wig, and wispy gray hair barely covered his balding pate. Still, she could see the resemblance to Trev in the sharp planes of his cheeks and cleft chin.

"You get nothing!" The earl's shout was slurred and nearly incomprehensible. "You cannot kill my heir and expect a reward! Leave, and I'll not… charge you with… kidnapping." The earl stabbed a stick in the direction of the exit with enough vehemence that he staggered. The manservant standing beside him had to grab his elbow to hold him upright.

"Why, so you can let him die just to accuse me of murder?" Trev demanded. "I'm back. Grow used to it. I'll not leave Laurence's side until he's well. Be happy that he's alive!"

Sinda supposed two male wolves circling their pack might snarl and snap with the same ferocity—until one either attacked or slunk off into the woods. She didn't think either of these two would slink anywhere. Maybe if she took a stick and swatted them over the head…

Instead, she plastered a smile on her face and gestured at the burly footman behind the earl. "I think Lord Lansdowne could do with some tea. If you would help him to the parlor, I'll ring for a maid."

She'd so startled both men that they shut up long enough for her to be heard. Before they could ignore her request, she caught Trev's elbow. "Is this what you want your cousin to wake to? Do you think he might not wish he were elsewhere and stay unconscious? Come along. You haven't had a bite to eat in hours. I daresay that makes you cranky."

"… blitherin' nonsense," the earl shouted. "I don't take orders from… doxies."

Trev heaved forward as if to grab the earl's coat collar, but not losing her grip, Sinda jerked him back with a force that surprised both of them. "You haven't introduced us, my dear. You cannot expect your grandfather to know who I am."

She thought Ninian gave a soft cheer, but she maintained a serene expression as she waited patiently for Trev's introduction.

"The Earl of Lansdowne, Lady Lucinda Malcolm Pembroke, my wife-to-be," Trev said.

Before Sinda could raise her eyebrows at that shocking bit of news, another male voice rang out from the doorway.

"Over my dead body, you scoundrel!"

Her father. Sinda rolled her eyes and exchanged a glance with Ninian. Perhaps she ought to just give them all swords and let them have at it.

Instead, she pointed at the bedroom door and in her best imitation of her mother commanded, "Out, all of you!"

Thirty-one

To Trevelyan's astonishment, the powerful Duke of Mainwaring and the furious Earl of Lansdowne both stalked out of the sickroom at the command of a faerie sprite wearing a pink and green gown and bright-pink hair ribbons. Actually, after a good washing, her hair was nearly pink as well.

And here he'd feared having his fey artist see this ugly scene. By Neptune, she was in command of it.

Accepting the nod of reassurance from the petite woman nursing his cousin, Trev allowed Sinda to guide him out after his elders. Not his betters. Sinda had taught him that. English aristocrats were just men—like him. Well, perhaps they were a little more polished, but that didn't make them *better*.

"Tea, please," Sinda ordered again, jarring the gaping servants into action. "And coffee."

Apparently the whole household was awake by now. It was just before dawn and many of them would have been rising anyway, but Trev assumed they had other duties besides anxiously lining the hall and stairs. At least, none carried weapons, although they appeared a little dazed.

Trev dared say they hadn't seen any man capable of ordering the earl about. That a dainty and riotously garbed female might do so probably strained their credulity.

"In here," he murmured, opening a nearby door to a sitting room. He didn't wish to have to carry his grandfather down the stairs to a parlor. They'd neither survive the indignity.

The room remained unchanged since he'd last seen it two decades ago. A footman hurried to light coals in the grate, and his grandfather's manservant assisted the earl into a moth-riddled chair near the fire. The Duke of Mainwaring paced up and down the faded carpet until Sinda settled onto a sofa facing the chair. She seemed the only bright spot in a drab room, and Trev dearly wished for the right to take the space beside her. With a defiant glare, the duke appropriated it.

So Trev remained standing, leaning one arm against the mantel.

"Mainwaring, you claim this... ninnyhammer for... daughter?" the earl asked in querulous disbelief.

"The only ninnyhammer in this room is you, old man," Trev said in defense. He shut up when he noted Sinda's disappointed look. What the hell did she expect of him? He wouldn't tolerate having her insulted.

"Your grandson has a point, Lansdowne," the duke said wryly, "although I'd prefer that he present it civilly. Since that seems to be beyond either my daughter or your grandson at the moment, let us set the example."

"He's not my... grandson. I'll not recognize... or grant him... my properties," the earl stated clearly, although with much effort.

Trev bit his tongue when Sinda sent him a warning look. She was the expert on social politics. In this, he would bow to her. He did so, giving her a grandiose obeisance of leg and dip, making her smile. In truth, the old man was such a fraction of his former self that he could not take any of this seriously.

Time had wreaked his revenge for him.

A servant appeared with tea and coffee, accompanied by a selection of fresh breads and fruits. The kitchen must be abuzz with gossip and speculation. Word of the confrontation would spread across all London before evening. Between his penchant for trouble and Sinda's for scandal, they could become more infamous than Robin Hood and Maid Marian. The possibility no longer bothered him. With a wife whose notoriety matched his, he wouldn't have to be as circumspect as he'd feared.

Trev waited for Sinda to serve her father and the earl before grabbing an apple. She was right. He was cranky when he was hungry.

While her father and the earl had their mouths full of hot beverages, Sinda brandished her verbal sword. "Sir Trevelyan has earned his own fortune and name and does not need yours, my lord," she informed the earl tartly. "And Papa, he does not need your permission to marry me. He needs mine. And at the moment, I don't think I shall give it."

Trev nearly choked on the bite of apple he'd just swallowed. While he coughed and spluttered and tried to recover his breath as well as his wits, his grandfather dropped his teacup from his shaky hand in fury.

"Why?" he shouted. "Think you're too grand for my family? You look like... Gypsy. The two of you... deserve... each other."

Family? Had he just heard the earl call him *family?* What the hell did that mean? That the earl liked to argue for the sake of arguing? Although Trev had to agree with the old man for a change. He definitely deserved Lady Sin. Cautiously, he studied her expression to see if she understood his grandfather's insult.

Sinda smiled that complacent smile of hers that Trev was beginning to recognize presaged trouble. He threw half a cup of hot coffee down his throat to clear any remaining blockage and tried not to wish himself back to his ship. Perhaps he could slip over to Laurence's room. He was desperate to see how his cousin fared.

If Laurence recovered, Trev could sail away easily enough, but even if he had to kidnap her, he damned well intended to take his Gypsy sprite with him. He wasn't entirely certain what a man did with a woman like Sinda, beyond the obvious, but he meant to enjoy finding out.

"My daughter is a sheltered lady. Your rapscallion grandson has ruined her, and I demand reparation," the duke said when Trev remained silent.

"They'll not see a farthing from me, you conniving thief!" the earl roared.

Interesting. The old man seemed to speak more clearly as the challenge escalated. Trev pondered that anomaly rather than follow the senseless argument. It very much sounded like two merchants haggling for the best deal.

"I'll see his claim to the title brought before Parliament on the morrow," the duke shouted. "I'll have you declared incompetent and your heir named guardian of the estate!"

"You can't do that you... cantankerous coxcomb..."

"Trevelyan?" Sinda smiled sweetly up at him as the argument railed around them.

He appreciated the mockery in that smile and lifted his teacup in a salute. "Yes, my love?" he asked in kind.

"Would you be so good as to keep an eye on your cousin and let us know when he wakes? One of us may as well be doing something useful."

"And miss the entertainment?" he asked in feigned disappointment, although he silently cheered her perspicacity. He needed to see Laurence. He didn't need to hear his elders argue over matters he could handle for himself.

Both earl and duke fell silent once they realized they'd lost the interest of their audience. Trev casually helped himself to a plate of pastries beneath his grandfather's glare. "I will take Lady Ninian some nourishment, but I'll be right back. Do not have too much fun without me."

"That's what servants... for!" the earl shouted after him.

Trev halted and cocked his eyebrow. "Caring for each other is what family is for. You might try it some time."

He walked out, realizing with a swelling sense of freedom that he wouldn't have to murder his grandfather after all. The earl was no longer the formidable monster that had loomed over his childhood.

What mattered was Laurence and the future. Trev shoved the bedroom door open with his shoulder and carried in the cup of tea and plate of pastries. The fair-haired Malcolm seated beside the bed sent him a look of appreciation, then rose from her chair and stepped out of his way so he could take her place.

Hope leaped instantly into his heart. Handing her the

pastries, Trev took her seat and reached for Laurence's browned and callused hand. Beneath the clean white bandage Sinda's cousin had applied, his cousin's eyelids fluttered.

Holding his breath, Trev prayed the wound had caused no permanent damage and that Laurence was returning to consciousness. With the exposure to time and weather, his cousin's pleasant English face had grown leaner and more mature. His gauntness worried Trev, but Laurence seemed to be breathing naturally. Someone had slipped a nightshirt on him, so Trev assumed no bones were broken or other damage done. He clasped Laurence's hand tighter.

A moment later, Trev was staring into the familiar blue gaze of his best friend. "Laurence?" he asked cautiously, fearing that after that blow, any response would be as unintelligible as the earl's.

"Trevelyan!" The voice was hoarse but filled with excitement. "You came! You're here. I…" He stopped and glanced around at his surroundings. "Where the devil is here?"

Trev bit back his fear and tried to sound casual. "London, in the townhouse. Not seen your old room lately I take it?"

The man in the bed gave a snort that might have been laughter. "Not bloody likely." He turned an eager expression to Trev. "Melinda? Is she here?"

Lady Ninian answered for him. "At the moment, she is birthing your child in Brighton."

Trev's eyebrows rose in surprise. How did she know that? He wouldn't ask. There were too many more relevant questions. Trev watched as his cousin absorbed the news. Did he realize what month it was? How long he'd been gone?

The shock on Laurence's face was swiftly replaced by determination. He started to sit up, but realizing he wore only thin linen beneath the sheets, he grabbed them up to his chin. "My clothes. I must go to my wife."

Trev pushed his cousin back down against the pillows. That it was a struggle to do so was testimony to Laurence's stubbornness than his strength. "You would terrify her into fits were she to see you now. The women would only throw you out anyway. They don't like men at birthings."

Before Laurence could respond, a quaking voice interrupted from the doorway. "Where have you... been... you mutton-headed fribble?"

Someone had notified the occupants of the sitting room that Laurence was awake.

Trev bit back an automatic defense. On his grandfather's acid tongue, the insult had almost seemed affectionate. Could it be that the old man had never learned to express his softer emotions?

For his forbearance, Trev was rewarded with the sweet scent of lilacs and a gentle hand on his shoulder. A charcoal-dusted hand.

"The footman tattled," Sinda murmured. "How is your head this morning, Lord Rochester?" she inquired politely.

Laurence blinked in puzzlement. "It pounds abominably. Should I know you?"

"My wife-to-be, Lady Lucinda," Trev said proudly. "How is your memory otherwise?"

"I demand explanations—" the earl roared.

Trev assumed his grandfather was attempting to wave a stick again because his roar halted abruptly. He didn't bother to look but answered the question in his cousin's eyes. "He had an apoplexy when you disappeared. You've had all of us in quite a stew for some months." No point in telling Laurence he'd been declared dead or his cousin was likely to have a relapse.

"I must go to Melinda. I had a fever and a dreadful headache. I couldn't remember—" Laurence squeezed his eyes closed as if he was still in pain. "How did I get here? I don't recall... I thought I was recovering. I remembered London and thought if I came here it might help me remember. But I don't—"

"You were set upon by thieves and received a blow to your head," a soft voice said. "Sir Trevelyan found you and brought you here. Sometimes a second blow can unaddle the brains. Or kill you. You were fortunate."

Trev recognized Lady Ninian's voice. He supposed he ought to learn her proper title, but he was more concerned with her reasoning. Had the blow unaddled Laurence's mind? Or worsened it? "How much do you remember?" he asked of the patient in the bed, whose brow was starting to wrinkle with frustration.

"I don't know," Laurence replied. "I don't recall arriving here. For a long time, I only remembered the storm and the mains'l toppling. I had nightmares trying to undo whatever I did wrong in the rigging."

"The first sketch," Sinda murmured for only Trev to hear.

"I was told a fishing boat found me and that I was delirious for weeks, but I don't remember it," Laurence continued. "When I started remembering bits of my past, I saved my coin and paid the crew to bring me to London. I was desperate to find my life again. And suddenly, I'm here, and I remember everything except why I'm in this bed. I need to see Charity and Melinda. How are they?"

"They're fine," Sinda assured him. "Trev has looked after them for you. As soon as Ninian says it is safe for you to travel, we'll order a carriage so you may go to them."

"Do you have... heir?" the earl demanded.

Rising to block the earl's access to his cousin, Trev placed a proprietary arm across Sinda's shoulders. "You'll have another grandchild," he told the earl, "a lovely child who will laugh in the sun and chase butterflies just like your beautiful granddaughter. It doesn't make a damned difference whether this one is a boy or girl. Appreciate what you are given."

From the bed, Laurence interrupted with defiance. "Until I have a son of my own, Trev is my heir. I will name him guardian of my children and my estate. And I'll arrange for him to have the damned title should I have only daughters. If I can lose one son, I can lose them all, just as you did. I will not throw away the family I have for a future I cannot control."

The earl sputtered and tried to shake his stick again. This time, the duke caught him before he fell.

"My fault," Lansdowne muttered, shaking his arm free. "Lost two sons." He suddenly looked haggard and no longer angry. "Glad you're back. Missed you."

"Perhaps we should take the discussion out of here so Lord

Rochester might rest?" Sinda suggested as shocked silence descended at his admission.

She asked it politely, but Trev noted that between her and Lady Ninian, they ushered out an earl, a duke, and a bevy of servants with a firmness befitting two generals.

He held back to give Laurence the reassurances a man needed. "I am sorry about the loss of your son. I hadn't known."

Looking pale, Laurence shook his head. "It was a shock from which I didn't think I'd ever recover. The storm may have taken some of my senses, but it returned others. I shall be grateful if Charity is all I ever have."

"Melinda will be so happy to have you alive that she will grace you with a dozen children," Trev said. "Your disappearance gave us a shock. I'm glad you're back."

Collapsing against the pillows, Laurence offered a skeletal grin. "Do you plan to stay and help me raise those dozen children, or has England grown too cold for you already?"

"It has its warm places," Trev admitted. "Will you mind if your children grow up with a rapscallion uncle present?"

"I've missed you," Laurence admitted, closing his eyes against the pain in his head. "But you've caught me in a moment of weakness. You'll never hear me admit that again."

Trev shouted with laughter. "Right you are, old thing. Rochesters wouldn't want to appear weak, would we?"

Satisfied they understood each other—and the earl—Trev strolled out after the others just to see what would happen next. That Laurence meant to recognize him as legal kin did not affect him one way or another. He'd already known his cousin was an intelligent man. He was more fascinated by the earl's admission of guilt. What did that portend?

Inevitably, instead of being herded anywhere, the duke had halted at the stairway. Trev tensed. This was where the real confrontation would occur.

"Lucinda, if we leave while it's still dark, we might avoid gossip. Come along now." Mainwaring gestured impatiently at his daughter.

Trev wanted to reach possessively for her, but her words earlier had hit home. He'd assumed they would marry. He was coming to realize that was a large assumption, one he'd made with tremendous arrogance. Sinda was her own woman, a rarity in that she could support herself if she wished to defy her father and all society. Despite her ethereal appearance, she didn't need any man. It would be reckless to believe she needed him as he needed her.

"Is this the gel what drew… that scandal… of a murderer?" the earl demanded, hobbling forward to place himself between Trev and Sinda.

"Lucinda is a talented artist and only your imagination conjured murder," Trev corrected his grandfather with all the formal politeness a gentleman might command.

"You… saved Laurence." Dismissing the reprimand, the earl focused his gimlet gaze on his disinherited grandson. His tone conveyed neither question or accusation.

"Lucinda did," Trev corrected.

"You lived," the earl continued, ignoring the interruption.

"No thanks to you," Trev agreed. He didn't think this the time or place for this conversation, but then, there might never be another. He crossed his arms and waited.

The earl's head bobbed. "Grief. Lost both sons. Angry. Blamed you."

"Me?" That was a new insight. He'd only been fourteen when his parents died. Wild with grief, he'd run away from his grandfather's stern presence. It had never occurred to him at the time, or since, that the powerful earl had been as distraught at the loss of his only remaining son as Trev had been at the death of his parents—and unable to handle the loss any better.

The earl struggled for words. "You were… uncontrollable. Told your father to send you to sea. He… got angry. Reckless. Drove too fast. Died. Because of you."

Trev stared at him in incredulity. "Because of you, you mean. I was a child."

The earl nodded. "Mistake. Should have looked for you. Did, too late."

Shocked at this new perspective of that horrible period of his life, Trev could only stare. The earl hadn't sent the impressment gang after him? He'd heard the argument between his father and grandfather, knew the earl believed he should join the navy. He'd thought…

"You looked for Trev?" Sinda asked, as he could not. "You did not give him to the navy?"

Lansdowne leaned heavily on his canes. "Angry. Waited too late. When I learned… what happened, I thought it was for the best. I couldn't handle him." As if to hide his admission, he straightened and turned his glare on Sinda. "You're no better. Won't have more scandal."

Recovered from his momentary paralysis, Trev intervened. "You have surrendered any right to direct my actions. Without Lady Lucinda, we would never have found Laurence."

"It is none of your concern," the duke replied in scorn, finally finding the right moment to assert his authority. "I'm taking her home."

"The earl is right in one way though," Sinda said, ignoring her irate father's tug on her arm to speak directly to Trev. "The portrait caused a scandal. My work will always cause gossip and outrage if only because it is mine."

For a woman who preferred quiet anonymity, she caught everyone's rapt attention.

"I would like to say that I will give up my art for those I love," she said, almost apologetically, "but without my drawing, the viscount might never have been saved. I'm beginning to think my gift has a purpose after all. That means I will likely draw more portraits and cause more horrific scandals."

Trev hung on her every word, hoping for some evidence that he fell under the category of "one she loved."

"I think it best to continue as I have begun by living alone under an assumed name to avoid harming my family." She raised her eyes to Trev. "And to avoid bringing scandal to you or your family."

Had she brought a bludgeon down on his head, she could not have smashed him flatter. Stunned, he watched as she lifted her colorful skirt and started down the stairs, followed by her father. Her ribbons blew in the breeze created by her rush.

He had just found his family again. He hadn't had time to

ponder the earl's apology, if apology it had been. Laurence was placing his trust in him as guardian. The earl and his cousin couldn't manage all their estates from sickbeds. His family needed him. Sinda had just said that she didn't.

She damned well did.

Without giving it a second thought, Trev took the stairs two at a time, grabbed his rebellious artist by her waist, hauled her from her feet, and dragged her out the front door before anyone could come to her rescue.

After one startled scream, Sinda quieted, but that did not mean he was safe or she was obedient. Oh no, he knew her too well for that. Without giving her an opportunity for protest or escape, he flung her into the carriage waiting at the front door.

The driver leaped to attention. The unliveried driver. In the growing light of dawn, Trev studied the black-haired, tall young man, decided he was an Ives of some sort, and frowned. "We need to go to Brighton immediately. Do I need to find my own man?"

"I'm just waiting for Ninian. If it's an emergency, she'll understand."

Wickedly, Trev said, "She'll understand," and climbed inside.

❧

Heart beating erratically, Sinda watched as Trev slammed the carriage door shut. She made no effort to escape. She shouldn't have hit him with her decision so publicly, but she had hoped he'd be so consumed by family and the shock of the earl's confession that he would hesitate long enough for her to get away.

That he hadn't hesitated at all had her foolish heart beating against her chest in joy.

"Do you think I care about scandal?" he demanded the instant the carriage rolled off.

"I think you missed your family terribly and now that you have them back, you would not wish to bring harm to them. You might even make amends with your grandfather. No matter how hard I try, infamy haunts my footsteps. You will have nieces and nephews who will look up to you with pride. Would you disappoint everyone with a wife who is the gossip of all society?"

"I don't remember asking you to be my wife." He crossed his arms over his chest.

"You called me your wife-to-be," she said, suspicious of his belligerent tone.

"That was when I thought you a reasonable woman. It seems you're not. So, how would you care to carry on? Would you prefer to live aboard ship while I trade with Holland? Or perhaps we could just settle in your cottage where my nieces and nephews can play at our feet while you pretend to be nobody?"

Puzzled, she leaned forward to study his expression. His dark brows were fiercely drawn down over his nose. The scar on his cheek whitened against his bronze coloring. He refused to look at her.

"You wish me to live openly as your mistress?" Admittedly, she had wondered if he might not come to visit her once in a while. She couldn't bear to think that he would cut her off entirely and that she would never see him again. But it wasn't a sentiment she dared speak aloud.

"Well, you have just told me that as my wife, you will harm my family, and you know society far better than I do. I accept your judgment. But I know myself better than you do, so you must accept that I cannot live without you. Therefore, we must live together in some manner. I'm open to your suggestions."

She gaped. "You cannot live without me? You have lived all your life without me."

He shrugged. "I have lived half my life with that ugly crew of mine. That does not mean I wish to live the rest of it with them. And as much as I love and admire my cousin and his family, I cannot say that I wish to live their boringly upright lives either.

"I would offer to take you to Jamaica," he continued, "so you need not worry over harming anyone here, but I suspect your family would raise strong objection to that. And you would not wish to be separated from them for long. I have duly noted that even in anonymity, you settled within reach of your cousin."

"I see." She settled back against the carriage squabs. She wished she had pencil and paper. She could not think properly without them in hand. Trevelyan Rochester made her head spin. "You've thought this out quite carefully."

"No. I'm thinking as we go. It seems the best way of keeping up with someone whose head is in the future. Or the past. What did you draw in the anteroom, by the way?"

He knew her so well, it was terrifying. She glanced down at her hands. "I really should erase it before your grandfather sees it. He will have another apoplexy."

"I would say no great loss, but now that the old man can't smash things so easily, there is some chance that Laurence might teach him manners. After all, you have practically tamed me. I doubt an earl would bother to enter a valet's room though. What did you draw?"

"I haven't tamed you," she said irritably. "You have just kidnapped me again. And with Davy driving. You are reprehensible."

"And you are avoiding the subject. What did you draw?"

She felt the blush creeping up her cheeks. "You and your grandfather woke me before I finished."

He waited. She thought he bit back a smile. Superior oaf. She flounced her skirt to a more comfortable position, wiggling her ribbons in the process. She hid a grin as he adjusted his legs to disguise his reaction to her. She loved this man, and she must have been out of her head to think he'd let her go without a protest. "I drew you," she answered.

He nodded solemnly. "Was I murdering someone?"

"You were naked."

That brought him up straight. He turned and narrowed his eyes at her. "How naked?"

"You are a large and admirable physical specimen," she said, trapping a smile with her prim tone.

Trev rapped the driver's door. "Turn around!" he shouted.

Sinda erupted into gales of laughter, covering her mouth

to hold it in. He grabbed her and settled her on his lap where she could bury her chortles in his shoulder.

"How large?" he asked, fighting the addictive snickers.

"Not *that* naked," she admitted. "You interrupted me, remember?"

He reached over and pounded the door again. "Forget that order. To Brighton, faster!"

"Witch," he muttered, before swallowing her giggles with a kiss that tickled her tonsils and swept her breath away.

"We'll catch the ship and be married in Scotland tomorrow," he declared moments later when he lifted his head for air.

"Not without my family," she warned before noting how his dark eyes gleamed with triumph and realized she'd been tricked.

"I accept," he agreed. "I'll simply keep you on the *Lass* and ravish you until all the preparations are made."

"I love you," she said, circling his neck tighter and pulling his head down. "Take me home with you."

"Wherever you are is my home," he murmured against her mouth. "And wherever I am, you will be free."

The dawn erupted in birdsong, but they didn't notice.

Epilogue

"Look! Charity is teaching Baby John to walk," Trev said, holding Sinda so she could lean to see around the mare's head to watch the two children maneuvering the pebbly beach. Her red-and-blue striped silk gown blew in the breeze off the water, covering Trev's knees like an exotic quilt. Her long silver tresses mingled with the horse's matching mane. The bright-blue ribbons taming her hair tangled with the red ribbons he'd tied in the horse's mane.

"I'm glad they could all come to the country for the fair," she said. "I think Melinda is finding her duties as the earl's London hostess onerous, even if Laurence enjoys his position as his grandfather's representative."

Trev had bought the horse to match his wife's glorious silver-blond hair—and because she'd told him she thought the silver horse she'd painted him on romantic. Who was he to argue with genius? He tugged her back against him just because he could. He would never grow tired of holding her.

"Melinda had best learn to run or Charity will be teaching the babe to swim shortly." He shifted her more comfortably across his lap so he could urge the horse through the waves to catch up with his straying niece and nephew.

Above them, Gypsies had parked their caravan on the bluff to trade with fairgoers and offer their peculiar skills. The streets were crowded with visitors come to take the water cure. And Duke Harry's fair was in full swing. The music of pipe and tambourine floated over laughter and the excited shouts of children. The air filled with the thick scent of meat pies and grease kettles and boiling candies. Flags waved atop tent posts, ponies raced each other through the streets, and out in the harbor, yachts bobbed and sailed.

After chasing the children back to the safety of shore and their nursemaids, Trev brought the horse to a standstill, and Sinda leaned back against the blue silk vest she'd ordered made for him. "Thank you."

"For what?" he asked, raising his brows inquiringly. "For waiting to leave for Jamaica until Christina safely carried Harry's screaming hooligan of an heir? For letting your cousin Felicity's husband install running water in the Willows so Aidan might return to his castle and sulk? I think your family might thank me for that one." He glanced down at the elaborate lace adorning his cuffs and jabot. "Or for allowing myself to be decked out like a macaroni for the baby marquess's christening?"

"For all that, and for taking me with you." She clasped her arms around his neck and kissed his nose. "And for understanding that I'm not ready to have children yet."

Trev hugged her close, and Sinda sighed in appreciation. Even after eight months of marriage, her husband still had the power to make her shiver with desire just by looking at him. The wind toyed with his black hair, tossing it across his prominent cheekbones. He still scorned wigs and powder, but she didn't mind that. It was the formidable man beneath the finery who held her interest.

Not until she admired the contrast of lace and dangerous masculinity did it strike her—her portrait had come to life!

And this time, she was a part of it, she realized with wonder and immense satisfaction. The oil in the gallery depicted *her* future.

"I am humbled that you are the first Malcolm to ever leave these shores and that you do it for me," Trev murmured, covering her face with butterfly kisses. "I would not wish to subject children to the travails of traveling halfway around the world."

"Besides, Mother would have both our heads should I have our child anywhere except home. So if you wish children, we must hurry back here."

"Remember that when you are lost in painting hibiscus and parrots," he warned. "As much as you might love the Willows, and I am grateful that Laurence sold it to me, it is not Jamaica."

He swung down from the horse, and Sinda slid into his waiting arms. "The Willows is our home," she said. "And I will be content to return to it when it's time. We will bring back more tropical plants for the orangery and be very happy there."

In sight of all the fairgoers, Trev bent to kiss her thoroughly and swing her in a mad circle until she laughed. "I am glad we have settled your nighttime terrors so that we can get some sleep. Your paintings these days are much happier, although the one of Harry's castle is nicer than the ugly relict deserves."

She wrinkled her nose at him. "I suspect my paintings are happier because no one close to us is in trouble. I still do not know how I picked up on Laurence's pain, and even his tremors from the fever. I would rather not experience it again."

"And so you shall not. I will hold you every night so you only have pleasant dreams," he declared. "Now here comes your family." He dropped her back to the ground. "Shall I signal for the rowboat before we are drowned in tears? I will do all that I can to keep you smiling."

She touched his pirate features and longed for the moment when they could be in his bed aboard ship again. Nothing could compare to lovemaking on a rolling ship with a sea breeze caressing them. They retreated there often when they craved privacy. "You know you love being the center of my family's attention," she admonished at his teasing. "And you will miss them fiercely while we are gone. Hug Mother, and watch her faint."

Trev roared with laughter, and she admired the way he

flung his head back without inhibition, living the moment with all the ferocity and joy within him. With all the passion for living that he was teaching her.

"I think after Aidan caused such an uproar when you painted a cloud over his castle, that your family would be grateful that I take you away for a while. The last I heard, they feared he was raising a Scots army." Trev glanced up the shore to where her family gathered.

"They are amazing, aren't they?" Sinda said with satisfaction as she too admired the display of silks and lace, tall men, lovely women, and lively children gracing the landscape. "Perhaps I can learn to paint them while we're away so that I always know what they are doing."

"I think I shall keep you too busy in bed to try," he said, giving a mock shudder. "Come along, then, the tide is almost in. Let us say our farewells."

Behind them, as they strolled up the path to say their good-byes, Trev's new ship, the *Malcolm Lass* bobbed at sea, waiting for the next adventure.

Author's Note

I enjoy historical research and travel, and attempt to adequately prepare the grounds on which I build my novels. But this is a novel and not a history, so I must make judgment calls on how much of my research aids the story and how much hinders it.

For instance, I am aware that Brighton was not called Brighton in the 1750s, but if I used the original name of Brighthelmstone, American readers couldn't pronounce it and most readers wouldn't recognize it. Since the original name does not add anything to the story, I used the name familiar to modern readers. I have also placed a jail in Brighton that I'm fairly certain was not there. Just as I have the characters note, Brighton was a crumbling fishing village at the time of the story, barely on the brink of becoming the tourist town it would become in the next century. Other towns and estates that were larger then but are no longer recognizable to the modern reader would have been more likely locations of a lockup. For the sake of simplicity, I have used the town that was already part of the story.

My apologies for any other encroachments on fact that I may have taken in my attempt to keep the course of the story sailing smoothly. I'm sure Trev would have appreciated the shortcuts!

About the Author

With several million books in print and *New York Times* and *USA Today* bestseller lists under her belt, former CPA Patricia Rice is one of romance's hottest authors. Her emotionally charged contemporary and historical romances have won numerous awards, including the *RT Book Reviews* Reviewers Choice and Career Achievement Awards. Her books have been honored as Romance Writers of America RITA® finalists in the historical, regency, and contemporary categories.

A firm believer in happily-ever-after, Patricia Rice is married to her high school sweetheart and has two children. A native of Kentucky and New York, a past resident of North Carolina, she currently resides in St. Louis, Missouri, and now does accounting only for herself. She is a member of Romance Writers of America, the Authors Guild, and Novelists, Inc.

For further information, visit: www.patriciarice.com, on Facebook: www.facebook.com/OfficialPatriciaRice, Twitter: twitter.com/Patricia_Rice, blog: www.patriciarice.blogspot.com, and www.wordwenches.com.

New York Times bestselling author

Merely Magic

by Patricia Rice

She has the magic as her birthright…

Ninian is a healer, but she's a Malcolm first and foremost, and Malcolms have always had a bit of magic—unpredictable though it is—to aid them in their pursuits. She knows she must accept what she is or perish, but then Lord Drogo Ives arrives, bringing the deepest, most powerful magic she's ever experienced and turning Ninian's world upside down…

But Drogo Ives has no time for foolish musings or legends, even if he can't seem to resist the local witch. Thrown together by a series of disastrous events, Ninian won't give herself fully to Drogo until she can make him trust and believe in her, and that's the last thing he'll ever do…

Praise for Patricia Rice:

"You can always count on Patricia Rice for an entertaining story with just the right mix of romance, humor, and emotion." —The Romantic Reader

For more Patricia Rice, visit:

www.sourcebooks.com

New York Times bestselling author

The Lure of Song and Magic

by Patricia Rice

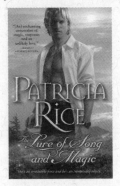

Her voice was a curse...

When Dylan "Oz" Oswin's son is kidnapped, the high-powered producer will do anything to get him back. Desperately following an anonymous tip, he seeks help from a former child singing sensation called Syrene, only to find she's vowed never to sing again. Immune to her voice but not her charm, Oz is convinced she holds the key to his son's disappearance—and he'll stop at nothing to make her break her vow.

Only he can make her sing...

She knows the devastation her talent can bring. There's more than a child's life at stake, but Syrene cannot unleash her dangerous siren's voice upon the world, even for a man who is impossible to deny...

"An enchanting concoction of magic, suspense, and an unlikely love." —Booklist *Starred Review*

"A truly terrific story... Rice brings you great characters, a dynamite plot, and plenty of magic." —RT Book Reviews, *4.5 Stars*

For more Patricia Rice, visit:

www.sourcebooks.com

New York Times bestselling author

Must Be Magic

by Patricia Rice

An explosive attraction…

Lady Leila Staines has always felt like an outcast among her magically gifted sisters. Desperate to discover her own talent, she seeks out Dunstan Ives, a dark and brooding aristocrat with a scientific bent who may hold the key to unleashing Leila's hidden powers.

Can create a spark that's pure magic…

Dunstan has shunned the decadent society that wrongfully condemned him of murder, and he's vowed never again to succumb to the spell of a beautiful woman. But the bewitching Lady Leila makes him a proposal no man in his position can resist.

"With Ms. Rice's skill for mixing humor, emotional intensity, and sensuality with a touch of the supernatural, Must Be Magic *is a highly recommended read and a 'keeper.'"* —RT Book Reviews, *4½ stars*

For more Patricia Rice, visit:

www.sourcebooks.com

New York Times bestselling author

The Trouble with Magic

by Patricia Rice

Is her magic a gift, or a curse…?

All the Malcolms have some magic, but Lady Felicity's ability to read people's emotions simply by touching them or their possessions overwhelms her. She's reached a marriageable age, but how can she ever wed when she can see so clearly a man's guilty secrets?

Only he can tell the difference…

Ewen Ives, itinerant rake and adventurous inventor, knows better than to underestimate the mischief of the Malcolms. But sparks fly when he encounters Felicity, and Ewen can't seem to refuse her plea for assistance…

"Rice's enchanting book is truly spellbinding." —Booklist

"You can always count on Patricia Rice for an entertaining story with just the right mix of romance, humor, and emotion" —The Romantic Reader

For more Patricia Rice, visit:

www.sourcebooks.com

This Magic Moment

by Patricia Rice

Everything about Lord Harry's easygoing life is about to change. After unexpectedly inheriting the title of Duke of Sommersville, he's also discovered it comes with a load of debt. To save the estate, he's going to need money. Lots of it—and quick.

Lady Christina has no problem with Harry marrying her for her dowry. After all, they've been friends since childhood. But gone is the laughing, charming boy she once knew. And she won't share anything of herself until she gets that Harry back. No matter how tempting he proves to be...

Praise for Patricia Rice

"Rice has a magical touch for creating fascinating plots, delicious romance, and delightful characters." —Booklist

"Charming and immensely entertaining." —Library Journal

"Rice bewitches, beguiles, and tickles your fancy."
—RT Book Reviews *Top Pick*

For more Patricia Rice, visit

www.sourcebooks.com